I0581507

The Dark Times Saga:

The Black Forest

The Dark Times Saga: The Black Forest

Book One

R. A. Revis

BRITON

1237 Glenwood TRL
Batavia, OH 45103

www.britonpublishing.com

ISBN
978-1-7353834-7-7 (Hardcover)
978-1-7353834-6-0 (Paperback)

Published by Briton Publishing
Distribution by Ingram Content Group

Acknowledgments

The Dark Times Saga, *The Black Forest* is a tale of dark fantasy and horror in a fictional world inspired by England in the mid-14th century. It takes place during a turbulent and apocalyptic time in our history on a fabricated new continent far west of England. It's a story that intertwines various myths, religions, historical events, and places within a familiar, but alternate fantasy world. While I tried to make it as accurate as possible using factual historic figures and places, there are certain liberties I have taken to fuel the story and stoke the reader's imagination. It takes place in a grim Arthurian world where monsters of myth and legend are all too real and the age of science is fast approaching out of necessity, forcing a time of renaissance and innovation. It falls in the same genre as Andrzej Sapkowski's *The Witcher* novels (a fellow Slav) and R.R. Martin's *Game of Thrones* with elements of struggle and hope like *The Lord of the Rings*. The story is primarily here to engage the reader's imagination and perhaps provoke thought, but first and foremost, to entertain. Set in a familiar world to ground you to something you know, with an added sense of dread and horror to stimulate. That said, The Black Forest is my first novel, hopefully in a series of many, and I hope you enjoy it as much as I did when writing it.

R. A. Revis

Contents

Prologue: Awakening

Voskavia is older than mankind. Its land is ancient and untamed. Gods walked these forests and mountains before humanity was even a twinkle in the eye of existence. You, outsiders, think you can tame this land. You think that you can bring it to heel like a rebellious pup, but you're a fool. What is wild will always be wild. No cage you build will contain it. No laws you make will control it. You push, and the land will push back harder and more violently than you can imagine. Brace yourself Englishman; this is but the quiet before the storm.

-Brom

I

Voskavia, the English Frontier.

Spring, 1348 A.D.

There it was again, the scraping on the cabin's door. Maisie's sandy brown eyes slowly opened and blearily tried to focus in the dark. The fire was still burning in the hearth, its dim light struggling to fill the cabin. She thought for a moment to get up and throw another log on its waning embers, but she was far too comfortable wrapped in her quilt like a cocooned caterpillar. Her little brother lay still on the floor next to the fireplace warmly buried in his bedding and although she couldn't see her mother through the privacy wall of her bed nook, she could faintly hear her rhythmic breathing. The cabin still smelt of berry porridge and biscuits mother had made earlier. Her teenage stomach was always hungry, giving a small groan at the thought of food. The wind outside was howling now, rattling the shutters on the windows. Flashes of moonlight fluttered in as the wood barriers resisted the gusts.

Another sluggish grind echoed from the front door, the hollow sound carrying through the stillness of the cabin. Maisie was wide awake now as adrenaline rushed through her body, goosebumps rolling down her arms. Her gaze locked on the wooden door as she tried to focus in the darkness, her mind filled with what-ifs. The frightened young lady tugged the covers up under her nose as a natural reaction, wanting to hide, wanting to run, but to where? Her family's shack was on the edge of English territory, deep in the frontier. Their hovel rested on the border to The Wilds, an untamed and often violent region of the continent. She was at least an hour's walk from the nearest settlement, and travel at night was dangerous, to say the least. Maisie had never believed the tales of the drunkards in the tavern about the forest being haunted, or the creatures the hunters claim to see lurking in the shadows.

That was until her father went missing. He had taken a job from the resident lord, Alistair Dumont, joining several other men to collect lumber for a shipment to the mainland. Most commoners would jump at the opportunity as a woodcutter. It was dangerous and hard work, but the men could make in one month what usually took them an entire season. They were to set up a lumber camp and bring in the first shipment within a week. Almost two weeks later, none of the men had been seen or heard from. Search parties failed to find tracks of the capable woodsmen, let alone a camp in the dense and highly overgrown forest that surrounded the trade outpost. The townsfolk feared animals had killed them, or worse. As of late, strange sounds emanated from the dark woods, and odd figures were seen wandering through them in the middle of the night. The people of Fort Dumont and its surrounding homesteads now huddled in their hovels when the sun set, fearing what might lurk in the woods that surrounded them.

There it was again. This time the light outside flickered as Maisie saw movement through the cracks in the wooden planks. Someone or something was out there. She gingerly moved a lock of her curly brown hair behind her ear with a delicate finger. With bated breath, she watched the door, too frightened to move or speak. Her knees were curled up to her petite frame as she gathered enough courage to prop her head up on a shoulder, the covers still pulled up as a barrier to what she feared might lurk out there.

"Edmund, do you hear that?" She spoke in a hoarse whisper. "Edmund, wake up!"

Her brother simply rolled over and resumed his snoring, either deliberately ignoring her or too deep asleep to hear her. She sighed and whimpered low to herself as she tentatively slid out of bed, her toes searching for her shoes, dancing on the cold stone floor. Her feet slid into her leather slippers, as dainty fingers quickly laced them up and reached for the lantern on her end table. Maisie's slender hands trembled as she curled a finger through the candle holder's ring. The flame inside swayed as she disturbed its rest. Shadows danced through the hut playing tricks on the young woman's eyes.

Everything was in place inside the humble abode, but was eerily quiet. Her breathing seemed louder than it was in the stillness. She didn't hear owls, or wolves, or insects, no animals at all, just the wind rushing through the branches of the trees. The sudden gusts rolled over her roof with a rumble, causing the fire in the hearth to flutter. Her pale hazel eyes turned to the door once more seeing movement, as the moonlight outside choked through the cracks. The floorboards of the porch groaned and creaked in protest under the weight of someone, or something. She jumped as the shutters rattled once more, her petite hand gripping the cross around her neck as she prayed they held through the storm. With a deep breath, she gently tiptoed to the door, passing the nook her mother now slept in alone, once shared by her father.

Maisie frowned as her thoughts drifted to their missing patriarch, wishing he had been sleeping in his usual place next to her mother. She smiled, remembering how he would snore while lying on his back. The cabin walls gently vibrating rhythmically as he breathed, forcing her mother to wake and get him to roll over. She felt safe hearing him. The family could always count on him to protect them, to shoo away bad dreams, or to put them all at ease during a fierce storm with a joke or silly story. It was up to her now; she was all the family had. While she wasn't the man of the house, she was still the eldest and had to protect her little brother and her aging mother. She did her best to puff up her chest, walking to the front door with renewed courage, carefully looking to see if she could tell what was on the other side. With a sigh of relief, Maisie noticed that the large oak bar was still in place across the entrance should the latch give way. Whatever was out there bumped into the door and caused the iron handle to shudder with a metallic rattle. She jumped; her svelte frame flinched noticeably as a small squeak escaped her mouth. She reflectively placed her free hand over her pursed lips, silently waiting to see if the person or thing outside heard her. Maisie's heart was pounding through her chest, as she was quivering in fright. That's when the voice eerily crept through the door like a shallow gust of air.

"Maisie…" The voice on the other side was faint, barely audible.

Her eyes went wide as she held the lantern higher, gasping as the gentle glow revealed an eye, glazed over and bloodshot, staring at her through a crack in the door. "Maisie…." The raspy voice hissed again coarsely, chilling her to the core, so familiar yet so foreign at the same time.

"Father, is that you?!" She said, her tone now changing from fear to elation as she placed the lantern behind her on the dining table.

She hurried back to the sealed door, removing the heavy oak bar with a little grunt, setting it to the side. *He must have survived whatever had waylaid them for so long* — she thought. He must be starved, exhausted, and happy to be finally home. Without hesitation, she excitedly flung the door open and although the figure was cloaked in the shadow, she immediately recognized the tall, brawny build of her father. She grinned as a tear rolled down her rosy cheek, seeing his beard knotted and unkempt, poke out from the shadows that cloaked his face. A wave of relief and joy flowed over her, like the wind outside, dry leaves blowing across her bare feet into their cabin. She thanked God he was finally home.

"Dad!" she exclaimed and joyously wrapped her arms around his broad shoulders, forcing her to stand on her tippy toes.

Her joy slowly faded however and in crept dread, her blood running as cold as the body she embraced. Something was wrong. Like a heavy rain cloud, it gradually came over her. He didn't hug back. The woodsman's tunic was heavily soiled, and as she pressed against his body, the young woman felt something moving within his chest, like snakes coiled and writhing. Her stomach twisted from his sharp, pungent odor, forcing her to retreat, feeling something cold and sticky against her linen gown. Her thin brow furrowed, looking down; the white nightgown her mother had made her for her nineteenth birthday was covered in thick, black, oily soil. Maisie's face went pale with horror as she looked up to her father's usually warm cheeks and saw it smeared with the substance. His jaw slanted at an unnatural angle. With horror, the terrified young woman gasped at his face that was barely being held together with vein-like roots which were pulsating with a thick black liquid. The right side of his skull was split wide open, revealing its visceral contents as the vines slithered throughout the rest of his body. She reeled backward, wanting to scream, but couldn't catch her breath. Maisie's eyes locked with her father's, which shone like silver coins, reflecting the light of the cabin's candles. With a sickening tear, her father's stomach pried open with a wet popping sound as the tentacle-like roots began squirming out, quickly reaching for her. She began to cry as her once-beloved father's jaw snapped and lolled open in a twisted fashion, a ghastly and inhuman voice poured from his shell.

"Trespassers, now you all suffer." A voice that was not his own hissed out the twisted version of the man she once adored; his mouth unmoving as black slimy vines slithered from his maw.

She trembled before her father, her protector, but ironically now, needed protection from him.

Maisie finally found enough breath to let out a scream but was cut short, as what was once her father grabbed her by the throat. Just as quickly, the roots slithered out of his forearm and up to her slender neck. Her slight form kicked and flailed, but the grimy impostor was too strong. The tendrils slid into her nose and mouth; the oily sap had a bitter tang on her tongue. Over Maisie's shoulder, she could hear her mother stirring and groggily calling her name, confusion in her tone. The creature quickly snapped his head to the new sound with a sickening crack. It glared inside at the others, his dead eyes reflecting the light like an animal. His head twitched rapidly with a sick joy and with a dull snap his gaze slowly returning to his daughter, his face warped with a horrific grin. His once gentle smile ripped open, his jaw detaching like a snake as vines swarmed like worms entangled in a bowl spurned from his blackened mouth.

"Take comfort, little one, in knowing you and yours will be united again." The voice of a dozen people rattled out of the wicked grin on the corpse it inhabited.

Maisie was frozen, not only by fear, but by the powerful grip of her once-doting father. She could do nothing as the sharp vines pierced her sleep gown, like threaded needles weaving into her flesh. They burrowed into her stomach, wiggling up into her chest as her body convulsed from the invasion. Her head dangled to one side as her slender arms dropped to her waist, her small form now dangling limply like the dolls she played with as a child. Her vision slowly closed in, blurring as the roots went to work, replacing all that was within her both physically and mentally.

Peering over her father's shoulder as the world was now a muffled jumble of sounds; she saw more movement making its way from the bleak woods. Several new figures emerged from the darkness that covered them like a mantle, their bodies ravaged and torn as they twitched and hissed. They were the other woodcutters that had accompanied her father, now shambling hollow shells of what they once were their limbs unnaturally twisted, as they trudged towards her once happy home. They surged forward, armed with sharpened tools from their camp unfazed by the weather's increasing hostility as the sky growled over their symphony of hollow moans.

A scream pierced the air behind Maisie as her mother became aware of the events unfolding before her. Edmund's bare feet padded along the wooden floor as he ran to his frightened mother, deeply unsettled and confused by what was happening. Both mother and son huddled on the bed embracing one another, too terrified to act as the room filled with flashes of light from the coming storm. Maisie slowly faded from this world and as she did, one thought echoed through her mind before the darkness overtook her; she wished she had stayed in bed and ignored the scratching on the door.

II

To her surprise, Maisie awoke for a second time this night. Her body felt odd, almost completely numb, yet warm and relaxed, almost sedated. Her once breathtaking hazel eyes were now dull black orbs, as they scanned her new environment with a content curiosity.

No longer in her cabin, safe and warm with her loved ones, she felt as if she was floating, her lithe toes dangling in the air, gingerly, wiggling. She was suspended, hanging like a discarded marionette from a large, blackened, hemlock tree. Usually, she would have panicked in a situation like this, but she was calm and at ease as something soothed her mind. All she felt was peace and serenity, as if she always belonged here. When her thoughts wandered to home, only this place came to mind. Maisie's dark and lush eyelashes blinked calmly as she took in her surroundings. Her graceful form, clad in white linen, hung before an enormous black oak tree that towered dominantly above everything else.

Even the older trees, the ancient residents that resided in the forest for eons, were dwarfed by its mass as its canopy overshadowed several acres. She instinctively knew this tree differed greatly from the others, as it was thinking and studying her and the others, who hung before it, like her mother and Edmund. Its powerful roots moved like tendrils grasping and burrowing through its dark domain, as small squirming acorns filled with dull embers of amber light gently pulsed, dangling from her ebony limbs. Maisie knew instantly somehow the powerful entity sprouted cautiously from a long slumber, a forced hibernation. Its roots uncoiled like fingers as it grew rapidly, digging through the soil, clawing towards the destiny it had been denied. She didn't know how she knew this, but she did, as she felt what it felt, knew what it knew. When she had a question, there was no need to speak. The answer was right there, gently placed in her mind. For a moment the young woman wondered if her thoughts were hers, but that was silly she thought as she recoiled at the notion, quickly dismissing the idea. Maisie knew she had always loved The Tree, the entity that gave her purpose and life. It was her family, her guardian, her goddess, and the only thing she ever needed or wanted.

Much like other plant life, its scent attracted other entities from near and far. Dark fiends and spirits gathered in the forest. Creatures from all over the land were attracted to the beating heart of the Tree, to its seductive whispers. The various creatures, both big and small, scurried through its omnipotent form like ants, never asking why just desperate to please. Over and over, its heartbeat thundered as the very ground shuttered, like a never-ending drum hammering in their heads. Like moths to a candle flame, they came entranced unable to remember how they arrived. The Mother had sprouted and matured, calling forth Her servants once more. As Her roots spread, they released sap that tainted the soil. The nearby trees were helpless as they had no choice but to feed on Her nectar, they gradually but surely would be corrupted, bending to Her will. To protect Her magnanimous form, she summoned vile things from the depths as Her roots dug down deep into the earth. The dark goddesses' glorious trunk swarmed with massive insects that grew to the size of dogs as they fed on the thick black sap, weaving their webs throughout Her forest.

On Her branches large blackbirds sat perched, the yellow-eyed sentries ever watchful and ever vigilant of their Mother. Swarms of vampire bats, large enough to carry off sheep joined the powerful birds, as they groomed one another, cleaning the gore from their fanged maws.

The Tree's greatest power however was Her ability to dominate and mold flesh. She planted Her seedlings, the pulsing acorns of vile energy, into the bodies of those she captured. Living or dead, it did not matter, they would bend the knee to their Matriarch and serve with feverish loyalty. These possessed vessels were known as "The Withered" and were a direct extension of Herself, Her mind, Her will, and Her emotions. The possessed humans and animals, all were enslaved to Her desires, as they sprouted from the ground around their mother like saplings, stretching to the sky as they were reborn from Her abyssal womb. These vessels were not mindless, like necromancer's reanimations, no not at all. They kept all their memories and knowledge stored in a hive mind as it connected them to their Goddess, their one Mother. They were Her eyes and ears, Her claws and teeth, what they knew, she knew. When injured, Her pawns burrowed into the viscous soil, replenishing themselves on the Tree's tainted essence, until once more rejuvenated and fit to serve. There was never any rest for the Withered Ones, for if they fell, Her roots would simply rebuild them. Their damaged limbs would be replaced with blades and spikes, natural weapons capable of brutality, their cycle of servitude never-ending, an infinite loop of horror and misery. Possessed vessels gently fell from Her limbs like ripe fruit. The entity's army was fueled by the corpses of endless conflict that plagued the continent. Each body gently plucked from their graves, harvested like corn. The tree gave the empty husks new life and a dark purpose.

Maisie looked back at the tree, her black and glassy eyes like polished marble; she had long forgotten her family. She now loved only one, The Tree, her Mother. Within Maisie's chest, a seed thumped in unison with the entity's heart. She felt adoration, love, and wanted nothing more than to please the entity. The black pulsating vines gently pulled her closer to the enormous sentient being as it towered over its territory with impunity. Maisie descended with grace just above the earthen ground, levitating like a dark angel as the vines now protruding from her back, her lithely petite form floating above the bubbling defiled soil. Her head slowly cocked to one side now as she was the eyes and ears of the Mother, her feet dangled and pointed at the ground like a dancer.

"My chosen, my vessel, my daughter of death, be my voice, my legs, and my eyes. We have much to do." The voice's raspy tone echoed in Maisie's mind as she smiled, feeling its embrace, her body, and mind in a state of bliss.

Among all those resurrected, there were three who stood out among the legion of the Withered. The warlord kings, Hrothgar, Vladislav, and Dragan. They were Slavic and Germanic native chieftains who had been betrayed by the English invaders. While still under the tree's influence, they had been given a gift. They were allowed to keep a portion of themselves, who they were, and most of all their memories. The Warlords remembered as their bodies seethed with hate and rage, their demise repeating constantly in their dark minds. They could still feel the coarse rope around their necks snap as they fell into oblivion.

Hrothgar, in particular, had a seething hatred for Baron Harmon and his allies. His rage burnt bright in his hollow eyes. The Withered Warlords had a deeper connection to the Mother, for they could hear more than just the thumping, never-ending thumping. They could feel Her will as Her commands were like whispers carried on the wind as they fluttered past like leaves. Her emotions flowed through them like a river, unseen, but felt all the same. The masses of The Withered stood staring in full obedience, their skins taught against their skeletal frames, reinforced with roots for muscle and vines for sinew. The Slavic kings and servants stood before their creator, their new god, reborn with a grand purpose.

"Go forth and spread chaos, my Withered Warlords, forgotten by time. Remind the children of Eden of what pain and terror truly are. Take your revenge and in doing so bring tribute to me." The voice came from Maisie yes, but was echoed by all the withered, thousands of voices speaking as one, in unison.

The three resurrected lords did only as they could; they bent the knee and slowly turned to gather armies of their own. This world would know fear once more, the pain, the misery, the horror the three lords faced at the hands of Lord Harmon. And the Dark Tree would reap the reward.

Chapter 1:

First Step Towards Destiny

I

Rohn had spent months at sea in the merciless turbulent waters, the squalls of spring hindering his journey by weeks. The constant rocking taking more than its toll on him, it twisted the young man's stomach. Barely able to hold anything down, the lad spent most of his day on the deck heaving over its railing, trying to keep what he had just eaten. A mist of ocean sprayed his fair skin with salt water, the air more bitter with the touch of frigid waters. He heaved again, his stomach retching tightening into a ball from the constant rocking, evacuating the meal he had just consumed. The taste of the stale bread and bean soup was far worse the second time around. Below he could see various fish feeding on the scraps of food he had just thrown up, darting about trying to steal their fill before the others ate it all.

Rohn was not an adventurer or a sailor. He had never been on a ship before; the closest he got to the ocean was when he and his late father had gone fishing. No, he was a scribe, an educated man, and a skilled artist. He spent his days pouring over books at the Queen's Academy, studying old manuscripts and sketching things that caught his eye. He didn't have the fortitude for a journey such as this, but it was far too late to turn back. His father, Edwin Durnham, had passed away a few months ago, leaving him alone in this big and often cruel world. The scribe had nothing left in England as he had sold everything to debtors as his father's business crumbled. What little silver remained from the auction was used to finish his education and afford basic supplies.

There was no lack of reasons to flee England either. War was brewing again, not only with France but a civil struggle between the great houses. It was no longer the enlightened land Emperor Artorius had envisioned. Instead, Lords bickered over land rights and made open threats over minor insults. A man of his age, in his early twenties, would be conscripted to die a gruesome death on a muddy and miserable battlefield over a long-forgotten slight made by some drunken noble. While the first horseman, war, approached the ancient kingdoms once again, its brothers would soon join in, delighted to aid their younger sibling in the destruction of civilization. Shiploads of serfs and lesser nobility alike fled for safer lands away from the creatures of the dark and the ambitious desires of the powerful.

Rohn's salvation came in the form of a surprise letter he received from a distant friend of his father. Sir Garrett Gerhardt was a Templar Knight, who was awarded land by Baron Edric Harmon for his services on the continent of Voskavia to the far west across the sea. The people of Britannia knew of the One Church's Templars all too well, from the stories told and songs sung by wandering bards of the holy warrior's rabid devotion. These men were deemed elite holy crusaders, feverishly loyal to God that could call on powers of the divine. They had often led the charge into new lands, culling the dark beasts that lurk in the shadows, cleaving out territory for their kinsmen to settle.

With a new Holy Crusade, known as The Purge, they marched with unfettered resolve across the newly discovered continent of Voskavia. Sir Gerhardt had led these expeditions into the unknown foreign landscape. They spoke of his bravery and loyalty even back home in England. Unleashing a brutal campaign as the Templar hunted anything deemed "unholy" and a threat to the Children of God by the Pope. They burnt pagan natives at the stake, wiping out entire nomadic tribes accused of witchcraft and devilry. These Holy warriors hunted ferocious monstrosities unheard of back home, impaling their heads on pikes bearing their banner, a not-so-subtle warning to survivors or would-be raiders. The corpses of the Purge piled taller than a lord's keep and burnt in pyres whose smoke blocked out the sun, as the Templar prayed to The One on bended knee. Their motto had become "Heads and Hearts" when facing the forces of darkness; two things to remove from a beast when felling it, to be sure it never rose again.

To credit the righteous violence, it made their land safer, for a while anyway. English settlements and homesteads sprouted all over Voskavia from farms to mines and even trading outposts. However, a shadow always reveals itself when the sunsets. The feral native tribes and ravenous primal creatures ebbed back in from the dark crevasses of the world. Greedily they consumed the doomed villages, taking vengeance on those settlers that were unlucky enough to be in their path. It seemed as soon as one homestead was founded another succumbed to the brutal and unforgiving frontier.

Rohn pulled his cloak tightly about his lean athletic form and curled into a ball, as he slumped down onto the damp wooden planks of the deck. He wiped his pale face of bile and looked out over the vessel, miserable, cold, and constantly nauseous. It was mid-morning; the sun trying to break through the dense fog that rolled over the ocean engulfing the large ship. The crash of angry waves slapping the side of the behemoth vessel as sailors and serfs alike scurried about tending to their duties.

While the ship was a fast war vessel, it was retrofitted to be a passenger boat, essentially gutted and stripped to the bare frame, to cram as many souls into its hull as able. Filled with hopeful settlers such as himself, all spending what little they had, carrying everything they owned, as they headed to an unknown continent in hopes of a prosperous new life. Packed bow to stern with peasants stuffed in like cattle. They slept wherever they could, huddled together in family groups, or if they were lucky, in a hammock precariously hung from the ship's hull as space was at a premium. The lower decks reeked of the pungent odor of body musk, pipe tobacco, and other unsavory scents with little ventilation to air out the cramped quarters. Buckets were constantly hoisted above deck from below, filled with excrement and other bodily fluids, and dumped over the side to avoid disease from contamination. Many of the peasants wouldn't survive the trip, either succumbing to illness, crime, or even going mad and committing suicide, as it wasn't unheard for them to succumb to cabin fever and jump overboard. The old and very young were always the most at risk during long sea voyages, as they hadn't the fortitude to survive such an unforgiving journey through harsh waters for so long. Those that died before landfall was given last rites by the clergy aboard, then quickly dumped over the side, becoming food for the sharks and other creatures that lurked in the depths below.

Needless to say, most of the passengers on the ship did not have the resources to make the journey from England. Instead, their travel was funded by local Lords or wealthy merchants who spent a pretty pence bringing them to the frontier.

There was no rest for them once they landed on the shores of the colony, they would slave away doing manual labor from dawn to dusk. Here they would work tirelessly to repay what they owed to their masters, many of them living and dying in servitude. The lucky ones worked hard and took side jobs if time allowed, usually extremely dangerous work that was more lucrative and paid well. This would help them work off their debt rapidly especially if all members of the household worked. If you could walk, you could plow a field, if you could sit, you could stitch clothing. With all this in consideration, they still had to contend with disease, famine, weather, barbaric raiders, and most of all the beasts, both natural and unnatural in this world.

While the Empire of Artorius was no stranger to the supernatural and paranormal creatures that dwelled upon the earth, Voskavia was a world apart. The settlers quickly learned this was a primal and treacherous landscape where ancient civilizations succumbed to the vicious beasts, harsh wilderness, and supernatural occurrences unique to the continent. The land was filled with horrors, but the lush temperate rainforest was also plentiful with both strange and familiar game, abundant with lumber, and its mountains filled with veins of precious metals, minerals, and gems. Many settlers braved the horrors of Voskavia's wilderness to exploit its untouched and almost unlimited resources, but more often than naught, the land claimed them as it had many others before.

Sir Garrett however was approaching his sunset and had sent for Rohn, insisting he needed his skills to document his memoirs and exploits. Rohn had no choice but to accept the generous proposal, excited to document the trials and tribulations of not only a Templar, but a highly respected commander. The generous knight had paid for Rohn's travel expenses in advance before he had even sent the letter. How could the young man refuse such a wonderful opportunity and the chance to escape war-torn England? With nothing to lose, Rohn traveled from Oxford to Pembroke and boarded the first ship to the frontier in the west.

"Feeding the fishes, eh, lad?" An aged brawny sailor chuckled, slapping Rohn's back. "You alright boy, perhaps a drink will settle your stomach?" He offered a leather flask of what reeked of rotgut.

"No, thank you," Rohn said, wiping sweat from his brow. "I fear it will make it worse." He tried to force a smile, his face pale and clammy.

"Suit yourself, lad," The sailor said, taking a big swig from his flask. "Hard travel, the ocean. This will be my second trip; I manned this vessel during the first pilgrimage."

"You've been here before?" The conversation began easing his nerves, taking his mind off the bobbing vessel.

"Oh, aye, been a sailor all my life, but this will be my second journey to Voskavia personally. Beautiful country during the day, just stay out of the forests at night. I've heard stories, that make the highland drakes and griffin prides back home seem like child's play." He chuckled.

"They're just animals, like any other big, strong, and dangerous of course, but animals nonetheless," Rohn said, shrugging. "Stay out of their territory and all is well."

"True enough, lad, but here? No, something is off. You can feel it when you set foot on its soil. The land doesn't want you here. Soldiers and sell-swords alike talk of things in the woods. There are monsters here, boy. The likes of which you've never seen. They've acquired the taste of human flesh. I've heard the stories the men tell in the taverns. Makes your skin crawl and if you're not eaten by a beast, then you need to watch out for the pagans. Godless heathens will split you open in the name of their feral gods. They make the highwaymen back home look like nuns." The sailor said, staring into the distance.

"So where you headed?" The sailor's attention darted back to Rohn.

"Gerhardt keep. It's a fief under the command of Sir Garrett." He answered, glancing to the letter tucked in his satchel.

"*The* Gerhardt? I know of him, not personally of course. He's a Templar, well respected and liked by most. People say he killed a dragon near Newcastle years back during the second Great Hunt; called upon personally by King Edward for the task. Slaying a dragon. Now that's a dangerous game. Of course not single-handedly, but he was one of three men left alive out of twenty if I remember the tale correctly. The survivors claimed he refused to leave his wounded kinsmen behind, nursed them back to health for almost a month. I suppose you'll learn if that's true eh?" He grinned at Rohn, his massive, weathered hand clapping the lad on the back again.

"Aye, my father would tell me the same tales. He was a close friend of his in England. The two had served in the same company when they were young. He and I sat around the hearth at night and he would go on and on telling me stories of their exploits as young soldiers. He always spoke highly of Sir Gerhardt, said he's a man of honor and God. A good man is a rarity it seems in this day and age. I am to travel from Port Eirburg to the fort, a driver has been arranged to bring me to his keep." Rohn said, finally his stomach calming as it got used to the slow rocking of the large vessel, the color returning to his face.

"Fort Dumont, the edge of the wilds that is, end of civilization. Untamed lands, even the natives steer clear of venturing too deep. It can be damned dangerous in those parts. Wonderful place for work make no mistake. Plenty of coin to be made and bursting with opportunity, but overly burdened with danger and death if you're foolish. A place better suited for mercenaries and less than savory personalities." He warned Rohn with a nod of his shaven head, now sprouting with a few days of peach fuzz.

Rohn took to his feet and offered his hand, "Thank you, sir, I never got your name."

"Gravy, they call me Gravy, 'cause I'm thick-headed and only useful for one thing." The man laughed, his mouth missing a few teeth as he grinned, shaking Rohn's hand with the grip of a giant.

"Rohn Durnham, a pleasure to meet you, sir," Rohn replied with a smile, wiggling his fingers to make sure they weren't broken.

"Aye, pleasures all mine. We should arrive soon, boy, get yourself together. You think the boat was rough wait till you arrive in Eirburg." Gravy laughed, slapping him on the back as he made his way to his duties. "God be with ye Rohn and be safe."

Rohn nodded in return as the man vanished back into the crowd of passengers and looked over the railing. His stomach was still touchy, but he could handle the waves if he focused on the horizon. The ocean was beautiful even in the mist, the light blue waves gently slapping the hull in a rhythmic motion. However, Rohn had heard stories about how deadly it could be as well. He overheard sailors telling tales of giant squids who would mistake a boat for a whale and bite a hole in the hull big enough to fit two men through. Rohn shuttered at the thought, staring into the black abyss under the boat, his imagination going wild, wondering what else might lurk down there.

"Land ho!" The sailor in the crow's nest bellowed as a bell began to ring, a flock of seagulls gliding around the vessel squawking a tale-tell sign of land nearby.

The English capital of Voskavia slowly peered through the mist. Its architecture solid and cold strengthened by ornate and monolithic pillars. Its granite walls blotted out the sun until late morning due to their sheer height and stood defiant against the water's frigid winds. The docks were made of stone blocks reinforced by timber to weather the harsh and unrelenting sea as it battered against its unyielding form.

Sailors ran along the railing as the ship began its sluggish drift into port, dumping speed as its sails collapsed. A rattling of the anchor startled Rohn as it plunged into the waters below with a splash careening to the seabed. The ship lilted into the dock; the sailors throwing ropes to dozens of dockhands lined along the pier, pulling in unison with a chorus of grunts as hard as they could to keep the vessel in position, as they quickly scurried about tying off their ends. With its anchor dragging into the seabed, scarring the sandy earth below, the ship glided to a halt with a defiant moan. As the galleon gradually came to a stop, its wooden frame groaned as the commoners erupted into cheers and jubilation. The ship's hands quickly laid several planks from the ship to the dock, and almost immediately the boat began unloading. People flooding off, thankful to have made the trip safely, eager to once again be on firm land. However, for Rohn, his journey was just beginning.

II

The young scribe was in awe of the capital; its walls rivaled even those of London as they encased the entire city in a thick stone barrier. He tightly wrapped his cloak around himself to fight the bitter wind that rolled off the water, as he slung his bag over a shoulder, gawking at his surroundings. The architecture was years beyond the mainland, but he supposed it had to be to withstand the harsh living conditions of the primal continent. As dangerous as the territory was, people fluttered about as ignorance was bliss he assumed. They toiled away day after day happy to be away from England's endless wars and famine.

The docks were brimming with laborers preparing boats for the day's work ahead as fishermen pulled in their hauls, returning from sea. Carts hurried past him to the market, filled with strange and familiar fish to be sold, their pervading odor lingering in the air as they passed. A group of anglers celebrated near the hanging corpse of a merfolk female. Its bloated carcass hung on the pier dangling by its tail like a trophy catch of the day as peasants shook the fishermen's hands and admired their prize. Its bladed finned arms ended in webbed clawed hands, dangling lifelessly still oozing from its various wounds. The smell of its dark mottled fleshy hide carried with the breeze, reeking like a low tide at the docks at home, as several bolts still protruded from its body. The creature's face was hideous. Big bulbous black eyes stuck from its skull and its mouth was half the size of its head, filled with rows of needle-like teeth.

The crowd, ever moving forward like salmon upstream, pushed Rohn on. He stared in marvel as he passed through the gates of the docks into the main portion of the city. The walls, covered to the brim with homes stacked several stories high, catwalks snaking in and out winding paths for commoners who scurried about like busy ants. The city was bustling with life, especially in the morning. Shop owners bellowed to the passing crowd, showing their wares and the familiar sound of a hammer hitting an anvil tinged from various sections of the city. Carts and wagons streamed through the dirt streets as peasants went about their day-to-day. Children chased one another barefoot with wooden swords, yelling and carrying on. Stray dogs rummaged through the garbage in a narrow darkened alleyway behind a pair of city guards as they leaned carelessly with their backs to a cleaned, whitewashed wall. It was overwhelming even for a city boy like Rohn. While he was used to the hustle and bustle of city life, England had nothing like it. It conformed to its tight and claustrophobic constraints in the confined space it had, instead of outward it raised upward blotting out what little sun shone through the cloud cover.

Rohn tiptoed, dodging the contents of a chamber pot doused in the street. Almost simultaneously he bounded to the side of the road as a wagon roared past carrying lumber to the docks. He wandered the streets looking for the carriage office mentioned in the letter he received. His search had him wander through a less than savory district. Ladies called to him, bearing their legs and shoulders, their faces painted with bright and alluring colors, as the scent of their spicy perfumes filled the air. Rohn quickly made his way past like a rabbit running through a wolf's den, the women cackling and laughing as they made bawdy comments and teased to pinch his rear.

"C'mon love! Long trip sure to leave you stiff! I can relax those muscles of yours!" A harlot called to him, winking her eye suggestively.

"No, thank you, madam!" Rohn said, spinning a corner and smacking his face into the back of a wall of muscle and ill-temper.

The brawny sailor turned and snarled at him. "The hell is your problem boy?" He growled towering over Rohn, a clay mug in his hand its contents splashed across his scarred knuckles.

"My apologies sir, sincerely, I was distracted," Rohn said as he tried to back away quickly.

The man's enormous paw reached out and grabbed him by the vest, "Fancy lad. You need to watch out where you're going. Easy to stumble accidentally into a man's knife if you're not careful." He said threateningly, with a grin. Most of his teeth were yellow or missing behind his ragged beard and one of his eyes was long gone, leaving nothing but a fleshy alcove that he bore with pride.

Rohn desperately tried to slip free, but was no match for his strength. "Please sir, I swear it, I meant no disrespect."

"Oi, Rohn!" A familiar voice came from behind the man as Gravy poked his head out of the tavern crowd nearby.

The brute eyed Gravy and then Rohn as he sneered, his breath overpowering with ale and salted fish. "Your tosser of a friend here needs to watch his step or he might get steel in his belly."

"That would be a daft thing to do, sir," Gravy interjected, "The young lad is on his way to his master. A Templar, if I'm correct." Gravy added, emphasizing his point.

The thug slowly let Rohn go immediately upon hearing who he served. "I've no interest in making enemies of the church. Piss off boy before I change my mind."

Rohn nodded and quickly joined Gravy as he drank his pint outside, the two scurrying off down the street. "You have my thanks again. If it wasn't for you, he would have killed me."

"Probably," Gravy said with a grin, "But then again your master would have had him chained and the damn fool would have been worked to death at the Stonestead quarry." He said slapping the boy's arm.

"So what do you think of this fine city?" Gravy said, motioning about, a bit of his ale splashing onto the dirt street and Rohn's boots.

Rohn nodded and smiled, kicking the ale from his rugged footwear, "It's amazing. I've seen nothing like it before. I would love to explore it more, but I'm afraid I must be off; I should meet Sir Gerhardt as soon as possible. I'm looking for the driver's guild on Reeves Street."

"Ah of course," Gravy said finishing a deep drink from his mug, "Bit pricey but it's a safe way to make it from town to town. As I said before, outside the walls of this city lurks some horrid beasts and nasty folk."

With a thick sausage finger Gravy pointed the way, "Just beyond those stalls, look for the sign, can't miss it."

"Thank you, let me pay for your drink at least." Rohn moved to his purse.

"No, lad, tuck that into your pants, don't let the folk round here know you got coin. You can pay me back some other time." Gravy said with a smile slapping him on the shoulder again the old sailor not knowing his strength as Rohn winced with the blow.

"Thank you, sir, and may God be with you," Rohn said as he made his way, hoping to one day see Gravy again.

Chapter 2:

Of Mice and Men

I

Aiden felt like he had been riding for weeks, but he had made the trip from Fort Dumont to Port Eirburg in but a few hours, pushing his nag to exhaustion. The young laborer was in his early twenties and had grown up on the frontier, usually spending his days loading wagons of goods to Eirburg for shipment to England, but today he had a more dire duty to attend to. He was alone in this world as his mother passed due to illness on the boat voyage here, and his father died a few months later of an injury. He had little left except for his one love, his betrothed. She lived on the outskirts of the fort with her family, and when he went to call on his dear Maisie, he had found her cabin ransacked and vacant. Pleading with his Lord, Alistair Dumont, he was sent to request aid from the capital. For the past few hours, he rode a scrawny farm horse he had won in a dice game, hoping Baron Harmon would send them more soldiers for protection. Luckily for young Aiden, Lord Dumont feared the wilds as much as his laborers did, rarely leaving the protection of his fort as he sent the lad out in his stead.

Although sore from the long, hard ride, the sight of the region's capital, Port Eirburg, still amazed him. The city was founded on the coast of the continent, on the only suitable land for miles. Most of the coast consisted of jagged cliffs covered in thick forests. Lord Harmon had put laborers, engineers, and craftsmen to work, erecting the massive stone castle, complete with layered walls. As more and more immigrated to Voskavia, the city grew, fueled by the labor of those who arrived. The port city had become a bustling and lively hub of activity. The center, and a true sign of civilization on the continent. Port Eirburg's design was planned out in great detail and expense. It was an oval or wagon wheel layout, with varied layers of thick walls that protected each district, acting as chokepoints should an enemy invasion or uprising ensue.

Well-fortified within its walls were its nobles, skilled craftsmen, clergy, and trained military. The common men and women ran apothecaries, bathhouses, taverns, and all sorts of merchant stalls and shops, from clothing to tools, and high-end brothels that were scattered throughout the capital. Eirburg was built during the early days of the frontier, a much different day and age when the horrors of the new world were prevalent. Port Eirburg now had become a massive exporter of quality lumber from its dense and endless forests. Silver seemed in abundant supply deep within its mountains, and its hunting outposts were sources of fur and rare beasts that were used for labor or even kept as pets.

Outside, its walls were protected by a moat that was close to ten feet deep in most areas. It was filled with pikes and whatever creatures swam in and out freely through the ocean. Seeing a bull shark slowly glide through the water wasn't uncommon for its residents. Eirburg's tall outer stone walls were almost ten feet thick and protected by massive towers that were manned by over two hundred city guards. They equipped the curtain wall with siege equipment, such as the ballista and catapults, capable of defending the city from invaders. Outside the ports defenses, were vast acres of farmland. The fields were tended to season after season, filling the castle's stores with wheat, barley, and other necessities to survive the harsh winters of Voskavia.

While the city's defenses were a magnificent sight to behold, they were rivaled by the One Church's citadel on the opposite side of the city to Lord Harmon's stone palace. The One Church funded a good deal of the frontier's infrastructure, mainly labor, which gave it a powerful hold on its people. While many looked to nobility for work and security, the people turned to the church for hope and spiritual guidance. The Church pulled in a healthy sum of coin from the lowly peasantry to its wealthier noble houses. Offering a variety of services, from medical assistance from its well-trained monks to the most benign blessing of livestock or new resource camps. One is not to worry if they can't afford to "donate" at the time of the church's services, as you can always work off your debts... which accrued interest especially if one needed food, clothing, and shelter. The Church also had a decent army of its own. Eirburg's citadel housed close to forty Templar chaplains that were trained in martial combat and spiritual warfare. They guarded its hallowed grounds with feverish zeal against both man and monster. The Templars, donned in heavy armor, were a force to be reckoned with as they aided Lord Harmon's soldiers in securing the colony's territory. The holy warriors would paint their faces white, marked with red crosses to insight fear in the natives. They soon got the reputation of being invincible, filled with the righteousness of their God; they stood against insurmountable odds and survived. Many had fallen during the Purge, but while vastly outnumbered, the Templars had a high survival rate because of their faith and bonds of brotherhood. It was a common belief that a small group of Templars equaled an army of the King's men.

As Aiden passed the center of town, he felt insignificant between the citadel's massive iron-reinforced walls and the Baron's castle that cast a shadow over an entire neighborhood. He noted how well swept and clean the streets were here. No beggars or drunkards littered the roads. Everyone was working, most of them because of the debts they accrued. He pitied them, realizing how blessed he was, and prayed he would never come to such recourse. Aiden shook off such thoughts and refocused his efforts on the situation at hand.

Castle Harmon was a grand structure still being perfected by its current resident. It's rumored the Baron had redone the blueprints for it over a dozen times in the first week of its inception, sending men to every corner of the map for stone and lumber. Aiden let out a sigh of relief as he finally made it to the gates of the castle; he dismounted and tied his horse up, letting the animal rest for the first time in hours. The poor beast eagerly drank from a trough after such a hard ride, its mouth as dry as paper. Aiden gently patted the beast before he made his way up the steps of the keep and over the drawbridge to the entrance. Massive double doors made of thick oak reinforced with iron bands stood as an imposing barrier to the gateway inside.

The palace was lavish and spotless, everything the young warehouse worker had expected. Its stone floors were washed daily and covered in ornately woven rugs. The air was filled with lavender and freshly cut flowers as the kitchens baked bread, and spiced meats flowed through the halls with an alluring and almost obscene aroma.

Aiden straightened himself up, spotting his reflection in a shield in the main entry. He removed his cap to straighten his hair as a posh and haughty gentleman approached him, wearing fine breeches, a satin tunic, and an upturned nose.

"If you are looking for kitchen scraps, dear boy, we hand them out after supper behind the servant's quarters," the well-spoken elderly man said.

"No sir, that's not why I'm here. I come with grave news and wanted to have an audience with Lord Harmon if possible. My Lord, Alistair Dumont sent me, sir; he sent word I would be arriving," Aiden said as humbly as he could, barely making eye contact with the man.

The steward looked Aiden over for a moment and then nodded, "Follow me. I will see if Lord Harmon has a spare moment, but he is quite busy."

"I assure you, sir, it's extremely important. Dumont Outpost may be in danger," Aiden pleaded, trying to keep his tone low as not to draw attention.

The man spun on a heel with grace and poise honed over years of holding court and led the young man down a side hallway.

"You had better be right, boy, or you're going to wish you had been here for scraps. You may wait in here until Lord Harmon summons you."

The herald ushered him into a room with another door to its far side, furnished with various plush chairs and sofas which he had only read about in tawdry books.

Before Aiden could thank the man, the door clicked shut behind him, and once again, he was alone. For the first time in a while, he sat down and rested, slumping into one of the overstuffed chairs as he rested his weary head on his hand. His eyes grew heavy, like bags of sand, and for the first time a few days, his exhaustion overcame him.

II

"Lord Harmon will see you now," The chamberlain said as he stood in the opposite doorway, this time more loudly, waking the boy from his slumber, and causing Aiden to jump from his sleep. "Wipe your face lad, and straighten yourself up. You'll not see Baron Harmon looking like you just awoke in the alley," he added snidely.

Aiden quickly took to his feet, straightening his dusty and worn attire as he wiped the spittle from his mouth. He skulked past the smug servant and through the ornate doorway into the audience chamber on the other side. The laborer couldn't help but timidly walk through the large hall, feeling well out of place next to the local nobility and wealthy merchants. They were dressed in the latest fashions of silks and satins and gently misted with perfumes made of juniper and coconut oil.

The palace was as ornate as its inhabitants. The room smelt of sage that slowly burnt to keep away foul spirits, its essence wavering through the hall like a ghost. Smooth stone pillars that were three times the height of a man held the massive room's clay tiled roof with unflinching strength. A tapestry hung from each of the stoic pillars, woven in bright colors displaying notable moments in the taming of Voskavia by the English Empire. In front of each pillar resided a guard in ornate well-polished plate mail, covered by a red and gold tabard decorated with the head of a lion, the symbol of House Harmon. In their right hand, they held a fire lance, a rare and exotic weapon from the east, only given to the most elite of the elite, the Royal Guard. The weapon resembled a halberd, but instead of a benign shaft, the end was a blunderbuss that could be loaded with iron pellets. They usually fired it from the hip, as it was not an accurate weapon and had a horse-like kick. Aiden had heard tales of it being used during peasant uprisings on the mainland. Just a few lines of Royal Guards could decimate an entire army of peasants in moments, shredding those foolish enough to be in the crowd's front to bits, spraying those behind them with their kinsman. That was usually more than enough to disperse the crowd and quell the uprising, and if not, the weapon could still be used to hammer, impale, and hack those who remained into submission. Their presence was intimidating to the weary young man, and as he passed each one, their steel-clad heads would slowly follow him.

As Aiden approached the Baron's table, the four noblemen stopped their conversation, appearing insulted by the peasant's presence. Their judgmental gaze crept over Aiden like a shadow at dusk, the crowd suddenly falling silent, as all eyes fell to the young man. He stood before the most powerful men on the continent, doing his best to not vomit from nerves. Aiden bowed to the best of his ability, but they only met his effort with chuckling and whispers from the crowd at his clumsy attempt. Lord Marshal Hendrik, commander of the castle's forces, scowled at the audience, his imposing form clad in battered but polished plate.

"Silence," he scolded them through a thick gray mustache, not so much for Aiden's sake, but the respect of his Lord. "You will show decorum and restraint in the Lord's hall."

Aiden's attention briefly drew to the Lord Marshal. He was in his late fifties, a large man, as even sitting down he was almost as tall as Aiden. He had bear's paw hands and thick pork chop sideburns that flowed into a mustache that he bore with pride as they were well-trimmed and neat. Aiden almost wanted to smile at the man, but was too fearful to even move. He quickly recovered from his daze and swallowed hard, not knowing where to start. It seemed like forever since anyone had uttered a word, as the silence was deafening now.

"Thank you, my Lord, for seeing me on such brief notice," Aiden forced out of his mouth with a trembling voice, as his tone bounced off the granite walls, the tapestries failing to muffle his voice. "I know you are very busy, Lord Harmon, but I fear something horrible has happened to a family in your province."

"Calm yourself, young man, and proceed," Lord Harmon said softly, his gaze not leaving Aiden, as he took a sip from a goblet on the table.

Aiden recognized the powerful Baron. His reputation was well known throughout the Empire. While not physically imposing at first glance, it was his demeanor that daunted most men. The Baron was of average height and lean build, in his late sixties. Confident, intelligent, and always in control of his emotions, Baron Edric Harmon had a reputation as a powerful negotiator and tactician. While not a cold person, he was calculated, logical and patient, which made him excel in his position. He knew more than he said, and even if he didn't, he made you think he did.

His legend was varied, but many portions remained steadfast. Once an obscure merchant, he had blossomed into a powerful trader and proprietor of goods, catching the eye of King Edward. The English Empire had needed more resources to fuel its military and economy, as it was still at war with France. The discovery of Voskavia to the west was a blessing from God. Edric had seized the opportunity and offered his services to King Edward, who was desperate to win what seemed like an endless conflict. Edric set out and successfully navigated his way to the new resource-abundant continent, returning to England with loads of lumber and precious metals. Edric talked his way into becoming the Baron of Voskavia, explaining that the King needed all his vassals by his side, and should send him in their stead. King Edward agreed and with the title of Baron, Edric settled the new land and sent its abundant resources to England. Everyone knew this colony was his life and his legacy, and he would let no one, take it from him.

"Yes, my Lord, as you wish, my Lord," Aiden stumbled over himself, unsure how to begin as small beads of sweat trickled down his brow. "My name is Aiden, my Lord. I work at Dumont Outpost as a laborer. There I met my fiancé, Maisie, who's gone missing. She would work as a barmaid, then return to her farm to aid her family. We were to be married in the fall, just after my twentieth birthday," Aiden said slowly, gaining confidence.

"We don't need your life story, boy. We are busy men. Be quick about it!" Bishop Varik spat out bluntly, interrupting the young man's train of thought, as his fat fingers played with the rim of his chalice.

"Yes, my apologies, your eminence." Aiden bowed slightly to the Bishop, trying to gather his thoughts.

Aiden became tense, struggling to find the courage to speak once more. "I went to check on her since she hadn't been to the outpost that week. She usually comes in by midday, as I would walk her home before dark. I figured she might have taken ill, so I went to visit her with some sweet bread and beet soup from the outpost, as it's her favorite." Aiden smiled but quickly caught himself when noticing the other men did not share his candor.

"I arrived at dusk and noticed the house was quiet. Not a soul was to be found. Even her little brother, who usually works the fields until dark, was nowhere to be seen. Her front door was left open, ripped from the hinges, and the shutters had been hacked to splinters. The cabin was a mess, as if there was a struggle, and the floors stained with blood. I searched the nearby woods for her, yet found no tracks, then quickly made my way back to the fort and informed Lord Dumont. I'm terrified barbarians have taken her, or even worse. Recently, her father and a group of woodsmen went missing as well, not far from her cabin. Please, my Lord, the outpost is terrified of what will happen next," Aiden finished, cowed in the council's presence. His eyes locked with Lord Harmon's, desperation on his face as he wrung his cap in his sweaty palms.

"Your concern is noted, young man. You have my thanks for bringing this to my attention. My council and I will decide what will be done, if anything at all. You are dismissed. God be with you." Lord Harmon spoke firmly but softly as he motioned the young man out the way he came.

Aiden bowed awkwardly, this time with no ridicule from the audience who were too busy gossiping in hushed whispers. Lord Harmon watched the boy leave and scanned the audience, noticing the change in those gathered. This would get out of hand if not dealt with swiftly.

"Dumont Outpost holds what, twenty men at the present? Sir Alistair knows he holds a major asset in this region, and we cannot let it come to harm or it would choke our supply chain. Word will spread, as will panic, and panic leads to less productivity. What will it cost to send a small company of soldiers to reinforce the outpost?" He asked, slowly turning his attention to the thin, pale, middle-aged man rolling a large ring on his right ring finger.

"Negligible, my Lord, though we could offer to help with coin, to hire mercenaries. Fort Dumont is riddled with them as it is so close to wild territory," Dusan, Lord Harmon's clerk, and bookkeeper answered as he gently brushed a lock of ebony hair from his face with long, thin fingers.

"If I might make a suggestion, my Lord?" Lord Marshal Hendrik asked, leaning back in his chair. "Sending soldiers to the area, while prudent, may cause more distress to the region than good. I can spare, say, fifty men, if needed, as mercenaries are expensive and wholly unreliable. Take also into consideration that peasants are easily startled, and merchants will avoid an area they think is troubled. Why not send a vassal of yours? I believe Sir Gerhardt is close to the region. He deals with the outpost often, does he not? He is more than capable of handling such affairs, and a smaller group of locals will rouse less intrigue from the common folk and thus less disruption to the region's economy."

"Aye, and who gives a piss if the bastard is ripped to shreds by beasts in the wilds? He dares to turn his back on the church. And on the Pope himself! Refuses to return to England, claiming his days of glory are well behind him. He dares to refuse the will of God, instead choosing to isolate himself in melancholy as a recluse with only his servants to keep him company. What a pathetic wretch he has become. Such a miserable existence, a life with no purpose, no hope," Bishop Varik snorted as he finished his goblet of wine, and glared at a nearby servant for not refilling it quickly enough, and anticipating his needs.

Lord Harmon stared out over the crowd in attendance, who were now assuredly concerned over the young man's message. He slowly brought his hands to his face, smoothing out his trimmed beard as he considered the options, and folding his fingers over his wrinkled lips. While Lord Alistair was a boil on his ass, he held the land's supply of lumber and fur trade in his greedy yet spineless hands.

"It seems I have little choice. Dusan, send a missive. I hope my old friend is still up to the task. We will play nursemaid to Alistair, but I'll not lose my foothold in the region. We have sacrificed too much to lose our grip on the continent," Baron Harmon stated, staring into the crowd.

"What of Stonestead, and Hweabrea? Should we warn the Du'Vales?" Bishop Varik asked hesitantly, holding his wine almost defensively.

"Of what? We know nothing as of right now. We're spread too thin as it is. Until more men and supplies arrive from England, we wait. We know little of the situation and cannot spare resources on 'what ifs'," Lord Harmon said with finality.

"I'll be sure the men at the fort are on alert. It is better to be safe than sorry," Commander Hendrik added.

The men at the table rose as Lord Harmon stood, all giving a slight bow as he made his way from the chamber, the Lord Marshal following close behind.

Bishop Varik turned to Dusan as the audience gradually emptied the main hall.

"It would be a shame if the outpost were to fall," Varik dared to quip as their lord was no longer at the table.

"Yes, it would," Dusan stated, curiously looking to the Bishop.

"If it did, I'm sure it would rattle the faith King Edward has in Lord Harmon. Of course, the Church would be more than happy to take control until a suitable replacement is found. Perhaps someone who has worked closely with Baron

Harmon would make a more suitable Lord," Varik suggested, slightly smiling to Dusan.

"Are you implying what I think you are, fat man?" Dusan replied dryly.

Bishop Varik scowled, a grimace lurking on his face. "You'll be wise to watch your tone pagan. You might have Edric fooled, but I've yet to see you grace the temple's halls. We still burn witches, several each month." He sipped from his goblet.

"And they behead usurpers." Dusan smiled as he gathered his things from the table.

"Oh, be calm, savage. I speak merely of a possible scenario, one of many. The Baron has no heir, no wife, his entire life spent to bring him to this point. Though should he fall from grace, or more likely, die of sickness or war, our King Edward would not just abandon this endeavor. Too much relies on it. God forbid France claimed this land, its mysteries, and resources ripe for the taking. England would fall like Rome. God forbid it." The Bishop crossed himself quickly and popped a grape into his mouth, squirting juice onto the table as he mouthed it like bovine. "He would, however, happily replace the fledgling Baron, perhaps with a… native? Who knew its peoples and was familiar with the English."

"You speak daggers, holy man."

"I speak hypothetically. We must have plans should our dearest Baron fall. Just ponder it, let it roll around in that pretty little skull of yours," he said, no longer gazing at Dusan as he finished his wine with a gulp.

"As you wish, my eminence." Dusan offered a slight bow to the Bishop as he left the hall.

Varik sat at the table alone now. A smile crossed his face, thinking of how wonderful it would be to do so day after day. All in good time, he thought. Good things come to those who wait.

Chapter 3:

Teeth and Talon, Steel and Wheel

I

The clanking of picks on stone throughout the tunnels was almost deafening, but when living in Stonestead you learned to shut it out. It became background noise, like the singing of birds to a farmer, or the roll of wheels to a merchant; static noise your mind erases from its conscious thought. It always surprised nobles what a serf could get used to, from hard pallet beds with minimal padding to the gruel they ate and the brutal work conditions they endured day after day. Most of the settlement was underground. Only the merchant quarters, soldiers' tents, and the nobles' keep were above on the surface, protected by a wooden palisade and thirty of House Du'Vale soldiers.

The workers all lived in close quarters in the mine. Eating, drinking, sleeping, even raising their children in the dark, dank confines of the intertwined tunnels and caves, only going to the surface as needed. Stonestead, while not as large as Port Eirburg, was just as vital. The mine supplied the cut granite for the port's walls, its iron ore for tools, weapons, and armor, and minerals like salt.

Baron Harmon had leased the land to House Du'Vale, offering Edgar vassalage, with reluctance, as the two had been rivals for many years in England. Edgar Du'Vale was furious when word had reached him of Edric Harmon's good fortune, and he claimed the Baron had gotten the title only because one of them traveled by land, and the other by sea, and Edric was in the right place at the right time; nothing more. Edgar had spent the past few years traveling Asia, purchasing rare and highly sought-after goods such as spices, dye, and fabrics. He then returned from the perilous expeditions to sell the luxuries to nobility at highly inflated prices, earning a hefty sum. In turn, the Du'Vales had to spend a tidy sum to purchase labor and soldiers to get the mine up and running, jumping at the opportunity to settle in the resource-rich frontier. A knighthood, offered by the new Baron of Voskavia, was nothing to scoff at. The merchant house saw a fortune that could be had. While it was not the preferred title Edgar desired, it was acceptable, and a step in the right direction.

"I don't give a damn if the men are tired. We need to fill the order before the end of the week! Do you want to be the one explaining why they were off task to Sir Edgar?" The foreman berated the small man, his breath thick with the smell of beer and onion soup as his voice echoed down the shafts of the mine.

"The men aren't just tired, sir, they're scared. Something is lurking in the mine. We keep hearing guttural growls and footsteps. We fear it may be haunted or even bewitched," the thin, older peasant said, desperation on his face. He held a pick in front of his chest, cradling it defensively in emaciated fingers.

"You get your worthless arse back to work, or I'll find someone who will. Ghosts and ghouls be damned!" He snarled, poking the laborer in the chest with a meaty finger, dust puffing off the serf's hemp tunic.

"If we could just bring some guards down here, it would make the lads—" He dared to interject but stopped short at the sight of the overseer's furrowed brow and gritted teeth.

"Did you not fucking hear me?! The soldier's man the fort above. If they come down here to swaddle your precious ass, then who keeps the natives from slitting the Lord's throat in the middle of the night? Then, the only one to care about your rotting corpse will be the dog who pisses on it," the barrel-chested foreman interrupted him, almost nose to nose with the sickly appearing serf. "Back. To. Work." His sour breath wafted in the peasant's face, almost enough to knock him back.

Just as the foreman finished his sentence, a scream echoed from deep in the mine. Both of their gazes snapped to the passage it originated from. "Now what?" The beefy man said, his thick arms shrugging in surrender.

He shoved his way past the frail miner who thudded into the rocky side of the passage. The foreman trod down the narrow corridor, blazing a path through a river of workers, their picks gradually coming to a stop as they watched the commotion. The taskmaster shoved them out of the way as he came through like a bull, head lowered, eyes narrowed, his candlelit lantern held high and leading the way.

"Back to work! No Gawking!" He berated them as he bowled by. The serfs flinched in response and quickly returning to their jobs, fearful of retribution by the hulking thug.

The clinking had stopped up ahead, infuriating the foreman even more and causing him to pick up his pace. In front of him, the passage opened to a larger area, the ceiling about twenty feet high and rimmed with wooden scaffolding. It was well-lit with torches and its form scarred with black smears as the flames danced on the ore-filled walls, but not a soul was to be found. The miners in Stonestead were mostly serfs. However, some were prisoners given the chance to complete their sentences early with hard labor. While the mine shafts intertwined throughout the mountainside, there was only one way in or out of the tunnels, and the peasants weren't above finding a dark alcove to sleep in, or play dice.

"Where the hell is everyone?" The foreman spat, drawing a short, barbed, cattail whip from his hip. "You had better not be slacking off, or it's the cat's claws that'll wake you!"

He cautiously moved into the open area, stepping onto the wooden planks that crisscrossed the cavern, each one making a low creak, groaning in resistance beneath the weight that bore down on them. The chamber was now abandoned; just a few minutes before it had been filled with the clank of picks and chatter of men as they chiseled away. Their tools lay scattered over the hard ground where they had stood as if dropped suddenly, abandoned like trash on the street. The taskmaster studied the earthen floor, his eyes narrowing as he searched, small patches of muddy dark soil leading him onward. The burly man was once more on their heels and raised his lantern, his whip at the ready as he made his way through the dark passage. His boots thumped as he walked for only a few dozen steps as his lantern revealed a foreign portion of the tunnel. A thick smell of musk filled the air as it flowed past him, almost as if in warning. This passage was new, as it bared no wooden beams for support, and its walls were raw and jagged. It appeared as if one of the miners broke through into a natural cavern, as it wasn't unusual to come across such natural formations in the tunnels. New caves and passages were discovered almost every day down here as the men scoured for precious metals, however, the smell that emanated from the inky black void was horrid, a mixture of body odor, feces, and decay. The foreman gagged and covered his face with the inside of his arm as he pressed on.

They are probably in there slacking off, he thought, the grip on his whip tightening as his knuckles whitened. With a growl, he ducked his head and shoved his enormous belly through the narrow passage, wincing as it squeezed his protruding gut.

Oh, they are going to pay, his mind thundered, as he tried to maintain his balance on the loose rocks, the soil sliding from under him. Halfway down the treacherous slope, his foot slipped on something wet yet thick, his worn leather boots losing their grip. The large man's back scraped along the stones and earth as he slid down the rubble, tumbling as he went, his whip and lantern scattering as he came to a stop on the cavern floor with a resounding thud.

He could only cough. Small plumes of dust lofting into the air around his mouth, his chubby cheek mashed by the weight of his head on the dirt. Groaning, the air gradually returned to him, filling his lungs. He pushed himself up to his knees, swearing up a storm as he did. His hands gripped the soft dirt in anger, the particles sliding under his already filthy nails. Still on all fours, he gasped to catch his breath, glaring into the dark like an animal, and spat on the ground, the salty, gritty taste of dirt on his tongue. His eyes began adjusting, his pupils dilating to absorb what little light there was, his surroundings revealing themselves little by little. He felt around blindly for the handle of his whip, but instead found a patch of sticky, muddy earth that oozed through his fingers. With disgust on his face, he frantically looked for his lantern, completely helpless without a source of light. With relief, he spotted its dim glow flickering in the inky blackness of the cavern, the weak flame surviving his fall. The foreman scurried on all fours, his efforts leaving a trail of dust that billowed in the air as he went. While he was in pain, he couldn't help but smile joyfully, once again reunited with the lantern's warmth. Only then did he notice his fingers covered in dark, viscous blood, painted with red chunks of dirt, stringy hair, and various bits of organic material. He wiped his hands on the leather jerkin in vain as the gore just smeared across his armor. Once again gripping his lantern, he felt more confident with its pallid light as he tried to compose himself. The room was larger than he had thought, as the ceiling was far from the reach of his vision. The walls were filled with tiny dark alcoves and large boulders that lay motionless on the surface of the cavern floor.

Carefully, he slung the lantern around the cavern and gasped in horror at the scene as its amber light created shadows that moved as though they were alive. The miners were everywhere, literally. Arms, legs, heads, and torsos were strewn about, tattered, and ripped apart.

Who in God's name did this? His thoughts scattered and panicked, his heart rapidly beating, pumping his body with adrenaline. Behind him, footsteps lightly padded on the ground, barely audible.

"Don't fuck with me, lads! I'll take your heads! I'm not to be trifled with. I'll ring your necks! You're going to hang for this!" He said, expecting one of the prisoners to rush out of the shadows at any minute and put a thick iron pick in his skull.

His trembling, sticky hand found its way to a leather-wrapped hilt on his hip, the short blade shimmering from the light of his lantern as he drew it from its scabbard. The void was pitch black; even the candle had a hard time piercing the darkness that seemed to move around him. His breathing was now heavy and rapid. His eyes darted through the cavern, trying to pierce its darkness as his panic grew. Another patter of footsteps sounded behind him. The now frightened foreman spun in the loose dirt to spot the origin, but the figure vanished in the dark just out of sight. He spun again, anticipating where the next noise might originate with his blade pointing the way. That's when he saw a small shadow dart behind a boulder, then gently peek out cautiously. Something was watching him, murmuring from behind the large rock, an arm's length away. He lifted the lantern; the light bleeding through the darkness and revealing an oval-shaped head and two black eyes that winced from the timid but blinding light. Its pale green skin, covered in blood, as it clung to the rock like a lizard, with clawed hands and feet gripping into the stone. Equipped with small but powerful limbs, keeping it steady as it stared at the man, its dark orbs studying him. It was the size of a small child, only a foot or two tall, but its head was large and covered in thick, coarse fur of various shades of black and brown, flowing down its small yet muscular frame. The creature's long, pointed ears protruded outwards, turning independently of one another and scanning for the slightest noise.

"What in the bloody hell are you?" The foreman said, inching towards it slowly, his blade hidden behind him, as it might agitate the small being.

The creature cocked its head as if trying to understand the odd noises he was making. It let out a small chitter from its throat in response, inspecting the disheveled human before him. The foreman moved carefully, with purpose, not taking his eyes off the creature as his muscles tensed and flexed, preparing to burst like a spring. Sir Edgar would reward him handsomely for killing the bugger who took the lives of the serfs he paid good coin for, and it was going to be hard enough explaining the deaths of ten men with nothing to place the blame on.

"Calm down, little one. I ain't here to harm you," he said, a quiver in his tone, as his fingers adjusted on the handle of his sword, the leather wrap conforming to his grip. "Don't you want to be friends, little bugger?" He forced a grin.

The creature cocked its head to the side, curious, as he watched the new infiltrator. With a sudden burst of motion, the man lunged out, slashing his blade at the goblin, but it was far too fast for him. It became nothing more than a blur of fur as it bolted from his sight in a cloud of smoke and sparks, as the blade hit nothing but the stone. The taskmaster stumbled in a pool of what used to be one of his subordinates, a man he had played dice with earlier in the week. He quickly regained his balance, standing in a defensive posture, blade outward as beads of sweat rolled down his pale face.

"Shit!" The man said as he watched the creature dart up the rock face with blinding speed, growling and snarling all the way.

His eyes following the beast as it scurried to safety, well out of his reach, its powerful limbs allowing it to climb across the stone completely upside down. The foreman's eyes were still adjusting to the darkness as he tried to focus on it as it moved, the dull light of his lantern little use. It was growling as it scurried from place to place in the dark, nothing more than a faint silhouette. To the overseer's surprise, a shadow next to his target moved, then another. Something dripped onto the foreman's shoulder as he stared at the ceiling. His gaze followed a chunk of flesh as it fell to his feet. It had once been an arm, but gnawed on, barely recognizable if it had not been for the fingers that remained.

Horror plastered across his face as he looked back up, his eyes focusing on the various movements above him. He narrowed his vision in the blackness, desperately trying to peer through the ebon shroud that hung above him. That's when he saw them. The ceiling was covered in the small creatures, their black eyes all blinking as they chittered and growled at the intruder deep within their territory. The goblins snarled, pulling their thin lips back to reveal enormous mouths, half the size of their heads, filled with two rows of sharp, jagged teeth that glinted in the dark. More revealed themselves from the numerous alcoves in the walls. The room filled with a malicious symphony of growls and screeches as the beasts closed in on their prey.

"God be merciful…" the man whispered, the color draining from his face as warm urine ran down his leg.

A screech resonated behind him, as the mob poured down in a flutter of chaos. The foreman flailed his blade in the air randomly, to no avail, as a flurry of hungry mouths soon doused him. Like bees they swarmed, clawing and biting. A sharp pain shot through his arm from his wrist as his blade fell to the ground still gripped in his meaty severed hand. They were unnaturally strong for their size, using their short arms and legs to grapple the man's limbs while they used sheer numbers to make him succumb with unnatural strength. He screamed as their teeth tore into him, stripping his limbs of flesh, the ivory color of his bones peeking out from the mob of feral creatures. Their bladed teeth made quick work of his thin armor, and their screeching drowned out the man's cries for help. His face rose to the heavens, staring at the ceiling of the cavern. The foreman wailed; the air escaping from his lungs as millions of tiny teeth sheared his body of its flesh before his world faded to black.

The frightened miner trembled in the cavern's entrance filled with wooden scaffolding, realizing now the foreman would never return. The chorus of screams and growls echoed through the large chamber from the darkness in the bowels of the mine. He flinched at each inhuman noise that was followed by a yell, thick with fear. Then it was silent once more. The only noise he heard was his heart thumping in his ears.

The thin man dropped his pick to the ground and was five steps from it by the time it fell fully to the earth. A lone screech came from the tunnel on the opposite side, where the armed taskmaster had wandered into, at the ready to dish punishment. An oval head, painted in gore, peeked from the darkness, joined by another, and then another. Their faces were messy and smeared with visceral matter as they carefully scouted the next room for prey. The old miner however would not see this and barely heard what was now long behind him. The sounds of horror itself were drowned out by his drumming heart and thumping footsteps as he fled past worker after worker on shaking legs. He didn't slow; he didn't stop to explain, nor answer their calls of confusion and shouts. He fled, happy to know he would not be facing what was lurking in the mines that day.

II

Rohn was pleased to confirm his ride to the fort had been paid for by his benefactor, as the next carriage out would be his safe passage to the outpost. The Wagoners' guild was busy with both serf and freeman alike, driving for themselves or their masters, ready to take jobs delivering supplies and passengers from one settlement to the next. It was good pay, but strenuous and often dangerous work. Wagoneers were constantly attacked on the frontier for their supplies, wealthy passengers, or simply as something's next meal. Smart drivers paid for armed guards and didn't skimp when it came to security.

Sir Gerhardt had paid well for a moderately comfortable carriage to take the young scribe to the outpost. While it was of fine craftsmanship, Rohn noticed there was more reinforcement than the carriages in England. Its walls were thicker, lined with iron bands, and its wheels were solid planks of wood. Its windows were but small slits about four inches wide and two feet tall. What caught his attention were the lightly armored soldiers that prepared to board the wagon as security. One sat on top to the rear of the wagon, armed with a light crossbow, as another took his place in the front, on the driver's bench. A worn, but thick brigantine coat protected both men, their faces obscured behind iron-nosed helms.

Mercenaries, Rohn thought to himself.

They carefully checked their weapons more than once, thumbs sliding across the blades, making sure they had edges, and greasing the strings of their crossbows with bars of beeswax. The driver was busy to the rear, loading several extravagant bags into a compartment among a few other packages wrapped in bland hemp cloth and tied with coarse twine. Rohn's nose wrinkled as his tunic smelt faintly of rum. His linen pants were dirty, smeared with greasy fingers from last night's meal.

"Are we expecting an attack?" Rohn nervously motioned to the guards, as the freeman tried to cram another bag into the compartment.

"Yes," the driver said with no hint of sarcasm, completely serious as he slammed the trunk shut and fastened its lock. "Roads are thick with brigands. Ye need to get in lad; you're not my only fair. Up you go," he said with urgency.

The driver ushered Rohn up and into the cabin and shut the door behind him, making sure it was secured. The young man scooted his way past the only other passengers in the coach, an elderly well-to-do couple. As Rohn took his seat, he could feel the plump wagoneer climb into the carriage as it rocked and swayed gently under his girth.

The inside was rather pleasant, albeit a little dark because of its window slits. Its leather seats were worn but cushioned, and still comfortable. The pair was in stark contrast to their drab and rough surroundings, as the older woman was dressed in a fine custom-made dress of bright mauve velvet and lace, and while in her late sixties she had much of her figure and beauty intact. Her silver mane tethered up and hidden under a matching ornate headdress made of the same fabrics as her posh gown. The man was a bit more elaborate, his brown hair speckled with gray but neatly kept, and his mustache curled upwards, teasing his nose. His clothing was made of luxurious furs and padded linen that was clean and custom fit.

"Lady, Sir." Rohn gave a polite nod to each as he tried to break the silence.

"See, I told you he looked well-bred, dear." The woman quipped to her companion, playfully slapping his knee, her rings gently clacking together.

"This is why we should purchase a carriage; I tire of traveling with the common peasantry," a feminine tone wafted from the elderly man, as he closed his book but kept his page with a thin finger.

Rohn looked back and forth between the two, confused about the conversation.

"Oh, for God's sake, ignore him, lad, he is always sour on long journeys," Lady Agatha chided. "Which house do you come from, child?" She finished, finding the questioning amusing.

"None, my Lady. I am not of noble blood. I am a scribe, a scholar from England. My name is Rohn Durnham, son of Edwin Durnham. He was a merchant in London," Rohn replied, trying to be polite about the interrogation of the rather inquisitive woman.

"Merchant, hah!" Agatha said with a matter-of-fact tone in her voice as she chuckled, elbowing her husband in the arm victoriously.

"Never heard of him," Edgar muttered, quickly losing interest as he returned to his book as if the conversation had never taken place.

"Bah, poor loser," Agatha playfully berated her companion, turning back to Rohn with a smile. "I am Lady Agatha Du'Vale, and this is my husband, Sir Edgar Du'Vale," she added, motioning to her husband, who refused to look up from his book. The carriage gently bouncing on the rough road out of the city.

"Well met," Rohn added, nodding to the couple.

As the carriage made its way out of the city as the two exchanged pleasantries, Edgar taking little interest in the young man, engrossed in his novel as he toyed with his mustache. The hustle and bustle of the city quickly changed to quiet farmland, and the air cleared and became crisper, filled with the smell of freshly tilled soil. First settlers had clear-cut acres of forest to make room for livestock and farmland that would be imperative to the survival of the colony. Fields of wheat, barley, even vegetables, and fruits grew just beyond the city's intimidating walls. In the fields, cattle and sheep grazed as herding dogs sat quietly, watching their wards, eagerly waiting for their chance to work. The carriage edged its way out of the open grass and gradually crept into the shadows of the ancient forest as if being engulfed by the maw of some massive beast.

The canopy towered over a hundred feet into the sky, almost completely blocking out the sun; only thin rays of golden light pierced through. As they traveled along, they saw large older trees greedily smothering others from its life-giving foliage as birds chirped, busily going about their business.

A familiar sound came from behind Rohn as the rear guard pulled the string of their crossbow, its limb creaking as it clicked into place. The driver snapped the reins; the horses neighing as the carriage picked up speed. A bang on the roof reverberated through the cabin of the carriage from the driver's bench, slightly startling all inside.

"Hold on! We'll not dally here!" The wagoneer bellowed, snapping the reins again and again, the carriage picking up pace rapidly.

Rohn's face paled slightly, anxiety roiling in his stomach.

"None to worry lad, they always hurry through the woods, as they're abundant with savages and creatures alike. So are you headed to work in a trade house in the fort, or perhaps as a smith or carpenter?" Agatha prodded, changing the subject.

"No ma'am, I will just be passing through the outpost. I am on my way to Gerhardt Keep. Sir Garrett needs a scribe, and I was offered employment," Rohn said politely, his deep hazel eyes staring through the window with paranoia, the trees blurring by like a dark green haze.

"Ah yes, Sir Gerhardt. Quite the gentleman, but such a dangerous burden placed upon him. I suppose that's why his keep was erected first. All he's been through, the poor soul. We spent a few days in our home in Eirburg as our manor is being built in our fief," she added, slowly fanning herself, the breeze causing small curly locks of platinum hair dangling on her neck to flutter and dance.

A horn's bellow suddenly interrupted the conversation as it poured through the air. The mercenaries atop yelled unintelligibly to one another, as the sharp thuds of their crossbows could be heard launching their bolts at something in the distance. The three passengers jumped as arrows thumped into the side of the wagon, sailing from the cover of the dark forest. Lord Edgar dropped his book as one of the arrows deftly buzzed through the window, sticking into the carriage wall between Lady Agatha and Rohn.

"Ambush!" the rear guard screamed to those below, leaning over to a window. "Get down!" He added, banging on the top of the carriage to those within.

Rohn dove to the floor of the cabin, Lady Agatha quickly joining him. The two huddled against one another as the war cries of the attackers whizzed by. Edgar tossed his book to the seat and peered out a window in disgust. Running alongside the wagon at a brisk pace was a large, grimy man. His hair and beard were long and unkempt, and he wore layers of flea-ridden furs and hides. With a grunt, the raider jumped to the wagon but misjudged its speed and fell under its wheels; the cart bouncing violently over the barbarian with a sickening crunch. Others moved from tree to tree deeper in the forest, releasing a volley of arrows at the carriage and its guards, most of them embedding themselves into the wood harmlessly with a thunk. The mercenaries returned fire with their crossbows, the driver's guard putting a bolt deep into the neck of another large blond barbarian as he struggled to keep pace alongside the carriage. The man's painted face drooped as he fell limp to the dirt and faded into the distance.

"My God!" Rohn said, "Sir, I think it would be best to get down!" he added as Lady Agatha curled up into the scribe's chest, arrows still pelting the wagon.

"Filthy, Godless heathens. I'll not be intimidated by the likes of them!" Edgar retorted, as a hatchet thumped into the side of the passenger cabin.

Before Rohn could reach for the elder nobleman, a powerful thud pounded on the top of the carriage. The rear guard bellowed out a stream of obscenities in response as a commotion broke out unseen above them. Sir Edgar was distracted by the scuffle above when a slender, dirty arm popped through the window, a filthy face glaring at him through the slots. The wild man clung to the side of the carriage, trying to get his footing as his legs flailed, dangerously teasing the wheels. Edgar slid to the other side of the carriage and began hitting the man's arm harmlessly with his book, making a disgusted face as he did. Rohn's eyes darted to what the wildman was reaching for, the bolt inside the wagon's door. The young man began frantically stomping the savage's hand to keep him from locating the mechanism.

A heavy thud reverberated through the cabin from the roof as the two battled atop. A chipped savage axe head pierced the roof of the carriage, splinters rained down on the helpless passengers inside. Repeatedly, it plunged into the roof, each time causing those in the cabin to scream. The wagon was now at full speed as it jolted into the air over the most minor bumps. Edgar still pummeled the brute's arm, but was interrupted by a flash of steel as it blurred past the savage's face between him and the window. The barbarian's right arm fell limp into the cabin of the carriage, the trio screaming in unison as the blood spurted over them from his stump. Rohn kicked the stunned raider's remaining hand, still gripping the passenger window. With a final stomp of the scribe's boot, the savage's soiled fingers cracked and twisted in an unnatural angle. The raider had no choice but to release his white-knuckled grip on the window, falling to the merciless ground below, and beneath the wheels, as they roared along the road.

A loud cry bellowed from above them, suddenly cut short, interrupted by a thump as something rolled across the roof of the cabin. A stump of a neck dangled over the side of the carriage, arms limply flopped as they barreled down the road. The barbarian's decapitated body slid off the side of the carriage with a grunt of the guard and a well-placed boot, flopping down into a ravine to join its head. With relief, the horns and guttural war cries faded behind them, the three passengers' hearts beating like a war drum in their chests. The carriage refused to slow as it was still at full speed; the trees were but a blur as they passed.

The head of the rear guard poked down through Sir Edgar's passenger window. "Everyone alright?" He asked, his rugged, weathered face bruised and bloody. "Yes, we're alright. Thank God it's over," Rohn said, clumsily getting up and removing his head from Lady Agatha's chest.

"Are they gone? Did you kill them all?" Lord Edgar demanded, straightening his elegant clothing. "This is completely unacceptable! It gets worse and worse. What the hell is Sir Alistair doing to quell these attacks?"

"Oh hush, you damn fool. Be thankful the uncivilized brutes did not take the carriage," Lady Agatha said, as Rohn helped her back to her seat.

"Are you alright?" Rohn asked to the inverted face of the guard.

"Aye, I'll survive, but the driver caught a spear to the chest. I fear he's long gone, but don't fret. We can get you into the fort safe from here," the guard said, as his face vanished back atop the carriage. Thumps echoed through the cabin as he made his way to the passenger's side of the driver's bench.

"Is this commonplace?" Rohn asked. The two nobles seemed far more composed than himself.

"Unfortunately, more often than not," Sir Du'Vale answered, his face still wrinkled in antipathy. "At least this time it was merely the pagans."

"Lucky us," Rohn added sarcastically, trying to catch his breath. "Who were they?"

"Remnants of ancient settlers. They landed here decades before us but failed to colonize the continent. The ruins of their defeat are littered all over the territory," Sir Du'Vale answered Rohn, obvious revulsion in his voice.

"They despise us English. They claim we are trespassing on sacred land. They demand we leave," Lady Agatha scoffed at the notion, as she finally relaxed and sat back in her seat. "They now live in nomadic tribes, and wander the continent aimlessly, raiding defenseless settlements and homesteads, demanding supplies and resources."

"Savages," Edgar added, wiping invisible bits off his long coat with a handkerchief.

"What happened to them?" Rohn asked as he dared to peer through the window, the outside of the carriage peppered with arrows and even a bone-handled throwing axe.

"We don't have a clue, and honestly I couldn't care less. Most likely gave into their true natures as marauders and uncouth barbarians," Edgar replied as he crossed his legs, trying to find his place once again in his novel. "Filthy heathens," He added, dusting off his book.

The three of them rode the rest of the way, regaining their composure, thankful to still be alive. The horses barreled down the rough road at full pace, the men not sparing the steeds in case the savages were giving chase. It wasn't long before the forest cleared and the sun began to shine down on the crippled carriage and its shaken passengers. In the distance stood the lone settlement, surrounded by a damaged and dilapidated wooden palisade. The carriage approached its southern gate; the horses coming to a trot, panting and whinnying, from the arduous ride. Rohn peered out his window at commoners who muttered when they lay eyes on the wagon, some even crossing themselves.

They finally came to a stop in front of a large manor made of heavy logs and a clay shingle roof, protected by a palisade wall. A clean and well-dressed steward ran to the wagon from inside and opened the door with a bow, then placed a small step stool. Lady Agatha disembarked first, with the aid of the steward who gently cradled her hand.

The mercenaries above pulled the spear from the cold and stiff corpse of the driver as servants moved to help them in removing the dead driver from the roof of the carriage.

"Bring me to Alistair at once!" Lady Agatha said, a scowl across her face. "As for you, my dear Rohn, I do hope to hear from you again. I'm sure you will serve Sir Gerhardt well and I look forward to our next meeting."

She smiled and curtsied, Rohn, bowing low with a hand on his chest in response.

"God be with you, my Lady."

"As with you, lad." She retorted with a smile, turning to follow the steward as he struggled to carry the pair's luggage into the manor.

Rohn once again found himself alone, still shaken from the encounter with the highwaymen. He felt safe, however, in the walls of the fort. Though they were worn and needed repair, they stood strong and had two thick gates to the southern and northern portions of the curtain wall. The southernmost led back into civilization and the northern gate opened to no-man's-land, a dark dense forest that lay beyond it.

Dumont was a bustling trade outpost, and well populated, mostly with hunters, mercenaries, and anyone looking to make a fast fortune in the deadly frontier territory. The place was energetic, as commoners flowed to and from various hovels and trade houses carrying goods and fresh game. Lively music fluttered out of one tavern nearby. A sign hanging from its doorway swung in a gentle breeze: *The Haughty Harlot.*

"I suppose this will do," he said as he entered the inn, thanking God to be in civilization once again, safe and sound, still shaken from his brush with the locals.

III

The Du'Vales made their way into Sir Dumont's manor, sore and shaken from the day's events. Older nobles passed one soldier after another. I stationed here most of the guards, standing about when not on duty, aimlessly looking for a distraction from the long day. Lady Agatha could only scowl as she entered, as its dowdy interior was drab and dirty. The stone floors covered in soil, tracked in by servants and hounds. Musk filled the air that smelt of wet dog and damp lumber, poorly concealed by cheap incense that gently burnt in each darkroom.

"Lady Du'Vale, you made it!" Sir Alistair greeted them, his arms splayed open, welcoming them as he made his way down the stairs.

Lady Agatha stuck a finger into his thick chest as he approached, stopping his attempt to embrace her. "Not with any of your help. We were attacked. Our driver was impaled," she scowled.

"My God," he quickly crossed himself. "I'm glad the two of you made it safely," he said, trying to sound genuinely concerned.

Edgar took a seat first, wiping the chair off with a handkerchief. "The road to the capital is not safe. How am I to do business if they constantly attack my wagons? Hire some sellswords in your taverns until more men arrive."

Alistair casually poured himself a goblet of wine, his pudgy fingers delicately holding the silver goblet. "Sir Edgar, of course, I would love to pay for their help, but they refuse. What I offer as payment isn't sufficient for these brutes. Their greed is limitless. Besides, I now have more mouths to feed because of your mine."

"What do you mean because of 'your mine'?" Edgar raised a brow, taking a metallic cup of berry wine, paying little attention to the servant who offered it.

"Your fief has been abandoned. A day or so ago, refugees flooded to the sanctuary of my fort, pleading to be let in. The Christian man I am, I, of course, let them take refuge within my humble walls, but at great expense, might I add," the balding knight stated coyly, sipping his beverage.

"Abandoned?!" Edgar Du'Vale's face flushed with anger. "Why the hell did they flee?!"

"They claim creatures came from the depths and killed a majority of the serfs. They refuse to return until the problem is resolved," Alistair responded, trying his hardest to not seem pleased.

"Fetch a carriage immediately!" Edgar commanded a nearby servant.

"Don't be foolish, Sir Edgar. They said dozens died in but a few moments. It would be madness to return," Sir Dumont calmly said, grinning behind his goblet as he drank once more.

"Agatha, let us go! We will not sit here a moment longer while our livelihood is sabotaged." Edgar's face cherry red now with rage.

"You think it prudent to return while the place is in danger?" His wife protested.

"I will not let my house crumble because of a few pests in my mine!" Sir Edgar roared as he made his way to the door, slamming his metal cup on a table, its contents splashing onto the surface.

"If you are so steadfast on returning, I'll take the next carriage to Eirburg and speak with Lord Harmon. I'm sure he will see the benefit of giving us more soldiers to rid us of the issue," Agatha spoke in a calm tone, knowing that returning without soldiers was a death wish.

"So be it, I'm leaving now. I'll not these fools bankrupt me!" Edgar said, storming out the door.

"Shall I make a room for you, Lady?" Alistair smiled, taking another sip, his eyes on Lady Du'Vale.

Agatha looked around, the rugged decor making her want to heave. "I suppose, though I wonder who is getting the better end of this deal, Sir Edgar or I?"

Chapter 4:

Things That Lurk in the Dark

I

It was almost dark by the time Sir Edgar's carriage came within sight of Stonestead. His gaze glaring through the windows of the beaten passenger cabin. The arrows and other projectiles quickly removed, its wood patched, but left scars peppered over its wooden frame. He had set out by himself and paid the two guards from earlier a small stack of silver to drive him to his manor with haste.

They arrived into his now vacant walls, usually lined with archers on patrol. As he approached, the sight of the settlement made Edgar seethe, off-white teeth flaring in sharp contrast to his mustache. The carriage came to a halt in front of his still-unfinished keep. The outer walls of the manor were up, but still, many unfinished details remained. They will stay that way until he can get workers to return. Only a small group of servants and guards loyal to House Du'Vale remained, quickly gathering in front of the manor, faces of dread etched on them as they waited for the carriage to park in front. Sir Edgar quickly disembarked as soon as the nobleman's cabin came to a halt, his face flush and hot as he saw the settlement in complete disarray. Caved in tents, buckets scattered and broken, benches littering the ground. Valuable tools and equipment lay strewn about as if the settlers fled at a moment's notice. Collecting their pay, the mercenaries unloaded Sir Edgar's belonging and then remounted the carriage, riding out as quickly as they rode in not wishing to linger in the settlement turned graveyard.

"Where the hell is everyone?" His voice high pitched, spittle coming out of his mouth as an old male servant ran to collect the knights' belongings from the muddy ground.

"They have fled my Lord," Beckett said shamefully, the large man avoiding eye contact with his Lord as he rubbed his shaven head.

"And why would that be?" his eyes narrowing as Edgar questioned the inept guard, "What the hell happened here?!" He demanded, his voice cracking from stress.

"Creatures from the mines, my Lord, they swarmed the tunnels, ravenous little bastards, killed a majority of the miners as the others fled. These beasts can strip a man's flesh to the bone, before the blink of an eye. We survived only because we took refuge in another portion of the tunnels, sealing ourselves in until dawn, we've been camping there ever since. We're all that remains, but I swear my Lord, I will soon have it back in order, Sir Edgar." Beckett explained, his tone failing to prove he had the situation under control.

"I pay you to protect my investment, my land. To protect the workers and I spend less than a week In Eirburg to return to an abandoned settlement. To a catastrophe! You have a day. One day, to clear the mines." Edgar interjected, his teeth gritting as he pointed a skeletal finger in Beckett's face.

"Sir you've not seen—"

"I don't care!" The knight stomped his foot. "Do you know what this is costing me? Do you even care?! Of course not you inbred buffoon. I want the creatures rid of immediately and the mine up and running before dusk tomorrow, or you will have far more to fear than a few beasts."

With a glare Edgar made his way inside the cobblestone keep, leaving Beckett outside to weigh his options. While the two-story manor was rough on the outside, it was almost completed, except for a few minor touches. The glass windows had been installed, costing a peasant's fortune, giving a quaint view of the outside settlement. Iron-reinforced bars had been installed on the outside of the windows to protect them from invasions, and the rods were adorned with barbs as Sir Edgar was paranoid of a peasant revolt and pagan marauders. While scaffolding still stood outside its frame, inside it had all the luxuries a noble could want. The main entrance was a vast open room, a feasting hall where the

Du'Vale's sat at the head table hewn from oak with matching plush armchairs. At the center of the room was a wide stone fire pit, acting to keep the hall warm, but also to roast large game and cook massive eloquent feasts, filling the room with the smell of spiced meats and roasted vegetables. Toward the back were the servants' quarters and storage room. The peasants slept in hay-filled pallet beds next to the dry storage; the serfs were crammed in, giving them almost no privacy.

Up the dual flight of stairs, to each side of the hall led to an open walkway that oversaw the great hall. Doors to the back led to the nobles' bedrooms, separated by request, but joined by a center door. Each room had a hearth in the corner to boil water for baths and warm the bed chambers during frigid nights. Tonight Edgar would relax in a warm tub and then dine on pheasant and potatoes, while his men ate dried meat out in the cold until they earned their wages.

II

The soldiers were huddled around a campfire within eyesight of the entrance of the forbidding mine. They warmed their hands as they stared into the darkness of the tunnel, fearing what would emerge from its bowels under cover of the night. The sun was quickly setting, barely peeking over the canopy of trees. Only five of the thirty footmen remained as the others were eaten by the creatures, or had fled to Fort Dumont as a refugee. Emmitt was Sergeant Beckett's second in command and dear friend who remained to watch his comrades back. Hewitt and Dudley were miscreants and only remained because they were owed three weeks of back pay. They refused to leave until they got it. Then there was Pudge. While Pudge wasn't his actual name, it was a nickname that stuck through his entire life; the chubby soldier loved his sweets and spends most of his pay in the bakery and taverns.

"We've only five men. I've seen those things rip through twice that in a matter of moments," Emmitt said, crouching to place his hands closer to the fire. The temperature was slowly falling as the sun's amber warmth faded from the sky.

Beckett stood with his arms crossed over his broad chest, watching in dread as the light slowly died like a candle flame behind the trees. "Well, we need to make a choice, and fast. The sun is setting and those things will come back. If we flee, there will be hell to pay, Sir Edgar will have us whipped, or worse."

"I say we piss off. Let the bastard fend for himself. Son of a pig needs to be alive to punish us, and those little bastards will shit him out before dawn." Hewitt chimed in, Dudley nodding.

"They've got two horses left in the stable. We grab them and ride all night." Dudley added.

"Horses can't carry five men, one of us would have to remain," Pudge said, already knowing the answer to his statement before he completed it.

"Sodding horse couldn't carry you anyway, I say we leave the heifer to the creatures and ride off," Hewitt said with a serious look on his face, as Dudley chuckled.

"I will leave no one behind." Beckett glared at the duo, "Besides, I can't leave. Not without the back wages he owes us, I need the money. I want to bring my wife here and she's with child." Beckett calmly replied staring at the fire his mind made up.

They were interrupted as a bucket tipped from a bench across the camp. The men jumped to attention and reactively drew their swords as their nerves were now on edge. The soldiers scanned the ravaged camp that had succumbed to the chaos of the brood, as the bucket rolled across the dirt.

"What the hell was that?" Beckett whispered, his blade held at the ready the others gathering near the fire, their backs to the blaze.

"Maybe it's just a stray dog?" Pudge said, his hand trembling as he gripped the handle of his blade.

"You've seen a bloody dog all day? We're it and those things!" Dudley chimed in, panic flowing from his cracking voice.

Before any of them could say another word, Hewitt ran for the stables, stumbling as he abandoned the others.

"Damn fool, Sir Edgar catches him he'll hang for horse theft." Beckett stated, "Let's go, we need to take shelter." He added as he made his way to the manor.

Emmitt followed his sergeant close behind, blade drawn as it gleamed in the waning sunlight. "In there, with him? Are you mad, he won't let us in there."

Beckett didn't let the man dissuade him as he made his way to the stone keep. "He has no choice, if he wants to make it through the night, he'll play nice. The keep is our best bet to see the dawn."

The four remaining men moved quickly, but cautiously, to the manor. In the distance, the stable doors burst open as Hewitt rode hard out of the front gates without a word to the others. Beckett grit his teeth hoping the man would send aid back. His train of thought was suddenly broken. Behind him, a scream shattered the silence. The other men jumped and spun on their heels, blades at the ready. Dudley was wailing his voice gargling and choking as one of the creatures had locked its jaw to the man's neck from behind. Muscles flexed inside the goblins' oversized head as it chewed and shook its body like a dog with a rat, blood spurting from the man's throat. The shadows came to life behind the poor soul as the ravenous brood lunged from the desecrated tents, seeing their opportunity, swarming like ants over the defenseless man. The others wasted no time and made a dash for the keep, Beckett cursed as the horde flooded over what was left of Dudley, only an arm left twitching in a pool of red mud as they fed.

Another yelp behind Beckett as Pudge wrestled with three of the beasts, no more than a meter tall, but unnaturally strong. The chunky guard fell to the ground losing his balance as they overpowered him clawing and biting. He desperately tried to get to his feet, sweat pouring from his brow as he grasped for the others with desperation on his face. The beasts quickly honed in on the vulnerable man as their fangs dug into his calves, the ground splattered in dark crimson. Pudge screamed for help, clawing into the dirt as the horde overwhelmed him, quickly covering him as they fed. Beckett slowed and glanced back to the swarm of coal-colored furred bodies that covered Pudge. The sergeant's face was racked with guilt as he watched his comrade-in-arms become engulfed by the ravenous swarm. He was their leader; he was supposed to protect them, and he had lost two more men in the same matter of moments.

Emmitt grabbed his arm, tugging on the sleeve of his chain shirt. "Leave him! It's too late."

"God forgive me." Beckett berated himself as he turned and fled to the keep, as they ripped the corpulent man limb from limb, his screams suddenly stopping.

The remaining guards slammed into the door; it was already barred from the inside. "Open the fucking door!" Emmitt bawled as a sea of tiny silver beaded eyes glared in their direction.

The men desperately hammered on the door kicking and yelling as the goblins snarled and flared their blood-stained teeth, bits of cloth and flesh stuck in their maws. With a groan, the doors finally opened enough for the men to squeeze through. A servant girl in her early twenties quickly backed away from the door as the remaining two survivors barged in their breath heavy and labored. They slammed the doors shut behind them as Emmitt quickly retrieved the large wooden bar to secure the entrance.

"Shut the damned windows, the shutters!" Beckett ordered as he and the Emmitt barred the front door. "Now!"

The terrified serfs quickly obeyed and ran to the windows, slamming the shutters just as small shadows scurried past crawling over the keep in a swarm of macabre grins. The horde excitedly chittered at the thought of what might be inside, desperately searching for a way in, their tiny bellies still growling greedily.

Sir Edgar almost spit out his wine as he sat at the dining table, his meal before him. "What in the name of God is going on? Get out of here! You have a job--"

"With all due respect, my Lord, you need to keep your teeth together and listen." Beckett motioned to the windows; they could hear claws clacking across the stone. "We're surrounded and vastly outnumbered. We need to barricade the manor and keep the fire stoked; the little bastards don't like fire." Beckett said his face cold as stone.

"And just how do you know that?" Edgar said, throwing his hands in the air.

Beckett turned to the aging merchant as he lifted a heavy bench. "How do you think we survived? Torches, braziers, anything that burns, get it lit."

Sir Edgar looked to the servants who were staring at him and then looked back to Beckett, the man sheathing his blade. "Go, make sure the other rooms are secure and get more logs on this fire, we're in for a long damn night," Edgar commanded with regret, as the sound of claws skittered across the windows, testing the defenses of the keep prodding it for gaps and possible entrances.

III

Hewitt wasn't going back; not caring if he hung for theft, as the bastards wouldn't make it to dawn, anyway. He saw what those creatures could do; and how vicious they were. Hewitt was so busy looking behind him, making sure he wasn't being followed that he didn't notice the fallen tree in the road. The base of it gnawed through. His horse reared at the last moment, leaping over the obstacle, as its rider fell backward to the dirt landing with a hard thud. The air shot from his lungs as the world blurred, the horses' hoofbeats quickly fading into the distance down the road in a cloud of dust.

"Dammit..." He whimpered as he made his way to his feet, gasping to catch his breath.

A branch snapped behind him and sent chills up his spine, freezing in place he stopped moving, even holding his breath. His eyes turning slowly to the area the noise originated from. Goosebumps bubbled down his arms as his blood ran cold. A massive wolf was creeping up slowly behind him, but its face was blunt and its ragged teeth stained with viscera as they jutted from its powerful jaws. *Wargs*, Hewitt thought. He had heard stories of them, bigger than a timber wolf and far smarter. Even worse, warg's didn't fear man. They assaulted anything, including humans that dared to stray into their territory. Traders claimed they even had the cunning to set traps, like creating roadblocks and separating people as they could mimic sounds such as an infant's cry. The beasts' golden eyes flared in the dark like topaz gems. Behind the warg, another powerful form bounded into view, then another. He drew his short sword and held it in front of him. The wargs flared their crimson-stained fangs in response, undaunted by the lone man as they slowly moved into position. The two newcomers skulked to the Hewitt's sides, blocking the road. The beasts were huge, close to four hundred pounds, and four feet tall at their shoulders. Their front paws were almost eight inches in diameter, with the dexterity of a bear capable of climbing or gripping prey.

"Piss off or I'll gut you!" He yelled waving his blade at them trying to keep them at bay, the animals unflinching and their eyes unblinking as they stared him down.

They knew he was alone and smelt his fear, the scent of his sweat lofting through the air. Hewitt suddenly slammed nose-first into the gravel road. It felt

67

as if a horse had charged into his back, as his face smashed and bounced off the unforgiving earth, his sword flying from his grip. Four hundred pounds of muscle and black fur pinned him to the earth, the beast's incredible weight crushing his back as its claws dug into his chain shirt. Hewitt gasped for air as dust billowed around his mouth like a suffocating fish. He felt one animal grab his right arm in its powerful jaws, its hot breath sweltering his skin as its teeth clamped down. The pressure unbearable as both bones in his forearm gave in and snapped like a twig. He screamed and flailed, gripping handfuls of dirt and stone with his free hand; reaching for anything he could use as a weapon. His left hand vanished next into a gnarled toothed maw, the warg shaking and growling as the bones in his wrist severed. Hewitt fell into shock, his mind telling him this isn't real, it's a dream, and you'll wake up soon. He could smell the breath of the beast on his back now as it lowered its powerful head downward, its thick saliva dripping onto his cheek. The smell of rotting death flowing into his nostrils as the beasts' putrid breath smothered him. The last thing the soldier saw was the inside of the alpha's mouth as it twisted his neck and, with a loud hollow snap, all went dark as Hewitt's body slumped lifeless to the earth. In a few moments nothing remained of the guard but his chain shirt, tattered and destroyed, lying alone in a pool of red mud to the side of the road.

IV

"So what are we to do now, sergeant?" Edgar demanded in a snide tone.

"We wait. We pray." Beckett answered not looking up from his blade in hand, as he listened to the creatures search for a way in.

Outside, a loud whinny echoed in the distance over the constant chattering of the goblins. The horse in the stables, Hewitt left the door open as he fled Beckett realized. Within a few seconds, the horse was silent, as those in the keep looked back to the fire, knowing the animal's fate. All that could be heard now was the constant chittering and growls in the distance as the monsters fed on the steed.

"Looks like we walk in the morning." Emmitt sighed, sitting on a bench in front of the fire pit. "If we see morning."

The servants were shaking, huddled together in a corner of the room. Beckett smiled at them compassionately. "We made it through worse than this, and with

68

less. We have stone walls and a big fire to protect us. Stick together and we'll be fine. Come, sit by the hearth and keep warm." He summoned them over with a hand, gently patting the bench next to him.

Tentatively the serfs moved through the dark of the large hall and slowly sat at the fire, its warmth and light comforting them a little. The anxiety of the dark slowly melting away as the fire licked through the air, snapping and popping gently in the pit. Beckett used his blade to adjust the fire, giving it more space to breathe.

"Damn fool Alistair. This is his fault. He knew we were in need and did nothing." Edgar said through gritted teeth.

"He took in the refugees did he not?" Emmitt dared to say.

"Oh yes, for a tidy profit, I'm accruing debt as we speak while he feeds and shelters my useless labor at the fort. Oh, you can bet they'll pay it off when all this is done."

"If you make it… Sir." Emmitt said a hint of malice in his voice.

Sir Edgar did not miss the subtle threat as he stood up. "I will be in my chambers. Keep your voices down, I've had a very stressful ride, and now I must deal with this. I need my sleep." And with that, he stomped his way up the stairs, slamming the door to his quarters, bolts clanging into place. The chittering grew louder; the sudden burst of sound arousing the horde.

"Well, at least we don't need to be his damned nursemaid all night. You closed the shutters upstairs correct?" Beckett asked the servant girl, receiving a nod in response.

The sound of glass shattering in one of the windows nearby startled the group, Emmitt stood drawing his blade as Beckett spun, shielding the servants behind him. The shutters fluttered and rattled as the tiny arms reached through the sharp broken glass and bars, clawing at the barrier, its bolts holding firm against the clawed hands.

"I don't know if they can get through the bars of the windows. I think we're safe." Emmitt said, moving to Beckett's side.

Beckett glared at the window shutters violently shaking. "For now."

V

In his room, Sir Edgar changed into a long flowing quilted nightshirt, preparing to retire for the night. He washed his hands and face in a bowl of rose water and blew his nose in a handkerchief, leaving it for the servants to clean up in the morning. Edgar moved to his bed and gently pulled down its illustrious covers, thick and quilted to fight off the chill of the mountain air. The knight gently blew out a candle on the bedside as he slid in the bed's warm embrace, the feathered mattress conforming to his shape and gently engulfing him. He would sleep this night wearing his jewelry; he didn't want the brutes downstairs grabbing them before they fled the keep in the morning. Edgar didn't care, though he would deal with them when the mine was up and running. Sir Edgar looked over his rings, using the only light in the room, the gentle glow of the hearth. By morning, his wife would be back with a company of sellswords he thought, as he snuggled under the quilt and closed his eyes knowing all would be well at first light.

The merchant noble knew many things. He knew how to corner a market; he knew how to choose fine wine and clothing and even knew the songs of rare birds he so much loved to watch flutter through the trees of the courtyard. However, there was one thing he did not know; that in their haste, the stonemasons had not yet secured the chimneys in the chambers with iron grating. The smoke, lofting its way up the stone shaft, into the cold night air, didn't go unnoticed by the small creatures. While it's true, they are fearful of fire, more primal urges can overcome fear such as an insatiable hunger.

VI

Beckett sat again at the large hearth, relaxing as the creatures moved from the windows, seeing it as a fruitless endeavor. The main hall once again fell silent as the horde scurried elsewhere, searching for a new means to get to their prey.

"Little bastards are clever," Emmitt said, as he tracked their movements as best as he could through the stone.

"That they are, frighteningly so." Beckett patted one of the servants on the back, giving them a reassuring smile.

"So, what do you plan on naming your boy? Or girl." Emmitt asked, trying to bring some levity to the tension-filled room.

"Not sure. Perhaps Martha if a girl, after her mother, or Edward if a boy."

Emmitt chuckled, "You think your boy will someday be king? Giving him a name like that is bad luck; he'll grow up humping trees and setting fires."

Beckett laughed his bass-filled tone reverberating through the hall. "Piss off; my children won't grow up like this, slaving away for twelve hours a day. No, they'll be better, strong, and smart."

"So they'll take after your wife?" Emmitt prodded not to waste the opportunity.

Beckett shot a grin at him, but a scream echoed from Edgar's room up the stairs. The men drew their blades as they made their way up the stairs and ran to the door, telling the servants to remain near the fire.

VII

They were flooding out of the chimney now, covered in black soot snarling and yelping as they fell over the fire. Their slight forms contorting and compressing as they squeezed down the narrow chimney-like rats. The larger ones waited on the roof, pacing as they glared down the stack, envious of those below.

Beckett and Emmitt pounded on the door, as it wouldn't budge the pair trying desperately to aid the doomed merchant knight. Sir Edgar curled up in his bed, terrified to move, cursing the architects with a slew of profanity as the creatures bounded to their feet, shaking their heads to regain their composure, and charged the bed with a horrid grin. With ring adorned fingers outstretched, he tried to stop the creatures from latching on to him. They clawed at his face, biting chunks from his scalp, and hands the goblins swallowing his fingers, rings, and all. Within moments he was covered in his bed, the air filled with blood-stained feathers and wool stuffing.

On the other side of the door, Beckett noticed the screaming ceased and grabbed Emmitt by the arm, halting his efforts, as they were now in vain.

"Wait! Stop! He's gone, they got him." Beckett scowled in a hushed tone.

Emmitt shrugged, stifling a smile, "That's a damn shame."

Inside the bellies of the goblins their meals churned and bubbled, their metabolic rates quickly absorbing the flesh of Sir Edgar. While goblins were adept at eating almost anything, certain things they couldn't digest. Certain minerals and metals had a severe reaction to their usually hardy digestive systems, gold being one of them. A few of them were sluggish and groggy as they scurried through the room, looking for a way to reach the other side. They moved slowly as their guts bubbled the room filling with their flatulence. Belching and growling as they whimpered, their stomachs expanding at a rapid rate, a chemical reaction creating far more methane than their small forms could handle. One by one, the goblins popped, like ripe little green grapes splattering the room with viscera and gore. The others scurrying about not knowing what to do, their stub tails tucked in fear as they watched their kin explode one after another. Gold rings and other jewelry that once adorned the merchant knight bounced off the walls as the goblins detonated like meat-filled bags.

Beckett and Emmitt looked to one another; the sounds inside horrific. The door shuddered and shook, the two men leaning on it to brace the only barrier between them and death. They could hear the door chipping away, then another detonation. The goblins were scared, trying to flee their exploding brethren. Not understanding what was happening, in a panic, they drove through the door.

Cold air swallowed the main hall across the guards' backs as they braced against the horde inside Edgar's room, Beckett looked over his shoulder, suddenly aware of the temperature change as his eyes went wide with fear. The two commoners had fled outside, leaving the front entrance wide open.

"No!" Beckett said, the color flushing from his face, now draped with horror.

The serfs didn't get far, as the larger creatures hopped from the roof onto their backs, gnawing and clawing. The servants screamed and flailed fruitlessly as they stumbled out into the night air. They were torn to ribbons before the men could even get to the stairs. One of the goblins ran away with the servant girl's head as her body fell to the ground like a rag doll. The other soon joined in chomping and ripping on her remains. The older servant fell backward as the horde overwhelmed him, his screams being drowned out by the growls and yips of the green mass flowing over him.

"Shit!" Emmitt said, "Damned fools!"

Beckett grabbed him by the tabard as he ran to the adjacent room, Lady Agatha's bed chambers. They sprinted across the walkway, seeing the horde pour in, clinging to the walls and ceiling. Behind them, the goblins ripped through the door from Lord Edgar's room eager to join their pack as they squeezed through the shattered barrier. The men stumbled into the inky blackness of the Lady's bed chamber and slammed the door behind them. They were just in time. A wave of claws and teeth snapped at their heels. The two men sighed and tried to catch their breath as they slid the deadbolts into place. Emmitt leaned his back to the entry, his heart pounding through his chest. Beckett braced against the barrier with both hands, holding it as it shuttered from the force of the creature's assault.

"We need to reinforce the door," Beckett said, as Emmitt stood staring into the chamber. "Did you hear me, grab some—"

Beckett stopped and turned, following his comrades' gaze. Something shifted and moved in the shadows. The two soldiers also knew many things. They knew how to handle a sword and ride a horse; how to deal with drunkards and even knew the best place to get a drink after a long shift. They knew they loved their families, and that they would be missed. However, what they did not know was that the stonemasons had also not yet put in place the metal grates to Lady Agatha's chimney, either. Slowly pairs of silver glinting eyes blinked in the room. The two men stared into the chamber filled with the creatures, which after watching their kin dive into the first chimney, they tried their luck down the other. At first, to no avail, the room empty and dark until two large men ran in, locking the door behind them.

The chittering in the keep slowly faded, leaving the surrounding area silent. The settlement was now dead quiet, just as the corpses that dwelled within.

VIII

Near Fort Dumont, deep in the earth under layers of soil and stone laid an old ruin, a temple to be exact. A place where the ancient natives paid homage to the gods that once ruled Voskavia long before the English landed on their shores. Like the deities of Greece and Egypt, the gods of this land once walked amongst their servants in flesh and blood. They ruled vast territories with great power and an almost unlimited supply of worshippers, all of their followers vowing to live and die for their chosen patron.

The once-great temple was in a state of decay now, its tapestries tattered and its mural-covered walls crumbling as it sunk into the earth. Now only a select few still wondered about its hidden halls. A brotherhood of loyal acolytes to the five great beings moved through its hallowed grounds like shadows in black linen robes, their cowls draping over their faces.

One stood above them all on a podium surrounded by disciples, watching them, and directed them from behind a black featureless oak mask, barbs protruding from his forehead, like a wicked crown. The Prince of Thorns wore a robe far more ornate than the others, as it was a deep shade of crimson, and embroidered from the base was the trunk of a massive black tree that wrapped itself around his frame, its branches splaying over his back like wings and ending in a crown on the rim of his hood. At first, his following could be counted on a single hand, but as his power grew, he also attracted more attention from those who hungered for power. The Brotherhood attracted those who were filled with wanting. It called those who were driven by lust, greed, hubris, fear, and even wrath. They all wanted control; the one thing humans strive for their entire lives and rarely obtain. Like sand, control could be had, but should you loosen your grip even slightly it quickly slipped from your grasp. The Prince knew this. The entity in the tree chose him, his new Mother. Of course, he wasn't ignorant or naïve as he knew the entity wasn't female, nor male, and certainly not maternal, but he felt safe near it. The Tree, unlike everyone else in the man's life, rewarded him for his service, treated him with respect and kindness. It also gave him powers beyond mortal men.

"All is in place brother?" The Prince said to his favored servant.

Ekart, a man as pale as snow, smiled from beneath his cowl and nodded to his leader with admiration, "Yes my Prince, the wheels are in motion. We have brothers in all corners of the colonies awaiting your commands."

The natural and unnatural obeyed Ekart's Prince, and soon his master would bring about a new age. Only those in Her good graces would be spared the wrath of the Old Ones. The antediluvian beings waiting to return to the world they once ruled.

Ekart walked the ancient halls, admiring the murals that remained as his brothers scurried about tending to their tasks. He would spend his free time trying to restore the works of ancient art; painstakingly he spent hours upon hours restoring the faded and aged paintings on the stone walls, slowly learning their stories and the past of Voskavia.

The biggest mural and the first Ekart had completed was that of The Mother. It spanned an entire wall, over ten feet long and six feet tall, dedicated to the greatness that was their Goddess. The Prince told him she had gone by many names through the eons. The Tree of Dark Eden, Black Yggdrasil, the Matriarch, no one knew Her actual name, or even where she had originated from; only that she preferred to be called Mother, and she was as ancient as the very soil she burrowed in. Under Her branches were five creatures of Her creation, Her children, Her allies, Her champions.

At first, the Mother's time on the planet was long-lived and unchallenged, but the Earth soon came under the eye of another. Humanity called him The Great One, The Creator, The One God. The Tree couldn't compete with such power, so she hid deep in Her forest, biding Her time. She despised being overshadowed and chased from Her territory, but The Creator was adamant on making this the cradle for his favored creation, Mankind. She would need allies if she was to survive, so she reached across the void and planted the seeds of envy, pride and jealousy into The One God's firstborn. With this new ally, she learned the weakness of humanity the great flaw and freedom God had bestowed on his favored. Freewill.

The first of humanity was warned of Her poison by The One. He spoke of Her false promises of power and knowledge and warned not to eat of Her fruit. But with the aid of The Fallen One, humanity could not resist Her whispers, Her promises, to make them powerful like their Creator. Handfuls of them fell from grace and ate from Her branches, lusting for power, demanding to be equal to their Creator. The Great One was disappointed in his favored creations, banishing them from paradise, and with no one to feed Her with their cardinal desires, she would wither and fade. Her first pupil, The Morning Star, was banished from the realm of Heaven to an abyss with his treacherous brothers, sealed in an abyssal prison, leaving Her alone once more. She needed children of Her own, born in Her image, loyal only to Her and controlled only by Her will alone. The mother would create them, mold flesh as man molds clay. She whispered once more into the dark places between worlds, calling for young spirits from the void. They seeped from the shadows, black wisps of smoke that vied for a material form begging to find their place in our realm. The Mother needed someone cunning to aid Her, a clever spirit, one wise and patient like herself. So the war between the Dark Entity in the tree and The One began.

Her children would need material vessels capable of holding powerful beings. She called forth a raven and a black cat to Her side. Her tendrils snapping out she embraced them in, snatching the animals into Her trunk; Her womb. From within She molded their flesh giving them a sample of Her power and Her first child was born letting the spirit take its avatar.

Sytal, the wise, the cunning, and the bearer of Her will. The spirit took the shape of a griffin-like beast. The rear of its body was that of a panther and the front torso of a raven. But Her power twisted and perverted when it created and instead of a bird's legs, he had the arms and hands of a slender human that ended in black wicked claws. He was the prince of the skies and all that flew answered to him shadowed by his massive ebony wings. He was to spread the seeds of sin and despair. Sytal knew patience, and that there was a time to act and a time to wait. He could twist men with fear, lust, envy, hubris, and greed. Seeds he would sow and then later reap the rewards. He despised humanity as much as his Mother and watched with great joy as they fell from grace, giving in to their primitive desires. He was proof all can succumb to their baser instincts and free will was the soil to plant his Mother's seeds.

Sytal enjoyed corrupting like his mother the Black Tree, and his favorite creation was from that of Cain, son of Adam. He took young Cain's lust for power and envy and molded The Vladene. Blessed with immortality, inhuman strength, speed, and telepathic gifts, the Sons of Cain were banished from the lands of man as they had to feed on their once kindred human brethren to survive. The One God condemned them for their betrayal to never again see the sunrise, as it would burn the flesh from their bones. They could never again feel the cleansing touch of water, as it would be acid to their skin. The vampiric tribes became nomads as they were banished from the lands of men and so they fled across the sea with the aid of Viking Kings whom they promised riches and immortality for passage across the harsh ocean. Sealed in iron tombs to shield them from the harsh spray of the sea and the burning rays of the sun, their Norse protectors brought them to new lands to the west, inhabited by primitive people easy to dominate and rule.

Soon they found their home on the most northern tip of Voskavia, burrowing deep underground in the frozen and harsh lands to the north where the hateful rays of the sun rarely shined. They built underground fortresses and ripped precious metals and gems from the earth, learning to exploit the greed of their allies with slaves and riches. Their empire grew deep and wide, under the watchful eye of Sytal, their patron.

The Black Tree now needed hunters to spread fear and chaos in the world of Man. Beasts who did not fear fire, or the sun's rays. The Vladene had promised the Norsemen who aided them in power, and it came in the form of Skadi, the Wolf Queen, the Bitch Mother. She relished the hunt and would slowly draw out her kills, savoring the intoxicating agony of her prey. The Vikings raided and pillaged in her name and, if proved worthy, would become blooded. Though Skadi's blessing was both a curse and a gift, while it gave them inhuman strength and the ability to recover from what should be fatal wounds it came with grave weaknesses. They had a ravenous hunger for both flesh and conflict as they relentlessly searched for new prey, and all of Skadi's children were damned to heed her call when the moon was full. Their mind and body would succumb to Skadi's will and an insatiable appetite for bloodshed and terror.

With The Mother's new allies, the guerilla war was going well and Her roots swelled with the fear and corruption of man, but the Tree was going to need a strong leader when the time came to reveal herself. She needed a general to lead Her armies across the world. Svaal, The King of the Beastmen, emerged next, Skadi's paternal twin, a twisted hybrid of a most unnatural nature, with the lower body of a powerful horse and the upper torso of a six-armed giant. His steel glowing eyes were sunk deep into his muscular head, adorned with horns and antlers of various beasts. He ruled the darkest places in the forest as his form thundered through the woods on clawed hooves. Svaals' power allowed him to bend the will of even the trees themselves, making them monstrous and hateful living weapons. His mortal followers wore the skull of a deer as a mask, decorated with fur and charms. They would dance around bonfires, summoning primal spirits and violent storms. Svaals' favored was the savage wendigo, wrath in its purest form. The possessed would become ravenous lunatics filled with the hate Svaal had for the realms built by the Sons of Adam and Daughters of Eve.

The Mother was proud of Her creations however the oceans were still turbulent and Her influence over them was absent. From the ocean depths, she bore

Mokosh, the Abyssal One. On his crab-like legs, he stood almost a hundred feet tall, his shelled carapace adorned with four arms that ended in powerful claws. Protected by the chitinous body, his bone-covered face had razor-sharp mandibles capable of crushing even stone. Mokosh was a gargantuan leviathan, the largest of Her children by far, and would have to be as he ruled the deep vast oceans with brutal and remorseless judgment. Men would succumb to his savage seas as his creatures would drag them to the abyss for judgment and rebirth. Mokosh lured humanity to his depths and created the Merfolk, abominations of man and sea life. The Deep Ones obeyed his commands with no hesitation, fearful of his retribution as they swam around his dominant form in the deep black of the ocean.

The last and most fearsome of all was Drahkal, the dragon that slept at the mouth of the Hellmaw, in the mantle of the Earth. Drahkal's obsidian hide was as hard as steel. His breath could melt stone and his wings could cause gale-force winds that could send an army into flight. He bathed in the fires that roared in the depths of the Earth, comforted by its hellish glow. He would awaken and climb from the depths to feed on the ash he left in his wake. When he had his fill, he would return to his lair and lay eggs that he curled around as he slumbered. As his brood hatched, they would crawl their way to the surface, to wreak havoc and torture the land of men. Arthur had led many hunts trying to rid his country of its spawn, but no matter how many they had slain, another seemed to take its place.

For eons, they ruled the continent of Voskavia, a haven for the wretched and vile creations forgotten by man. Undeniable and unquestioned, they roamed the ancient continent to the west. But they had incurred the wrath of The Great Creator, and for five days it rained fire from the sky. Her champions were forced to flee and hide, while She and Her great forests burnt to ash. To quell the raging fire a great flood smothered the land, drowning it in forty days and nights of rain. While she was uprooted, she refused to be forgotten and so easily erased from this world. There was a reason she chose a tree, an ancient species that had inhabited the planet since time was time. Resilient they were, reborn with just a seedling or twig it would one day rise again from its ashes. Nothing could stop this process, the saplings capable of even splitting stone.

She would wake Her spawn and once more rule the continent. Soon Her tendrils would gather enough pain, enough misery to strengthen Her fully, and in return,

She would awaken the others so a new age could begin. The titans grew restless as their Mother's heartbeat echoed through the continent. They began shifting in their ancient resting places, hearing the call, like a drum beating through the Earth. She had a new unlikely ally in the world of man, Her Prince of Thorns, Her carrier of seedlings. And with his aid, she would once again rule Eden.

Chapter 5:

Home Sweet Home

I

As the sun rose over the outpost, its rays were desperately trying to pierce the overcast skies. The old fort awoke slowly to another day. Sounds of birds chirping and a rooster's crow carried through the area. The air was crisp from the rainfall the night before. A murder of crows called to one another, eagerly waiting for the scraps the butchers and taverns would toss out from the night before. It was constantly busy at the trading post, as men and women woke to seize the new day, happy to see the daylight once more. Commoners slowly flooded the muddy streets. Some headed out to hunt the durruk herds, which were even more profitable a business than working at a lumber or stone camp. The durruk is best described as a mix of rhino, moose, and buffalo. While hard to take down, the five-ton behemoth's furred covered body was worth more coin than most men could make in a month. Of course, you needed to survive its horned head first and males were brutally territorial, while females were even more dangerous if they had offspring. Many hunters have never returned from the hunt due to being impaled or trampled to death by a rampaging durruk, its hide resisted all but the sharpest spears and most powerful crossbows.

As the winter faded and the snows melted, bands of long-hunters once again geared up to head into The Wilds, hoping to fell any of the many creatures that dwelled in the untamed region. Those who did not leave the outpost to hunt usually did so to prospect for rare metals and resources, cutting paths through the newly discovered territory to set up camps that harvested the dense temperate rain forest of its lumber.

The women of the outpost also had their hands full as spring arrived, as they went about their daily chores if they wished to remain home, or opened shops to sell home-crafted wares made during the bleak winter months. Some even joined their husbands on expeditions into the wilds north if their children were old enough to tend to themselves. Though life was tough in the land of Voskavia, the people were hardy and thrived in its lush landscape. English settlers were a rough sort, hardened by the day-to-day life of being frontiersmen. They worked hard to put food on the table, and at night they drank and sang their worries away in the local tavern. This caused Rohn to stick out like a sore thumb. Well kept, soft-spoken, and highly educated for a man in his early twenties he would have a hard time fitting into their rough society like a rose in a bramble patch.

Rohn checked out of the inn after a night's good rest and a warm bath. He had slept well despite the nightmarish ride to the fort, his mind tired and weary from the attack on his carriage. He took in the sights and sounds with an unconscious smile making his way to a nearby warehouse, his boots gently splashing as he walked through the streets nodding in greeting to those he passed. He was to meet his driver, William, near the storage yard where merchants were loading their deliveries and purchases for the day. A large burly man approached Rohn with a limp and a pipe hanging from his smiling bearded face.

"You must be Rohn. The names William, but everyone calls me Will." The driver said as he offered the young man his weathered and calloused hand.

Slightly taken aback Rohn wondered how he knew and then noticed he didn't exactly fit in. His clothes were well kept and none of them bear signs of being stitched together or patched. His nails were clean and trimmed and he had bathed at least once in the last twenty-four hours.

"Yes, sir, well met." The young scribe shook his hand and tossed his bag to the back of the wagon.

William couldn't help but snort a bit at the smooth skin on the young man's palm. "Must have been a long trip, eh, lad? Never been fond of the sea myself. How was your stay at the inn?" Will said, as he helped the laborers load the final crates into his wagon.

"Good. It did me well. It was nice to have a hot bath after such an ordeal; quite a terrifying encounter." Rohn added.

"Aye, it can be rather rough in these parts. Surprised to see a lad like yourself around here. Well-educated man, that is. Not a shit shoveler like the rest of this lot." He chuckled in half jest, looking over his shoulder to the surrounding folks in a hushed tone.

Rohn smiled gently, lifting another satchel of provisions onto the wagon, and nodded. "Yes. It is a great honor Sir Gerhardt wishes to make use of my skills, explaining he had much work to be done. All that is written of him is vague and mostly conjecture. It would be an honor to write from the perspective of someone who helped found the frontier. From a person that saw it firsthand, let alone a member of The Order itself."

"Aye, the old bastard has his quirks, but he's a good man, seen more than his fair share of war and bloodshed. He's an honorable soul. Never had him try to fleece me over his order or refuse to pay me for delivery. God-fearing people, the Gerhardts." The driver bellowed out a cloud of smoke from his pipe, as the pair heaved the last of the supplies into place, securing it with old hemp rope.

"Hop on boy," the driver said, as he hoisted himself onto the driver's bench, "it's about a half day's ride from here to his land. Once we get into his fief, we should be safe."

Will offered his paw once more down to Rohn and helped him up. After the wagoneer finished adjusting his wide-brim hat and puffed smoke from his pipe, he snapped the reins, lurching the wagon forward that was pulled by two draft horses. The noble beasts whinnied as they drove forwards, towing the wagon with little effort. Rohn had never gotten used to the aroma of horses especially how they would just defecate at a whim. Although the wagon moved swiftly it wasn't dangerous, but Rohn gripped the sides of his seat as if he were careening around a narrow pass at full gallop still on edge from the last ride he had.

"So what is it you studied at the Queens College?" William asked, shifting his pipe to the other side of his mouth.

"History, philosophy, and science are some of the most popular subjects at the academy. I wanted to be a writer, documenting history but I would happily take the job of a clerk, or accountant," Rohn chuckled nervously, "I was afraid I would be drafted into the war, that was until Sir Garrett contacted me. I was immensely surprised, to be sought by a man with a reputation like his. It was a blessing for certain." Rohn looked down at his journal and made a few sketches using a bit of coal before they faded from his memory.

"I heard you were attacked yesterday; people were gossiping in the tavern last night." Will scoffed, "Sir Alistair is a useless fat bastard, worried only for his purse. Roads are thick with peril, and you think he'd do a damn thing? Last week one of the lads at the outpost checked on his girl. She worked as a barmaid, or such, in the tavern. He came back panting like a hound and carrying on, said he found her shack abandoned. Claimed it was overgrown as if it had been deserted for years." Will puffed again as another cloud of smoke billowed from his mouth as he slowly shook his head, keeping his eyes forwards on the road. "Damn shame, they were good people. Knew their father. He was a good man. God-fearing and never hesitated to help a person in need."

Rohn sat back, scanning the landscape that surrounded them. It was all so picturesque. Mountains laid before them were capped in snow-tipped peaks that had yet to thaw. The mountains gradually leveled into the tree line below and flowed down into deep thick forests which opened to the vast plains he and Will now traveled through. The landscape was perfect for farming and raising livestock, a beautiful countryside, untouched by the hands of man.

"Where does Sir Garrett live?" Rohn asked, daring to take his eyes off the surrounding forest.

"In the mountains before us, deep in a valley. Not a lot of farming land, but decent lumber, stone, and wild game up there. Sir Garrett had his choice of land as a gift from Lord Harmon, and the old sod chose a small valley in the middle of the mountain range. Man's a brilliant soldier, but with picking farmland, his head is up his arse." Will laughed, "Don't tell him I said that." He retorted half-jokingly.

"Perhaps he wasn't looking for farmland…" Rohn said to himself as he stared at the mountains before him. "You said he lives there with family?" Rohn added, trying to not yell over the hooves beating the ground and the rattling of the wagon, still terrified of falling from his seat.

"Family of a sort, not by blood shared but by blood spilled. Tight-knit group, the lot of them. Ayla is like a daughter to him, he kept the lass on when her mother passed, as she's a physician and damned good alchemist. You should get along just fine with her. She's educated like you always nose deep in a book. My wife had serious gut rot a few weeks back. She could blow the bark off a tree by breaking wind, and it was coming out of both ends. No idea what brought it on, I swear it was her cooking, but she refuses to admit it, but Ayla gave her a tonic. Within a day or so the wife was back to normal, nagging me and finding all sorts of work for me to do around the house. Bless Ayla and curse her." Will said, grinning through his scruffy beard.

"She sounds like quite the person. I can't wait to meet her." Rohn retorted, trying to get over the graphic picture Will described of his wife.

"Aye, she's a kind but tough lass. Then you have Bromislav. Now that bastard is a piece of work. Loyal as they come and good-hearted, but as rough around the edges as a saw. Something about him makes me feel uneasy, like when a fox smiles at a chicken in the henhouse. He's a native, one of the wild-man tribes I hear, Sir Garrett will swear he saved the man's soul, but I say once a barbarian always a barbarian. Brom drinks, swears, and womanizes, but one hell of a hunter, as heathen as they come, that one. But out in the wilds, I wouldn't want anyone else watching my hide. Hunted with him once or twice a few years back, I swear it's almost like that man can smell the deer. Just don't piss him off and keep on his good side and you'll be fine." Will puffed again and snapped the reins again as the road steepened.

The chill of the mountains flowed down through the trees as they entered the forest at the base of the range. Rohn pulled his cloak about him tighter; more frightened than cold as he slowly scanned the forest. His anxiety only heightened as he could barely see anything because of the density of the trees and overgrowth that nestled the ground.

"Are we close?" Rohn asked not taking his eyes off the thick woods with an unshakable feeling of being watched.

"Aye, just a while longer and we'll be on his land, soon as we enter the mountains," Will yelled over the whinnying of the horses and the wind cutting through the pass as it now took more of his attention to keep the beasts on the narrowing and more treacherous road.

Soon the two found themselves surrounded on the canyon road between two mountains. The sun was slowly setting behind the massive peaks, and Rohn worried they would fail to arrive before dark, as he certainly did not want to spend the night out here. Who knows what lurked in the shadows? Humans were helpless in the wilds, with no teeth or claws to lash out with, no hide or fur to protect us, just pink little mice scurrying from place to place hoping not to get eaten.

Suddenly Rohn was snapped out of his haze when Will began bellowing out for the horses to slow, pulling tightly on the reins, forcing the horses to whinny in defiance. Rohn followed William's gaze down the trail until he saw what forced them to stop so suddenly.

"What in the name of -" William stopped short, slowly taking his pipe from his mouth, staring at an enormous mass in the way about twenty to thirty feet from the wagon. A massive dog was lying in the center of the road. Not wounded or injured, but just resting as it gently panted, stopping only to lick its pearlescent teeth. It was enormous for a domestic canine; its body was at least two hundred pounds covered in thick, coarse black fur, while a large mane protected its neck and throat from predators.

"What should we do?" Rohn asked, staring at the dog, as it just calmly stared back nonchalantly.

Before William could answer, a thud shook the wagon coming from behind the driver's seat. From the edge of Rohn's vision, he could see a fist gripping a thick large knife as it quickly found its way under the jaw of William. The husky Wagoner slowly raised his hands upon feeling the cold steel under his chin, causing him to drop his pipe in his lap. Rohn could only see part of the intruder from his peripheral vision as the highwayman had his face covered and his cowl pulled low. The man was wearing thick fingerless hide gloves. They were worn from use and stitched back together more than once. Rohn tried turning his head left, sneaking a peek backward, where the man had landed in the wagon. But before he could, a muffled voice stopped him in his tracks, almost causing him to lose control of his bladder.

"Wouldn't do that pup. You see who I am, and I'll take your tongue and eyes. Hate to ruin such a pretty face as yours. Let's do this quick and painless. Coin and cutlery first." The voice commanded in a low Norse accent.

"I ha-, have no weapon, sir, I am unarmed. I have money though, a few shillings. Please, we'll tell no one! We swear, take what you wish." Rohn said shivering with fear unable to believe his luck, being attacked twice in two days.

Will gritted his teeth and silently contemplated trying to take the brigand, but couldn't do so with his blade so close to his neck. "You heard the boy, take what you will and leave us. We're of no consequence." Will stated with great restraint to not antagonize the knife-wielding brigand.

"Ah, you aren't, but the pup is." The cutthroat let out a chuckle. He continued toying with them, "I know someone who is looking for a scribe, looks just like him. Pretty little pup lost in the woods." The Highwayman hissed.

Rohn swallowed hard, trembling, wanting desperately to flee, but out of the corner of his eye to the right, he saw another massive hound sitting in the forest, staring at him like he was anticipating his movements almost daring him to flee so he could chase him down like a rabbit.

Will and Rohn eyed the road once more in front of them. As the sound of hoofbeats rounded the bend in front of them, they both braced themselves, preparing for the worse. Rohn took in a deep breath. The sound echoed off the mountainsides, like a thundering drum. He wished he had a sword, hell he wished he knew how to use a sword. His heart skipped a beat as not an army of brigands and cutthroats rounded the bend, but a young woman in her early twenties with hair the color of a campfire. She rounded the pass with remarkable horsemanship as Rohn got a better glimpse of her. The woman's hair was braided into a ponytail that reached her waist. Her fair skin complimented with rosy dimpled cheeks. Her emerald eyes scanned the man and the merchant. She was curvy, but with an athletic build that suited her frame. The young woman ran her mount almost nose to nose with the two draft horses, pulling the wagon before rearing her steed to a stop.

"Brom, Stop torturing them this instant! William's heart can't take such antics and you're going to make the poor lad shite himself. You can see they're petrified!" Her voice like a melody thick with a heavy Celtic accent.

Will's eyes suddenly went as wide as saucers when he realized he was the butt of what he considered a horrid joke and a torrent of obscenities poured from his mouth as he clumsily tried to spin around, waving his arms at the now very familiar assailant.

"Son of a whore, I'll skin your scrawny ass! Make you wish you'd never be spat out from the devil that bore ye." Will yelled as he flailed his arms almost tumbling from the wagon as he did.

Rohn quickly reached out grabbing the driver's cloak desperately trying to keep him upright through his tantrum. "You miss me old man?" Bromislav playfully replied, easily dodging the portly mans' reach.

"Getting slow after a winter of thick stews and pot pies. Nice to see your wife didn't kill you with her cooking before the crows got their chance to pluck your bones clean in the road after a night of too much drink." The ranger jested as he hopped out of the back of the wagon while sheathing his knife in one swift motion on the bandolier across his chest.

Brom let out a quick whistle as he casually walked around the passenger side of the wagon, the burly bear hounds more than happy to return to their master's side and as Brom gave them a heavy pat on the ribs. His horse slowly sauntered over from its hiding place behind a few trees and brush to complete the quartet. He removed his hooded disguise, revealing a man in his mid to late thirties. The large man had a full beard braided into three locks; one on his chin and two from his mustache. It was kept neat, with thin strips of leather wrapped at the base to hold them in place. The sides of his head were clean-shaven, the top of his scalp left long and braided, reaching the base of his neck. He was agile but a well-muscled man with broad shoulders, thick arms, and a neck like a tree trunk. Brom mounted his horse still grinning more than pleased with himself that he should have been.

"I knew it was you, I just didn't want to ruin your fun," Will said trying to save face in front of his passenger while adjusting his clothes and brushing pipe tobacco off his pants. "Next time I'm going to make you swallow your teeth, you cheeky bastard!" Will finally sat back down, putting his now empty pipe in his mouth. He grabbed the reins and snapped them excitedly as Rohn tried to catch his breath and make sense of what just occurred.

"Sorry about that. Brom's a mischievous bastard at times. He's not that bad unless you piss him off." Ayla said as she rode up alongside where Rohn sat puzzled on the wagon. "You get used to him… sort of." She gave Rohn a cheeky grin, that put him at ease.

"Don't think we've exchanged pleasantries, have we? I'm Ayla. You met Brom. I sent his arse down here to make sure you made the pass without too much difficulty. It can get dangerous when the wind cuts through the mountains." She offered her hand, and Rohn took it gently. Her firm grip surprised him.

"Rohn, Rohn Dunham, at your service." The scribe could barely speak, entranced by the women before him.

Ayla snorted, "Well met Rohn let's get you two back to the keep before nightfall; get some warm stew in your bellies. Miss Shea makes some of the best meals on this God-forsaken continent."

Rohn couldn't help but stare at her as she rode off; unbeknownst to him his mouth was slightly agape.

"Close your mouth, boy." Brom interjected suddenly beside the lad, appearing out of nowhere, "You keep your pecker to yourself pup, or I'll make good on my threat from earlier." Brom grinned and winked at Rohn as he quickly rode off, flanking Ayla, leaving the boy with an expression of terror.

"Don't worry lad, Brom won't do a damned thing to you," Will said to Rohn putting him at ease. "You try to anything with that lass and she'll have you swallowing your teeth before you can blink." he finished with a hearty laugh.

Rohn forced a smile. He looked back toward the darkness of the forest, wondering if he should have stayed back home and taken a simple job at a coinage house. The young man had no idea what he had gotten himself into.

II

The encounter with Brom and his hounds still shook the young scribe. Though he was happy he had met Ayla. She was a sight to behold. Most of the women he met at the university were not worldly. They were children of rich aristocrats who focused on gaining more prestige and power for their families, either through manipulation, marriage, or a little of both. To many, the university was a simple social gathering of the noble's children, a way of making connections into other houses and perhaps strengthening alliances or creating new ones. Few sought knowledge there beyond information to fuel their ambitions. Rohn wanted more. Obsessed with the unknown, he wanted to learn all he could.

"We're here lad. God be praised." William rejoiced with a hearty chuckle as they rounded a bend of the mountain pass.

Below them snuggled in the scenic valley lay Gerhardt Keep. The defiant structure sat aloft on a small plateau in the center of the lowland, encircled by a river that flowed around it, creating a natural moat that was fed by a roaring waterfall pouring forth from the mountains to the north. The surrounding land was not only lush, it was protected by three sides of the steep, hazardous mountains. Rohn now knew why the Templar chose such a location. The mountain runoff supplied endless freshwater, and there was plenty of land to feed livestock. The mountains protected the homestead from severe winds and native raids with plenty of lumber and stone, and only one safe path in and out. It was a perfect place to build a secluded fort, protected from prying eyes and wandering miscreants. The mountains alone were sure to be filled with precious ore. He spotted a gathering of tents near a cave entrance to the rear of the valley that seemed to be occupied with miners hard at work extracting ore. The keep was self-sufficient, as it had all it needed within walking distance.

"I think I'm going to like it here, after all," Rohn said, with an unknowing grin.

"Good, because I don't feel like hauling all your shite back to the outpost," William said with a chuckle, as he slapped Rohn on the shoulder. "Though you'd do well to know that this road is closed during the winter months, damn near impassable with the snow. You're my first delivery since the thaw. If you wish to spend the winter here lad make sure you're ready to hunker down for a bit." William finished with a nod as a puff of smoke erupted from his mouth.

Rohn just nodded, considering the advice, but again quickly overwhelmed at the beauty that surrounded the stone manor. It wasn't long before making their way into the valley. Finally arriving at the main entrance to the keep that faced the roaring waterfall. The young man hopped off the wagon with ease still staring at his surroundings in amazement.

"Aye, it's a pretty view, isn't it? Our little piece of heaven." A familiar voice stated as Ayla walked up behind him, handing the reins of her horse to a stable hand.

"That is an understatement, my Lady." Rohn retorted, turning back to her with a grin still fixed to his face.

"Ayla, plain and simple. Garrett's not big on formalities, and all the servants are here on their own accord. You won't find serfs here, just freeman. We're a family here, Rohn. We look after one another, unlike the city folk. Let's get you inside, they'll be done unloading the wagon in a bit, and I'm sure everyone is dying to meet you." She smiled, happy to see Rohn's reaction as she led the new member of House Gerhardt up the stairs and into the keep.

III

Rohn was overwhelmed as he entered the main hall. Its entrance was massive with a huge double staircase in its center which led to the upper floors of the multistory manor, surrounded by various pathways that flowed into more hallways littered with rooms. The smell of fresh-baked bread and pies flowed through the manor, making Rohn's stomach growl. He was nearly trampled as a mixed pack of dogs ran past him almost sending him head over heels as they chased a small terrier mutt mix carrying a stuffed leather ball in his mouth.

"Rowdy, place nice!" Ayla yelled at the small dog leading the pack on a rampage through the keep. "Always the small ones that are the biggest problems you know? Garrett can't say no to a stray. That's why he brought home Brom." She grinned.

"At last!" Came a voice at the top of the stairs stood.

A regal man, in his late sixties, his face strained and worn from seeing so much in his lifetime although he bared it well. Though in his sunset, he was still handsome and had a powerful physique honed from years of military campaigns. His hair was slowly paling from its usual chestnut hue and his well-groomed beard succumbing to the same inevitable march forward in time.

"Thank God you made it in one piece my dear Rohn. I knew I could trust my family to bring you safe and sound. I do hope the long journey was not too much of a hardship." Sir Garrett stated as he offered his hand to the young man who eagerly took it, surprised by the powerful grip the Templar still had.

"Rough, yes, but none the worse for wear." Rohn gave a glance to Brom as he passed the group who just responded with a grin, "I wanted to thank you again for the opportunity. I have been hard-pressed to find a unique subject to write about in the cities back home; I was speechless when you offered a position here in your home, Sir." Rohn said.

"Please call me Garrett; I've no stomach for formalities. Most of the people living in this keep have been with me for decades. I am honored they wished to remain and help me build such a wonderful home. However, I have a feeling you will have more than you can handle here when it comes to inspiration for your books. Your training alone will fill a novel or two I hope." He said putting his arm around Ayla and giving her a gentle kiss on the forehead.

"Training, Sir?" Rohn said with a bit of surprise, "If I may be so bold, what type of training Sir Garrett?"

"Yes lad, no need for concern we will speak of it more later. Why don't you find your room? Get comfortable, then meet us down in the dining hall in a few minutes? We'll speak more then." Sir Garrett stated.

"I'll show him to his room," Ayla said, as Garrett excused himself from the two. "Let's go get you settled in Rohn, you should find your quarters more than adequate. You have a fine view of the waterfall you adore so much." She said with a friendly smile.

"As you can see the keep is rather large, Henry, our resident engineer, and architect is a master of his craft. Been building structures since he could walk. He claims the keep mimics various aspects of nature and the strength it naturally exudes. I'm sure you'll get to meet him soon enough. He can be a bit gruff, but he is tasked with keeping this magnificent home of ours standing upright and secure. You might need to just bear with him at times." Ayla chirped as she led him down the hall decorated with thick rugs, old tapestries, family portraits, and even hunting trophies, well-lit by various candelabras and lanterns. "Here we are," She grinned as she opened the double doors to his room.

It was more than Rohn had ever had imagined. To the left of the entrance in the wall was a large, warm hearth that contained a cozy fire. In front of it sat a plush, ornate sofa accompanied by two end tables. The room's walls were end-to-end bookshelves stuffed with manuscripts and various novels, only leaving enough room for the two glass double doors that lead out to his private veranda, which overlooked the northern reach of Sir Garrett's land. To his right, there was a large feathered-filled bed, smothered with pillows and warm blankets held in a cherry bed frame. Hidden behind a privacy screen was a wooden bathing tub that could be filled with hot water from the fireplace and a dresser for his clothing. The floor was made of smooth, strong lumber but protected by various furs and woven rugs.

"I don't know what to say, Ayla, it's fantastic. This is more than I had expected." Rohn stated shocked and almost in tears.

"Aye, Garrett went all out, as he usually does for those he wants to stay. So you're one of us now, Rohn, family, you just don't know it yet. He doesn't just pick anyone at random, you're here for a reason I'm guessing. And if you try to run, I'll have Brom track you down and hogtie you." She added as she wrapped an arm around his shoulders and then gave him a playful squeeze. "Get freshened up and meet us downstairs. Got a big meal planned for you, and plenty of introductions to be made." She chuckled as she walked out, gently closing the doors behind her.

Maybe this won't be so bad after all — Rohn thought to himself, gawking over the innumerable tombs, novels, and scrolls that almost poured off the shelves. He wondered if a man could even read so much in his lifetime, but with a huge grin he swore to himself he would die trying.

After a few moments, Rohn had finished putting away his clothing and belongings and poured water from a decanter into a basin left on a dresser for him. He gently washed his face, the water cool and refreshing, as he checked himself over in a mirror that hung on the wall. He couldn't believe he had done it, traveled from one continent to another, and survived to speak of it. The future both excited and scared him. This land wasn't like home. It was new, untamed, and far more uncivilized. England was dangerous enough, but this place was unknown and foreign. While his new employer seemed pleasant enough, what if he was a beast, what would he do? He had little money left to go elsewhere, and the area was dangerous. And training? Rohn was no fighter he didn't even own a dagger.

No, stop, he thought. *Faith, I must have faith. All will go well. There is a reason I am here.* He took one last look after he calmed his nerves, straightened his unruly mane with a brush, then he made his way out and down to the main dining hall.

Rohn couldn't help but be in awe of the decorations and trophies now that he could stop to admire them. Creatures and animals of all kinds were stuffed and mounted on display as he made his way down the hallway. Some he had never heard of like the Rock Ogre. Its head was the size of Rohn's torso and had three eyes on its scarred face, one dead center, and two adjacent to each side giving it a wide range of sight. Its teeth were jagged and its skin mottled gray and heavily calloused. The scribe couldn't help but wonder how the knight had gained such a trophy.

Sir Garrett's collection of trophies taken from combat was impressive as well. Various axes, swords, armor, and other instruments of war hung from the walls of the various clans of Voskavia. Wooden stands displayed the locals' armor, heavy leather, and lamellar he believed the same Brom had been wearing when they first met. It was surprisingly lightweight, allowing those who wore it to move freely, but its overlapping plates provided a powerful defense for their vulnerable flesh and bone. While by no means primitive, they were brutal warriors that had adapted well to the harsh and dangerous world they lived in. Their armor was lined with furs and thick hide. Underneath, they wore heavy chain coats, as an added protection from barbed arrows or large claws. Their swords were thick and broad and far heavier than the English long swords. Some sabers could slice a man in two with a single blow. Their tools of war were far stouter and more finely crafted than he had expected.

He finally managed to pull himself from his exploration, hearing a commotion downstairs as it reverberated through the halls of the keep. The ruckus slowly became clearer as Rohn made his way down the dozens of stairs, into the entranceway, and down another winding hallway behind them. The noise came from a large dining hall at the end of the corridor, as people were finding their seats, pouring wine, and setting the table in the grand dining hall. In the center of the large room, was the roasting pit where a fat boar was rotating among a few plump game birds and vegetables that boiled in a stew pot. Along the dining table sat various loaves of bread, jugs of wine, meads, and bowls of fruit. The scent was overwhelming and intoxicating. Never had he seen such a feast as his stomach immediately chimed in and growled eagerly to indulge in the meal before him.

"Behind you, behind you, watch yourself, the table will not set itself and I've four pies cooking in the kitchen that need tending to!" The plump French woman said as she playfully bumped him to the side with her rear, "Find a seat boy we'll be starting soon."

"Ah Rohn, come sit here next to Ayla," Garrett said, motioning to a chair to the right of him. "We'll begin grace when we all have seated ourselves; we just need to wait for Miss Shea to finish in the kitchen." He said as he scooted up the table in his high back padded chair.

Rohn took his seat and gently placed the vermilion napkin placed before him in his lap, as he shifted, getting comfortable in the padded armed dining chair. Brom and William sat next to one another directly opposite him, the two in a heated argument over who gets the snout of the pig.

"Shall we?" Sir Garrett said, raising his hands to Brom and Rohn simultaneously as everyone else at the table also joined hands and gently bowed their heads.

"We wish to give thanks to you, Lord, for the meal in which we are about to receive and for the friends we are about to share it with. I would also like to thank you for seeing William and Rohn safely through the pass, even if they had been waylaid by a bandit," Garrett threw a look out of the corner of his eye to Brom, as the ranger elbowed Will for snitching. "We give our thanks for your guidance, blessings, and mercy Lord. Amen." All at the table raised their heads, smiled, and said "Amen.", almost in chorus. "Let's eat," Garrett said with a gentle grin. The table slowly erupted into varied conversations as people began digging into the feast before them.

"I wish to introduce you to a few people here, Rohn. While everyone is vital, these folks are imperative in the day-to-day and act as my liaisons throughout the keep. First is Henry Bosc," Garrett motioned to an elderly man as he scooped a mouth full of beans with his only remaining right arm, Henry just nodded slightly to Rohn in return and went back to his meal, "Henry is my architect, he tends to additions, repairs, reinforcements and even the placement of its defenses. He keeps the roof over our head, quite literally. Next is Shea Roues, Shea tends to the manor while in my absence, she makes sure we have adequate supplies and that they are properly stored and kept, and that the rooms are tidy and kept neat. You have her to thank for your accommodations, as she spent almost a week getting it furnished and decorated. Not least of all, she is a fantastic cook. Without her, we would eat far less luxurious meals.”

“Ah, you are too kind Garrett and it is a pleasure to meet you, Rohn,” She replied giving a brief wave, “No one goes hungry here while I am running the kitchen if you ever need something just ask sweetie.” Her voice a symphony in a thick French accent.

“Next we have Bromislav, or Brom as we call him. He’s like a brother to me and a close confidant.” Garrett said, smiling at his old friend.

“A much younger and better-looking brother,” Brom added, ripping a mouthful of meat from a chicken leg.

“The two of you have already met, I believe, but despite his reputation, he is an enormous asset to me. Brom oversees my land as its game warden. He keeps an eye for unwanted visitors and tends to our animals and anything else that goes bump in the night. You can thank him for all the roast meat Miss Shea has prepared for us tonight. One can sleep safer knowing he is out there keeping a sharp eye out.” Sir Garrett said, resting a hand on Brom’s shoulder.

“Ah yes, I had caught another little piggy today, but it smoked too much and had a foul temper, so let it go to drive its little wagon another day,” Brom said laughing into his cup, as William caught on, he turned and gave the ranger a dirty look as he chewed a mouth full of mutton.

“You’ve already met William. He’s delivered goods to us since the founding of the manor. Will goes far and wide for us searching for anything we might need and usually arrives the first week of every month, so if there is anything you need just prepare a list, I’m sure he can handle it.” Garrett said, cutting another piece of meat and placing it into his mouth.

“Aye, might take me a bit to find more difficult items, but I can scrounge up just about anything ye might need lad, and I charge a fair price too. I won’t fleece ye like some other traders at the outpost,” William said with a smile and a nod, and then went back to enjoying his meal.

"Last but not least is Ayla. She's our resident alchemist, botanist, and physician. Ayla studied under her late mother and aided her during the expansion into Voskavia. She also adores sticking her nose in old books much like you I hear." Garrett said as he gently smiled at his adopted daughter.

"Aye, I'll have to show you my collection when we have the time. I've some books you might find interesting about ancient Rome, such a fascinating civilization. Unless you're into those gushy love novels where the stable boy has a tryst with the lady of the house." She grinned her dimples on full display.

"No," Rohn chuckled, "While I enjoy almost any subject, I prefer nonfiction. History, mostly. Tales of knights of old, the great battles society has faced and overcome through the years, even perhaps forgotten knowledge and lore. Again, I am deeply thankful for the library in my room. It's wonderful. I am extraordinarily grateful, Sir Garrett." Rohn finished placing a hand on his chest to emphasize his gratitude.

"No need son, we are honored to have you. I'm glad you came, your father was a dear friend, and when I heard you were looking to move to the frontier I jumped at the chance. I'm sorry to hear of his passing as he and I served together. I owe him a great deal; the least I could do was offer my home to his boy. As I said before, Rohn, I require a squire. I saw this as a sign. I'm not as young as I once was and could use your skills. A well-educated and well-mannered young man as yourself will find little difficulty filling in as my page."

"While I am deeply grateful Sir, I know nothing of combat. I can barely ride a horse." Rohn admitted his face red with shame.

"There is far more to knighthood than swinging a sword and riding a steed. I have a sense for these things and I am rarely wrong in judging character. I am glad you came Rohn and none too soon either." Garrett said, drawing the attention of Brom and Ayla as well, "I received a message from Lord Harmon. It appears a family has vanished off their homestead and he wishes me to investigate their disappearance. I would like the three of you to accompany me." He said motioning to Ayla, Brom, and Rohn.

"Of course, but I thought Lord Harmon considered your service complete?" Ayla said, taking a sip of wine.

"Lords will always be lords, your service to them is never done. Present company excluded of course," Brom said, "Of course I can see Alistair won't get off his fat ass and check on it himself. The damn fool is frightened of his own shadow."

"Men are cut of different cloths, Brom. Some made of silk, others of canvas," Garrett said with a chuckle. "I happily serve; my duty still lies to the people and above all God. Enjoy yourselves tonight. We leave at first light. I wish to reach Outpost Dumont and gather information before we head to the farmstead."

The three nodded in agreement and soon lost themselves in good drink, food, and company. The rest of the night was a blur of laughter, drinking games, and songs. Rohn finally felt like he belonged after such a long time being alone. He never thought he would feel at home after the death of his parents, and while he couldn't explain it, this felt like home. Rohn wished the night could last forever. That the bliss he felt now would never end.

Chapter 6:

Rules of the Wildlands

I

The exhausted hunter rose from his tent finishing a chapter of his book, his shelter nothing more than a canvas tarp held upright by two wooden poles. Jaro scratched his stomach as he rose with a long yawn, making his way to the dissipating campfire. He sighed wearily as he grabbed a log from the nearby pile and dropped it into the fire. Flames danced from the rough wind that gusted through the camp. It was his turn to keep watch of the fire, and in the wilds beyond the fort, there were rules. Not for decorum, but for necessity in hopes of one day returning home. In the wilderness you didn't travel alone, you didn't travel unarmed, and you didn't let the campfire go out. These rules kept you safe, kept you alive, and only a fool ignored them.

Jaro sighed again, rubbing his face as his eyes burnt; the thick forest around their camp was dark, a sea of shadow that moved as if alive. The campfire barely lit beyond the other tents that circled it. From time to time, movement caught his eye, only to be a branch waving in the wind. He yawned again; this time far more drawn out as he rubbed his heavy eyelids. Genuinely tired from a good day's hunt, they had taken down an old durruk male without injuries, a rare feat anyone should be proud of. They had worn it down from above in a nearby ravine it had wandered into looking for soft shrubs; the men expelling at least a quiver of bolts each before the beast succumbed to its wounds. He looked over to the trees, with a slight smile filled with pride, where the durruk's hide stretched after cleaning. He rubbed the stubble on his face, admiring the day's work.

The durruk's thick pelt was going to fetch a nice price at the market, as it was mostly intact. Its meat would feed their families for months when properly smoked and salted. Even the durruk bone and guts were of high value for alchemists and hunters who used it for scent bait to take down some of the continent's larger predators. Jaro poked the fire again with a stick, his eyes heavy and watery as he leaned on a knee. Just a while longer and he could wake one of his partners, as it would be their turn to stare into the dark and babysit the fire. Again, he sighed, moving back into his tent; and curled near a lantern with enough light to read a book.

It was a sultry tale of a noblewoman, with an insatiable appetite for peasants, while her husband was away at war. Even with reading the titillating novel, he was having a hard time keeping his eyes open. Slowly they kept dropping as the wind gently rocked his tent, acting as a natural lullaby, his eyes getting heavier and heavier until they finally didn't open again.

II

Jaro jumped from his sleep, swearing he heard a scream. His eyes quickly darted to the darkness outside his tent, the fire nothing more than embers.

"Dammit!" He muttered with a flinch, his tent flap slowly dancing in the breeze as thunder rolled overhead.

He moved to slide out of the flap of the tent, but stopped. Something was growling in a menacing tone. As it moved, he could feel the ground shutter under its girth. A low rumble of thunder rolled overhead, as a flash of lightening above lit the outside of his tent. There he saw the silhouette. It was huge, two to three meters in height, and dragging something behind it. He heard what sounded like large branches snapping, wet hollow branches. A sharp scent flowed through the air as the beast chewed, whatever it was cracking and crunching in its powerful mouth. Another growl, followed by a huff.

Jaro slowly moved to his hunting sword, a long sharp broad blade with no guard and a four-foot handle mostly used to land a death blow on wounded animals. He could hear the beast sniff, snorting with its head raised to the sky, its lungs heaving as it took in each scent that wafted in the air. Another low rumble of thunder and a flash of light quickly blared through the camp. Nothing but silence surrounded the tents. The shadow was gone. The forest was eerily still and silent. Only the whistling of the wind through the branches of the ancient trees dared to make a sound. The hunter's gaze went back to the open flap of his tent, it gently snapping in the wind as the storm began its gentle release of droplets. He sat in silence, dragging his blade near to him like a favored blanket, hugging it to his chest, as he slid his legs under him in a low crouch. He stopped and listened… still nothing. Just wind and thunder, the soft sound of rain gently thumping on the ground and bouncing off his waxed canvas tarp. He slid forward cautiously towards the entrance; using his blade, he pushed the flap to the side. Willit was lying in front of the campfire. Or what was left of him. His head crushed inward, and his body torn in half. Recognizable only by the tunic he had been wearing.

"Shit!" he screamed instinctively, far louder than he would have wanted to, as he gagged from the sight.

As if responding a large three-fingered paw, four times the size of a man's reached into the tent and grabbed him by the head, its rough palm covered the huntsman's face. Jaro's blade fell to the dirt as his legs flailed and kicked. The hunter tried to grip the creature's arm, but it was far too wide for his human hands, as it was the width of a small tree trunk covered in calluses and thick, rough fur. The grip of the monstrous hand tightened as Jaro could feel pressure in his head, as if a wagon was slowly rolling over it. His tent fell to the side as the beast lifted him with little effort, a full-grown man, two meters off the ground.

Through the beast's thick fingers, the hunter saw the monstrous face. It had a blunt snout, two beady charcoal eyes that scanned him carefully, and a pair of thick ivory tusks protruding from its drooling maw. A forest troll, a male Jaro determined because of the large tusks, as they used them to spar for mates during the spring when they were the most aggressive. The four-armed monstrosity huffed, snot flying from its nose as it let out a growl as its two lower arms balled up and slammed into the dangling man in rapid succession, hammering into his torso. As his sternum caved in, Jaro whimpered, his ribs shattering like twigs. The hunter finally stopped kicking, his legs hanging limp. He could barely breathe now, as he gasped for air in random gurgling pants. He looked down to the ground as he panicked, positive he had just lost control of his bowels. There laid his kinsmen, brutalized and beaten to a pulp. His eyes slowly crept back to the troll his eyes full of tears begging for mercy, as the pressure in his head became overwhelming.

The troll gave a sharp yelp suddenly wincing to the side, throwing Jaro in anger. The wounded man sailed through the air and bounced from a tree like a child's toy. With what little strength the huntsman had left, he lifted his head from the mud as the rain pelted him. Through blurry eyes and fading vision, he watched one of his remaining hunting companions succumb to panic as he was trying to reload their crossbow, kneeling halfway outside their tent. The troll's smaller arms pulled the protruding projectile from the side of its torso with a snarl, glaring at the new contender. The larger, more prominent arms were almost the size of a man; slammed down, repeatedly crushing the hunter. Red mud splashed into the air and onto the face of the rutting troll as the battered Jaro whimpered, watching his kinsmen shatter and fall like a marionette with the strings cut. He could only whine in horror as the beast's powerful arms pummeled his savior into nothing more than a muddy puddle of fabric and gore. There was nothing the remaining hunter could do but lay there and pray it would forget him as the pain slowly left his body, a warmth ebbing through him now as he went numb.

Trolls weren't the brightest, but were more cunning than your average animal, akin to a great ape. The hunter coughed as blood-infused spittle sprayed from his mouth. His breathing was much heavier now, and labored. The troll casually turned back, hearing the whimpers of the survivor. The large hole the bolt had made in its side was almost closed now as its metabolism rapidly increased, healing the wound.

Such a gift came with a cost. In order to heal so quickly, the massive creature had to feed. Again, Jaro rose above the forest floor, the giant three-digit hand gripping his head, his body limp as he dangled helplessly. This time thankfully he couldn't feel the pressure squeezing his skull. All he could hear was a hollow cracking as the troll grinned in his face, its maw filled with sharp crooked teeth and its breath hot and musty like a cellar of rotten food. One last thing went through Jaro's mind before it sprayed out of his crushed head like an egg. The hunter wished he had kept the fire going.

III

Early in the morning, Sir Gerhardt and his party rose, as the sun barely graced the morning with its rays over the keep, hidden in the mountainous valley. Each one of the adventurers prepared for the journey in their own special way. Ayla gave her cat, Mia, a gentle scratch on the head which in return Mia leaned into as she sat perched on the end of her master's luxurious canopy bed. Rohn packed a few books and tried to calm his nerves unsure of what might lie before him. Sir Garrett stood in the keep's entranceway with a crowd of his household staff, leaving instructions to the other members to be carried out while he was away. While Brom, still at his cabin near the stables, checked the edge of his weapons and slung his composite bow over his back. He told his pair of Ovcharkas to be good and could only grin, knowing they would ignore the orders.

Slowly one by one each of the party met outside in the chilly mountain air near the front steps. Ayla was the first to arrive as usual with a hop in her step, obviously a morning person. Rohn soon followed the bright-eyed and bushy-tailed Irish lass as she hopped down the stairs wearing her favorite riding boots and a pair of sturdy canvas breeches, lined with quilting for comfort. Over her tunic, she wore a custom-made set of hardened studded leather to protect her if she should come to harm and to top it off a thick hooded archer's cowl made of heavy wool and arm slits in the sides so she may use her crossbow without being hindered. On her belt were two separate quivers of bolts, one in particular, caught Rohn's eyes.

"I've never seen bolts like those." He motioned the lower quiver with fewer bolts and small clay capsules on the ends.

"Ah, a little invention of my making, one of many. Pray to God we don't need them." She said with an air of mystery.

Rohn just nodded, and his attention drew to the stairs as he heard boot steps again. Garrett was next to make his way down with a few bundles from Miss Shea, packed full of provisions to keep them well fed on the road and draped over one arm a set of leather armor, much like Ayla's. He wore his day-to-day outfit that Rohn had first met him in, his worn but well-stitched breeches and long quilted coat. His chest was protected by a sturdy and polished breastplate, layered over by a snow-white tabard decorated with a large ornate red cross.

"Glorious morning is it not? I hope the two of you slept well." The knight said, handing the provisions to the stable boy to load onto their horses.

Ayla nodded, "Aye. Well enough."

He looked to Rohn and playfully shoved the leather armor into his arms. "For you, lad. Until I can get you fit for something more appropriate. It was mine from when I was a young squire."

"Thank you, Sir," Rohn said, investigating the armor. It had been worn, but its previous owner had taken great care of it.

"I pray you will have no need of it, but it is always to better to err on the side of caution. Protection is prudent." Garrett patted him on the shoulder with a smile.

As the three exchanged greetings, Brom thundered up, riding his big, burly steed. Both mount and master were impatient as his large warhorse cantered in a small circle wearing leather and chain barding as it snorted and huffed eager to ride.

"Are we going or shall I go back to bed?" Brom asked, his horse rearing hastily to leave.

All of them were wearing armor, and this worried Rohn. Brom had donned almost the same armor he had seen in the hall among Garretts collect of trophies, a broadsword on his belt and sheathed on his saddle rested a large crested broad axe with a pick and flanged butt. On the front of the ranger's bandolier was his favorite hunting knife that William had a close shave with the day before and, on his back, Brom's quiver and bow. He was armed to the teeth and dressed in dark earth tones to match his surroundings. The ranger had smeared a black strip across his eyes, making them seem more intense, and him all the more menacing.

"Morning to you as well, Brom." Rohn dared to say, getting a laugh from the duo.

"Not bringing Fen and Elka on this trip?" Ayla asked, referring to his two favorite mountain hounds.

"You mean the roadblocks made of fur?" Rohn added, with a chuckle.

Brom moved his large mount around again in a circle, getting impatient. "No, I want them to mate, so I am leaving them here. If he is as virile as me, Fen will have her pregnant before I leave with you fools."

The three of them laughed as they mounted up, joining their Slavic friend. Shea, accompanied by Henry and a few more of the household, bid them farewell as they waved from an upstairs balcony. Sir Garrett nodded to those gathered as the group rode off, Brom in the lead, his horse eager to run, as they rode out of the valley to the fort below.

IV

Somehow the outpost seemed different Rohn noticed. The mood had significantly changed since he was last here, as had the weather: thick gray clouds hung in the sky, threatening to pour at any moment. The people were silent, scared, and on edge. Fear lingered over their heads like the ominous storm clouds in the sky, and the sight of Sir Garrett and his party reinforced the locals' paranoia. If they had suspicions that something was wrong, it was confirmed now, especially for the knight to arrive armed and with reinforcements. Rumors began swirling through the outpost as the group rode through to its center.

"Ah, I am glad you made it, I hope your travels were pleasant Sir Garrett?" Sir Alistair exclaimed, the extremely homely, yet incredibly wealthy older man was shadowed by two large well-armed guards and a small entourage of servants and handlers. Terrified of what lurked beyond his palisade walls, Alistair was far too greedy to miss an opportunity to line his pockets and had made a small fortune taking over the fort when Sir Garrett left it in his hands.

"All is well, the pass has thawed nicely," Garrett responded with a smile, looking down on the man, noticing his hair had gotten thinner since the last time they had met.

"I am, of course honored and deeply grateful Lord Harmon has sent you with haste. Unfortunately, I'm far too busy to handle such affairs myself. It would appear we have a situation at one of the nearby farmsteads. But let us speak of it in a more comfortable setting." Alistair said, trying to lure them back into the tavern.

"I wish to speak to the lad. I would know what he saw, from his mouth." Garrett commanded, as the sky began rumbling with thunder.

"Of course, yes by all means… Aiden!" Sir Alistair clapped as a young man behind him stepped forward removing his wool cap.

"I'm Aiden, sir. I was the one who found the cabin."

"Good, you can fill us all in on the way there." Garrett motion Aiden to hop onto his mount.

"It's going to rain soon," Brom said, "It will be hard to track anything if it's a heavy downpour. We should move quickly."

"Hold on, boy," Garrett instructed Aiden as he snapped the reins of his steed, eager to leave the place filled with so many terrible memories. The others quickly followed suit; Sir Alistair stumbled out of the way almost being trampled by Brom's steed as the wild ranger gave the merchant knight a cheeky grin.

V

"This wasn't here before. This makes no sense." Aiden said, completely confused, looking at the forest before him. "Their cabin was near the forest edge, not in it."

"Are you sure this is the way, boy?" Brom said, growing impatient.

"I'm positive, it was only an hour's walk at most, I had been there many times Sir, I swear," Aiden said on the verge of panic as he scanned the surrounding area, slowly beginning to doubt himself.

"A forest doesn't just sprout up overnight, certainly not a fully grown one," Rohn added, riding closer to one of the trees for inspection trying not to act like he was purely focused on controlling his mare.

"At least not naturally," Ayla added, flanking Rohn.

They were your normal fully grown hemlock, spruce, and oak trees, albeit quite a bit larger than average. However, something seemed off about the forest. The trees almost seemed agitated Rohn thought, silly as it was. There was a constant interruption of creaking and snapping limbs. The forest constantly moaned as if resisting strong wind, but made no visible movement.

Ayla thought she saw something move within the bark and as she leaned in she saw a small translucent vine, or worm perhaps, slither back into the tree as her presence startled it. She drew her dagger and took a sample, cutting a small branch off the trunk, noting the sap was thick and dark, almost black. She wrapped it in a burlap sack and tucked it into her saddlebag for later as she caught up to the others.

"None the less, we should get going, the storm will be upon us soon," Garrett stated as he gently kicked his horse into action.

The others followed each in turn, falling in line behind Garrett heading in the dark menacing woods as the storm gained momentum around them the wind picking up speed suddenly. Even Brom was uneasy in this forest; as he drew his broad axe from its place on his saddle, he felt better with its weight in his hand. The ranger glared into the distance, watching for any sign of movement, listening for the slightest sound.

"You hear that?" Brom stated as they made their way deeper into the trees, navigating the silent foreboding woods, each person listening intently now for what Brom's keen ears picked up.

"No, I don't hear anything," Rohn said, using a hushed tone barely above a whisper.

"Exactly. Where are the birds, the squirrels? It is the first month of spring; this forest should bustle with activity. No scat, no tracks of any kind." Brom said, looking to Aiden, "What forest has no animals in it?"

Aiden shifted uncomfortably on the back of Garrett's mount, his mouth now dry as he found it hard to swallow, worry clearly showing on his face. "Maybe we should turn back? Get more men from the outpost?" he said, sounding shaken as his voice quaked.

"Too late," Ayla interjected, and point ahead through the colossal trees.

Off in the distance, a small cabin sat quietly. Almost completely hidden in the trees and overgrowth. As they approached, they noticed it had become overgrown with vines and appeared as if it had been abandoned for months. Brom quickly rode ahead; still armed with his axe as he dismounted swiftly, hitching his horse to a nearby tree a few hundred feet away, and moved low and quickly to the cabin.

Garrett motioned the others to follow his lead, hitching their horse close to his, as they prepared for the worse.

Brom quickly crept up to the cabin with the stealth of a seasoned hunter, each footstep calculated. Neither branch nor leaf met his stride as he deftly moved to the structure. Within seconds he was in the doorway, his broad axe at the ready. The warden stopped for a moment, completely still as he listened. Still nothing. No birds, not even vermin. The forest animals were still as stone. The constant snapping and creaking of tree limbs were enough to drive a man mad he thought.

Shaken from his thoughts by what sounded like a whimper. Someone was here. He could hear their erratic breathing; whoever they were, they were afraid. Slowly he moved through the home, hearing his allies taking positions around the cabin, the creak of Ayla's crossbow being cocked and the slight slink of Garrett's blade unsheathing. Nature had overtaken the one-room domicile, leaves had blown in over the now weather warped floorboards, the front door lay ripped off one of its hinges dangling uselessly. He felt inside the hearth, stepping over furs and bedding in front of it. The fireplace was stone cold, but plenty of ash. He noticed melted candles near the beds, but they were smaller ones, usually used at night as they gave off less light, just enough to see where you were going. Two pairs of shoes left abandoned, a pair of day boots on the table's bench, and adult slippers usually worn by women lay in front of the large bed. Three beds total, one large enough for two people stained in dried blood. He sighed, seeing the splatter, a sizeable amount, far too much for them to have survived. Nothing left behind, no scat, no viscera, not even bones. Wildlife couldn't have done this.

"You can come out. I don't feel like dragging your ass from under there," Brom said to the man he saw hiding under the main bed while checking the hearth. He carefully looked over the place, making sure he hadn't missed anything.

The trembling serf slowly scooted out from under the bed. He smelt of ale and piss covered in dirt, as his hair was unkempt and matted. The frightened looter slowly raised his hands as he dropped a dagger to the floor.

"I am unarmed, please; I just came here for shelter. Out of the rain. Like you, sir. Please." The haggard man said, eying the door.

"You're a liar. There are but a few reasons to be out here, in this cabin. You sure as hell don't look like the owner or the boy outside would have identified you." Brom said, as Garrett and the others came into view. "Either you are looting, or hiding from the law."

"Either way, you need to come with us," Garrett interjected. "This place is dangerous, no place for anyone," Garrett commanded as he threw Brom a bundle of rope. "Secure him please, nicely, and then join us outside. We spotted tracks."

"Of course, me lord," Brom sarcastically joked, poorly imitating an English accent even adding a little bow.

Garrett walked back to the others and explained the situation. Brom soon joined them after tying the man's hands together, thinking better to be safe than sorry. He handed the rope to Aiden to tend to the bound man to lead him around like a dog by his wrists. While no one is sure what Brom said to Aiden, they were positive it was some sort of threat seeing the reaction from the young man and the captive as the ranger walked away.

"So we follow the tracks or bring the man back?" Rohn asked Garrett.

"What do you think we should do young Rohn?" Garrett asked deciding to use this as an educational moment.

"Me? I don't think I have enough experience to make such a decision."

"Why not? Ayla would have her input as would Brom, shouldn't you as well? What do you think of the situation?" Garrett pressed him.

"Well," Rohn took a moment and looked to Ayla who just gave him a cheeky grin as she folded her arms over her chest waiting for his answer, "We could send Aiden back with the looter, as we've no use of him now, no more reason to put him in harm's way and a strong lad like him can easily handle the captive until he is in custody by the local watch. We can follow the tracks as far as they take us, perhaps they will lead us to a hideout, or lair of some sort. We can then return better prepared and with more men." Rohn finished, nervous he had made himself sound a fool.

Ayla looked to Garrett, smiling and nodding in approval. Garrett grinned at her reaction and then clapped Rohn on the shoulder also in approval.

"Sounds good, do we have any objection?" He said to Ayla as Brom approached them.

"We need to move quickly if we are to follow these tracks, they are faint and the rain is going to muddy them up damn fast," Brom said as a roar of thunder echoed through the forest accompanied by a gradually increasing fall of rain to accent his point.

"So be it," Garrett said as he turned to call over Aiden, but gasped in shock, reaching for his long sword. "Aiden, look out!"

Behind the young laborer, a hulking figure charged on its knuckles like an ape, its two small secondary arms tucked under into its chest as it snorted and huffed. The monster was over twice the height of a man. Its skin covered in muscle and calluses, scarred over from being injured and then quickly healing throughout its lifetime. It huffed and let out a bellowing roar as it swatted Aiden away from the captive, sending him a good twenty feet as he slid into a tree, knocked out cold. The bound looter stood no chance, before he had the opportunity to turn around the troll had him by the head with one massive arm and by a leg with the other. The troll's lower two arms began punching the helpless individual in the face and chest with the force of club each hit making a resounding thud stopping only to then slammed him into the ground like a fish with his powerful upper limbs.

Ayla began replacing the iron-headed bolt with a clay-tipped projectile filled with pitch. Her education kicked in and she knew the troll would regenerate lost limbs within a few days and severe wounds within a few moments unless burnt with acid or fire. Brom growled and charged the beast, sliding through its legs now flanking it as the monster was distracted ripping a massive chunk from its prey's abdomen with its crooked teeth, spilling the captive's steaming intestines into the wet mud.

"Rohn, tend to Aiden, get him away from here," Garrett ordered, drawing his long sword as he moved in to aid Brom and the doomed looter.

Rohn couldn't move though, he wanted to so desperately, but he froze in fear at the horrific scene before him. Never had he witnessed such brutality, such savagery. The creature was horrific, its tusked maw slowly chewing what it bit off almost oblivious to the others. He wanted to run, to vomit, to hide and scream all at once.

"Rohn! To Aiden quickly!" Ayla reinforced as she positioned herself, lining up the sight on the crossbow, trying to find an opening.

Rohn quickly snapped out of his stupor and ran to Aiden who lay unconscious at the base of a tree. The scribe hastily picked up the unconscious young man under his shoulders, struggling to keep his balance in the slick mud as the rain beat him from above. The scribe slid his arms under Aiden's and wrapped them around the man's chest. With a grunt, he lifted and scurried backward to where they had tied the horses, praying to God it was out of the way of the ensuing battle.

Brom finally found his opening, and with a guttural yell, he buried his axe deep into the calf muscle of the troll. The beast roared and screeched, ripping the rest of his meal in half, dropping the prisoner's legs to the ground to free one of his massive, more powerful arms. It spun clumsily, swinging a barrel-sized three-digit fist into Brom's side connecting with a thud, but Brom was not such easy prey. The man's master-crafted armor combined with his quick reflexes and training helped him absorb the blow as he flew to the side, his axe never leaving his grip. The ranger tumbled into the mud with a splash ducking into a controlled roll easing the momentum and slid to his feet prepared to strike once more.

As Brom had distracted the monstrosity, Sir Garrett found his mark and thrust his long sword upwards into the armpit of the monster, bypassing its thick rib cage and piercing its vital organs. Garrett immediately retracted his blade, sending two more quick horizontal slashes across its abdomen before it could retort, and prepared to parry the troll's rage. None too late, as the creature's larger right arm swung wide to fend off the new assailant. Garrett however was already prepared for it, his feet firmly planted he slashed upward in a parry, not only deflecting the powers of the beast but cleanly cutting off his three-digit hand, sending it and the corpse it held flying over his head into the forest behind him. He quickly retreated backward, holding his blade in a defensive stance and keeping low, knowing Ayla should be ready by now.

As if on cue, Ayla slowly squeezed the trigger of the crossbow and with a thunk the bolt sailed through the air, slamming into the beast's chest with precision honed over years of practice. The pitch pot on the tip shattering on contact, splashing the thick black tar all over the creature's forest green hide, the bolt now protruding from his chest. She didn't hesitate and began reloading as soon as the first bolt left the crossbow. The troll's smaller, lower arms tried to pry the projectile loose, smearing the pitch all over itself as it panicked.

"Rohn, I need a torch! Light a torch!" She yelled back to him as she heaving the string of the crossbow back into its trigger cradle.

Rohn quickly moved from Aiden, propped up against a tree out of harm's way, and ran to her horse frantically digging through her saddlebags and sighed out of relief as he felt the rope wrapped head of the torch. He tucked the object under his arm and cradled it as he quickly made his way to a nearby log. With a stumble, Rohn slid to his knees, protecting the torch's tip with his cloak from the downpour assaulting them. He gripped the handle under his arm and fumbled through his belt pouches, finally pulling his set of flint and steel from his dry belt pouch. With urgency, he began snapping them together over and over, watching as the sparks bounced off the slowly dampening torch's head, the fight behind him thundering through the forest as the beast roared in rage. He knew the damp air would hinder lighting it with each second it was exposed, and he furiously and more closely snapped the flint and steel together trying to overpower the humidity of the air.

Brom had regained his footing and pulled the clasp to his cloak, letting the mantle fall to the mud. He could move freely now unhindered and bolted into the fray with a burst of speed, seeing the beast's imposing right hand being cleaved from its body, he grinned noting the now weakened side. He quickly reached into a pouch on his hip and pulled a leather bola that ended in three heavy wooden balls adorned with studded silver spikes. With a quick snap of his wrist, the bola got up to speed as Brom jogged closer to the enraged creature, now slamming the ground trying to take his rage out on his old friend. The hunter let loose, and the bola swooshed cutting through the air, wrapping around the troll's wide head. It let out a roar, as the leather straps entangling itself in its fang-filled mouth as the balls smashed into its face and head with a stinging thud. The beast was now beyond rage. In full fight-or-flight panic, it began flailing its limbs at random, at anything or anyone who was near. It stumbled into a young hemlock tree, felling it with a roar, as it bellowed, grasping at the leather straps wrapped around its face.

Brom dropped to a knee and slid at the last second, swinging his axe with his free hand, using the other to keep his balance he cleaved into the back of the creature's knee. A bright crimson burst sprayed freely from the tree trunk-sized leg, causing it to buckle and fall to a knee. As the troll tried to regain its footing, Garrett struck again, slashing the monsters opposite heel with three blurs of his steel blade, a loud snap followed by the trolls rumbling bellow as its Achilles tendon tore forcing the beast to both knees, his powerful front arms barely keeping him upright as he trembled with pain. The monstrosity looked up, snarling in rage and fear, refusing to accept its fate.

Ayla seized the moment and sent another bolt through the air; its feathered end whistled as its clay pot tip sailed through the trees and thudded deep into the monster's right eye. The troll let out a deafening screech as the bolt shattered, the thin clay tip it was housed in, splashing its tar contents all over the monstrosity's face and oozing into its bellowing maw. The creature writhed in pain as it bawled at the sky, forcing Garrett and Brom to stumble back covering their ears.

"Hit him with the torch, Rohn! The torch, light him!" Ayla tried to scream over the troll's constant cries of pain.

With one last stroke of the lad's almost depleted flint, the torch roared to life in Rohn's arms. Stuffing his remaining flint and steel into its place, without hesitation he stood to his feet, running past Ayla as she prepared another pitch bolt. Rohn stumbled as he slipped in the slick mud, his leather boots getting little to no traction as the torch danced dangerously close to the drenched mud. With all his strength, he slung his arm to the side, letting the torch go at the last moment. With a prayer, he let the torch fly. Everyone held their breath, watching the flaming projectile glow as it spun through the air, the shadows of the trees fluttering and waving in its wake. With a resounding thump, the torch bounced into the creature's chest, the sticky pitch erupting in a burst of amber light. They all exclaimed as Rohn found his mark, but the troll had enough as the fire seared his skin. Now a hulking, burning pyre of unbridled raged it swatted Rohn with its remaining left arm, its claws ripping through the scribe's lightly studded breastplate into his chest and stomach. The young scribe flew a good ten feet into a tree nearby and landed face down where he remained unnervingly still.

Ayla screamed in both rage and terror and let another bolt loose, this one hitting the troll in its shoulder as the pitch exploded outwards in a puff of flame and smoke. The troll desperately trying to regain his footing but Brom and Garrett took turns closing in, slashing, stabbing, and then retreating. Overwhelmed by the fire and constant barrage of blows, the troll's regeneration couldn't keep up. It weakly roared, as its massive frame thudded into the muddy forest floor with a hiss as the pitch on his chest doused itself.

"Quickly Brom, the head and heart!" Garrett commanded, Brom already moving into position.

"Yes, yes, this is not my first dance old man," Brom said as he began hacking at the neck of the smoldering corpse, like a log in the middle of the road.

Ayla dropped her crossbow, seeing the creature fall, and ran to Rohn. She slid on her knees to him, quickly turning him over, placing her fingers on his neck looking for a pulse. She grinned and sighed trembling, feeling responsible for the unprepared man's fate, tears welling up in her eyes as she felt his heart still pumping through his veins, albeit rapidly. Quickly she removed a bottle of strong, clear alcohol and several bandages from her satchel to her side, and went to work.

"Will he make it? Is he ok?" Garrett said as he dropped at Ayla's side, clearly worried the young man would have been disemboweled or worse.

"Yes, the claws grazed him, but he needs to be cleaned and bandaged to stave off infection. Check on Aiden, please. I have Rohn." Ayla said calmly as she doused the wounds with the alcohol and began folding bandages over his two wounds to stem the blood flow.

This spurred Rohn awake from the sting of the wound cleanser, as he gasped and instinctively tried to get on his feet. Ayla gently held him down while putting pressure on his wounds. "Be still Rohn, you took a hard hit and are wounded, but I have you, you'll be ok! Relax." She reassured him, wiping the hair from his brow as he settled back to the cold ground exhausted, both mentally and physically from the entire encounter.

Rohn faded again into unconsciousness. The last thing he saw before he passed out was his fiery-haired guardian angel smiling at him, relieved, wiping tears from her freckled cheeks.

VI

"What the hell happened?" Aiden said sitting up holding his head the world spinning and his stomach turning, "I feel like I've just woken from a week's drinking."

"Move slowly boy, the troll smacked you good, sent you a good ten paces at least, right into a tree," Garrett said, bandaging the shaken young man's head, covering the small lump covered with scrapes and minor cuts.

"The troll?!" Aiden said, looking around suddenly paranoid.

"Be still! We've taken care of it, I need you to remain here until it's time to leave." Garrett ordered, the rain finally letting up as the thunder rolled in the distance.

Brom was having a field day. It only took him a few moments to cleave the head clean off. He then heaved the massive beast onto its back and sliced its belly open with his large hunting knife. Coughing and gagging, but with a huge grin still on his face he shoved his hand upward into the ribs, his face showing a bit of awe as he gripped the creature's heart slowly still beating, trying to reanimate its master.

"No little beasty, you're done. Well fought though, well fought." He grunted, tugging the heart from the chest with a wet rip.

Brom stood at as a horrific sight. In one hand he held the troll's head gripped by its hair and on his shoulder its heart that must have weighed close to eight pounds alone, his favorite axe, slung on his back. His body and face covered in a mixture of mud and blood, and a grin ear to ear on his face, the wild man having the time of his life.

"You alright?" Garrett asked Brom, eying him warily, though amused.

"Oh, hell yes! Damn good time and to think I was considering staying at the keep!" Brom said, as he made his way past with his trophies.

"Well, I am glad you had fun Brom, that's all that matters." Garrett said sarcastically, "Stow those and come help us get Aiden and Rohn ready to travel, I will need to fashion a travois to move him."

"Tough pup isn't he, though he'd be cleaved in half, Good arm on him too. He just might do." Brom stated, shoving the heart into a burlap sack he pulled from his horse and tying the troll's head to his saddle with its long, thick mane.

Garrett made his way to Aiden and helped him stand. The man was still shaky, but able to walk on his own. After Garrett got him mounted on the back of his horse, he helped Brom complete the travois and brought it over to Ayla and

Rohn. The two men gently lifted him and set him on the make-shift structure like a stretcher. Ayla quickly bundled the still-unconscious young man before Brom carefully dragged him over to Ayla's mount and fastened it to her saddle.

While the others prepared to leave, Garrett walked over, picking up the looter's remains, and placed him with respect on top of the troll's corpse. He closed the man's eyes, folded his arms over his chest, and quietly gave him his last rites as he gently doused the pair in flammable oil.

"God be with you; may you find peace in the next life you could not find in this one." He then snapped his wrist, sending sparks from his flint and steel into the odd pair. They, in turn erupted into flames. Garrett crossed himself, making sure the fire caught, and then made his way back to his waiting family. Tired, sore, and still shaken with their brush with death, the party said nothing on the way back to the outpost.

Chapter 7:

The Scion's Son

I

The party, exhausted and wounded from its encounter with the forest troll, made its way back to the outpost arriving by midday. The first order of business was to explain the situation to Sir Dumont. Garrett believed they would need at least a company of twenty to thirty soldiers to reinforce the outpost and send out scouting parties. While trolls were usually aggressive, he had never seen one come so close to a human settlement and stand its ground against several humans. They had become brazen and fearless of humans in their exile.

"Ayla if you could arrange for a wagon to take Rohn to the keep. Brom and I will speak with Sir Alistair and catch up with you on the trail. And Ayla, Thank you. You did well out there. I couldn't be prouder." He said, pulling her close with an arm around her shoulders. "Thank God you weren't harmed. I don't know…" He stopped short not wanting to think about losing her.

"Aye. Don't get sentimental on me now," hugging back, "we've much to do. Go deal with Alistair; I'll tend to Aiden and Rohn."

Garrett smiled, seeing how strong Ayla had become. Of course, living on the frontier, you would have to be strong. Before he led the Purge, encounters like the one with the troll were commonplace. Most days commoners remained huddled in the cities. Rarely venturing out during the day, fleeing back to the thick walls of their villages before nightfall. Creating a homestead in the wilds would

117

have been suicide. Garrett was afraid the peace they had created would not last, that the land would return to its natural and dangerous ways. So he chose the place he had for his keep. It was remote and covered with natural fortifications, with plenty of resources. He just prayed it would hold out to whatever was coming their way.

II

"We bring grim news," Brom said as he entered the trade house where Alistair spent most of his time.

The large warehouse was filled to the brim with supplies of all types, from food to fabrics, tools to toys all packed nicely in crates waiting to be purchased and sent out. The balding knight turned to Brom and Garrett, a worried look poured over his face as his eyes rose from his trade manifests. "What do you mean?" He snapped, part of him not wanting to know the answer, his gaze falling to the enormous head Brom had just tossed to his feet, getting gore and blood all over his newly polished leather boots.

Alistair jumped backward as it landed with a thud, taking shelter behind one of the large gruff guards who reactively gripped the handle of his blade.

"I ran into that bastard out at the homestead. While I don't think he killed the folks there, the fact that the forest has expanded its border a few hundred feet in no less than a week is a slight concern." Brom said, loving the attention.

"I strongly suggest you request reinforcements," Garrett said, trying to keep the plump knight calm. "This could have been an isolated incident. But the forest, spreading at an alarming rate, is not natural." Garrett finished.

"Well, how am I to protect against an encroaching forest filled with beasts?" Alistair said, still hiding behind his guard with a hanker chief covering his mouth.

"You have a town full of eager mercenaries; I suggest you let your bloated coin purse do the talking," Brom growled.

"I will return soon when my squire has healed. I will come back to check on the outpost and help with its fortifications. Until then, I suggest you tell the

118

population that they should remain within its walls at night and venture out only if necessary." Garrett suggested, trying not to upset Alistair.

"Not go out? I have a busy trade outpost to run Sir Garrett! How am I to tell them to remain inside?! This will choke the King's revenue, and you expect me to hire more men? This will not do! I will write to Lord Harmon immediately." He fled to his office near the back of the warehouse, motioning the guards to deal with the mess.

"Choke his profits he means. People could become corpses, and he worries over silver." Brom walked over and picked up the troll's head from the ground and lobbed it back over his shoulder, the guards staring at him with shock.

"You're going to keep that," Garrett said not at all surprised.

"Damn right I am an old man. This will look great over my mantelpiece. If you're nice, I'll give you a tooth, you can show off in the keep." Brom grinned as they both shared a laugh before heading back to Ayla.

III

The laborers' barracks had helped Aiden by letting him rest a day or so as he regained his senses. Ayla had more than a little trouble finding another driver to take Rohn and herself back to the keep. The commoners were frightened to leave the walls of the fort. They found another hunting party dead just a half day's travel from the outpost. However, a healthy stack of silver can change a man's mind rather quickly.

Ayla hired an older man she had dealt with before in the trading post. He offered a fair price since it was just them and Rohn who were wounded. She tethered their horses to the rear of the wagon, then hopped in the back as they got Rohn settled. Ayla sat next to her ward, resting against the driver seat covering the wounded scribe with his wool cloak keeping him comfortable, as the wind was still chilly and bitter near the mountains.

She sighed rubbing her face; the day had been rough. The image of the poor looter burnt into her mind. At least she got Rohn and Aiden back to safety. For the first time today, she managed to relax and rest, though she still held her crossbow across her lap cocked and ready for loading at a moment's notice. The lass wouldn't fully let her guard down until they were within the halls of her home once more.

Rohn winced slightly as he shifted from the pain and groggily opened his eyes the sunlight blurry and blinding. He was happy that the first thing he saw was Ayla's dimpled face looking down at him with a smile as she gently patted his shoulder to comfort him.

"Well, look who's up, ye rest well?" She said playfully.

"Thank you, Ayla. Without all of you, I would have ended up—" He stopped. Thinking of the poor sod that was devoured. "My God, what happened to him," Rohn said, the memory of the horrific encounter coming back to him.

"Hush. Don't you worry, Rohn, as I said, we're all family here. We take care of our own." She smiled, rubbing his hair back from his face. "You did well. Damn fine throw." She chuckled a bit gently patting his head. "When you get back, I can make a poultice out of the troll's heart. I'll have you back to your old self soon enough."

He sighed with relief, the pain bearable but sharp and constant if he moved. "I noticed Garrett wanted to leave the outpost almost as soon as we arrived. Not wanting to pry, but I'm honestly curious. Why did Garrett wish to leave the outpost so quickly?" Rohn asked.

"Aye, that. We honestly don't like that place too much. Not due to anyone there, just bad memories. It was the place we lost my mum. Outpost Dumont was a stronghold and the first line of defense in protecting the new lands, specifically Eirburg. It still is, although most of the creatures fled as civilization spread. They built the walls at Eirburg when Garrett commanded the fort. A place to defend the territory. Some sort of commotion occurred almost daily. Whether it be a native raid, territorial Wyverns, or Fomorians trying to bully the settlers, something was pecking at the palisade's wall." She sighed, brushing her auburn hair from her face, looking out to the forest. "Was never really safe. I think that's why he wanted the manor so secluded, hidden, and independent. He was afraid the old world would return one day. He wanted a safe place for him and his family." She finished, smiling down at Rohn, wiping a tear from her eye.

"All of you have suffered much here. You deserve a place to go where you can rest, laugh, and be content. A little piece of heaven." Rohn said, longing for the same thing.

Sudden hoof beats interrupted the two as Brom rode up beside them nosily looking into the wagon.

"Just making sure you two aren't getting bawdy." Brom teased.

"My God, Brom, do you ever stop being yourself?" Ayla said her face twisted from wincing at the low-hanging sun.

"Only when I'm dead, girl." He said snapping the reins of his steed, taking point.

"I'm glad to see you up. You gave us all a serious scare lad." Sir Garrett said to Rohn.

"Aye sir, I'm sorry I couldn't have been more helpful," Rohn stated as he tried to sit up, but a sharp pain forced him back down.

"Oi! Don't move Rohn, I've just patched you up, you'll tear the wound," Ayla ordered, forcing his head back down.

"Rest Rohn," Garrett ordered. "You need to heal; I need you back on your feet, lad." And with that Garrett nodded, smiling proudly at Ayla as he rode past.

Rohn had to admit he was exhausted; his body sore and his wounds were sensitive. He laid back and gradually fell asleep once more to the gentle humming of Ayla, the rocking of the wagon aiding him to relax.

IV

The party returned to the keep just before dusk. Brom and Garrett helped Ayla move Rohn to his quarters, as the rest of the household doted over the lot of them hearing what had happened. The scribe slept comfortably in his room, as the others went downstairs and cleaned up. Before Ayla had supper, she took the heart of the troll to her laboratory and began preparing a thick salve that would help Rohn heal. Troll blood, when boiled down and mixed properly with herbs and diluted with pure liquor could become a powerful remedy for deep wounds and dire afflictions. The monsters' constant hunger was a side effect of the rapid metabolic rates; it wasn't unheard of to hear a troll had eaten an entire flock of sheep, or a small family group wiped out an entire herd of cattle. Though they usually were not as brazen as to attack a large group of humans, especially when alone.

Ayla had spent much of the night finishing the poultice for Rohn and would apply the ointment in the morning when she changed his bandages. Ayla realized her eyes were burning as it was well past midnight. She sighed and began putting away her notebooks and decided she would unpack her saddlebag in the morning, but right now she was sluggish and too weary. The alchemist walked out of her private laboratory gently closing the door and headed down the hall, noticing a light in Garrett's study. She poked her head in with a tired smile her eyes barely open.

"Rest well and don't stay up too late." She said with a smile, still admiring his gusto.

He chuckled, "I won't. Just a few things I need to take note of and go over. Then I'll head to bed."

She nodded and left him to his books and headed to her room as quietly as she could. Ayla passed out as soon as her head hit the plush pillow, her cat Mia, curling up in her red wild mane to join her.

V

Rohn slowly opened his eyes, his chest aching but not nearly as bad as before. He had to pee so badly it hurt and despite the pain of moving he had to make his way to the chamber pot. Rohn cautiously lifted himself from his bed careful to not agitate his wounds, and limped over to the small pot in the corner near the door to his veranda behind the privacy of the wooden room divider. Carefully he maintained his balance and sighed as he relieved himself, almost filling the pot to the brim. He tied his pants back up but couldn't help but notice his stomach growled with a low rumble, hungry from the day's events. He had slept right through the evening meal, exhausted both mentally and physically and wondered if perhaps Miss Shea had left some pie, or rolls out on her preparation table, so he grabbed his tunic and tossed it on as he headed out the door, closing it as silently as he could.

Making it to the kitchen was a feat all its own. He was careful not to fall, taking one stair at a time. Balancing a candle in its holder was far more difficult when wounded. Despite the struggle to the kitchen, the reward was well worth it. The master cook had left out a little less than half a cherry pie. He grinned and looked for a knife, quickly slicing into the thick crust as cherry oozed from the sides. Rohn took a seat at the large table in the center of the kitchen, carefully sliding onto a stool, grinning at his treat as he bit in.

"Pie for dinner?" Garrett said, walking in with a lantern, shadows dancing on his face.

Rohn tried to swallow his mouthful quickly, embarrassed at being caught.

"Don't worry lad, I came for a piece myself. Shae's pies are heavenly." He said, sitting down next to Rohn, cutting himself a slice as well.

The squire smiled. Not sure what to say. He took another bite, a cherry bursting in his mouth with a sweet pop.

"Rough day. I'm sure you're not used to such excitement, especially coming from a university." Garrett started taking a small bite then placing the pie down. "You handled yourself well, considering. The torch, I mean. Well done indeed lad you fit in well here, I hope you see it."

Rohn nodded, thinking about the looter. The horror on his face. Defenseless as the creature sealed his fate.

"What happened is done. The man is in a better place." Garrett saw the strain on the young man's face. Being in this state of mind many times himself, he could read the boy's thoughts.

"I can't stop thinking if I had done something different. If I hadn't frozen, or perhaps tried to distract the beast." Rohn said, feeling guilty for surviving.

"No, sometimes no matter what you do, where you go, you can't change the fate of someone else. We were all given free will, Rohn. He made his choice to be there, and he knew it was dangerous." He patted Rohn on the shoulder. "You did very well. Edwin would be proud."

Rohn nodded. He looked down at the table; the moment repeating in his mind.

"We lost my Abigail in the same area. At the outpost. We were to be married, but never were we able to see the day." Garrett spoke in a somber tone.

Rohn looked at Garrett. "Ayla told me a little, but no details. Said you lost her when it used to be a military outpost."

"Aye. She was a physician." He smiled, "I was seriously injured in one of the wild-man raids. Bastards brought Fomorian giants with them, probably bribed them to join their cause. We killed the giants and the remaining natives fled, but I had been gravely wounded in the battle. Because my men feared I wouldn't make the night, they sent me back to Eirburg to be with Abigail and Ayla. They managed to find a path around the main road; it was a longer route, but hidden and relatively safe. When I had arrived at the capital, only Ayla was there to greet me. Abigail had come to my aid taking the main road when she heard I had been injured. They didn't send word of me returning in fear of ambush. So the two of us just missed one another."

"That was brave of her. Strong woman. I can see where Ayla gets it." Rohn said, trying to ease his pain.

"Aye, she was. Tough as steel, smart as a whip, and beautiful to boot. The morning she arrived at the fort; the men had suffered a serious attack from the hill clans. She had heard they sent me back to the capital to recover. Abigail however remained at the fort to aid with the wounded. She was always putting others before herself. It was her nature." He added as pain seeped into his tone, "The wild men returned, this time in far greater numbers as they overran the outpost. My dear Abigail had defended the wounded to the death. They found her body in the infirmary entrance, with her short sword nearby. The lass had fought to the end."

"My God, I'm so sorry Sir," Rohn said, not sure how to console him.

"She's in a better place, and it left me with her little angel to watch over me." Garrett smiled, wiping a tear from his eye. "I think she sent you as well, lad. I haven't been totally honest as to why you're here."

"I had my suspicions," Rohn said, bracing himself mentally.

"I'm getting older and I have no one waiting to carry on what I do here or tend to my land and its people. I would leave it to Ayla but the other nobles would contest it and surely they would take it through force or litigation as she is not of my blood." Garrett said, "But I have a son." He added bluntly.

Rohn looked up at him, confused. "A son? Brom?"

"No lad, I met Brom on the battlefield when he was a young man, around your age. He was a prisoner for a while, but he abandoned the old ways of his people, and now aids me instead, leaving his brutal culture behind. Mostly behind." The knight chuckled. "I mean you, son." He said seriously.

"My father is Edwin Durnham, buried back in England." Rohn corrected, confused and slightly shocked.

"No Rohn. Edwin raised you, yes, and did a fine job at that. Made you a strong, moral, and decent man as I knew he would. However, he raised you in my stead. He wasn't lying when he said your mother died at birth, but it was my wife he spoke of, not his. His wife died of illness years before, a bitter winter that claimed many. Edwin and I were close as we served together, but my talent drew the attention of many nobles. Soon I was offered a position as a squire and rose quickly through the ranks. A bloody path I cleaved as well." Garrett stared at the cherry pie as its shade of red reminded him of some dark memory.

"You left me behind? Why?" Rohn asked, feeling rejected.

"I knew I couldn't take a newborn out here. It was far too dangerous. Worse than I had thought. The Age of Darkness in England was nothing compared to what we faced. What we may yet face. I did not wish to abandon you lad. I loved you and your mother, but I admit my duty was more important at the time than my son and my grief. To be honest, I was running from losing Elizabeth, abandoning you as I did. Duty was a convenient excuse. I am regretful now, not being there for you. Not mourning Elizabeth, as I should have. I loved her deeply since we were young and I was so proud when I found out she was with child." Garrett's eyes began welling up, but the seasoned templar kept his emotions in check.

Rohn could see this was difficult for the seasoned warrior, and allowed the Templar time to compose himself.

"The days passed, and all was going well for us. I was rising in the ranks. Every day they opened a new position because of death and failure. My name even caught the eye of the One Church's higher echelon. When your mother went into labor, I rode all night to be at her side, arriving as you were being cleaned and swaddled. But Elizabeth had lost a lot of blood. There were complications and she did not survive your birth. It devastated me, but The Order made me an offer, to promote me, to make me a commander. So I had a choice to either give you up for adoption or place you in the care of someone I trusted. Edwin gladly accepted my responsibility. In return, I made arrangements that you and he would be taken care of financially and when you came of age, you would attend the University in Oxford and get a proper education. You would be someone great, educated, and well-versed. When I had heard of Edwin's death and that you had wanted to serve in Lord Harmon's court as a scribe or bookkeeper, I knew it was God's will bringing you back to me. I told Baron Harmon who you were and, that I wanted you to return to my side in your rightful home. And here you are. The only blood kin I have left. My son, my legacy. That is why you are here. I wish for you to carry on my work, my duty."

Rohn just sat there, taking it all in. "How can this be? I cannot defend people; I've read books all my life, prepared ledgers for trade deals."

"You share my blood, I am part of you and it is part of me to be a guardian of the people since my fathers, father. It was my calling to stand before the creatures that lurked in the darkest places of our blessed Eden. Now I wish to train you to do the same. Pass on my legacy, my name. All that is mine will be yours, *is yours*. I know ask much of you, Rohn, but I saw something in you today. Just as I saw in Ayla and Brom. Just as theirs, your spirit is righteous, Rohn. You can be the people's guardian, their shield. You have it in you. Think about it, please. If not, I'll respect your decision and send you where ever you wish to go."

"I have no place to go. Everyone I know is gone." Rohn said, staring into the distance.

"Brom, Ayla, myself, we will train you. A shield does not make itself; it is forged. You belong here, boy. With me, with us, and you know it, you can feel it. Abigail sent you, Edwin sent you, your mother sent you and God sent you lad. Can't you see that?" He wrapped his hand gently behind Rohn's neck. "Give me a few weeks. It is all I ask."

Rohn slowly looked to Garrett, taking a measure of the man. Rohn knew he had nothing to lose. No family to return to. Garrett had nothing to gain either as Rohn wasn't rich, he wasn't powerful and it was true; he felt like he belonged here. Since he first saw the keep, he knew this is where he belonged. He had found a family.

"When do we start?" Asked Rohn, with determination chiseled across his face.

<h1 style="text-align:center">VI</h1>

On the other side of the kitchen door, a small figure slipped back into the shadows as Rohn came to his decision. Ayla had mixed emotions about what she heard. Why wouldn't her father tell her? Didn't he trust her and know what would become of her? Ayla was always his champion, his protégé. When Sir Garrett wished to marry her mother, she objected, insisting her father was dead, but Abigail had told her, "Family is not always who you share blood with, but those who will shed blood with you." She made her way back to her chambers and laid in her bed thinking on that, as she stared at the hearth's flickering light and slowly drifted back to sleep cuddling Mia in her arms like a teddy bear.

<h1 style="text-align:center">VII</h1>

It was late in the day as the sun was just passing its apex, gradually making its descent in the sky. Rohn spent most of the past few days lying in bed resting. Ayla's salve, while potent also had a side effect that acted as a sedative. Rohn thought this might be deliberate to keep patients bedridden as they recuperated. He had finally found enough energy to move his way to a comfortable sofa that temptingly sat in front of the fireplace warmly lighting his room. He enthusiastically grabbed a book from the shelf at random; this one was a fictitious novel of a bard who was struggling with newfound fame in London. He had only sat and read for a few moments when a gentle knock reverberated on Rohn's door.

"Come in." He said, looking up from his book.

Shea peeked through the door as she slowly opened it. "Bonjour, I came to bring you something to eat. Sir Garrett said you will be bedridden for a few more days to heal your wounds." The words dancing through her playful French accent.

"Thank you, ma'am," Rohn stood, taught always to do so in the presence of a lady, wincing past the pain.

Miss Shea quickly brought the tray of stew over to a table near the sofa. "No, do not strain yourself, Mr. Rohn. Please sit, you must rest." She quickly ushered him back into his place on the sofa, easing the young man into the cushioned embrace of the comfortable couch.

"I fear it will be a few days or so before I am well again. Though I am lucky to be alive. God saw fit to save me that day." Rohn said, with lingering guilt.

"We must not dwell on what was and must focus on what can be Jeune monsieur." She said taking a seat on the sofa chair next to him, a smile playing across her plump cheeks. "We are all so happy you will be staying with us. Sir Garrett still mourns the loss of those he loves; It is a blessing to see him surrounded by family and friends."

"Yes, though I'm not sure how well Ayla is going to take it," Rohn said, taking a sip of the tea Shea had just poured, its bitter taste hidden behind a spoonful of honey.

"Do not worry, Rohn, it will be rough at first, but she will come around." She added, resting a hand on his arm. "For now, you must focus on getting better, Sir Garrett will rely on you and the others soon enough."

A knock on Rohn's door sounded through the room. It slowly opened wider. Sir Garrett entered with half a dozen books under his arm.

"Glad to see you up son, I see Shea is keeping you well-fed." He smiled at both of them.

"Yes, it is a pleasure to keep the household well-nourished, but so many mouths to feed. I am blessed with work, speaking of which I must say goodbye, for now, my dear Rohn." She said rubbing Rohn's arm as she stood, "Be patient young Rohn, all will be well. God may not give us what we want, but He always gives us what we need." She winked as she made her way out.

Sir Garrett gave a gentle bow as she made her way past; he then turned his attention to Rohn who was blowing on a spoonful of stew.

"I brought you these books lad; you can still study while you rest. I want you to start with this volume first. One is of long sword techniques and theory, a good read, I learned much from it. And a few manuscripts, some from the church that covers the various types of creatures that inhabit our world, and biology notes from scholars on the known beasts of the land. Study them well, memorize them. The knowledge in these tombs could mean the difference between survival and death Rohn." Garrett said, adding an edge of seriousness in his tone.

"I will, I assure you. And thank you again." Rohn replied smiling, "Do the others know?"

"Brom has known for some time, he says we smell alike." The old knight chuckled.

"Ayla?" Rohn asked hesitantly.

"I believe she does, though I've yet to speak with her on the matter. She has locked herself away in her laboratory, a telltale sign something is bothering her. When her mother died, she wouldn't leave her study for days. She will come around soon enough." He smiled reassuring Rohn.

"I don't know why she is upset, the last thing I would wish to do is offend her." He replied with sincerity, finishing his tea.

"I know, but for so long it was just the three of us. Perhaps she feels like I am replacing her, but the truth is I now rely on her to help train you. She has the healer's touch like her mother, perhaps even more so, and her skill in alchemy is unparalleled. I don't know where she comes up with such things." Garrett chuckled.

"Perhaps I should speak with her…" Rohn said, as more of a question than a statement.

"It is best to let her be, she will be fine. For now, I need you to study, your combat training will begin soon and you will need to be at your peak. We have a brief window to prepare you and cannot afford to ease you in." He patted Rohn on the shoulder and made his way to the door.

"Did you love her? My Mother?" Rohn asked suddenly.

Garrett paused at the door. "I loved Elizabeth with all my heart. I look forward to the day I will once again meet those I loved so dearly and lost." He said over his shoulder. Then he made his way out of Rohn's room as the sun set over their valley, leaving Rohn to his thoughts.

Chapter 8:

The Day of Many Deaths

I

A few days later, Rohn slowly awoke before the sun rose over the valley. His wounds had healed quickly, nothing but two thin scars remained, thanks to the poultice Ayla had made. Though the fiery young woman had been worrying Rohn as of late. Her demeanor had changed, even when she came in to help him change his bandages. Her replies were curt and brief. She was now more withdrawn and gave him but the most basic greeting as they passed usually just a smile, or she would hide behind a book she was reading. He didn't know how he had wronged her or offended her, but he wanted to make things right. After all, they were all going to live together under the same roof, and they needed to get along. Rubbing his eyes, slowly looking around the room, he froze as he noticed someone was in bed with him.

"Was it good for you love?" Brom asked batting his coal-lined eyes curled up next to the young scribe.

Rohn screamed, falling out of his bed, his heart pounding like a drum. "The hell is wrong with you?! I almost shit myself!"

"Oh, aren't we a sweet talker," Brom said, rolling off the opposite side of the bed. "Days of lying around reading are over, boy. Time for you to begin your real training. Books can only teach you so much."

He walked over, standing almost directly on top of Rohn. "Get your armor on boy, today you're mine."

Brom let out a boisterous laugh as he made his way out the door and down the hall as Rohn took a deep breath, trying to ready his nerve for whatever Brom had in store for him. He looked to his repaired leather chest piece laying on a chair in his room. Brom must have put it there when he prowled in to wake him. He sighed, his chest still sore and wondering if it wasn't too late to flee back to Eirburg and catch the first ship back.

II

"Nice of you to get your ass down here, pup. Sun's almost up already and we've not even made you sweat, let alone bleed." Brom said, as Rohn made his way down the stairs to the front hall. "Here, we need to eat and run, lots to do." The ranger tossed an apple to Rohn.

"Bleed?" Rohn said, catching the apple. "What exactly are we doing, Brom?"

Brom said nothing, making Rohn even more nervous. They both made their way around the side of the keep. Past the stables to an empty animal pen, most likely housing pigs from the smell of it. It surprised Rohn to see Ayla waiting for him in the corral. She wore her studded armor and carried a quarterstaff; the ends wrapped thickly in cloth and leather. Her face all business as she donned a leather helm.

"Lesson one boy," Brom said, grabbing a wooden sword leaning to the side of the newly created arena and tossed it to him. "Hop in and try to not get your skull caved in." Brom grinned as Rohn carefully climbed into the pigpen, smiling at Ayla.

"I didn't know I would train with you. I've seen little of you in the past few days—" Ayla cut Rohn short, charged him, staff spinning over her head, whooshing past his face, missing his nose by a hair as she let out a growl that even impressed Brom.

Rohn stumbled back as she pressed her attack; clumsily, he tried to parry her assault. Left, right, left, right, she batted at him, finally a spinning backward thrust

132

landing square in his gut. As the wind shot out of his gaping mouth, he froze and fell to the mud, or at least what he hoped was mud. For a moment he laid there, hearing Ayla walk back to her ready position.

Brom leaned over the pen peering down at him and took a big bite of his apple as the juice ran down his beard. "Going to have to do better than that, boy. By the way, you do something to piss the girl off? She seems a bit riled up?" he grinned cheekily, chewing his apple like a cow.

Rohn spent a few moments catching his breath. Stars still swirled in his vision. He slowly got back to his feet, covered in thick, sticky soil. Reaching down with a groan, he picked up his practice sword, but before he could raise it in defense, Ayla's staff came careening down. Her quarterstaff narrowly missing his skull as he ducked and rolled to the side, her pole smacking the wooden post with a loud crack.

"Good instincts, pup!" Brom smiled, enjoying the show.

"God Almighty! Ayla, calm down!" He said raising his sword with both hands in front of him. "You're going to kill me!"

Ayla ignored the laughing of Brom as she turned back to Rohn. She wanted to make a point and make sure he didn't forget it. She bolted forward, giving a feint thrust, then another feint to his head, throwing Rohn off-center as he tried to block both false attacks. He wobbled and slid in the thick mud, not able to keep his center as easily as Ayla with his poor footwork. When satisfied that he was off-kilter, she stepped in, planting her staff behind his foot and throwing her full weight into a shoulder charge at the same time.

The next thing Rohn saw is her standing over him, a few stray strands of fiery hair flowing down over her face.

"I don't need you to protect me. Hell, you can't even protect yourself. You just think you can walk in here and play lord of the manor?" She snarled her face almost as red as her hair.

"Ah, so she knows. Now, this is going to get interesting!" Brom said, putting his hand over his mouth, feigning coyness.

Rohn ignored Brom's comment and quickly rose to his feet, now head to toe with pig wallow. "What has gotten into you?"

"I heard you and Garrett, in the kitchen. Now that he has you, he's no need of me." Ayla said her eyes welling, though she hid it well.

"God no! Ayla, is that what you think? I'm not here to take anything." Rohn pleaded, tossing the practice sword to the ground.

"Well, I don't want you thinking you need to save me from anything. I can fend for myself. I don't need a wet nurse." She said, now on the defensive.

"Never Ayla. I know you can, I saw it for myself." He walked over, cautiously putting a hand on her arm as the lass was still fuming. "I've lost what little family I had Ayla; I see myself blessed to have found more." He smiled with sincerity.

"Aye alright then. If you're sincere. I'm sorry I tried to split your skull." Ayla said slightly embarrassed.

Rohn smiled, "Come here!" He grabbed her in a big, muddy bear hug before she could protest.

She gasped as the cold mud splattered on her and could only laugh out loud, her face smeared in the soil as she wrapped her arms around him, accepting the muck-covered embrace. It was nice having someone her age around, someone she could rely on.

"If you two are done whining like a bunch of children with skinned knees, can we get back to his training?" Brom said, leaning on the fence.

The two looked at each other, grinning; menacingly looking back to their clean friend.

"Don't you dare," Brom said suddenly on the defensive. "I'll have you hung by your feet you get any of that shit on me!"

"Get him!" Ayla playfully commanded as Rohn hopped the fence.

The duo charged for the ranger, slipping and sliding about each one, trying to corner the fast native, as Brom weaved and dodged their attempts to wrangle him.

"Piss off," he said, trying to stifle a laugh as the two worked in unison to corner him.

Inside the keep, looking down from a window, Sir Garrett watched the three as they played. His heart swelled seeing them enjoy the noonday sun. Little did the family know the trials and tribulations ahead of them. Lord Harmon had once again summoned Sir Garrett, needing to speak with him, but Garrett wanted to make sure his new squire, his only son, would have a fighting chance against anything the Baron placed them against. He refused to lose another person he loved and would die before that happened again.

III

Rohn had been training now for several days with Ayla and Sir Gerhardt, his footwork was greatly improving and his technique was much better. He now knew the basics of swordplay. It was give and take, like chess. He made a move, causing a reaction which he was to expect and counter.

Sir Garrett had shown him how to deflect blows with his sword, using the flat of the blade to spare the sharpened edge. He also showed him how every aspect of the sword was a weapon, not just the blade. The hilt and even pommel could land deadly blows. The three of them taking turns in the dance. Even though Ayla was extremely efficient at combat with a variety of weapons, Rohn was learning quickly as he noticed each weapon could only move and flow in certain ways, allowing him to calculate her next move. Each attack, each riposte could only be one of a few, depending on her stance, distance, and position of their weapons. Rohn learned to calculate these variables quickly and anticipate their movements. While sparring with Ayla and his father was fun and a learning experience, he made his way to practice and saw none of them this day. Only one figure stood in the fields behind their stronghold. Brom smiled at Rohn as he chewed on a stalk of grass, the grounds huntsman crouched, arms leaning on his massive broad axe. The mountain wind blew through the valley as the two stood facing one another, twenty feet apart. The grass of the plains rippled like waves in the ocean.

Today Rohn faced off with Brom, the day he had long dreaded and prayed never came. He had become used to Ayla's fast but light attacks and his father's explanation of various techniques. That's why he was sure the two did not show up to practice today. Instead, Brom stood alone in their place.

While the native was a large man, he was fast. Very fast. Rohn remembered how quick he was when facing the troll. The man was a blur, nothing more than an ivory grin that swung a broad axe with lethal precision. Brom gripped his favored weapon. One side of the axe's head was a crescent blade, thick and honed to a razor's edge as a man could use it to shave. The opposite, a sickle with a tip capable of piercing even the thickest of plate mail. As if it wasn't deadly enough, the butt of its handle was flanged like a mace capable of smashing armor and bone alike, and the top pointed to a spear for thrusting attacks. The weapon was almost as terrifying as he was. Even more so in his capable hands. Both men wore armor this day and used their proper weapons. When Rohn had objected, Brom explained it was best to use the weapon you will always use, so your body and mind learn its weight, its movement, its unique feel. Let your body memorize it so one day it will no longer be just a weapon but an extension of you, like an arm or leg. Brom told him of archers who could fire an arrow as quickly as they could point a finger, and with far more accuracy. This was all from practice.

"Let's see what you have learned pup." Brom moved slowly to a ready stance his axe held to the side, two-handed.

"And what if you kill me?" Rohn asked, obviously nervous.

"First off, that is highly unlikely. It is more likely you will kill yourself swinging that blade like a buffoon stumbling out of a tavern. Second, if I did, an enemy would have surely killed you in battle anyway if I had not. If you can survive a tussle with me, then your odds grow ever better out there." Brom said, pointing his axe to the outside world beyond the valley.

"Shouldn't I use a shield?" Rohn interjected, buying time.

"Shields are for children and the old. You will never win an actual battle hiding behind a hunk of wood. Speed is your greatest weapon when facing the creatures in this world. If you can dodge the blow from a beast or the snap of its maw, then you will easily dodge a man's blade or even his arrow." Brom settled once more into his stand, his left foot forward, his right toes dug into the ground, his axe held low. "Hit me. Do not insult me. Do not hold back." His face stone serious, his breathing measured now and controlled.

Rohn gripped his long sword in his right hand. It gently trembled, terrified he might miss, or worse he would hit his sparring partner. He pulled his blade back over his head. He quickly swung low, but long before the blade landed harmlessly in the dirt, Brom was on his right side, well out of the path of the blade. Rohn felt a tear in his pants, on the inside of his right thigh. Feeling a sudden breeze, he stopped and looked down. A small red streak of blood peaked through his britches.

"Damn it, Brom!"

"Your pants can be stitched, unlike the inside of your thigh, which if you paid attention to Ayla's lessons you would know an artery runs through. If I had severed it, you would have bled to death long before I finished this sentence." Brom said grinning again pleased with himself.

"You couldn't just tell me that?" Rohn sighed, looking over his favorite pair of trousers.

"Pain is an excellent teacher. Pain makes sure you never forget the lesson." Brom said, tapping the side of his temple. "Again."

Rohn had to admit, he was right. The thought of bleeding out within a few seconds before he even landed a blow was terrifying. While he knew Brom as an excellent combatant, probably second only to Garrett, it horrified him that a fight could be won and lost so quickly over such a minor oversight. If this had been a fight for his life, in a genuine conflict, Rohn would be dead. That stuck with him as he looked down to his scratched thigh, the wound from a blow that he never witnessed, or even saw coming. This is when it finally hit Rohn, that this wasn't a game. It wasn't like in the books. It was real. Life or death. One false move and he was done, much like the poor looter at the cabin. Brom smiled at the young man as he saw the look on his face. Rohn had got the point.

This time Rohn's attack was more calculated. He didn't telegraph his approach so hastily and even tried to feint to throw Brom off guard. Of course, the seasoned warrior saw it, but it impressed him that Rohn was learning. He was adapting to his new sparring partner. This was the hallmark of a survivor. Rohn feinted left, then right, lunging at Brom with a stab to his chest. The ranger smiled as he ducked the blow, the cold steel gently but harmlessly grazing his mail hauberk. Before Rohn could retract his blade for a second strike, he felt the razor edge of Brom's axe under his chin. The wild man had closed the distance in just a step and had placed his blade perfectly, where it would meet nothing but flesh, no bone to slow its progress as it cleaved his head from his shoulders should he had chosen so.

"Again," Brom said, and the two repositioned.

Over and over Brom showed Rohn that the fight should be done quickly, one misstep of the enemy should mean his demise. With Brom, there was no give or take, nor dance. Just death. If Rohn's strike failed, which it always did, Brom's axe was perfectly placed for a killing blow. Checkmate. Again and again, they did this. Rohn's muscles burnt, but most of all, his lack of skill frustrated him. When he fought Ayla, he could land a blow here and there, his confidence growing, but now, he was even more scared. Rohn stabbed his blade into the ground and slowly rested on a knee, catching his breath.

"What did you learn today, pup?" Brom said, sweat barely running from his brow.

"That I have a lot to learn." He said, between gasps to catch his breath.

"You learned nothing from your many deaths?" Brom teased, resting his hands on his axes head.

Rohn reactively glared at him, but the same smile crossed Brom's face, as if he was waiting. He was educating him, Rohn realized. Each of Rohn's mistakes was common for the average soldier, and Brom had shown him how to counter them. Over and over, he instructed him. He wasn't embarrassing him, not on purpose. He was giving him a chance to learn, instead of holding his hand, he was teaching him in a way he would remember. His many deaths were lessons that were his to see and recognize.

Brom charged Rohn suddenly, his axe held high above his head like a madman, reminding him of one pagan who attacked his carriage on the first day of his arrival. Caught off guard, Rohn quickly dodged to the side, rolling on his right shoulder easily dodging the blow. He recovered on one knee his blade up again ready to riposte. Brom tugged his axe from the ground and again charged, pulling his weapon back over his right shoulder. This time Rohn calculated its arc, its path. He dropped low, deflecting the bladed head away to his right, and noticed how perfectly his blade tip now aligned with Brom's throat. Stopping his sword at the last second, its cold edge laid on the wild man's shoulder.

Brom grinned as Rohn was learning. He was seeing his mistakes through Brom's exaggerated movements. Rohn looked for telltale signs of an attack now. Instead of watching the blade, he watched Brom's shoulders. His chest. When they flinched, he anticipated their subtle movements, instead of waiting for the weapon to be cocked into position he already knew where it was going and where it could strike.

"You learn quickly, boy, and a fast learner is much harder to kill," Brom said, clapping the young man on the shoulder. "You've done well today and should be proud," Brom said, as the two smiled and had a chuckle.

"So what do you do if your adversary is a troll or ogre?" Rohn said with a puzzled look.

"What has no legs cannot move and what has no arms cannot strike. If the bastard is taller than you cut him down to size." Brom added, plucking another blade of grass selectively to chew on.

Rohn smiled and nodded, pleased with himself and learning more about his rowdy companion. While Brom was bestial and untamed, he also had a focused side to him. He knew why Brom was rarely serious. For Bromislav and the natives, life balanced on the edge of a blade. Death at any moment, with no warning. It was best to enjoy every second you had breath in your lungs, blood in your veins. Brom knew how dangerous this place was, he knew how quickly it could all end. That's why he enjoyed every minute of being alive. Rohn had learned this today, thanks to his many deaths.

Chapter 9:

Bubbles and Blood

I

To the south of the continent lay the town of Hweabrea, a tiny fishing village in the fief of Lord Harmon himself. It survived on the vast and deep body of water that it nestled on the edge of. Within its calm glass-like water a meaty royal blue seaweed grew, but unlike its saltwater cousin, this form of lake weed had a variety of uses. Fed by the rare algae created by its inhabiting fishes' waste and minerals in its waters, the herb could be harvested and dried. When ground up it provided remedies for ailments such as severe colds and touches of flu and even aided in curing black lung when inhaling its vapor. It also provided relief from pain as it soothed the minds of those that ingested it, relaxing them and sending them into a euphoric state. The lake weed was highly sought after not only on this continent, but sold for ten times it's worth in England. It could be farmed year round but only harvested at certain times during its cycle, as culling the plant too quickly or incorrectly would cause the death of the algae and that around it. Harvesters of the lake plant were carefully trained by herbalists brought in from the mainland.

Dale was one of these men. The local botanist trained him well, but waiting for a plant to grow left him with a lot of spare time. Most of the year the fisherman happily spent his days casting and reeling in his fishing nets in the deeper areas of the lake. Accompanied by his son, Oswin, the two would row out, keeping one another company. The two only having one another as Dale's wife was taken by illness last winter. Her grave lay peacefully under an oak tree by their small hovel.

141

It was night already, the moon slowly rising in the black sky, stars slowly poking through the veil of darkness as insects chirped merrily. Dale was bringing in the fishing nets, methodically checking them as he did for snags and tears that he would need to patch. His son was securing the boat, pulling it onto the beach, and securing it with a rope to a wooden pole he had set in the sand. Dale smiled, thanking God he still had Oswin as he watched the boy work hard. Only in his tenth season of life, his son was a hard worker and obedient young lad.

"Don't forget to clean the fish, I'll get the fire started inside," Dale said, as Oswin nodded with a smile, a few of his baby teeth missing from his mouth, and a bruised eye from tussling with his friends.

Oswin watched his father walk into the cabin, his lantern light creeping through the tiny home, giving away his position. He turned his attention back to the fish; a few bass they had caught earlier in the day. They were not huge fish, but they will do well fried. A few potatoes sliced around them, and some ground herbs will help to dull the tangy taste. The boy quickly went about his chore. Cutting the heads off the fish and tossing them into the lake; feeding them back to the other fish. But something caught his eye. A black spot floated in the water, not too far from his home; about fifty feet out from the beach. At first, he thought it a log covered in algae, but he had never seen black lake moss. It almost looked like a head, gently peeking from the water, staring at him. Oswin squinted, focusing on the blot of black as it didn't bob in the water, two silver beads staring back at the boy, and then it submerged once more. Without a single bubble, it was gone. Chills ran down the lad's spine. With urgency, he went back to cleaning the fish, tossing their guts into the lake as soon as he stripped them in one swift motion. Just as he had finished cleaning the last of the day's catch, he saw small wakes of ripples tap the shore, gingerly rolling over his feet. The sound of bubbles gurgling as the water churned just over his shoulder. He tentatively turned his head, terrified of what he might see, his fishing knife gripped so tightly in his hand his knuckles were white.

The black blot had returned, silently floating on the surface its hair scattered like the tentacles of a sea creature. Its pale silver eyes stared at him unblinking from the flat water, but this time closer, too close. Its milky white skin stood out in stark contrast to the dark lake, as its twisted face slowly breached the water. Oswin wanted to run, he wanted to scream, but he froze as his body trembled, locked in the entrancing gaze of the creature. He prayed to God it was just his imagination and shut his eyes tightly, rapidly saying the Lord's Prayer in a hushed tone. It was on the shore with him now, dripping wet, it's breathing heavy and labored in the oxygen-rich air that now reeked of low tide.

Dale had finally gotten the fire roaring in the hearth and quickly placed a butter-laden cast iron pan in its warm embrace. With a smile of contentment, he patiently waited for his boy to return with tonight's meal as he watched the slabs melt into the black iron with a sizzle. Dale wiggled his fingers, warming his hands in the fire's glow proud of the day's catch. *What is taking that boy so long?* He stood with an ache from a hard day's labor, looking out the window expecting to see his son cleaning the fish on the shore. However, Oswin wasn't there. The water just gently rippling onto the sand of the water's edge, as if it knew a secret but couldn't inform the fisherman. The smile slowly vanished from his face as he peered through the window for his boy, panic slowly bubbling in his stomach.

"Oswin." He called, with only a response from the crickets and insects chirping through the swamp.

He hastily made his way down to the edge of the lake, his breathing heavier now as he scanned around the cabin. He spotted Oswin's knife on the sand of the bank, next to four, expertly cleaned fish. His father knew he wouldn't have left his knife, the two being inseparable, as the slender fishing blade was a gift from his late mother. Dale crept to a squat. He took the smooth handle into his grip, almost too small for the grown man's hand. His eyes turned to the lake, a low mist slowly floating over the smooth glass-like water. He saw it, a black blot, slowly drifting towards the shore.

"You fall in boy?" Dale said, waiting for his son's answer. "Bit late for a swim." He chuckled.

The blot didn't answer, just slowly floated towards him, wake gently rippling out as it made its way once more to the shore. That's when their eyes met. The glassy beads in the sunken skeletal eye sockets and black hair stuck to its wet, slimy face.

"Jesus almighty…" Dale muttered crossing himself as his skin went cold, his instincts telling him to run, to flee to the safety of the cabin.

Dropping the knife without thinking; he spun on his heels, his feet dug into the soft sand, propelling him forward with a sluggish start. He could hear it burst from the water. It was cackling, laughing in a distorted, inhumanly feminine voice. The hag trudged behind him, her long lanky legs thumping into the sand, her bony, webbed clawed hands reaching out grazing his legs as he fled. The cabin seemed so far yet so close, the world standing still as he moved, his heart hammering in his chest as he ran.

Crying and trembling, he burst through the door of the cabin. Spinning as fast as he could, he saw her face as he slammed the thin wooden barrier into place, a wretched smile on the hag's twisted mouth. Her sharp, crooked teeth glistened in the moonlight. She hammered against the door, growling, her voice distorted almost gargling.

"Fear not Son of Adam, I come to take thee away to paradise." She cackled maniacally, shoving the door harder and harder her fish-filled breath wafting through the gaps. "Do not fear me Christian man, I come to bring you bliss!"

Dale crossed himself and prayed. His legs trembled as they collapsed under him. The door shook and shuttered from the water hag's strikes as she threw her weight into the barrier. Its weathered surface cracking from her relentless assault. He had nothing to fight her with, to defend himself. No sword, no bow, not even a hatchet as he scanned his humble hovel bracing the door, the only thing between him and her. She was cackling louder now excited with glee, as she moved around the outside of the cabin, like a cat that had trapped a mouse. Her tall thin body having to crouch to peek into the windows, as her slimy long ebony hair stuck to her putrid skin. Her sunken face grinning as she peered in, licking her thin lips with a bulbous purple tongue. The club, Dale thought, the one he used to put the fish down as pulled them from the water.

"Does he wish to see his boy? Oh, the bubbles they could make together!" She cackled, hobbling around the cabin, her nails scratching across the wooden walls of the hovel as she circled the shanty, taunting him.

"You bitch! Whore of the devil!" Dale bellowed as he charged to the side of his bed, tossing the fishnets aside searching for the club, the front door shaking, its hinges now rattling in its frame about to give way.

He fell to his knees, desperately searching for the wooden bludgeon, tossing rope and fishing net aside in a feverish search for its grip. Finally, it revealed itself, tangled in a net, far under his bed. He winced as he stretched, his fingers gently tapping its leather grip just out of reach. The door rattled heavier now with constant pounding, as the hag saw the man through the small window. Wood nails tinged to the floor as they shook loose from the barrier that was slowly giving way.

With a grin, Dale breathed deep as the club rolled into his hand. He spun as the front door flung open, wooden splinters spraying into the air as the hag burst in cackling and laughing. Dale swung the bludgeon as hard as he could, connecting with her thin, emaciated form. The witch let out a screech as the club bounced off her shoulder, then with a thunk off her soggy head.

The hag quickly spun about, her long black locks acting as a cloak, the only thing she wore on her sickly form. Dale jumped to his feet barely able to stand from the sheer terror. Again, he swung, the club whooshing through the air, as the hag leaned back out of reach. She retreated a few steps and grabbed the table in the center of the room. Now on the defensive, she threw it at him, hissing in defiance. Dale guarded himself, raising his arms to block the blow of the projectile losing sight of the intruder. He stumbled back into the wall from the force of the heavy dining table and shook his head, dazed, and his vision blurred. The room was empty. He gripped his club tightly and ran to the front door, long footsteps leading to the lake's edge. Nothing but ripples flowed out over its glassy surface. The hag and his boy nowhere to be seen. Dale fell to his knees sobbing, as lights from the town slowly closed in, the rest of the village coming to see what the noise was, armed with torches and tools. However, they were too late, as Dale sobbed in front of his now-empty home.

II

"Another attack? This time a boy was taken!" Lord Harmon said, tossing the message onto the large oak desk of his study. Dusan and Marshal Hendrik sitting opposite him, looks of worry on their faces.

"I have a few men I can dispatch my Lord. Twenty or so, they will arrive in Hweabrea in a few days, sooner if at a forced march, but it may be prudent to keep them well rested in case they encounter the hag." Hendrik said, tentatively.

Since the attack on the boy and his father, the swamp village had discovered a lake hag, or water witch, had taken residence somewhere close by. Hags were corrupted vassals of dark spirits. Usually, women who lusted for power, who had made a deal with evil itself for innocent souls. In return, the corrupted woman was given limited powers aided by their dark patron. It came at a cost however, as their beauty and humanity slowly drained from them, leaving nothing but a bitter, hateful creature with the form to match. It was the last straw when a farmer lost his leg to a large fanged eel that now resided in the swamp. The beast obeying the commands of the witch, acting like guard dogs protecting their master territory. The town was helpless as they never knew whose home would be invaded next and its occupants dragged screaming into the murky waters.

"Twenty men," Edric shook his head in dismay, "There could be one or one hundred of these daughters of the devil in the area, not to mention what they have conjured. Because of my ignorance, almost half a dozen people have gone missing in the village over the past few months. Now as this dark practitioner shows herself, this is more than coincidence." Harmon said, his head leaning on his hands bearing the guilt of those taken.

"Perhaps the men will frighten the creature off, hags are brazen when they have the advantage but quickly cower when they lose the upper hand," Dusan said, quill and paper ready.

"Send them, by all means, but tell them to escort the villagers back here. We are to abandon the hamlet until we can find someone to deal with the hag." Harmon said with a sigh.

"The church could dispatch Templar's my Lord they are—" Dusan began, interrupted by a look from his Lord.

"The church will remain out of this. The Bishop is looking for any reason to take control of this colony, this is just what he will be looking for to make his move. We use the Templar's and I'll be up to my neck in debt." The Lord corrected him.

Lord Harmon's face visually tensed, his jaws clenching. "No, send the men to escort the survivors back, evacuate them. When Sir Garrett finishes preparing with the fortifications at Fort Dumont, I'll send him and his men to handle the outlying settlements. His duty is to God and his people, not to the church. I can rely on him to handle this."

Both men knew of their Lord's view of the church. While a man of God, Baron Edric Harmon distrusted the corrupted institution and its hunger for power and influence. King Edward gave this task to Lord Harmon alone until the Pope offered support, including coin and Templar's aiding in its success. Of course, King Edward was pressured into allowing the Church to join into the excursion, as it would seem blasphemous to deny them the "chance to spread God to the poor souls of Voskavia," However the Baron had known better, it was their way of interfering as they always had done, seeping into whatever crack they could as they vied for power against the crown and its people.

"Dispatch them immediately, Lord Marshal. I want them to return with the survivors as soon as possible. We are quickly losing our grip on the territory, as if the land itself is poised against us. You are dismissed." Baron Edric stated with finality, the two men looking to one another as they stood.

"And what of my husband and our fief?" A voice interrupted from the doorway.

Lady Agatha stood; her arms folded over her chest. "I have lost much Lord Harmon, and invested even more into this endeavor for our King, but I will require aid. The scouts inform me that the manor at Stonestead is in shambles, covered in vile filth, and the remains of those they had little taste for."

"Lady Agatha, I assure you, as soon as the frontier is secured once more, I will send aid to your settlement, but as of right now we are spread too thin. I need more soldiers, more men. What little I have must be sent to secure the fort, in case this is something more than just chance, dare I say, invasion."

"Invasion." She scoffed as she made her way through the door, becoming bolder with each step. "This is no invasion; it is simply beasts being beasts. Monstrosities have always haunted those swamps; it is just now they are emboldened by lack of protection around the hamlet."

"And the attack at the homesteads? The creatures from your mine?" Harmon interjected. "No, these attacks are poised at the primary resources needed to proceed inland. Medicine, iron, stone, and silver. Something is cutting off our supplies."

Lord Marshal nodded in agreement, "My Lady, if I may, it appears this may be coordinated. Many of our major settlements have been rendered vacant. My suggestion is to reinforce the fort once again as the mainline of defense. We can then dispatch soldiers from the outpost to wherever they need to be."

"So you would protect your assets instead of aiding us? I should have seen this as a ploy to rob us of our labor and what little our house has." Lady Agatha stated puffing out her chest.

Lord Harmon slowly stood and sighed. "Not at all, Lady Agatha. We must regroup. Stonestead, Hweabrea, and its surrounding homes must return to Eirburg at once. When we have again secured the territory, we will deal with each settlement as needed. You have my word; I will give you my full resources to aid you in retaking the mine."

"Your word?"

"Absolutely. From my mouth to God's ears. You will reclaim your home, Lady Agatha." The Baron promised with sincerity.

"So be it. I hope my faith in you is not misplaced." She sighed defeated, and turned quickly, vanishing out the way she had come.

"I will do all I can my Lord. I will dispatch the men immediately to evacuate." Lord Marshal Hendrik stated as he bowed, placing his helm under his arm.

The two men walked from their Lord's chamber after being dismissed, Lord Harmon going back to staring out a window of his study. He knew this day might come once again. The Purge he knew was only a temporary victory. The creatures would return, and most likely in larger numbers. He knew this was the trickling of the dam before it burst.

III

Outside, Dusan moved before the Lord Marshal when they were safe from the prying ears of those nearby. The two stopped to speak candidly, far from the ears of their Lord who may think the conversation something it was not.

"You think it wise to abandon the settlement? It is a large portion of income for the colony. Almost a third of its trade income." Dusan stated, receiving a glare from the Lord Marshal.

"I've served Lord Harmon since we landed on this continent, and I'll not start questioning his orders now. You had best follow my example." Hendrik stated, almost a threat in his tone.

"Of course not, I have nothing but faith in Lord Harmon's leadership, it's just… this will not bode well with King Edward," Dusan said, trying to keep his tone hushed, looking about as he spoke.

"Horse shit! The Emperor chose Baron Edric for a reason, a damned good reason, he'll not lose faith in him so quickly. It would take an act of God to remove Lord Harmon from his rightful place, and I'll not hear another word of it." The Lord Marshal said with a growl, as he turned and left Dusan alone in the palace's hallway.

"An act of God indeed," Dusan said to himself. As a native, he knew these attacks were not uncommon, but Lord Harmon spoke the truth; they seemed coordinated. Planned. They were striking their main sources of income, strangling their economy. While Baron Edric was favored by King Edward, he could quickly lose his liege's good grace if the colony began costing more than it produced. It was a game of give and take, of politics. It seemed though as if someone or something was hell-bent on dislodging Lord Harmon's efforts in colonizing the continent. Dusan just wondered who.

Chapter 10:

Wolves in Sheep's Clothing

I

The messenger had been riding hard all night, his horse breathing heavily as its hooves pounded into the dirt road, flanks of soil thundering into the air. The courier was veiled in a thick black cowled cloak, made of heavy fabric, all but their eyes covered to hide their identity. They rode hard into old the old territory. Deep into forgotten lands littered with failed settlements and old ruins abandoned long before the Englishman arrived. It seemed this land hated anything mortal men tried to create. Even the natives were reduced to roaming clans of nomads; some even turning to cannibalism. Torchlight came into view and the rider slowed, their horse desperately clamoring to catch its breath. A man draped in furs, his black beard and wild hair flowing freely, stood on the side of the road.

"You were expected yesterday. Why the delay?" Dimah said, his voice thick with a Slavic accent.

The rider did not reply.

"So be it. Remain on your horse, it is safer if I lead you. We must be quick. He is waiting and in a sour mood." Dimah turned, holding the reins of the messenger's horse, taking the rider off the main road into the depths of the dark forbidding forest.

The torch desperately tried to pierce through the forest's dense overgrowth, its weak light little match for the oppressive canopy. Without the ember of the waning flame, the woods would be pitch black, an inky abyss; few creatures would be able to see through. The rider knew this land though, as he had been sent here many times over the past months. He knew this territory in the wilds of Voskavia. Perhaps not as well as the locals, but well enough.

This area was once the seat of power for the natives; the long-ruined kingdom of their people's empire. Before the English arrived, there had been cities of stone and supporting villages dotting its landscape. They too had tried to tame the wilds but failed, now haunted by the constant reminders of their past. The natives struggled, finally bending a knee to the Old Gods, the Horrible Ones. One clan resorted to ancient pagan rituals, summoning the favor of an Old One, begging for the ability to survive in the harsh environment. They were granted their wish, but at a significant cost. The locals would become as brutal as the land they walked upon, merciless and unforgiving. This new clan slowly absorbed many of the others through savagery or fear. Slowly they grew, day by day, birth by birth, their numbers swelling.

"Stick close to me," The wild man warned more out of concern than a threat, "As long as you are near my scent, most beasts in the woods will leave you be. They know another monster when they smell it." With a wolfish grin, the wild man looked back.

It took almost ten minutes, but the two finally arrived at the well-hidden camp in the old ruins of a long-forgotten castle, overrun by the forest. Figures moved freely through the decayed stone, like ghosts haunting their ancient home, the natives clad in furs and ragged hemp spun clothing. There were few fires in the camp, this was not only because of the need to remain hidden, but most of the clan did not need the fires to see. Their eyes were adapted to the dark, as their silver-colored orbs absorbed even the smallest amount of light when the sun faded.

As the two got closer, Dimah handed the torch to the rider, knowing he needed it far more than himself. While the messenger had dealings with this clan many times before, slowly gaining their trust, he never got used to the eyes in the dark. Like small glints of diamonds, blinking slowly, moving around him like a pack of wild animals ready to pounce at the slightest provocation.

"Come, this way, he awaits you deeper in the castle." Dimah motioned for him to dismount as he tied his horse up in the middle of the courtyard of the ruined castle to a long, empty fountain, filled with soil and wildflowers. The rider was quickly surrounded by feral men and women, who silently glared, even smelling the air as the rider passed, muttering taunts and jokes at his expense.

Dimah led the messenger down into the belly of the crumbling structure. Through winding corridors, the man could only see what the torchlight illuminated. Eyes followed him from the shadows as he made his way through its narrow tunnels, as they finally arrived at a room that was dimly lit by candles. This must have been a feeding ground. The floor in this immense area was littered with bones from various animals and even human skulls of varying sizes. Still, the courier remained quiet, steadfast, and resolved in his mission. These messages were far too important to be sent via carrier pigeon, as his master could not risk having them intercepted.

"Go." Dimah motioned the rider to enter the room first.

The messenger did so, but hesitantly. Scanning the entrance of the room, and its dark corners before entering fully.

"Still you do not trust me, outsider?" A massive hulking figure said in a deep, calm tone, sitting on a log-carved bench in the center of the room.

"After all this time, you still think us little more than beasts?" Scavin growled as he stood, easily clearing over two meters from the ground.

His shoulders were wider than most door frames, with the girth of a black bear. The scars on his face were the only part of his skin not etched with pagan tattoos of wolves devouring men. His thick unnaturally crimson beard was tightly braided and secured with leather strips, reaching just short of his chest. There was something feral in his eyes, dangerous and primal. Scavin gazed on the black-clad man, his nostrils sniffing in his fear as beads of sweat gathered under his dark ensemble. The barbarian grinned, his large ivory canines glinting in the fire's light.

"Do not worry little one, we don't bite and if we did, you wouldn't be alive to feel it," Scavin remarked, as he and Dimah laughed at the rider's expense.

Still, the rider only offered silence as he reached into his cloak slowly, knowing better than to make quick movements, and offered a small scroll container to the giant man. Scavin motioned Dimah to take it, staring down the silent messenger, glaring at him with savage intention. Dimah took the case, the only one of them capable of reading the English language. He unfurled it and quickly deciphered the message, understanding only a rudimentary portion of the foreign language; no more than a child.

"I grow weary of your cloak and dagger games rider. I grow tired of waiting in the dark like a mongoloid child in his families' root cellar." Scavin said slowly pacing back and forth clearly agitated and deeply frustrated.

Each step covering almost twice what a normal man would, his hulking form crushing bones scattered on the floor. "And I grow tired of you!" He snarled suddenly, grabbing the rider by the throat in a blur of muscle, lifting him well off the ground and face-to-face.

The rider struggling to no avail. His feet frantically kicking as his hands grabbed the bulky man's forearm. His fingers were unable to wrap around the warlord's wrist as it was the size of a small tree. "We trust your master, we wait, we remain silent. We 'behave' and in return are treated like dogs. We are fed your criminals, your peasants. Promised glory and revenge. For what?" Scavin's fist tightened, as his sharp fingernails dug into the emissary's neck.

"Let me see who you are, Who I speak to…" Scavin said, about to rip the courier's mask from his face.

"They wish us to prepare our army!" Dimah blurted out as he finished reading the letter. "It is time!"

Scavin grinned at the rider and playfully cocked his head to the side like a curious pup. "You're a lucky little bunny, you get to scurry away with your life." Scavin dropped him on his feet, the shaken runner gasping for air as he clutched his throat.

Their time had finally come. They would bath the land in English blood once more. "I will have an army by the next full moon," Scavin spoke in a growling laugh as Dimah grinned widely. "Then I paint the land in your kinsman's blood, my speechless little rabbit."

II

The carrier rode quickly back to his master, still shaken from the close encounter with the savage warlord. He snapped the reins over and over as the forest passed by in a green haze. He didn't care if the horse perished from exhaustion; he just wanted to reach the safety of the outpost as soon as possible. The courier had no wish to prolong his mission any more than he had to, as God only knows what lurks out here now in the darkness. Although he was a servant of the Mother, in no way was he protected from the other beasts that lurked in the shadows. He smiled with relief when the lights of Fort Dumont appeared in the distance, but instead of heading directly to the outpost, he veered left, down an old game trail. Winding through the overgrowth and jutted boulders, he made his way to another entrance that had been recently made to accommodate him and his brethren. In a ravine nearby, he slowed his horse to a gentle trot not wanting its hoof beats to draw attention.

"Greetings, brother," Ekart said. "I assume all went well?" He asked in an eerily calm tone, as the rider nodded, dismounting the exhausted, sleek black steed, impressed the animal had not succumbed to the arduous ride.

"The Prince is eager for your return," Ekart said, taking the reins of the horse and leading them down into a cave entrance not far, hidden by the thicket of trees and winding serpent-like vines.

The duo entered quietly, the pathway dark for the first few dozen feet to remain undiscovered. It was then lit by black iron braziers and matching torches crafted in the settlement above. They came to a thick iron door with a small porthole protected by a cage. The barrier had been securely built into the natural stone of the cavern that had been expertly carved for its placement. Ekart knocked twice, then paused and knocked twice more. The eye-slit creaked as it opened. All that could be seen in the dim light was the sight of a crossbow aimed through the porthole's iron gate.

"Ascension is at hand," said the voice behind the crossbow.

"Old Ones be praised," Ekart stated.

As suddenly as it had opened the porthole shut tight, various locks and bolts could be heard sliding out of place before the heavy door sluggishly opened. A pale hand in a black robe motioned them inside, his face obscured by a mask made of a wolf's skull.

"Well let's not keep him waiting shall we," Ekart said, keeping his pace walking past the doorman.

They had to enter through another heavily fortified entry, each one tightly shutting behind them, protecting the sanctuary behind thick iron barriers that would take an army to breach. Ekart and the silent rider traveled down a winding staircase large enough for two men to walk shoulder to shoulder its gray stone lit by iron torches in holders along the wall. At the end of the stairs, the temple opened up to a large room; the walls covered in ancient murals depicting the First People and their ancient gods. The old sanctuary was coming along nicely, its murals almost completely restored and its halls once again busy with acolytes.

Ekart walked before the courier, his hands tucked in his layered robe. The duo passed through another set of black iron double doors that had just been refurbished to their ancient glory. These however were guarded by what the Prince had deemed his Death Knights. The terrifying figures wore black armor that resembled human musculature and bone under tattered hooded robes, and the feverishly loyal warriors were armed with wicked blades that curved like a snake sheathed on their hips. Ekart's pale face grinned at the sight of dozens of masked faces. The population of their once small brotherhood had exploded. Each member now wore masks depicting the Old Gods in the murals, the ones the Prince had Ekart restore at great expense. Each one gave the pale enforcer a gentle nod of respect as he and the silent rider passed to the front of the main chamber. At the front of the hall appeared the Prince from a door to the rear, hidden in one of the murals. The messenger walked before his master and gently fell to a knee as everyone followed his example.

The Prince's coal eyes stared at the mute horseman, the sorcerer's gaze sending chills down the courier's spine. "Welcome back, brother. I do hope the ferals were not too much to handle. I know they grow impatient."

The silent one slowly rose and approached carefully, removing the scroll case handing it back to their patriarch on a bended knee. With the gentle calmness of the quiet before a storm, the Prince took the sealed case from his servant. The veins on the cult leader's hands were coursing with ebon blood, his nails had become long and sharp, resembling blackened claws or thorns.

"Were you followed?" The Prince questioned his voice distorted and eerily inhuman.

The rider shook his head staring at the stone floor of the citadel not daring to meet the gaze of the magus, as Ekart stood behind the mute waiting patiently for his orders. The Prince opened the case, sliding the message out and unfurling it, looking for Scavin's mark as the brute could not read or write. A smile grew across his concealed face as he scanned the ledger.

"He wants to know which settlement he is to start with. Quite the ambitious brute is he not?" A laugh flowed from behind his mask as others in the hall quietly joined in. "He's hungry. Good, a well-fed dog is useless."

The Prince made a simple motion with his hand, Ekart immediately handed the rider another sealed scroll case from his robes he held at the ready. He was adamant about sending a missive instead of face-to-face meetings with the Skadi. While the Mother protected him, he knew how volatile Scavin was, and once released he would be difficult to rein in, but every tool kit needed its hammer. Without a word, the rider took the case and made his way out of the ancient buried citadel. A sea of masked faces watching him leave, each one eager to see their avatar, their chosen demigod in the flesh, and bring glory to the world.

"So it begins my Prince?" Ekart asked the masked man.

"Yes, my dear Ekart, now we finish what she started so long ago before you and I were even dust in the void. This is but the first step to bring about a new age." The Prince said, grinning widely behind his mask, feeling great satisfaction in fulfilling his destiny.

III

For the second time tonight, the mute rider rode hard for the warlord's ruins. On a fresh horse, he rode at full speed, wanting to be home again, safe in the citadel behind its thick doors, sturdy walls, and most of all, secretive location. The rider didn't mind them taking his tongue. He could live without it. He knew a good messenger was one who never told a secret. It was hard to reveal confidences when you couldn't read, write, or speak. His sacrifice would be rewarded in spades when the Old Ones returned. His wants and needs would be known and he would have no use for a tongue, he thought as he smiled to himself under his dark veil.

He recognized the portion of the trail that veered off to the old ruins and skillfully steered his horse down the narrow path, slowing only enough so he wouldn't be thrown off his steed. He wished to be done with these savages, uncouth barbarians. Once more he saw the eyes glinting in the distance, but the silent rider did not tremble this time. This would be the last time he had to endure the bestial humans, as the Prince's plans were now in motion. He reared his horse to a stop; the clan taking interest in the rider's newfound confidence. The horse was tethered to a dead tree, and he removed a torch from a nearby wall as he made his way through the clan, ignoring the snarls, growls, and even snapping jaws as he made his way down to Scavin's lair. He was elated. This would be the last time he ventured into the dilapidated shell to deal with the wolves in sheep's clothing. Dimah and Scavin were carrying a conversation in their old dialect when the rider entered the room abruptly, his torch fluttering in one hand and a scroll case in the other. The mute held out the message to Dimah not intimidated by the pair now, happy this would be his last time dealing with them.

"Back so soon my mute friend?" Dimah said, taking the case and removing the scroll, leaving Scavin to sit glaring at the rider, the two staring one another down.

Dimah suddenly laughed, coming to the end of the message. He grinned at the rider, then casually walked over to Scavin, whispering something in his ear. Scavin's mood slowly changed from impatient and aggravated to calm and appeased. Some would say even happy. The beast of a man stood and walked to the rider, now holding the parchment in his hand.

"Do you ever read these, mute?" He asked with a grin.

The rider didn't answer, tired of being bullied by these animals.

"You should my little rabbit. According to Dimah, there is a lot more here than orders. Your master has also given me a gift of good faith. To solidify our bond, you could say." Again, the wolfish grin found its place on Scavin's face.

Visibly tensed, the rider was not liking where this was going. The Prince wouldn't dare, would he? The mute had sacrificed so much for the Brotherhood. His fears were confirmed when Dimah stood in the doorway, blocking the rider's retreat, a sly grin across his face like a fox in a henhouse.

"He gave me one last gift before we begin. One last meal to show his gratitude." Scavin said, dropping the parchment on the dirt floor, littered with brittle white bones.

The barbarian's face twisted and distorted, muscles spasming in a painful ecstasy as his bones snapped and resettled instantly. His human mouth popped as it disjointed, stretching into a maw filled with large sharp teeth. His ears filing to a point now covered in thick black fur that sprouted across his muscular frame ending on his in powerful clawed hands. While it was a painful process, Scavin reveled in it as it was almost orgasmic to him. The pain fueled him and made him feel alive. While the other children of Skadi had to wait for the moon to be full, Scavin was Skadi's chosen. The man was filled with so much rage and hate he could transform by just giving in to his bestial nature, as it was harder for him to remain human than succumb to the beast.

The rider stood terrified now. His hands trembling, his knees were shaking and weak. How could the Prince do this? What had he done? Before he could come up with a reason, Scavin's massive mouth snapped out, crushing his head like a grape, and began shaking like a dog with a rat in its jaws. The mute's headless, lifeless body flew into a wall like a rag doll, as Scavin released an ear-shattering howl that reverberated through the ruins. The clan had a fine meal that night, and at first light, they would send runners for the rest of his clan. Their numbers would swell with dozens of blooded warriors joining his ranks by tomorrow, and the fort the Englishmen huddled in would burn in the light of Skadi's blood moon. *So many settlements and so little time* — Scavin thought as he cracked one of the messenger bones in his bloodied maw.

Through the night the Skadi chieftain drove his pack to a feverish bloodlust, cleaving through the land like a living blanket of iron and teeth. Their faces smeared in crimson red paint, fueled by the knowledge Skadi, their wolf goddess, was watching to deem them worthy. The sun rose to a sky filled with black smoke and scattered screams that faintly haunted the air. Scavin marched ever forward, savoring the path of destruction they left in their wake as they headed to Fort Dumont. Using the soupy, almost supernatural haze that oozed over the territory as cover as the clan burst forth, again and again, on unsuspecting homesteads, camps, and farms that littered what was once Skadi territory. They had ravaged homestead after homestead, feeding as they went, arriving at one last feast before they approached the outpost. Scavin watched as a large family fled into their hovel, its once whitewashed walls splattered with red and thatch roof smoldering as the rogue embers from the other huts grabbed hold. He smiled and almost felt bad for those inside. Almost.

"This is far too easy, I expected more of a fight from the Englishmen." Dimah scoffed.

"Burn it down, kill them as they flee," Scavin commanded, glaring at the home.

His kin quickly went to work, throwing torches onto the roof laughing at the screams of those huddled inside. A young man ran from the entrance of the building, to only be shot down by a hail of arrows. The clan bellowed in joy, each betting how many more would come out. A woman burst out of the billowing smoke next, it swirling around her form like a gray spirit of death; she shuttered coughing and choking as flames quickly consumed the home.

A spear sailed through the air from the Skadi war pack without hesitation. The unfortunate settler stumbled into the open as the spear found its mark, impaling the unsuspecting woman through the chest, causing her to crumple where she stood. A hoot came from the gathering, the Skadi female who threw the spear, walked to claim her kill with arms held high in the air victoriously.

"We will eat well before nightfall," Scavin said, half-joking as the others agreed.

Scavin was interrupted by a hail of condemnation upon him from behind. The clan turned to see an old man approaching them, stumbling as he made his way. Barely able to walk, his face black with ash and soot, cuts and bruises adorned his frail body as he approached the lycan war chief, completely unarmed yet standing defiant before the ravenous horde.

"God will punish you for this. His judgment will be swift." The old man warned Scavin, stumbling just a few feet from him before falling to his knees.

Scavin let out a booming laugh, impressed by the man. "You have more balls than all the men in this village combined, I'll give you that old man." He said slowly, clapping to applaud the man's gall as his kin laughed.

"You will reap what you sow," The old man said, exhausted and wounded, his face smeared in blood and the ash of those he loved.

"Here," Scavin said as he approached him, handing him a water skin. "Drink. You've earned it."

The old man used what little strength was left in his meager form to slap the container away. "I'll make no deal with the devil. I'll be reunited with my wife tonight and dine with her in paradise."

"Is that so?" Scavin said, getting annoyed as his patience quickly faded, his temper gradually rising. "I have a little secret for you. Your God is not here. This land is angry. Hungry for revenge. You were damned the moment you set foot on its soil. Your remains will rot in the noonday sun, mourned only by flies that buzz around bathing in your stench." Scavin hissed in his face with contempt for the frail harbinger of his doom. "You and all your kinsmen will die before the next snowfall; this I assure you."

"You will meet the His champions, murderer, and we will find you wanting… that I assure you." The old man said with a defiant tone, glaring into the eyes of the feral warlord.

Scavin stood up straight, his temper broiling as the peasant challenged him. "Let them come! I'll split them nose to navel! As for you old man, let me reunite you with your wife." He said pulling a war axe from his belt. "Send my regards to the rest of the village." Scavin grinned as he slammed the axe down into the man's head, splitting it in two down to his neck.

His pack howling intoxicated with bloodlust, they dispersed throughout the village to finish what they had started. Scavin looked to the sky as ash gently rained down like snow. He smiled, pleased with himself, knowing Skadi would be proud, and let out a bestial howl that ripped through the air, his pack quickly joining in. Tonight, he would strike the first blow to the invaders and burn their outpost to the ground.

Chapter 11:

Death on Swift Wings

I

Some time had passed since the troll attack and the people of Dumont were still on edge. The arrival of a small contingent of soldiers put the trading post slightly at ease, but they still feared the ever-encroaching forest. They knew it was getting closer each day as the trees were bigger and more numerous, and saplings sprouted from the now blackened soil. The constant creaking, cracking and moaning of tree limbs were enough to make you go mad. Wild animals fled the area, abandoning their once fertile home, as dogs just snarled and flared their teeth at the border of the woods, refusing to enter.

Although Lord Harmon had sent reinforcements, offering another fifty men to Sir Alistair, he had no answer as to what they would do to the forest's supernatural encroachment. Upon arrival, the new force immediately went to work in the construction of much-needed fortifications and repairs to the neglected settlement. They toughened the walls with dirt mounds, dug a shallow moat around the outer curtain, and placed wooden stakes that protruded out as a deterrence to any creature foolish enough to charge the bulwark of the fort. The outpost had turned into a fortified forward base almost overnight now under the command of Sir Gerhardt.

For the men, their discipline had been kept in check and morale was decent, as the fort was still well supplied from its last delivery from Eirburg. Lord Alistair had spent his day, as usual, complaining. He whined often about the lack of

163

soldiers offered, or the profit he was losing by cutting back hunting and lumber camps in the area. Garrett quickly reminded him of the troll and what would happen to others should he ignore their Baron's commands.

It was midday now; the air was thick and humid, as a dense fog lay motionless on the forest floor. A few hundred feet from the outpost they had erected a covered watchtower near the edge of the ever-encroaching forest. It was to act as an early warning, and two guards were posted at all times taking shifts. On the outer territory of the outpost, they had sent rangers on patrol, scouts that were well adept at moving silently through enemy territory, the men in the tower keeping an eye out for their return.

"This is horseshit," the scrawny disheveled guard complained aloud staring out over the outpost barely able to make out those who scurried back and forth going about their day below. "Weeks now we've been at the Outpost and I've seen nothing. The ale is warm as piss. The women uglier than the livestock, and more boring than… reading."

His compatriot was sitting on a stool nearby that he had smuggled up during his last shift. The larger, broad man let out a sigh as his partner began complaining again. The burly guard whittling away at a small chunk of wood, trying to make the shape of a dog but failing with his burly hands.

"Well, my apologies for having higher standards than this wretched place." He spat over the side, looking with contempt to the people of the settlement, leaning on a beam of lumber supporting the covered tower. "Vermin. The lot of 'em. I belong in Castle Harmon, a royal guard. My grandfather was a damn soldier, I come from a long line of warriors. Probably back to Emperor Arthur." He spat as he bawled, working himself into an ego-fueled frenzy.

"Yes," the sitting guard quickly responded, "I hear they have a position at the ready for a pig farmer's son, such as yourself." He chuckled to himself, slowly coming to a halt as a large raven landed next to him on the railing of the tower.

For a moment, the two just stared at one another, waiting for the other one to blink. With a flailing hand, the plump guard shooed it off, the bird trying to ignore him at first before finally fluttering away. The slender guard ignored the two as they growled and exchanged dirty looks behind him as he glared at the town, folding his arms across his meek frame.

He watched the fools go about their day-to-day, nothing more than shadows in the fog, and thought about how he missed hooting at the prostitutes in the brothels, as he walked his patrol through the streets of Eirburg. The smell of the taverns as they prepared for nightfall, the scent of baked bread and stew wafting through the air.

"And so many damned birds! They must be attracted to the stench of all the game meat. I've never seen so damn many. More flying vermin here than back at the city. So damned unsanitary." He bellowed out as he picked his nose, desperately flicking his hard-earned prize from the tip of his finger.

His snot flew into the air down sailing below making the uncouth guardsman grin, only to be interrupted as another bird abruptly landed right in front of him, causing him the jump back with shock. The small creature cocked its head at him as it had no fear of the armor-clad footman.

The pudgy guard turned his attention from his distraction and gazed over his shoulder, stifling a laugh at the fool, only to quickly fall silent in shock as he peered over Fort Dumont. He stood in awe, his mouth agape as he dropped the whittled mutation he had been working on and gawked in terror. He could barely see the trading post through the thick miasma that lingered around them. Almost like a living entity, it rolled through the small village. A new shadow dwelled over the fort, however, this one far more ominous. The once golden thatch roofs were covered in a blanket of black feathered bodies and haunting eyes. Various blackbirds, from ravens to crows sat in silence, watching the settlers on the ground below as if patiently waiting. He grabbed the thin man's shoulder before he could draw his blade, the fool completely oblivious to the situation developing around him as he squared off with the amused animal.

"You ever seen birds do that?" The large man shook his partner's shoulder.

"They're just birds. No, better than rats." He snarled as he drew his sword from its sheath menacingly, still focused on the small creature before him.

"They're not making a sound though, just watching. Bloody vexing that is."

Another raven took his place on the wooden railing, joining his flock on the perch. Soon came another, then another. The two men looked up to the wooden roof of the tower. The sound of dozens of clawed feet waddled along its surface.

Their tiny claws scraping about, but not a one made a sound, silent and unafraid the birds refused to vocalize.

The thin guard's face fell pale as the realization swept over him. This was not natural. "Should we sound the—" The frightened guardsman began, only to be interrupted as two ravens lunged at the large guard raking at his eyes, their screeching erupting through the air as black feathers clouded the guard's vision.

He could only flail his whittling knife in vain, as he stumbled back, thrown off balance and blinded by the feathered assailants. The tower's railing snapped from the heavy girth of the large man, as he plummeted to the quickly approaching earth below. His screams ceasing with a sickening crack as the full weight of his burly frame landed on an odd angle of his neck.

Seizing the moment of chaos to its advantage, a crow darted at the last watchmen, ducking its small feathered head as it dove past the foot soldier's yellowed teeth as he screamed and shoved itself down his throat. The disheveled guard tried to shout, but couldn't as the small bird wriggled its way past his uvula, pecking into the soft and vulnerable pink flesh of his throat as he did. In terror, the guard dropped his sword and before he could grab the small black legs they kicked and clawed their way down his esophagus.

The man could feel the animal move through his body like a worm burrowing through soil. The bird's brethren just watched as the small creature toppled a man hundreds of times more his weight, its small beak pecked and pierced his heart from the inside. He fell to the wooden floor of the tower with a thud as the silent birds watched with heads cocked in interest, almost amusement. The soldier's arms fell limp to the deck of the tower as his body became still as the surrounding air. Coal-colored feathers floated gently from the air, like snowfall, resting on the man's cadaver. The birds glared at their victim, as his stomach stretched toward the sky, the small beast working its way out. A small ebon beak poked through the man's belly button, like a hatchling breaking through its shell to the cold world for the first time.

The avian assassin made its way from the dark viscera it had burrowed through, covered in a crimson viscous liquid. The flock stood eerily silent and watched with calculating eyes, heads cocked to one side as they watched their smaller brethren preen himself on the stomach of the corpse. Their gaze gradually moving with a sinister motive to the fort below.

"I need you to help me get the war wagon ready. Garrett wants it in the outpost before nightfall." Brom said, as he led Rohn quickly to the stables.

The stable hands were preparing four large draft horses in chain-clad barding, which unsettled the scribe as he followed his companion to the back of the barn. Rohn and Brom had remained back at the keep to continue his training. Garrett and Ayla were down at the outpost aiding with the fortification and preparations of the trading post; once again turned fortress. While Sir Alistair was knighted under Lord Harmon, he was no combatant and made no insinuations of ever wishing to become one. He feared his own shadow let alone what might lurk out in the wilds, but he had a gift for making a profit and Lord Harmon knew silver meant power.

"Did you say war wagon?" Rohn asked curiously with a hint of disbelief, following Brom into a part of the barn Rohn had honestly ignored until now.

"Yes, or as Garrett has aptly named it, 'Ironclad'. He used it as a mobile stronghold if you will, or forward base camp as he pushed the unholy hordes back during the Purge. Sir Garrett and Ayla spent months working on it, perfecting it, as it has become a tradition for it to evolve with each repair and refit. Becoming stronger and more fierce. They wanted a safe place to stay in the wilds when traveling in Voskavia, a castle on wheels if you will. While not as big, the war wagon does just fine. And if I am honest, I don't blame them. It's always nice to bring your coffin wherever you go." Brom finished with a sarcastic smirk.

Brom made his way over to the form of a hulking-covered carriage in the back corner, stored purposely from prying eyes. The large wagon was covered in a thick dusty canvas tarp forgotten by a time when the continent was even more brutal than it was now. Rohn had always considered it nothing more than a simple wagon, but honestly had never paid it any mind, as he quickly aided Brom in removing the canvas covering the bestial carriage.

The scribe was amazed at what sat before him, a means of transportation he had never seen before. It was far more than a carriage that the pompous nobles would ride in, with their noses in the air. The behemoth stood over ten feet tall and was over six feet wide. It was built on top of a large heavy delivery wagon chassis and while nothing fancy as it was little more than a massive wooden box; it was reinforced by oak planks, and metal strips hammered into its sides. Thick coiled springs ran along its frame between the wheelbase and its flatbed that held the cabin. This kept its weight balanced and centered as it absorbed the shock of the roads it would travel. The wheels were made of thick sturdy lumber, almost three inches wide, and had been wrapped in iron bands thinly adorned with triangular spikes on its sides and base. This would crush and impale anything it ran over and giving it the traction to be pulled over less than smooth paths and obstacles.

The roof was lined with sharp-pointed boarding spikes to deter anyone or anything from trying to jump aboard the cabin during its travels, and a small metal hatch allowed its inhabitants to access its top with relative ease. The most innovative portion was the carriage's elevated driver's chair. It was accessible only by a heavy door on its side, and a smaller hatch inside allowed the rider to crawl inside from the carriage. It was almost completely encased but for a six-inch tall window that wrapped 180 degrees around the driver's cabin, protected by bars vertically and horizontally to shield its driver. A small hatch below the portal windows allowed the driver to control the reins of the steeds that pulled it, while a passenger could be free to do as they needed such as fire a crossbow or aid in navigation.

"How did he make such a thing?" Rohn said in awe his jaw dropped from its sheer size.

Brom finished gathering the old tarps and placed them aside nearby. "Ayla has a creative mind, and with Sir Garrett's resources it slowly came together."

"What could pull such a massive creation?" Rohn asked as he ran his fingers over its frame.

"No less than a team of draft horses. Once they get it up to momentum, it's easy enough, stopping is the issue. Ayla placed a large brake on the side to keep the horses from being run over by the carriage."

Rohn noticed the ornate iron crosses on each side of the wagon. "Nice touch." He smiled his fingers slowly tracing them.

"They are more than decoration. Some creatures fear the symbol as if they know what or who it stands for, but a symbol is only as powerful as its wielder. A cross is little more than wood or metal without faith." Brom stated, checking the wheels with a firm shake.

"Is it true, what they say about you, Brom? That you converted?" Rohn dared to ask.

Brom sat still for a second, making Rohn nervous. Then turned to him with a serious demeanor for the first time. "My people are a shadow of what they once were. Long ago we were civilized, we had a social structure much like yours. Towns, villages, and even kingdoms. However, we were waging war on one another long before the English came to our shores. My ancestors worshiped animals and ancient gods to no avail, desperate for power to overcome the wickedness of this land. We remained in the mud, slaves to our ideology and those we called masters and gods, with nothing to show but conflict and suffering. When I fought Sir Garrett, I was overcome by his zeal. He *knew*, he was righteous, and that made him unbeatable and terrifying. Wave after wave, he cut through my allies as if they were nothing but a mere obstacle for a rolling landslide. We outnumbered the English Templar and his kinsmen at least ten to one. Yet he and his men stood their ground fearless and absolute in their belief. Time after time they repelled us and anything else that battered his walls." He nodded, thinking back, "I faced him in one-on-one combat and while I'm a damned good fighter, better than most in this world… he was beyond me. Instead of killing those of us who were left behind during the retreat, he showed us mercy. He treated us well, gave us a warm place to sleep, food to eat, and offered us his wisdom and compassion. He still mended our wounds even after we spat at him or insulted his God. None of my kin would have done the same, especially if they had been victorious. Garrett was different. His God was different. Many of us saw our chance to once again rise from the ashes of our past misdeeds and ignorance in the new empire on our shores. If anyone or anything had a chance to bring peace to this horrid world, it was Garrett and his mighty God. That is why I follow him and why I have faith in him." Brom finished a look of sincerity on his face.

"So you believe in God?" Rohn pressed.

Brom laughed at the question as he went back to checking the wagon over, "After all you have witnessed how could you not?" Brom added.

"That didn't answer my question though, Brom. Did you convert?"

Brom grinned behind his golden beard. "It is easy to believe in heaven when you've been through hell. And I am no fool, I wish to be on the winning side."

III

Sir Garrett walked the palisade behind the curtain wall of the Dumont trading post as old memories flooded his mind from when this fort was his. The monsters, the savage barbarians, constantly pounding at the walls. Not a day went by that someone or something did not harass them. However, now all seemed calm, even the wind stood still and a thick haze laid docile in the air. So soupy he could barely make out the other watchtowers in the distance. A numerous amount of crows and ravens in attendance gave him apprehension as they were silent, but their presence was a normal occurrence for spring. They would usually come seeking the scraps the taverns and butcher shops would throw out, just usually not in this number. The winter must have been hard on them as well he thought as he made his way across the wall.

"Reporting in Sir." The young soldier quickly saluted Sir Garrett, accompanied by his partner. Both men wearing standard-issued light mail, a kettle helm on their heads, bows in their hands, and a quiver of arrows and long sword on their belts. Garrett nodded, seeing them ready for their shift.

"At ease, men. Are you well-fed and rested?" Sir Garrett asked sincerely.

"Aye, sir, ready for our watch. Where will you have us?" The first soldier asked.

"Relieve the forward watchtower. They must be going mad with boredom." He smiled at the lads.

"Aye, sir." They both saluted and immediately made their way through the line of soldiers on the wall and hurried out the front gate, as it sluggishly opened with a heavy moan.

Sir Garrett watched the young soldiers fade into the mist their bright red tabards of House Harmon fading into the blurry fog. He scanned the horizon, waiting for the two relieved soldiers to return and debrief them. The knight stopped for a moment, seeing movement through the miasma opposite the tower. He narrowed his eyes and stared at the figure not too far from the edge of the forest. A dainty form, dressed in what appeared to be a nightgown. He wondered if the girl had gotten lost, or was coming from a nearby farmstead.

Suddenly his concentration was interrupted as screams flooded the air from the forward tower. Their attention turned to the disruption in the distance. The soldiers gripped their weapons like a child would clutch his favorite stuffed bear, making them feel safe and secure knowing it was near. Sir Garrett moved into a better position on the wall, quickly squeezing past soldier after soldier, the thick fog choking the sounds that emanated from the field of screams and… caws.

"What was that, Sir?" A soldier asked, his hand trembling on a nocked arrow, waiting for orders, obviously frightened.

"Longbowmen, at the ready!" Sir Garrett ordered, suddenly behind him a flurry of activity as the archers obeyed, readying their arrows, preparing for further orders.

Out of the fog, a lone figure emerged, stumbling, falling, and then clumsily regaining his footing as he made his way back to the security of the fort. He gripped his throat as if he was choking his face the shade of a plum. Within moments, the footman was in the walls of the palisade once more, his comrades spewing obscenities as they moved to his aid, looking for a wound. It was the young soldier Garrett had just dispatched, his face bloodied, one of his eyes missing, and his clothing torn to shreds. Garrett ran to him and cradled the wounded man in his arms as he fell. The boy wanted to scream. He pointed to his mouth. A black feather stuck to his lips, fluttering as he tried to gasp for air. The soldier began convulsing, his body shuttering violently not making a sound.

Sir Garrett began searching for a wound, but the soldier suddenly fell still, his eyes glazed over. A low, cracking, gasping sound slowly echoed from the corpse's mouth. Garrett leaned down and slightly turned his head towards the sound as it reverberated from the soldier's body, eager to get a better listen. Ayla quickly cut her way through the muttering crowd, wearing her healer's apron and carrying her satchel at the ready. She fell to her knees opposite her mentor and adopted father.

"My God! What happened?" She asked, Garrett quickly looking up at her, then back to the wounded soldier.

"I've no idea, do you think—" His question cut off and as a blackbird's head popped out of the man's mouth with a squawk.

The crowd gasped and quickly jumped back from the man as they muttered in horror, crossing themselves. The bird slowly wiggled his way out of the soldier's mouth, covered in gore as it casually hopped onto his chest. Without fear, the tiny animal stood brazen in its actions, its eyes glimmering in a bright yellow. The tiny creature shook its body as it preened itself, small droplets of blood spraying onto the man's surcoat that it stood on, gently misting his face in bright crimson as it shook the matter from its oily feathers.

"Witchcraft!" One of the laborers yelled, the crowd erupting joining in. "He's been cursed! A spell has been cast on him!"

"It's God's wrath!" Another voice bellowed. Those gathered yelling unintelligibly as they riled themselves up into a panicked frenzy fueled by fear and ignorance.

Garrett ignored the onlookers and raised his gaze upward. The roofs were covered with avian creatures. Hundreds upon hundreds of birds. Ravens, crows, and even smaller blackbirds littered the stray rooftops like a living shadow of feathers and glaring eyes. They sat there, silently watching, heads cocking slightly from time to time, as they studied the crowd below. He looked back down to the blackbird that had emerged from the man, a few laborers moving into position to grab it, still yelling, bellowing about the devil and God's wrath. They lunged for the bird. A clumsy human, with the feeble grace of a sheepherder, stumbled forward. The little bird was far too fast for men such as them and darted into the air, the crowd's eyes following it, as the animal ascended beyond their reach into the overcast sky above. The onlookers gasped as a silence swept through the assembly, their eyes welling with tears as they gazed on the rooftops. Whimpers and whines were all most of them could manage as they crossed themselves and prayed feverishly. With an explosion of movement, the roofs erupted as all the birds took flight simultaneously in formation, pouring into the sky like a fountain in perfect unison. The air erupting with unnatural screeches and caws, as feathers gingerly fluttered to the roads. The crowd burst into screams of panic and terror.

"To shelter! Find Shelter!" Garrett ordered, screaming over the thunder of the beating wings and unnatural screeches, cover his ears from the piercing calls of the murderous flock.

Ayla didn't hesitate quickly running to Garrett's side, taking shelter under his mantle as he protected her from the oncoming swarm of beaks and claws. Garrett headed for the nearest doorway, ushering others to do the same as the flock twisted like a winding serpent bound for the heavens. The congregation of death now circling the outpost, their numbers so great they blotted out what small amount of sun seeped through the fog. People desperately ran, trying to find shelter, but were cut down as the mass of the birds flooded the streets. Pouring through the settlement like a rushing river of feathered projectiles, as they pierced into peasant and soldier alike. Their beaks as sharp as the head of an arrow, tore through flesh and clothing alike, a red vapor spraying in the air as they collided with their targets. The birds were scraping and pecking at the eyes of one doomed woman as she collapsed in the middle of the road, two small black legs quickly vanishing down her throat. The soldiers had broken rank and were panicked at the horrific turn of events. Archers began firing at random losing all discipline, many of them planting their arrows in innocent settlers instead of the small black blurs that were assaulting them.

Garrett finally burst through the open door, following Ayla, as the birds clawed and pecked at their backs. He slammed the wooden door shut and hastily moved the latch into place, the other side of the door erupting in a flurry of clawing and guttural unnatural sounds. Garrett pulled the table in the center of the room on its end and with a grunt slammed the thick barrier against the entryway.

"The shutters, Ayla!" He pointed to the wide-open windows, the pounding sound of a million wings ripping through the air.

Ayla charged to the open portal and began to close the shutters. She couldn't help but gasp in horror at the scene outside their haven, as the vicious animals homed in on those not yet able to find shelter, ripping at them as their brethren thumped into the vulnerable settlers like black bolts from a crossbow. As those outside fell from the onslaught, she managed to get the shutters free just in time as several crows veered and made a dash for the open window. Ayla slammed the wooden shutters into place and secured them as the birds furiously pecked at the thick barrier screeching in frustration.

"It's the end of days! God is punishing us for our wickedness!" One of the refugees in the stone hovel claimed as he took a seat on a nearby stool in the middle of the room, his hands shaking as he buried his face in them.

"Calm down, we can't lose our senses," Ayla said, panting, her hair wild and untamed.

Garrett moved to a woman holding her two young children and placed a gentle hand on her shoulder, "Remain here. My daughter will look after you." He said to the terrified woman. She nodded. Her eyes welled up with tears.

"What? Where are you going? It's madness out there!" Ayla said stepping in front of him the shutters shaking and rattling as the creatures swooped by.

"Aye! Don't open that damned door. Those things will get in and kill us all!" The man pleaded with Garrett.

"These people are under my protection," The Templar said, grabbing a wall torch nearby. "I refuse to hide in here while others are at risk. Look after these people, Ayla. It is our duty." He finished rubbing the worried healer's arm with his free hand, "You can do this, my dear. Have faith."

Ayla nodded and prepared to move the table back into position when the templar made it through. Garrett grabbed the piece of furniture and slid it to the side as it groaned along the floor. He had just enough room to squeeze by, holding the flickering torch in one hand and his blade in the other. He nodded to Ayla, giving her one more reassuring smile, and dashed out the door into the street as the room momentarily filled with the guttural cries of both bird and commoner. Ayla heaved the door back as the middle-aged man moved to help her. With a grunt the two shoved the heavy table back in front of the door, taking a moment to catch their breath, as once more the birds pelted the wooden entryway, chipping at the barrier.

The sound of the birds' calls was deafening as much as it was terrifying. The shutters rattled on their hinges from the sheer force of numerous animals flying by in unison. Ayla slumped against the wall, placing her head onto her knees as she prayed Garrett would again return. She looked up and met the gaze of the woman cradling her two small children. She could only offer a tired but cheery smile at the family, who had let her take refuge in their home.

Ayla took to her feet and checked over the door, finally sighing, satisfied it would hold in place as she listened to the incessant flutter of wings beating by the domicile. Her thoughts drifted to the outside as a look of worry clouded her face. While they were usually benign animals, in mass and guided by a malevolent force, they had become a terror to behold. She turned back to the woman embracing her children. "Just stay here, it's safe, I'm sure they will disperse soon." She assured the family in a calm, reassuring tone.

Ayla had spoken too soon. Fluttering came from the chimney and echoed down its shaft. *God no*, she thought, as several blackbirds erupted from the hearth, spraying cinders and ash as they burst from the chimney. The crows quickly regrouped and went for the woman who tried to shield her children from the animals.

Ayla ran to their aid, swatting at the birds with her hands, as the mother and children screamed and flailed their arms. She used her mantle as a weapon, smacking the birds off the boy with her cloak like a whip. The beasts turned and viciously retorted, turning their fury on Ayla in a frenzy of claws and beaks. She snatched one off her face as it pecked and bit her hand, drawing droplets of blood. Out of sheer pain, she reactively threw it to the ground, panting as she quickly checked her wounds. The creatures quickly regained their composure and hopped to the fireplace, fluttering their wings as they swooped back up and out the way they had come.

"My God." The mother said, "How would they… they've no damn fear of us!" She stammered.

"I told you it's the end of damned days!" the panicked man sobbed huddled with his knees to his chest.

Ayla grabbed a nearby bench and flipped it onto its side, blocking the mouth of the fireplace, and then slumped against it.

"Why is this happening?" The woman said to no one, in particular, her voice choked with fear.

"I wish I knew…" Ayla sat there breathing heavily.

She watched the light through the shutters flicker as the possessed beasts fluttered around, seeking more prey. Ayla closed her eyes and leaned her head back, praying Garrett would return soon.

IV

Almost an hour had passed since they began preparing the wagon. Brom instructed the servants and Rohn as they checked the structure and loaded it with all manner of supplies, from day-to-day such as soap, bedding, extra clothing, and dry goods, to weapons, tools, and ammunition. Brom had to follow a very strict and detailed checklist of items that made it into the wagon. Each item was essential to either the family, its horses, or the wagon itself.

"Quite roomy in here, more so than your average gypsy wagon," Rohn stated as he stood in the wagon's passenger compartment with a few inches to spare above his head.

"You've spent time in a gypsy wagon? Don't be shy, let us hear of your exploits." Brom teased.

"You know what I mean. Besides, a gentleman does not speak of such things." Rohn grinned, making the ranger laugh out loud.

The inside of the wagon had a few benches that pulled out into beds and held storage beneath. Tables folded out from the walls to act as workbenches or supper tables. When night fell, you could start the small iron stove in the corner for heat or to cook a meal, while hanging in your hammock from the ceiling enjoying a book or a night's rest. It was quite the home away from home. Brom had told him the top of the wagon could be mounted with a Scorpio, a weapon from the roman empire that Ayla had researched. It was a miniature ballista capable of firing a variety of ammunition, all of which were Ayla's and Garrett's designs.

"Yes, Garrett also required Ironclad to be equipped with certain comforts for extended stays in the wilds. I am used to simply sleeping beneath the stars. To each our own I suppose." Brom said, placing crossbow bolts in their place. "I think we are about done, he said, looking about. Time to go."

V

Garrett held the torch high, his blade out in a defensive posture as he waded through the blur of ferocious beaks and talons. At first, the birds careened around him, trying to dodge the fire he wielded, but one at a time they began colliding with either his blade or the burning rope head of the torch. His face was peppered with feathers and blood as the beasts split in half, careening at full speed with his long sword. The animals could see attacking him head-on was foolish and began veering around him as he edged his way to a group of soldiers in an ally.

A scream came from his left side as he moved to the men. Still holding the torch high he ran to a nearby woman who had three of the creatures on her back, pecking away at her neck. He slashed at them, slicing two in half, the third fleeing to join his brethren. Garrett shook her, trying to get her to awaken, yelling for her to stand over the screeching of the birds. Garrett quickly rolled her over onto her back, staying low as a stream of blighted beaks passed him. He crossed himself with his sword arm. The woman had no eyes. Her skull hollowed out. All he could do was pray for her. He moved to the group of soldiers, who were huddled in an alleyway behind some crates.

"Where are your bows, men?" Garrett demanded.

The men scoffed at him in disbelief. "Are you mad? We can't fight these things!" One of them said, his voice quivering.

"You can and you damn well will. Find something to burn. These creatures still know to avoid fire." He said with absolute authority.

The men looked at one another, then one by one they grabbed their bows, as Garrett crossed himself before he began ripping pieces of cloth off a nearby dead man. He returned to the soldiers and tossed the fabric to the men. As he peeked around the corner, the blur of animals was gradually thinning.

"Wrap the tips of your arrows, we're going to wait for the next wave. We will draw their attack away from the citizens." Garrett ordered, his tone calm and steady.

The men nodded, wrapping several of their arrows with thin strips of cloth. "Here," a gravelly voice said, "This might help them burn." One of the older soldiers pulled a flask from his surcoat.

Sir Garrett raised a brow, eying the older footman, smelling the potent alcohol as he popped the cork.

"For the cold night's Sir, you know how it can be."

"Of course," Garrett said with a smirk, as the man began dousing their arrows with the liquor.

He waited for the last few animals to fly by and watched them arch upward in unison, perfectly synchronized. He knew within a few seconds they would be ready to strike again. It was now or never. Garrett moved to the middle of the street. Other men, seeing the knight and their fellow soldiers' bravery, left the safety of their hiding spots to join their commander, weapons at the ready.

"Formation!" He ordered, as over two dozen men lined behind him, forming a firing line.

The soldiers nocked their arrows, nervously looking to their commander, and then back to the swarm overhead. Garrett lit the archer's arrows with his torch, each one helping ignite each other's down the line. He turned, facing the black mass that was now careening down at him and his men.

"Ready!" Garrett commanded, the men lifting their bows, drawing the string back to their cheeks.

"Hold." He waited for them to bunch up, the denser the mass the better.

"Lose!" Garrett stood defiantly as he felt the air of the arrows snap over his head.

The projectiles soared through the air into the oncoming mob; men cheering as most of the projectiles found their mark. The fiery arrows bounced off the incoming wave or stuck into a feathered body as its smoldering corpse succumbed to gravity. The animals screeched as their brethren ignited, bumping into others; the flock scattered momentarily losing momentum.

"Fire at will men!" Garrett said, quickly lighting arrows as fast as he could, the men firing their bows in rapid succession.

Birds rained from the sky one after another, screeching as they fell to the ground and bounced like burning charcoal, their black mass now in disarray. The flock let out an unnatural shriek in unison, almost as if possessed they dove into the men who dared to stand against them. The soldiers dropped to the ground, covering their heads. Not all were fast enough, though. Some stood trying to fight the swarming birds as they flew in. Their blades singing as they cut through the horde in a flash of blood and steel. The gravelly voiced soldier slowly dropped to the ground stiff as a board, a crow impaling itself into his right eye and deep to the back of his skull, the bird's legs still twitching.

The soldiers began praying, muttering to themselves as the black mass tore through the street inches from their faces. Garrett crawled near his men, offering protection with the torch, swinging it into the air, swatting birds as they flew past. What was only a few seconds felt like an eternity. The flock careened by. This time as they took to the sky, they turned into the forest, cawing in defeat, safe from the soldier's fire and metal.

Sir Garrett took to his feet cautiously, urging the men to stay low until he was sure it was clear. One by one the shaken warriors rose behind their commander with apprehension, their eyes scanning the foggy sky, intently listening. Nothing but silence surround the fort now, as black feathers danced from in the air, onto the macabre scene below like confetti. The fort was littered with corpses and smoldering bodies of the possessed birds. Air thick with the scent of burning flesh and the mercurial musk of blood. Slowly others came from their hiding places, their sanctuaries, from the onslaught. Ayla came to the seasoned warrior's side and hugged him, burying her face into his chest. "Are you alright?!" She asked, tears streaming from her cheeks.

"Aye, I'll be ok. Are you alright?" He held her face, looking her over as she nodded in his hands.

"Yes, I'll be fine, just shaken up is all." She smiled wiping her face, "Not everyday birds try to murder everyone you've ever met." She chuckled.

Garrett smiled and squeezed her tight, wrapping his arms around her. He then took in the gruesome scene that surrounded him like a horrid nightmare, a deep sigh escaping his lungs. Soldiers patrolling through the streets stabbed and stomped the birds to make sure they were dead, spitting and cursing as they did. Garrett didn't blame them. This was odd, even for Voskavia.

"Do you think it's druids?" Ayla said, gaining her composure.

"No, druids are usually more controlled and targeted in their efforts. They would never send the beasts to their deaths so easily, they respect life and we would have been offered terms before it resorted to this." Garrett responded,

"No, whatever or whoever caused this did so to scare us, to sow fear. We are dealing with something yet to be seen."

He looked from the horrific sight before him. Then said to Ayla with a faint smile, "We'll be fine if we stick together. It will take more than a flock of birds to rip our family apart." Garrett pulled Ayla closer, hoping Brom and Rohn were on the way with the carriage as he had a dire feeling, they were going to need it.

VI

Maisie stood silently at the edge of the forest as the birds flew overhead frantically and confused. The Mother saw through her eyes now, glaring at the Outpost. Rage bellowed in her as they dared to stand against her. *So be it* — she thought, pain educates and she would be their teacher. Slowly, a smile cracked across Maisie's face. Tonight the children of Skadi will arrive empowered by the red moon. She wanted to hear their screams as they were ripped limb from limb, but she was needed elsewhere. Still much to do, for she had been dormant for so long. The entity grinned as she vanished back into the shroud of the forest, thinking of the horrors that were in store for them. This was just the beginning.

VII

A few moments later, Brom and Rohn were geared up and ready to head to the outpost. They took their places in the wagon's driver's cabin, squeezing in through the small side doors. It was a tight fit, but roomy enough for them to sit comfortably. The two men looked to one another, then to the reins.

"You ever drive a wagon?" Brom asked.

"Once," Rohn said, worried about where this was going. "But it was a one-horse cart. Nothing of this size and assuredly not a four-horse war wagon."

"Well, you are, after all his son. Should anyone survive telling him he lost control and sent it into flipping into the forest it would be you." Brom grinned, and he shoved the reins into Rohn's chest.

"If I live to tell him," Rohn said, accepting the responsibility.

180

He took a deep breath and looked to the stairs of the manor. As if there wasn't enough pressure on him, the entire house was watching as he gently snapped the reins. The massive horses jolting forwards, their harnesses creaking and groaning as they pulled Ironclad, its thick wheels slowly grinding into the dirt.

"C'mon, boys! Again Rohn!" Brom commanded, shoving the young driver playfully with a grin on his face.

Rohn smiled and snapped again, this time with much more gusto, the horses getting the message loud and clear. Before they knew it, the wagon was racing down the road. The men and women at the keep cheered but were drowned out by the commotion of the horses and wagon. Rohn got the hang of it quickly, gently pulling to slow them as they made turns and then snapping again to drive them on. The wagon was well built and handled the turns well. Its thick, wide wheels reinforced with iron drifted through turns as the horses charged on. Its weighted hull shifting and rocking as it kept its balance thanks to the large iron springs and heavy wheels. Before the duo knew it, the outpost was within sight, both hooting and hollering as they rolled into the settlement in style, a sight to behold.

VIII

"The hell happened here?" Brom said as they dismounted the wagon in the middle of the fort.

The sight was shocking. Settlers walked about picking up dead birds with pitchforks, throwing them into a small cart to be added to a nearby pyre. Bodies were strewn about, as remaining kin mourned over them some kneeling and sobbing the air still thick with the scent of death. Rohn and Brom made their way over to Garrett who was directing the recovery of the outpost.

"Are you alright?" Brom asked, not taking his eyes off the spectacle.

"Yes, I'm fine, and Ayla is helping the wounded. Something foul is at work here. Something we've no knowledge of." He said as he nodded to Rohn. "Glad you two made it, especially with Ironclad. I fear we'll need it soon enough."

"Finally, you two get here. Damned birds went berserk. Attacked the outpost." Ayla said as she made her way to the trio; finally finished with her work in the infirmary.

"What do you mean berserk?" Rohn asked worriedly.

"We've no idea. But the beast seemed possessed. They fled for now and I've still no idea how we're to stop the encroachment of the forest, nor what is causing it." She added.

"Cut it down, burn it and salt the earth," Brom interjected, picking up one of the dead animals casually to inspect it.

"I haven't tried that." She said, her face lighting up.

"No need for sarcasm," Brom said, spreading the animal's wings eying it over.

"No, really!" She said running back to the war wagon, "Did you bring it?"

She bounded into the rear door of the carriage eagerly searching the wagon, rummaging around inside, as all three men followed Ayla curiously, watching her sudden enthusiasm.

"Aha!" She grinned wide, holding up a small barrel.

The men stared at her, not following at first, then saw it. A barrel of salt.

"You are going to cook the forest?" Brom said, half-joking half questioning.

"No, don't be foolish. I have a sapling with me, from the troll encounter. I want to see something." Ayla excitedly said as she prepared a working surface in the wagon.

"Let us know what comes of it, Ayla. Brom and Rohn will be preparing for nightfall." Garrett said, motioning the two to follow, "With me lads. I fear things are going to get worse."

Garrett took them down to the palisade gates as he explained the situation. Rohn was far more shocked by the events than the native warden. Brom spat to the side and glared at the dead birds littering the streets, "Stories of the land turning on men are not uncommon. Our elders told legends of such things. When men began to build and ravage the land, it would send beasts from the wilds. The animals became monsters with the cunning of men. Hunting anyone who disobeyed the old laws." Brom stated.

"Old Laws?" Rohn asked.

"The old kings of this continent spoke of the soil becoming ill and aggravated." Garrett explained, "They spoke of a time when their fathers, fathers were just boys and they had erected large settlements. Their shamans warned of the Old Ones, who claimed to rule the land. And any man who built here would bring upon themselves devastating plagues and horrific monstrosities." He finished looking to Brom.

Brom returning the notion with a sigh. "What do we do if this is true?" He asked Garrett.

"We survive. We hold out, stick together and dig in." Garrett insisted confidently. "We have been through worse."

"Have we?" Brom asked, "Monsters and beasts are one thing Garrett, but I know the stories of the Old Ones. If they are more than simple wives' tales…" He drifted off, seeing the worry on Rohn's face.

"We will be fine," Garrett assured them. "Have faith. God will see us through this."

The men nodded hopefully, but not as sure as their leader. He clapped them on the shoulders. "We have work to do, men. Sitting and worrying will do nothing for us." He motioned them to follow. "The fort still has areas that need to be reinforced and repaired. We need to set an example for the settlers. Show them we are unafraid and in control, if we are to inspire courage and faith."

Brom and Rohn looked to one another, again unsure this is something they could face with so few men. Especially not knowing what was in store for them.

"It works!" Ayla said, hopping out of the wagon. "It worked!"

She ran quickly to the others, showing them a small shriveled stick.

"I'm sure a local dog would love to fetch that for you," Brom said sarcastically.

"No, you smart ass!" She held up the sapling. "Salt, purified salt. It has a severe reaction to it. The sapling was growing, unnaturally and thick with this black liquid. When I pulled it from my pack, it was several inches longer…"

"Oh, I bet it was—" Brom smirked, interrupted by a glare from Garrett.

"But when It touched the salt, it began to wither and became as brittle as coal." She finished, ignoring Brom. "If we scatter enough of this, we can halt the growth, at least temporarily." Ayla was grinning widely, proud of herself.

"Well done, Ayla." Rohn patting her on the arm. "You may have just saved the outpost. We should send word home, warn them and inform them of what's going on." Ayla nodded in response and went back to the wagon where she would prepare a carrier pigeon to bring a message back to their keep.

As they celebrated the good news, the sun's auburn glow doused behind the mountains. The moon was slowly rising, filling the sky with a sanguine hue. In the distance, guttural and primal howls, far too large for a wolf, gradually erupted from the forest.

"Maybe not boy," Brom said his face now tense as his jaw clenched.

The group looked to the forest from the palisades walls a knot forming in their stomachs as the tree line fluttered with movement. He recognized those howls. They weren't from wolves or dogs. He gritted his teeth, pulling his axe from his back.

"What is that," Rohn asked, putting his hand on his sword.

Brom glared with keen eyes into the forest, seeing the silver reflections staring back.

"My kin," Brom answered bluntly.

Chapter 12:

The Blood Moon

I

The sun had fully set over Dumont Outpost as a menacing storm crept over the fort, thunder rumbling through the thick rain-filled clouds dyed red by the vermilion moon. Slowly the world was bathed in a red hue as the full moon rose, a herald for things to come.

Ayla ran to the wagon and began gathering what silver bolts they had stored in Ironclad, and loaded pitch pots into a hemp bag. Moving to the small table in the wagon, she flipped open a large book and carefully read the ingredients as she mixed a concoction of silver powder and wolfsbane. The blend would burn those tainted with Skadi's blood, as the allergic reaction would cause wounds to burn and fester. Once the mixture was complete, Ayla carefully stuffed ripped pieces of cloth into some clay oil pots, sealing them with a cork. When lit, the cloth would ignite the grease pot upon impact, causing the liquid to splatter and douse an area in flame. The sticky substance would burn anything it landed on and act as a good deterrent to keep the lycan warriors at bay.

Hopping out of the wagon, she quickly found her three companions. The men readied themselves, double-checking their weapons and armor. Garrett grabbed a kite shield from inside of the Ironclad, decorated with a metal cross on its face and adorned with small spikes along its edge. Ceremoniously, he placed his great helm on his head, keeping the visor up so his commands would carry through the air unhindered. It had been a long time since he fully armored up, preparing the fort he once guarded brought back memories, both horrible and happy.

"Here," Ayla said, handing them a vial, "Cover your weapons." She added handing out cloths to spread the oil evenly on their blades.

Garrett and Rohn quickly did as instructed. The silver glinted in the moonlight as the wolfsbane oil caused it to stick. They coated their swords as best and as quickly as they could, "You must be careful," She added, "The oil will wear down with use and I've no more of it. Let the soldiers deal with the men; save your blades for the beasts."

"Most of the Skadi are not blooded. They will fall just as easily as any man. It is the blooded ones we need to worry about. They will be much harder to kill." Brom told Rohn, as he finished polishing his blade with the potent oil, being extra careful not to touch it.

"Blooded?" Rohn asked as he hefted his kite shield to his side.

"Lycanthropes lad, werewolves. They embrace the sign of the beast and are cursed with the lust of bloodshed." Sir Garrett answered. "When one falls, quickly remove its head, or douse it and ignite the body. I have instructed the soldiers here to do the same. They regenerate like trolls but are far faster and more cunning. While bestial, they retain their human gift of rational and thinking while in hybrid form."

"Wait, Brom said these were his kin. Does that mean—" Rohn stopped, looking to Brom, his mouth slightly agape.

"Don't worry boy, I don't bite unless you pet me wrong." Brom's said, his grin wolfish.

"He will be fine, just stick close to me, lad. We will make it through the night, God is with us." Garrett said with a calm, steady tone.

The war-hardened Templar made his way through the crowd of nervous soldiers to the palisade wall and stepped onto a crate with an arm gently raised in the air. The settlement slowly hushed as they gazed at the knight in his full battle garb.

"Many of you know me, or have at least heard of me," Garrett said, addressing the soldiers and settlers alike. "You know I will not bow to the monstrosities of the dark. I will not be cowed by the evil that lurks in this world and nor should you. For we are righteous. We are chosen. Though they may be many, we are blessed with great purpose. God will see us through. He walks with us this very night. I held this outpost many times before with Him at my side. My men and I slew two giants in this very spot, and tonight is no different. We stick together, we fight together and we send these godless heathens to hell!" Garrett finished raising his sword in the air, the entire settlement cheering, suddenly energized.

The soldiers quickly dispersed and moved into position along the walls, spears, and shields in hand. The archers taking position behind them, preparing their bows and stuffing arrows into their quivers. Ayla instructing them when to use the flaming projectiles she was handing out, as they were too precious to waste on the Skadi whelps.

Rohn was surprised to feel a powerful slap on his back that jostled him even in his armor. Brom nodded to him as he turned around to see where it had originated from, "I'll see you after, boy." The ranger said with a smile, hoping he was right. "You survive this and you'll survive just about anything."

"Of course. Try not to take them all for yourself." Rohn said, clearly nervous.

Brom laughed, "Don't worry, boy, they'll be plenty to go around. You stick with Garrett. He'll see you through this." His words comforting Rohn as he vanished in the hustling settlers and soldiers preparing for the attack.

Rohn made his way to the wall next to Garrett who greeted him with a warm smile, putting his large gauntlet-covered hand around the back of his neck and gently squeezing. "I could not be more proud," the knight said, "of you, Ayla, Brom, and everyone here. Greater men have fled from less, but you stand strong. All of you, especially my family. I am blessed." He said to Rohn contentment on his face, knowing his family was near. The Templar had nothing to fear.

"Thank you, for having me. For bringing me here, for everything. Even on a night like tonight, I am happy. Once again, I have a family. It is best to stand against the dark knowing you are surrounded by those who love you." Rohn smiled and looked out to the forest. "Let them come. We are surrounded by those who love us. How can we lose?" He said, lowering the visor on his helm a slight tremble in his voice.

Sir Garrett smiled, lowering his visor as well, happy to know he had made the right choice. Rohn was definitely a Gerhardt.

II

Scavin stood at the edge of the restless forest, its branches constantly writhed in anger. His kin stood at the ready, rhythmically hammering their weapons into their shields as they grunted. Their bodies were freshly painted in red, the blood of the fallen settlers who were unfortunate enough to be in their paths.

"You heard the old man, my brothers, and sisters. Tonight we dine on chosen ones." He said sarcastically, as laughs erupted throughout the army. "We feast here, then we move on to the main course. Their whore infested abomination on the coast. Tonight we show Skadi our true worth. Tonight, we feast on Englishmen!" He roared.

Scavin's clan was now in a fevered rage as they charged the palisade gates, as allied archers rained fiery death on the fort from the tree line covering the warriors who charged the gate of the palisade. The berserker's moved under cover of a shield wall, carrying a hewn log they had fashioned into a battering ram with rope. A few of the savages carried oil made from pig fat in large containers they would douse the gate with and ignite it, weakening the barrier. They laughed as English arrows thumped into their shields. Casually hopping over their fallen brethren without slowing, reveling in the bloodshed and chaos they were causing.

"Fire at will, men. We cannot let them get in!" Garrett ordered as his soldiers let fly a stream of arrows peppering the invaders as they barreled at the curtain wall.

The archers picked off of the Skadi whelps one by one, as they crumpled and slid through the grass lifeless, leaving nothing but a red smear as their legacy. Another volley of arrows and more invaders were culled as the projectiles thumped through their makeshift armor, easily bypassing the weak protection the hide provided. Boiling pots of water flowed over the side of the palisade splashing in a fountain of steam as it scolded the barbarians below, their fair skin flaking off as the water seared their flesh. Corpses of the Skadi slowly piled up, used as nothing more than stepping stones by their brethren.

"Burn in hell!" An English soldier roared down at the invaders as he threw his spear into the crowd below only to catch an arrow in his throat, falling back and off the ramparts to the dirt below.

Pig oil pots shattered onto the burning wood as the front gate burst into flames. The Skadi yelled and howled with joy, moving closer to those within. The wildmen were ruthless and cold, even pointing and laughing as one of their own fled the gates, as he had been too close to the oil when it ignited, his body burning as he flailed his arms. Caring not for their own. Why would they care at all for anyone else? All that mattered was appeasing their goddess and sating their lust for conflict. The weak were to be culled especially from their ranks.

"Douse the gates! Water buckets!" Garrett yelled over the buzz of arrows gliding past his head.

Rohn dropped from the palisade offering shield cover to the settlers who were running water to the gate as a torrent of arrows steadily rained into the trading post. The projectiles burnt like careening fireflies into the parched thatch roofs. Commoners scurried about, passing buckets spilling over with water, trying to douse the blazes before they got out of hand, but were slowly losing control as the ravenous fire consumed anything it could to remain alive. The heat coming off their homes was almost suffocating, as serfs winced, taking their turn trying to quell the fires that consumed what little they had, then running back to refill their bucket from the rain barrels. Rohn did as best as he could to protect them with his shield as they ran to and from carrying buckets, but the hailstorm of projectiles was overwhelming as serf after surf fell to its constant barrage.

Lord Alistair watched from the protection of his manor. Arms folded defensively as he drank from a chalice of strong wine. The smell of burning wood and echoes of screams flooded through his glass pane windows, as those within the walls of the fort fought for their lives. He was a coward; he knew it, and they knew it. With enough supplies to last the night, he sealed himself in his manor; accompanied only by a few guards and servants to tend to his needs. Should the fighting get too fierce and spill into the walls he had a hidden passage ready for just the occasion that would lead him out and far from the fort. He would not die here, nor would he die for these commoners.

Behind the palisade wall, Ayla stood at the ready in the street near Ironclad, with a small group of archers armed with the flame pots and burning ammunition. She knew not to waste the ammunition by blindly firing over the wall at the first wave that was primarily fodder to weaken their defenses. She had to conserve what they had for the most dangerous of the Skadi. Garrett had expected the large force to breach the gate and funnel inward. That is where Ayla and her forces would rain death on them and fall back to Ironclad if needed, still capable of providing cover fire.

The soldiers on the wooden ramparts rapidly dropped heavy stone onto the savages from the palisades, the large rocks bouncing from both shields and heads as they plummeted to the invaders below. Gerhardt's men were fighting valiantly, but the savage's axes combined with the fire and battering ram were making quick work of the entrance of the palisade. When one of the Skadi fell, another was right there to happily take their place, vying for the honor of their goddess. The wooden gate chipped and splintered, slowly rocking back and forth with the thunderous rhythmic pounding from the onslaught of the barbarians.

"She's going to give!" Rohn yelled to Garrett trying to protect the settlers as they fell back with his shield the faces of the Skadi now clearly showing through massive gaps in the blockade.

"Secondary stations!" Garrett ordered, as most of the men flooded from the walls to the street. "Shield formation!" Garrett roared again, as the spearmen and footmen took their positions. "Make them pay for each step they take men!" He added, the formation grunting in response.

As if on cue, the front gate burst open in a flurry of burning splinters and rolling embers. The barbarians charged through like hellish warriors, their faces twisted and covered in the crimson paint of their victims, relishing every moment, screaming as they poured through like a flood of animals.

"Fire!" Ayla ordered, slowly squeezing the trigger of her crossbow. Her bolt joined in the air by dozens of arrows, as they thudded into shield and flesh alike.

Ayla's bolt pierced clean through one of the savage's throats and stopped in the chest of the man behind him. She didn't celebrate or even take notice; immediately she began to reload her weapon.

A steady flow of Skadi whelps charged through the gates for their chance to prove their worth, none of them hesitating as they charged into the hail of arrows and the shield wall of spears and blades. Some of the raiders tried to jump over the barrier of soldiers, only to be met with the steel of the rear guard and Garrett's long sword. Brutally rewarded for their efforts, the barbarians fell to the ground clutching their amputated limbs and screaming before being put down by another soldier's blade. The shield wall held fast, the men's feet digging into the ground as they grunted and roared in defiance of those that wished to take everything from them. A horrific chorus of weapons and shields clashing accompanied by screams filled the air as they met in a clash of metal and grit. The Skadi breaking out in a war chant as their horns bellowed through the fort desperately trying to gain ground.

Rohn soon rejoined Garrett at his side after he made sure the peasants had been seen to safety, falling back to the security of the walls of Alistair's keep. The Templar and his squire smiled at one another with a quick nod. Shoulder to shoulder they aided the foot soldiers in maintaining the shield wall as long as possible and cutting down any of the Skadi warriors that managed to flank, or breakthrough as spurts of red fountains burst into the air misting the two opposing forces.

"Pots!" Ayla called, as her archers quickly grabbed their firebombs and lit them on nearby braziers.

"Loose!" Ayla ordered as she let fly another bolt, it thudding into a Skadi warrior as he tried to jump the shield wall, his body lifelessly landing behind the formation with a hollow thud.

The pitch pots soared through the air, glowing like miniature meteors as they found their marks, shattering on the shields and heads of the feral attackers. With a whoosh, they ignited, the amber glow consuming the barbarians as they cried out and flailed, their lines breaking apart. The invaders ran aimlessly trying to douse themselves, but just smeared the burning sticky liquid all over with their frantic panicked movements, their dry furs embracing the flames like summer firewood.

Scavin gently chuckled to himself, watching the spectacle from the tree line still as a gentle rain began pouring from the heavens. He knew the rain wouldn't stop the grease bombs from burning, as it was far too volatile, but it would douse the flames of their braziers. The Englishmen would have a much harder time lighting their pots and arrows.

"The second wave, ready!" Scavin ordered, as he dropped his axe to the mud and violently ripped his clothing from his hulking form.

Joined at his side, by his nude kinsmen, each one slowly twitching as their muscles spasmed in joyful agony. Their bones shattering and reforming as their bodies embraced the gift of their goddess. The air resounded with a terrifying chorus of howls and yips as the werewolves were eager to taste the blood of the Christian settlers.

Garrett finished off another burning barbarian with a quick thrust of his blade, the muddy ground littered with corpses from both sides. "Rally on me!" Garrett ordered, seeing the glowing orange eyes in the distance. "Shield formation!"

Scavin's first wave had done their job. The whelps created an opening and softened the fort. Now it was time to finish it. Scavin was well over eight feet tall now and covered in blackish-red fur, as he released an unnatural howl in his werewolf form. His kin burst from the forest in a blur of muscle and claws, running with unimaginable speed on all fours, their new forms terrifying to behold.

"Hold!" Garrett ordered, "Stand fast men!" He repeated, seeing the men look to each other as the monsters charged for the wide-open gate.

The clouds now released a steady flow of rain, pummeling the outpost and all in those in the battle. Ayla knew they had to protect their greatest weapon against the Skadi, and it had to be done quickly.

"We need the fires! Feed the braziers!" she demanded. "Switch to fire ammunition men, we must burn them!" She ordered over a crack of thunder, gaining a glimpse of the bestial horde as a flash of lightning revealed the monsters that barreled toward them.

Her archers were panicking, their courage fading like the embers of the fires they used to light their arrows and pots. "Look out lads!" She yelled, desperately tossing a pitch pot into one of the braziers. Its sacrifice fed new life into the fire as it flared and roared back to life.

"Fire at will. Light, and fire! We have to weaken them!" She ordered, igniting a bolt of her own and placing it into her crossbow as she anxiously saw the pack closing in, a steady blur of radiant eyes, claws, and fur bounding at them at a rapid pace.

There was a sudden silence, a momentary calm as the world stood still. The rain slowly thumped onto the ground. It was almost as if time slowed, as the beasts lunged through the gate of the palisade, their maws wide open, clawed hands outstretched, eager to rip apart the soldiers before them. The Skadi's impact into the shield wall was deafening as they bowled in like cavalry with a deafening collision. The shield wall fractured as a sea of fur and muscle plowed in, slashing and hacking at the footmen, red mists filling the air with shield splinters and bits of mail armor.

Some of the Skadi's blooded climbed the walls outside, quickly ascending upon the palisades and pouncing on archers who focused on the beasts within. The werewolves tore through the oblivious bowmen, ripping them limb from limb, shaking them like rag dolls in their mouths as they were ripped in half and discarded to the dirt like leftovers from a banquet. The Englishmen screamed in horror when they realized they had been flanked. In a desperate act, they jumped from the walls, their arms and legs shattering from the impact.

"Damn it!" Ayla yelled. "Focus fire on the wall! Shoot the beasts on the palisade walls!" she frantically pointed and then began reloaded as the archers nodded.

The bowmen immediately altered their aim and let loose a volley of burning projectiles into the werewolves ravaging the hapless men. The beasts screamed and let out roars of pain, some of them managing to pull the projectiles from their flesh before they did more harm. Their monstrous gaze was quickly directed at Ayla and her troop below, their eyes narrowing in rage as they leaped from the ramparts, heading to their next targets.

III

Another battle was ensuing in the tavern nearby, but this one was far more personal. Brom's breathing had grown heavy and labored. The call of Skadi pounding in his chest and head like a drum, the world blurring as it twisted in his vision. His axe lay on a bench next to him, as his nails dug into the wood of the table he braced himself on. He had removed himself from his kinsmen fearful he could not contain what hid within him. His muscles twitched and begged to be released from the false confines of his flesh as the moon, red and hungry for blood pulsed in his mind screaming for him to join in the hunt. His eyes narrowed and radiated like gold rings around his pupil. The beast was begging to be set free, demanding to be released. *No!* he said to himself, *be calm. Need to be level-headed.* Gradually his breathing came under control, his body calmed, the low growl in his throat subsided. He let out a slow, quivered breath. The beast was at bay for now.

IV

Garrett and Rohn whirled around one another back to back to ensure they were not flanked, their blades thrusting and slashing as the shield wall collapsed around them. The father and son duo desperately fended off the remaining whelps with a blur of silver-coated blades, as the Blooded cleaved their way through the soldiers of the fort. It had become every man for themselves, as the werewolves were far too much for the guardsmen to hold against.

The lycanthropes casually picked up men by their heads and threw them aside, tearing off their limbs and cackling as they beat them with their extremities. Out of the corner of his eye, Rohn saw a blur of burning pots careening towards him and Garrett. He quickly lifted his shield as he threw himself onto his father, both landing face down in the cold mud. The projectiles exploded all around them as they impacted the lycan raiders, shards of silver spraying into the air. The werewolves yelped in searing agony, as the vicious tar stuck to their coarse fur, igniting them like candle wicks.

Some of the unfortunate Skadi inhaled the silver mist and began choking and convulsing as the insides of their throats swelled and inflamed. The thick silver slivers hissed and boiled as they dug into their flesh. The beasts recoiling as they desperately tried to swipe at the venomous bite of the metal in their skin, clawing and raking into their hides to dislodge its ferocious effects.

Rohn looked up to see Ayla with her archers nearby grinning ear to ear seeing the tides turn. She gave the young scribe a wink as she led her soldiers into the war wagon where they could fire from relative safety.

Garrett quickly rolled to the side, dodging a clawed foot as it slammed into the ground, just missing his head. The knight rose to his feet, swinging his blade low, lopping off the leg of the monster, and thrusting his blade hilt deep into the creature's chest before it even hit the ground. With years of experience and skill, Garrett weaved his way through the Skadi clan, cleaving off limbs and heads as he went, their claws raking across his armor as fragments sparked into the air.

Rohn set his shield before him, its front slowly burning covered in pitch. The beast before him hesitant to attack the ignited barrier as it took a step back and flared its bloodied maw. With a belly-filled roar, Rohn charged with his shield up and blade forward, burying his sword deep into the creature's stomach. The scribe pressed his shield into the beast's chest, twisting the grip of his weapon violently, satisfied as he could smell the sharp tang of the silver's reaction in the lycan's body. The abomination of man and beast roared in agony as the silver slivers embedded themselves into its torso, burning like acid, its insides covered in pustules. Rohn retracted his blade and stabbed again and again only stopping when he felt the creature fall to the mud with a splash, its head flopping to the side, as its tongue rolled out of his motionless mouth.

Rohn had little time to celebrate as he felt a huge paw pound into his back from behind and instinct kicked in. Instead of fighting the force of the blow, he rolled with its momentum, shoulder first he tumbled into the ground and quickly found his footing on one knee, his shield raised, blade leveled reflectively. Behind the visor of his helm, his eyes widened while his jaw dropped. It was Scavin. The hulking monster trudged towards him, batting soldier and whelp alike to the side with little effort. Rohn lunged forward, thrusting his glinting blade towards the chest of Scavin with a grunt, but a tremendous paw-like hand gripped his wrist as he impaled his blade into the Skadi alpha.

Scavin grinned slowly lifting the young man by his arm, Rohn kicking and flailing, hitting the beast in the face with his shield to no avail. The blade was clean, as no more oil remained on it. Scavin batted Rohn's shield to the side effortlessly, the smoldering bulwark shattered against a cobblestone wall.

Scavin's bestial face twisted from elation to pain as he spun around, releasing a roar of agony, throwing Rohn into the side of a cart a dozen feet away. The Skadi alpha turned to see Brom retracting his axe from his back, the crescent head doused in his blood.

"You miss me, uncle?" Brom said as the monster drooled, its teeth flaring in his face. The beast's breath was sweltering and thick with the scent of death.

Scavin lashed out, his paw nothing but a blur, his thick black claws skimming the mail hauberk as the ranger deftly ducked the blows. Brom rolled to his right, under Scavin's attempt to decapitate him, and as he recovered, embedded his axe into the back of the tree trunk-like thigh of the werewolf, quickly withdrawing and preparing another assault.

With a roar, Scavin kicked Brom with the opposite foot, desperate to distance himself from the rival, his blow landing center of the ranger's chest. Brom sailed through the air and crashed through the shutters of a window into a nearby home, his axe sliding along the ground in the other direction through the streets. The furious monstrosity turned his attention back to Rohn. The scribe was still confused, his vision blurred and the world nothing more than muffled noise.

Scavin gradually closed the distance between himself, and Rohn swatting soldiers aside as he trudged towards his prey. The Skadi chief snarled as he watched his brethren being slain one by one, cut down by silver death and burning salvos of ammunition, his kin writhing in pain as spears and swords skewered them. Scavin fought well-armed and prepared soldiers at the fort under the command of a seasoned Templar, not peasants armed with pitchforks and wood axes.

No matter, he thought. The Skadi elder, the Bitch Mothers chosen, would deal with the boy then move on to the rest, personally culling this chattel from his territory. He lunged for the helpless young man, the ground trembling as he charged on all fours, his mouth agape and hungering for its first bite. The young man was unaware of the wrath that was heading his way as he stumbled to his feet.

A sudden flash of pain shot through Scavin's head just before he clamped his jaws on the defenseless squire, sending him staggering to the side. He was interrupted by a blur of iron, a crossed shield smashing into the side of his face. Its spikes biting into his jaw and temple. Scavin wobbled away from the helpless squire, as he tried to shake off the powerful blow, his vision blurred and scattered now as his head rang like a church bell.

"Get the fuck away from my boy!" Garrett demanded, seething through his teeth, his voice reverberating in his helm as he stood waiting for the beast's reaction, shield, and blade at the ready.

Scavin growled and snapped his jaws as he rose to his full height, towering over Garrett, grinning down at the aging knight. Standing his ground between the creature and his son, the Templar unafraid as he hammered his blade into his shield, taunting the monstrosity, and began closing the distance with his new adversary. The giant lycan roared spittle flying from its bloodied teeth, as Garrett charged, shield up and sword ready to strike. They clashed as fur and sparks flew into the air. The two warriors trading blows in a flurry of attacks, each one trying to get the upper hand. Garrett was quick, his blade finding its mark over and over, but the oil on his sword too had worn off.

As fast as he was striking, the wounds were gradually closing. He knew he couldn't keep this up for long as his muscles began to burn from the strain. The knight spun around the ungodly figure. Tufts of fur with crimson splashes of blood trailed his blade. He had to finish this quickly, but couldn't find the opportune moment to land the final blow.

Brom's eyes slowly blinked, his face on the cold dirt of the hovel he had landed in. The ranger rose on his hands, gasping for breath on his knees. He could hear muffled screams and shouts around him, as sharp pains jutted through his body his muscles spasming and contorting. *No, please no!* His thoughts were a flurry of what-ifs. Could he control his rage, his hunger? It mattered not. It was too late; the transformation was already well underway. The native warrior's bones snapped and surged through his skin, his face twisted as his jaw popped from its place, his teeth gnashing as they jutted from his mouth. No matter how badly he resisted he knew in the back of his mind, Skadi's call must be answered. The terrified family in the home huddled against a wall. All they could do was just watch in horror at the spectacle before them.

Garrett was gasping for air now, his lungs burning as salty sweat ran down his face like a river through a map. He was slowing, as he could feel the weariness of battle weighing down on him, his shield and sword getting heavier by the second. In a moment of distraction, he felt a pain in his stomach that jutted upward through his body. All went still, voices and screams muffled as Garrett looked down to see Scavin's claws impaling him. The knight looked up now face to face with the monsters, as Scavin lifted him from his feet, his fanged mouth grinning.

Garrett's shield dropped to the ground with a clang, and with the last of his strength, he buried his blade into Scavin's shoulder. The werewolf winced and roared as the defiant knight twisted the blade with a grunt. With a snarl, Scavin smashed his huge furry fist into the chest of Garrett. The Templar's breastplate dented as he slid across the muddy ground several feet away. The world was fading from the knight's eyes. Garrett was afraid. Not for himself, but for Rohn. For Ayla. For Brom and the settlers of Dumont. He was fearful he failed them. Scavin grinned, seeing the fear in his eyes. He could smell it. Thick musk, like a rutting dear. He relished it, wafting it in, but his ecstasy was interrupted by a scream.

"No!" Rohn yelled shakily on his feet, his blade in hand.

Scavin again squared off with the young squire and let out a massive howl that shook the nearby abodes, his wounds already healing from the bout with Garrett. He would relish this kill, bleed the boy slow, make him scream for his God.

Rohn's eyes grew wide as he saw another head raise behind Scavin, as another werewolf leaped onto the alpha's back. The challenging werewolf's fur was a stark silver sheen that stretched down his back like a warthog's mohawk. Scavin roared as Bromislav sunk his teeth into his uncle's neck and shook his head, trying to tear a chunk from his prey. The alpha lycan yelped in pain, flailing with his clawed hands, trying to grab the traitor. He stumbled backward and slammed the smaller werewolf into the walls of a storefront, cracking their planks with his might.

Brom just kept biting and raking his claws into his kin's spine, not slowing even when the ivory glare of bone peaked through the coal-colored fur of Scavin's back. With a last-ditch effort, Scavin let out an inhuman screech of pain, grabbing Brom by the scuff of his neck and tossing him to the ground more than ten feet away. The transformed ranger rolled and slid with grace on his feet, his clawed toes digging into the earth, leaving scars in the mud. The two lycans glared at each other, baring their teeth and flashing their claws. Scavin moved with a limp, his back heavily torn, his backbone protruding through his blood matted fur. Brom was relentless, his blood boiling with rage as he bolted forwards with inhuman speed, fast even for an animal, even for the Skadi.

Scavin braced himself, roaring with open clawed arms, but Brom still had his wits about him and knew diving directly into his arms could be a lethal mistake. At the last second Brom darted left with a feint, then pounced right, running on all fours along a wall, boosting himself off. He bolted into a dive directly into Scavin's vulnerable throat. The two colliding with a thud, as Scavin fell onto his back, Brom pinning his arms in the blood-soaked mud. The silver maned Skadi buried his fangs into Scavin's neck once more, snarling as he squeezed with all his might as the behemoth monster gasped for air, his warm salty blood filling Brom's mouth with a gush.

Rohn saw his chance. Quickly the fledgling warrior picked up a nearby spear as he removed his helm, the cool air wafting over his face as he took a deep breath. He had full vision of the beast as he charged, the spear's broad head leading the way.

Witnessing the turn of events, Ayla deftly reloaded, a silver-tipped bolt glinting in the light. The war wagon was covered in lycanthropes as they clawed and bit at the reinforced frame. Splinters of the wagon flew into the air as the rabid monsters frantically ripped at its armor, their jaws snapping as they tried to squeeze their heads through to the meat inside. However, Ayla was still. Her breathing slowed, the roars and guttural cries muffled out as she watched the two Skadi blooded do battle. She focused as her eyes narrowed. Her heart gradually slowed as the chaos ensued around her, the wagon rocking from the onslaught. None of it mattered, just this shot. Out of the corner of her eye, she saw Rohn charging in to aid their lycanthrope ally. A smirk grew across her face as she waited, eyes locked on the two battling werewolves, her sights steady and patient. *That murderous bastard wouldn't live to see the dawn,* she thought.

Brom jerked and twisted his head, trying to control Scavin's arms with his own, but struggling against the much larger werewolf. Even in his wounded state, the alpha was a formidable foe, especially with his wounds healing and muscles restructuring before their eyes. Brom's ear perked with the sound of a war cry, a familiar scent wafting past his nose as he heard the young squire's approach. It was time to finish this. With a hard tug, he felt Scavin's throat give way, as a torrent of red splashed in his face. Brom reeled back, as Scavin flailed in pain, his claws raking into the silver werewolf's chest and face sending the ranger airborne dozens of feet away. Brom landed on the ground with a yelp and slid into a jumble of crates as they shattered into kindling.

The massive Skadi warlord stood gasping, choking, clutching the gaping hole in his throat as the world slowly blurred. Scavin could smell fear again, but this time the sweet musk was his own.

Rohn let out a roar as his spear impaled the beast through the side as it stumbled confused. Its steelhead plunged through the thick hide and abyssal black fur as red poured down the shaft of the weapon. Rohn screamed out of rage and fear as he twisted the spear violently. Scavin let out a horrid yelp and stumbled, reflectively swinging a backhand that sent Rohn skidding across the muddy road, muck spraying into the air.

Ayla didn't flinch or even blink as with a click her bolt lunged from its cradle, gliding through the air. Its silver tip shone like a star at midnight as it passed soldier and Skadi alike, focused on a particular target. Scavin stopped suddenly as his body went numb. He glared at the fiery-haired girl smiling at him as she lowered her crossbow, a look of pride on her face. The massive werewolf looked up and saw the tip of a bolt protruding from his forehead. With a thud, over five hundred pounds of fur, muscle, and teeth collapsed into the mud.

A final vision went through Scavin's mind before Ayla's silver-tipped bolt seared away his failing neurons as it protruded from his face. The old man from the village they had raided earlier walked calmly through the outpost to his murderer, unseen by others, visible only to Scavin. He stood in the middle of the fort in a brilliant white pair of linen clothing that flowed in the wind. His face was at peace as he blinked slowly, a smile on his face.

"Reap what you sow," The elderly man repeated. "His judgment will be swift." Those last words were the last thing Scavin heard before he faded from this world.

The rest of the Skadi fled, seeing their chieftain fall, the soldiers of the outpost cheering as the barbaric remnants ran to the safety of the forest. Rohn made his way to the body of Scavin, dragging Brom's axe behind him. He wanted to make sure this was ended for good. Garrett's voice echoed in his mind, *heads, and hearts.* The weapon was heavier than he imagined, its blade still wet with the blood of the Skadi alpha. He hefted the massive axe over his shoulder and let out a loud grunt as he hacked into the neck of the Skadi alpha. Again and again, he chopped until finally, Scavin's monstrous head rolled from his neck, a silver bolt still protruding from his forehead.

Rohn let the axe fall to his side and urgently stumbled to Garrett, Ayla joining him sliding on her knees in the thick mud. She fumbled through her satchel as Rohn carefully removed his layers of armor and clothing. The wounds were deep, one almost went clean through. Ayla quickly poured a clear liquid over the wounds, Garrett wincing as it sizzled, the scent of the fluid strong and sharp.

"We need to get him help!" She said, trying to remain calm as she prepared bandages.

"To the keep?" Rohn asked, helping her stifle the blood flow, putting pressure on the deeper, more severe wounds.

"No, Eirburg." She said quickly, looking for a means of transport. "The monks at the temple will be his best chance."

The war wagon was still in working condition, but its horses had been stabled and it would take too long to harness the four steeds required to move the war wagon. Before she could ask, Rohn rushed to a stable and within a moment returned leading a horse out and was quickly harnessing the animal to a nearby hay cart.

"Help me carry him, you can tend to him while I get us to the capital," Rohn said, confidence in his voice.

Ayla nodded, then stopped. "Wait where is Brom?"

"I'm fine, just a few scratches," Brom replied now back to his human form stumbling across the street groggily.

He was stark naked as he plopped down on a nearby barrel holding his wounded chest, his teeth showing through a hole in his jaw. The two stared at him in amazement. "Are you entranced by my pecker? Go! Before Garrett bleeds out!" He demanded, the hole in his mouth slowly closing before their eyes.

The two didn't hesitate a moment more, Ayla hopped into the back preparing to stabilize Garrett, as Rohn snapped the reins, "Hold on Ayla!" he said as the cart jerked quickly forward.

"Just keep us on the road." She said as they rolled through what was left of the smoldering trade post, praying they could save their patriarch.

Brom waved them off as he stood, tired of the cold wood on his bare buttocks. His body sore from transforming back and forth he rolled his neck trying to work a kink out of his broad shoulders. He was worried for his friend, but he was in the hands of God now and those better trained to save his life.

Besides the transformation had drained him and while in pain his stomach growled and his throat was dry as sand. He made his way to where his axe lay on the ground; the mud squishing between his toes reminding him of when he would go frogging in the woods as a boy. Brom paused for a moment, glaring down on the head of Scavin, its tongue dangling out to one side, its lifeless eyes staring out in the distance. He picked up the head of his father's brother and sighed, "Never liked you anyway." He quipped.

He plopped the head on a nearby stack of crates and made his way to the middle of the street to a crowd of soldiers standing about, still shaken from the fight. While nursing his jaw with a hand, he motioned to the corpses with his broad axe, "Alright boys, we need to take the heads and hearts, burn the rest before they get back up." He said, completely naked but with authority and confidence, only Brom could have.

The soldiers just stared at him awkwardly too afraid to question the nude warrior unsure how to handle the situation. "Let's go! Off with them! Don't be shy it's like dressing a deer. If we don't, they'll be up on their feet within moments. Quickly!" The nude ranger ordered the soldiers, who jumped from the tone of his voice and quickly got to work.

Brom made his way down the street with his axe resting on a shoulder to a nearby shop as a few older women gawked in shock at the sight. "Don't judge me, it's rather chilly out tonight," Brom said half-jokingly as he gave them a nod, the women gasping as they crossed themselves and hurried off.

"Damned English can't take a joke." He said as he strolled into the abandoned store looking to do a little clothing shopping.

Chapter 13:

An Army Reborn

I

The road was longer than they had remembered. Perhaps it was because they were in a rush to get Garrett aid, but the trip seemed to take forever; even with the horse at full gallop. The golden rays of the sun were slowly rising over the horizon as Ayla did the best she could to stem her beloved surrogate's blood flow. Sir Garrett was pale and getting cold. "Faster Rohn!" She said desperately, the young man snapping the reins in reply.

Rohn hollered for people to move as he barreled down the road, not daring to slow. Rohn could only apologize as they raced by, the cart kicking up mud and dirt as the commoners dodge the racing cart. They blurred past the guards at the main entrance to Eirburg, as the soldiers yelled and demanded them to slow down, but not daring to get in front of the cart's steed.

Through the streets the horse galloped, bumping into trade carts as Ayla shielded the Garrett from baskets of fruit as the screams of peasants rushed by. Rohn yanked hard on the reins as they came to the Citadel's gates. He wasted no time running to a nearby Templar, alerting him of his wounded father. The young Templar recognized Garrett immediately and ran into the temple quickly returning with several robed men, one carrying a stretcher. The group of monks rushed the pale knight into the temple as the Templar cleared their path, ushering people to the sides.

Ayla finally collapsed to her knees in tears on the pale cobbled path of the temple entrance, the night's events and exhaustion finally catching up to her. Rohn quickly ran to her side wrapping his arm around her trying to comfort her as best he could. "You did well, I think we made it in time Ayla, he is a strong man, he'll be alright!" Rohn said, trying to assure himself as much as Ayla.

She nodded, the magnitude of what just occurred finally hitting her. "He's lost a lot of blood." She said looking to her hands and clothing now dyed red, "I've never seen him in such a state." She sobbed.

"He's survived worse, he can do it again. He's at the best place he can be, thanks to you." Rohn said with sincerity. "Let's get inside, we'll send word for Brom when we know something." He said as he helped her to her feet, the two still sore and filthy from the confrontation with the Skadi as they made their way inside, Ayla curled in Rohn's arms.

II

Word had reached the castle of a rampaging cart making its way to the Citadel; a young man and woman, carrying a wounded knight in tow. When Lord Harmon heard, he immediately made his way to the temple; while the Church and he were not on the best of terms, the two disagreeing on many things, he placed politics aside. He had to see Sir Garrett and check on his old friend and compatriot. The Baron briskly walked through the rows of pews in the massive main hall and stopped, seeing Ayla and Rohn huddled together, covered by wool blankets as they sipped mugs of hot lavender tea. The pair's eyes were swollen from crying and lack of sleep, their clothes were muddy and covered in blood.

"I came at once when my steward told me of your arrival. You made quite the entrance." Lord Harmon forced a smile, taking a seat next to them. "How does he fare?"

"We don't know," Ayla answered, helplessly looking to Lord Harmon.

"How did… what did this?" Lord Harmon dared to ask, not wanting to know the answer.

"Lycans. Clan Skadi, I think they were called." Rohn answered, staring at the stone floor of the temple.

Lord Harmon sat back slowly nodding, crossing his fingers in his lap. "Yes. I know of them. We drove them from the territory years ago. I should have known they would return. Does the fort still stand?." Harmon asked with fear in his voice as to the answer.

"Yes, but barely," Rohn stated, "The Skadi attacked during the blood moon and in mass. Their blooded, I believe father called them, ravaged the fort, many did not make it through the night."

Harmon noticed what Rohn had called him. "So he told you."

Rohn and Ayla nodded. "We all know the truth now," Ayla informed him.

Lord Harmon nodded, "Good. Secrecy has no place within a family. Why don't the two of you head to the castle, bathe, get something to eat, and rest. Sir Garrett is in the best of hands here, children. Worry not."

The two sighed, and after looking to one another Rohn politely declined. "We must stay with my father should he call on us."

"I understand." Edric nodded.

Gentle taps of feet quickly grabbed their attention as it approached the trio. The three looked up as a monk made his way to their pew his arms folded in his brown linen robes, bracing themselves for the news with anticipation; the monk's face giving no hint of Garrett's fate.

"He is stable at this moment." The priest finally stated in a calm tone, "It appears his armor softened the blow, and the beast's claws missed his vitals. God was with Sir Garrett this day. Though he is still in a fragile state, he has been sanitized with a poultice, bandaged, stitched, and cleansed. Now he must rest. Infection is still a worry, and his recovery lies with him and Almighty God. Pray for him children."

"You do whatever it takes, spare no expense. He is your top priority." Lord Harmon commanded.

"We will do all we can for the Templar. As he is also a fellow soldier of God." The monk added, his tone flat and almost challenging. "God be with you." The clergyman blessed the trio and said a brief prayer in Latin, before making his way to another family.

Edric turned to the two Gerhardts, "I will see he is tended to by the best physicians." Lord Harmon said, resting his hand on their shoulders. "When he is well enough to be moved, I will have him brought to the safety of the castle. He is my responsibility now." Harmon said, his tone resolute.

"Thank you," Ayla said softly, her face reddened from crying. "You're too kind, Lord Harmon."

"Yes, thank you," Rohn added. "We are in your debt."

"No, it is I who am indebted." Lord Harmon said slightly, bowing. "Twice now I asked him to put his life on the line for that cursed place, and twice he has. Sacrificing all for this colony without complaint or hesitation. I must return to the castle to right this mess. If you need anything, come to me directly, my hospitality is at your disposal." He said, giving the two a faint smile, making his way out of the temple as quickly as he arrived.

Rohn and Ayla took their seats once more, sipping from their mugs as they played the waiting game, praying Garrett would recover.

III

Lord Harmon walked into the castle's audience chambers, calling an emergency meeting of the council. Dusan, Hendrik, and Varik stood as he entered. "We are to evacuate the post immediately." Lord Harmon said not wasting a moment. A look of shock coming over Dusan and Varik.

"After Sir Garrett's triumph? The local merchants will be most upset my Lord." Dusan said.

"I'll not have more blood on my hands. We must regroup and discover what is causing these attacks." Harmon stated.

Varik did well hiding his glee. "This will of course cause you to lose favor with nobility, not to mention the King."

"That does not matter, people's lives are at stake. We must rally together now. Prepare a message to the mainland. We will need supplies, more soldiers, and a larger workforce." Baron Edric commanded.

"Agreed, we should band together within the strong walls of Eirburg until we know just what in the hell is going on." Hendrik nodded, thumping a meaty fist on the table.

"I'm not sure we should be so hasty my Lord. Perhaps there is a way to salvage the situation," Dusan said, trying to calm the Baron.

"A red moon, Skadi rampaging across the countryside, birds attacking settlements, goblins pouring from the depths, and now a witch has infested my fief. Shall we wait for more evidence something is wrong, that something wicked is poised against us?" Lord Harmon glared at Dusan. "These are no coincidences. Send the message."

"As you wish, my Lord," Dusan said, swallowing hard under the Baron's gaze. "It will be done immediately."

IV

"You're going to bring all of this?" Brom said, shaking his head at Sir Alistair, who was berating his servants as they loaded a wagon. "I'll not wait for you to bring your entire home."

"You think I'll leave this all to nature, or worse yet savages? You're mad!" He said, glancing at Brom scoffing at him before he turned his attention back to his help. "Careful with that you mongrel that is worth more than you and your family!" He slapped one of the peasants across the back as they almost dropped a painting.

"Damned fool. Willing to lose your life over such paltry items." Brom said, turning back to the settlement.

The outpost was busy, as they had just barely finished the pyres for the Skadi warriors. Most of the soldiers and barbarians still laying in piles or scattered throughout the fort, when the messenger arrived dictating, they must abandon the post and return to Port Eirburg at once. Many were relieved that Lord Harmon cared for their well-being, but hated leaving the place in such a disarray. They hadn't even time to bury their dead.

"So you're all leaving?" Aiden asked Brom.

"You're not? This place is lost, boy, look around you, it reeks of death." Brom said, getting the horses harnessed and securely attached to Ironclad.

"This is the only place I know. I've been here since I can remember. Hate to leave it behind." Aiden sadly said.

"Well, whatever you choose boy, good luck." Brom patted him on the back made his way to Ironclad.

Brom took his place in the driver's cabin and grabbed the leather straps, cracking the reins, and the war wagon was off, limping out of the front gates to the capital. Gradually others fell in line behind him as they headed to Eirburg in a mass exodus. Some left on foot, others on a wagon or cart, if they were lucky. Leaving all they knew behind; their future uncertain.

V

A hooded priest walked through the trading fort, arms tucked into the folds of his robes. His flock was long gone, sobbing as they passed the bodies of their fallen, the air filled with ash and decay. Dogs fed on the remains of the bodies that laid in the cold mud; growling and snarling to defend what was now theirs.

Ekart had spent the day giving last rites and helping the wounded find a place on wagons and carts, tending to them as best as he could. The night had been a brutal one, but one he had expected and even counted on. The priest kept his head low and remained humble as to not attract unwanted attention as he moved throughout the Bishop's parish. While not as powerful as knights or Barons, priests were given power of their own. He listened as men and women confessed their sins and prayed for absolution. Temporary forgiveness is what he offered to most, but for some, he offered a different solution to their trespasses. Their sins became a currency for the priest, a way to control their wants, desires, and influence. Especially the nobility. Such naughty little lambs, he thought with a smirk on his pale lips. He removed his cowl with thin, milky white fingers, revealing his smoothly shaven head and face. His Prince had been right. The ferals were indeed more useful when starved as the carnage on both sides was stunning even to one who worships death.

"Father Ekart, are you remaining behind?" Aiden asked with concern, as he sat on a scrawny nag.

"For a while, child. I must tend to the flock and be sure the dead are given their last rites." Ekart replied, a gentle smile on his face.

"As you wish, Father, but it's dangerous here. You should return to the capital as soon as possible." Aiden warned, "God be with you."

"As with you young Aiden, as with you." Father Ekart offered a blessing to the lad before he rode off with the last of the settlers.

It had been a long day Ekart thought. He watched the remaining refugees vanish into the distance on their long walk to Eirburg. He sighed contently, as he was the last living human in the fort to remain.

As Ekart stood in silence admiring the work of his Prince, a feathered body landed gently on the priest's shoulder. A large raven sat perched. Giving a little shake as its feathers. The animal was calm, as if he was a long-lost friend, its beak and feathers still spattered with blood and viscera. "All is well, Mother. The Prince is safe and still well hidden. The fort is destroyed and left in ruins. It will take time for the Skadi to recover from this, but I am sure with time a new warlord will rise." Ekart said, his eyes still on the victory before them.

"That is of little concern." A raspy voice echoed behind him in a hollow tone.

Ekart smiled without turning around, recognizing the voice, even in its new form. "Punctual as usual, King Hrothgar." He prodded sarcastically.

The Withered Warlord remembered this place as he walked through its scorched streets, joining the pale priest. It was a fort when Sir Garrett summoned him and his allies long ago. Gerhardt blamed the three for the crimes of his kinsmen, still sour from the death of his wife to be. The Templar had the three warlords hung and then buried in unmarked graves, stripping them of their honor. Their claim to the afterlife was denied and given a coward's burial. The Warlord's clans scattering to the wind in their absence, the last of the native tribes that were not tainted by the continent's living deities. Hrothgar's clothing was worn and tattered, musty from years under damp soil, the same he wore on the day of his betrayal. He was much stronger now though, his corpse rebuilt through the Mother's grace. King Hrothgar was far more powerful now than in life. His hands ended with clawed fingers that gripped an ancient war hammer. His commanding form blackened and leathery, thorns protruded from his skin as the seedling inside took to its host. Hrothgar no longer feared the wrath of fire or ice as the viscous black liquid made him and all the Mother's children quite resistant to the brutal elements.

As the Withered warlord and Ekart made their way through the fort, the corpses of both the English and the Skadi twitched and jerked. The small seedlings that Ekart had placed in them as he gave them last rites, quickly took to their new hosts. Sprouting as they twisted their vines through the deceased vessels, slithering in the shells of those on both sides caring little for the politics of the two.

Death was death, and that is all the Mother required. Whether it was those that served Her willingly, or the loss of who defied Her, in death, they would bend the knee and serve Her will. The Withered corpses rose with moans and hisses, thorns popping through their skin, arms and legs being replaced with wicked sickles and blades, tools of death granted to them by their goddess. Their hollow eyes glowed faintly with an amber light within, staring at Hrothgar. Waiting patiently for orders.

"It is time," Ekart said, staring at the port city in the distance, nothing but a blurry speck. "You have waited long enough for your promise. Take your vengeance Hrothgar, may the Mother guide you."

The Withered fell in line as they began following their new commander, King Hrothgar. Their hive-mind linking to one another's. Like ants, they followed and swarmed as they made their way through the empty trading post. Hundreds of them lurched forth, hollow eyes focused on the city of Eirburg, as they growled, groaned, and hissed with Her rage. The sky darkened with the black mass of feathers and claws, as the murderous flock escorted the Withered Warlord and his army to the capital.

"Tonight the city burns." The priest said, glaring at Eirburg in the distance.

Chapter 14:

Roots Run Deep

I

"You know I always thought myself a coward," Rohn whispered. Breaking the silence, not wanting his voice to echo through the temple.

Ayla looked at him, her eyes were still red and slightly puffy. She gently pulled the wool blanket tightly around her as a chill swept through her.

"I was afraid of everything. Illness, travel, conflict, failure, the list goes on. I spent my life with worry, fretting away the good times, with problems that may never come to pass." He added, looking to his empty mug of lavender tea.

"Now look at you." She said slightly, smiling. "Slaying trolls and werewolves."

"Yes, all thanks to the man in there." He motioned with his head; his face still dirty from the night before.

"We stick together and we'll be fine," Ayla said, trying to convince herself as well.

The two were interrupted as a commotion erupted from the front of the temple. Brom loudly entered the Citadel, thankfully clothed back in his hauberk. His weapons jangled as his boots thumped off the marble floor, everyone turning their eyes on him as a small monk scurried next to him, trying to get him to lower his voice and calm his boisterous nature.

"No weapons in here, sir! It is a house of God! A place of peace!" A monk said trying to hold his tone low but firm, leaving hustling to keep pace with the brutish warrior.

"And it's safer with me here, armed to the teeth," Brom replied, no indication of disarming as he searched for his friends.

"Brom!" Rohn called for him, giving him a warm greeting, gently waving to get his attention.

"Ah, there they are!" Brom grinned as he made his way to his companions, with his usual swagger. The monk finally gave up trying to reason with the warrior and scurried off. The three united with a warm embrace and checked one another over.

"Your back to your old self," Ayla said with a warm smile.

"Aye, sore as a whore's ass but I'll make it." Brom added, "So how does he fare? You've not yet buried him, so that's a good sign."

Rohn couldn't help but chuckle, "He is has been stabilized but still weak. We are waiting for him to wake."

Brom nodded about to sit down as a nun approached the trio. "Sir Gerhardt is awake and wishes to see his family. Would you kindly follow me?"

The ranger motioned for them to lead the way. The group headed into the back through thick, ornate mahogany doors as the three quickly made their way to the infirmary. Its space was large and well-lit by dyed, stained glass windows. The long room was lined with beds, each patient separated by a white linen curtain. Nuns and clergymen moved about the room, seeing to each of the patients under their care.

It wasn't long before they spotted a familiar face, Lord Harmon, accompanied by Bishop Varik and Dusan stood at the foot of Sir Gerhardt's bed. Garrett was clean and his wounds dressed as he laid comfortably, his head gently propped up by a stuffed pillow. Lord Harmon stepped aside with a smile, as the others took their places next to the wounded knight. Although he couldn't move too much without sharp pain, the knight was happy to see the three together once more.

Brom eyed the Bishop who gave him a sharp look in return, the two recognizing one another as a cat and dog would.

"How are you?!" Ayla quickly flung herself over Garrett's chest, embracing him with a tearful smile, the wounded warrior wincing in pain but happy to hold her once more.

"I knew you were too damn stubborn to die," Brom said with a grin.

Rohn stood at his father's side, placing his hand on Garrett's shoulder. "You should rest. Your wounds are deep."

"I'll be fine, I needed to speak with the three of you." He said, mustering what strength he had.

"You now know the truth about Rohn. Should I not make it—"

"You'll be fine." Ayla interrupted, not wanting to think about that day.

"No, I want you all to know, my estate is yours. My only son, my dear Ayla, and my brother in arms. Those dearest to me." He coughed and then regained his composure. "Lord Harmon, his scribe, and Bishop Varik will attest to this as witnesses, as will the three of you."

"I will have it noted in the castle archives, but I don't think we'll have to worry about such things for a long time yet to come." Lord Harmon said nodding slightly. Dusan took notes of the encounter, his fingers rapidly writing on a piece of parchment. "If you will excuse me, I have matters to attend to. Please join me for dinner at the castle, as honored guests." He said with a smile.

Varik's brow lifted as he gazed from the Barons to Brom, almost glaring at the ex-pagan with a warning. Brom smirked at the Bishop, "Oh you are too kind my Lord, I cannot wait to feast in your great hall." Brom said to Lord Harmon, his gaze never leaving Bishop Varik's.

Ayla and Rohn both offered respectful bows to the Baron, "Again thank you for all your help, Lord Harmon." Rohn added.

"Aye, we owe you greatly," Ayla added.

"Think nothing of it. Sir Garrett is a dear friend to me. If you will excuse me, duty calls." He gave the group a nod as he made his way out, shadowed by Bishop Varik and Dusan.

"This turned out to be a blessing after all!" Brom laughed as soon as he was alone with the Gerhardts excited at the invitation. "Overstuffed feather mattresses, food from lands you've never heard of, and enough ale to drown a man twice. Eirburg beware…" He grinned ear to ear, wringing his hands together.

"Behave, Brom," Garrett warned. "We are his guests and will act as such."

"Aye, no need to be a stick in the mud, your brush with death should leave you hungry with exuberant joy!" Brom exclaimed, his voice reverberating through the hall.

"I will leave you as his escort, Rohn. There is something I need to look into," Ayla said, giving them a faint smile. "I will meet you at the castle, later tonight for supper. And as for you old man I don't want to see you on your feet for a few days." She warned Garrett as she kissed him on the forehead and then made her way out, leaving nothing but a faint scent of her presence.

Rohn sadly watched Ayla leave, as Brom draped his arm over the young scribe's shoulder. "Let's go, Garrett should get some much-deserved rest. We've got a city to explore, woe be them." Brom wiggled his brow still grinning.

"I will see you later, father," Rohn said, shaking his patriarch's hand.

"Aye lad." He smiled, gripping his son's hand. "Now go rest, you've earned it."

With a nod, Rohn and Brom headed out through the temple into the bustling city streets, their sense assaulted by the change in atmosphere. The air filled with enticing odors, both foreign and familiar; sounds of bards playing in the taverns and vendors peddling their wares. The pair made their way to the castle, laughing and joking all the way, ignorant of the tide about to crash into the walls of Eirburg.

Ayla walked with purpose through the local academy, her clothes still stained with the battle the night before and her fair face painted with dirt and dried tears. She paid little mind to the nobles who gasped and wrinkled their noses at her as she passed by. The forest was still at the forefront of her mind. Something told her its rapid growth had to do with what was occurring; the sudden surge of bestial attacks. She had to find out what was happening to the trees and what was causing their mutations.

The city's library was stuffed wall to wall with tombs and scrolls as robed scholars wandered its silent halls, reading or quietly discussing various topics. Nobility sat at tables with their noses in books or using it as a social gathering away from the peasantry of the city. Ayla however was here for a much different purpose.

She headed to the main directory and immediately asked for books on horticulture and botany as the elderly scribe looked up and gave her a smile in greeting. Not long after she made her way to a table with a stack of manuscripts and took a seat quickly devouring the information as she tied her hair back in a ponytail. While disease in trees was not unheard of, none of it matched what she and the others had witnessed. No ailment could cause a tree to sprout from the ground overnight. *Perhaps what is happening is not natural, but indeed supernatural,* she thought as she heard a gentle voice behind her.

"Is there anything else I help you with child?" The old woman's voice was low and rather soothing.

"Yes, I was looking for a book on native lore, on prophecies, or superstitions of the local clans before Voskavia was colonized." She said, blowing a stray strand of auburn hair from her face.

"Come with me." The old woman instructed, carefully waddling to a room towards the back of the library.

They made their way through the main hall, through rows and rows of manuscripts, leisurely heading to a side hallway. The portly woman wobbled on stubby legs as she walked, her weight too much for her slight frame. They finally stopped at a large oak door, reinforced by iron, as the woman fiddled with a key ring on her belt and smiled with a content grunt pulled a single key from the hoop. With a quick twist of the librarian's wrist, the door to the room opened, sucking in the fresh air in a gasp.

The scribe looked to Ayla. "Would you be a dear?" She asked, motioning to a candlelit lantern nearby outside.

Ayla obliged and gently handed her the light. Its warm glow slowly pouring into the room, drowning out the darkness. It was musty and had a smell of old leather and parchment that was dry and brittle. Little particles of dust floated through the room, as the old woman eyed stacks of ancient journals and scrolls.

"Few books on the subject. What we have was recently written, but there are a few old journals down here from previous explorers that have yet to be transcribed to a more legible manuscript." She said, setting down the iron lantern and began digging through the stacks of documents, the room filling with dust as it was disturbed.

Ayla coughed and waved the cloud from her face, fighting the urge to sneeze, waiting patiently on the elderly woman's search. One by one the librarian examined the book in her hand and shook her head as if looking for a particular one. "I know it's here." She said, tossing another to the side on an adjacent stack of books.

"Here, the journal of Sir Ruthger. He spoke with some of the clans before we settled here." She said handing her the thick leather-bound journal, pages of notes slipping out. Ayla gently stuffing the loosed pages back in as she took the book from the aged woman, hoping it contained something useful.

"Thank you," Ayla said, the woman nodding in return.

She quickly left the scribe to her duties and walked to a table to get a better look at the manuscript in the large hall lit by various windows and candelabras. Ayla sat in a chair as she quickly flipped through the pages, scanning the entries. All mundane at first, they started like all journals. Trials and tribulations of the arduous journey. The illness at sea, lack of food, and petty bickering. Then entries flowed into the elation of landing on Voskavia's abundant shores, the men thanking God as their supplies were running low. It appears they had been sailing in a fog for several days until they heard the crash of water against a cliff-side. Carefully they followed the shoreline, looking for a safe place to anchor and begin their investigation of the new land.

A few days after arriving, a local tribe approached Sir Ruthger and his party. They spoke a familiar dialect, and one of the expeditions linguists had translated for Sir Ruthger. It was an old form of Slavic and the native men who spoke it were wild-eyed, wearing nothing but furs over their weathered skin. Their shaman spoke for them, their faces covered in faded tattoos and berry paint. They had claimed the land long ago landing on its shores when they were taken from their home to be slaves by the men of the north, hoping to one day tap into its abundant resources itself, but the land refused to heel.

They warned the Englishmen to leave while they could before the woods claimed them as it had many of their people, that the forest itself was alive and angered by their presence, claiming it was evil and malevolent. The druids warned the earth was bitter and its soil tainted with venom. Their ancient ancestors had fled their inhuman masters and took refuge on an island off the coast where the forest and its beasts could not reach them. They lived off the abundance of the sea and what they could snatch from the wilds their warriors would bring back from hunting expeditions on the mainland. Not long after finding their salvation, their ancestors witnessed a firestorm bathe the continent from the sky and drown its smoldering forests with a great flood. Their people had been spared though, as the Great Spirit had warned them to prepare for the deluge of rain, so they build large rafts to live on. It wasn't long before the sea once again receded and they ventured back onto the continent.

Ayla slowly turned the page, to see it was filled with a drawing, scribbled in black of a massive tree across both pages. In its trunk were the faces of various monstrosities, its roots spreading through the land for miles. The druids warned of disturbing the entity, telling the men to return where they came from, that the continent already had masters that needed to be kept dormant. They urged the knight to leave and never return, that their presence would wake the being once more and it would feed on the pain and suffering they brought to its shores.

Ayla slowly looked up, the growth of the forest finally making sense. The wars between locals and the English settlers must have awoken whatever the entity was. Perhaps a virus or a disease, it spread, consuming life as it did to fuel its expansion. She grabbed the journal and quickly made her way to the palace. The sun now high in the sky almost blinding her, making her way to the castle to share what she had learned with the others.

"So this is what it's like to be a Baron. I wonder how you go about getting such a title?" Brom said, sitting in a padded armed chair, his leg dangling over the side, a leg of chicken in hand and ale in the other.

Rohn chuckled, taking a sip of his flagon. The two refreshed after a hot bath and a warm meal. The castle was indeed grand, with every luxury a person could ever want. Servants to full fill every need and minstrels played soft, soothing melodies with their lutes and harps. Rohn could get used to this as the two sat in a private dining room separate from the larger gathering hall where banquets were usually held. Servants quickly fluttered in and out, refilling their cups, clearing their plates, and placing new meals before them.

"We have a dire problem!" Ayla said, finally caught up to the two bursting through the doorway of the room.

"Relax Ayla, sit, have something to eat, and be merry," Brom said partially drunk, waving a drumstick in his hand to the melody.

"What is it?" Rohn said still smiling, his body warm from the strong ale.

Ayla laid Sir Ruthger's journal on the table, a small tuft of dust plumbing around it, on the spotless dining linens. She quickly flipped to the marked page, as Rohn sipped deeply from his cup.

"Here," She said, placing a finger on the page of the drawing. "A tree. A gargantuan tree. But the locals say it's more, it's a living, thinking creature. A being from before man was man. The druids warned Sir Ruthger of it. Claimed it would once again awaken if we were to return."

"That they did." Lord Harmon said, walking into the room, gently taking his place at the head of the table.

"My Lord I didn't—" Ayla began but was silenced by Lord Harmon's raised hand.

"It is fine my dear. I suppose you have earned the right to the truth." He said as the servant placed a bowl of soup before him.

"Sir Ruthger told us of the warning as he deemed the continent uninhabitable, but Britannia is no stranger to the supernatural. England has called for a Great Hunt to slay giants to dragons. Such things are a way of life; so we paid little heed to the warning of a few frightened shamans. It was my hubris, hungry for a new challenge that let it get to this point." He said bringing a spoon of soup to his mouth, gently blowing on it to cool it.

"So you knew of this?" Rohn asked, sobering up from the revelation.

"Yes. That is why I was sent here, King Edward put full faith in me and I refuse to fail him. While the natives succumbed to the land, I will not. I have sent for more soldiers, supplies, and workers. We will double our efforts and retake the old fort, then expand outwards once more. With the aid of your house of course." He said, sipping his soup.

"My Lord, did they not tell you? The forest spreads. It grows day by day; it will soon be outside the very gates of Eirburg." Ayla added.

Lord Harmon put down his spoon and waved away the soup. "Yes, I've read the scouts' reports. It is truly disturbing, but we cannot fail. England is at war and famine haunts the countryside. King Edward demands wood, food, and goods to trade with Asia to fund his claim to the throne. I refuse to return home empty-handed, back to my life of lugging lumber across an ocean only to haggle for a paltry profit. I have made something of myself here. I have a destiny here, as do all of you. Do you wish to just discard it due to a few trials and tribulations, or rise above and seize your future?"

"People may die. There are things in the forest we've never encountered in England; nor has been recorded in ancient Albion," Rohn added.

"Aye, some evil beasts lurk out there, and I don't mean wild animals. Vicious creatures, that loathe men, especially Christians." Brom stated as his buzz began wearing off.

"I am well aware of the situation." Lord Harmon said, his tone becoming more forceful. "But we are burdened with great purpose, it is our destiny to spread the English Empire to the edge of the map. I have already dispatched ships to return to England. They will return with more men and supplies. We *will* not lose this colony."

"If you're so determined to remain, my Lord, I think I figured out a way to hold the forest at bay," Ayla said, sitting down slowly, almost as if she were giving up trying to reason with the Baron.

Lord Harmon looked at her, waiting for her solution, as he sat back in his chair, fingers folded around its padded arms. "Go on."

"It seems the growth is deterred by salt. It reacts the mineral, like lycanthropes to silver." Ayla pulled the dried sapling from her satchel and placed it on the table before Lord Harmon.

"Is this true Rohn?" Lord Harmon asked, eyeing the branch carefully, its withered husk looking like nothing more than a burnt shriveled twig, brittle to the touch.

"Yes, my Lord, Ayla discovered it just before the attack at Dumont by the Skadi," Rohn said, sitting up straight in his chair. Ayla smiled at him, grateful for his confidence in her. "I believe this will at the very least slow the invasive woods." He added Lord Harmon, nodding slowly in response.

"Let's not forget where she got the idea," Brom said, lifting a mug at them in a silent cheer.

"This would also make sense why it never spread from the continent." Ayla added, "The salt of the sea hindered its growth. It was us, our settlements and conflicts with the locals that awoke it."

"So be it. I'll have my men prepare a barrier around the walls of the city. I do hope you are right Lady Ayla, as we will have to spend a great deal of the colony's resources on this endeavor." The Baron said as he stood from the table adjusting his clothing before making his way to the doorway. "I will make arrangements based on your observations, young lady, let us pray it works."

"I'll send word home. Warn the keep and inform them of all that has happened." Rohn said, standing from the table. "Well done, Ayla." He rubbed her shoulder as he walked out of the room just a few paces behind Lord Harmon.

"Again, it was my idea!" Brom slurred, as the others made their way out to prepare for the evening.

III

The sun was fading over Eirburg as most citizens moved indoors, Lord Harmon called for a city-wide curfew. No one was to be on the streets after dark unless necessary. One by one the city's windows glinted to life as lanterns inside homes were lit, the families taking solace in their warm abodes. Huddled around their hearths, the commoners unwound from the busy day reading books, playing games, or knitting new garments for themselves and their loved ones. Many found shelter in local taverns, huddled around mugs of ale as they told bawdy jokes, or shared the latest rumors as they would sleep with their heads on the tables in a deep alcohol-induced slumber.

Even with the curfew, the streets still bustled with activity. Watchmen patrolled in small groups preparing for what may come. The city guard and soldiers spent hours walking the city confiscating salt, loading wagon after wagon. They went from home to home, shop to shop, and even confiscated salt from the Citadel itself. Barrel after barrel, the men directed a workforce to lay a barricade of the mineral in front of the moat which had been now opened to the sea, letting saltwater pour in. The soldiers on the wall of the castle chummed the water, calling in predators from the ocean to act as natural deterrents in the murky barrier. For the past few hours, wagons slowly streamed in and out of the capital as the footman of the city guard finalized the salt barrier. The people of Eirburg felt safe behind its large ramparts and streets filled with armed men ready to do battle with whatever may come to their doorsteps.

IV

"I'm telling you, the Baron is going mad. What fool would have us pour salt in front of a forty-foot wall and its moat? It's madness." The footman complained again, tossing another empty barrel to the back of the wagon.

The sun was now setting, its radiance dimming behind the tree line as small patches of torchlight flickered around them, the other wagons dumping their payloads. The two soldiers had been at this for what seems like hours now, scooping out handfuls, peppering the ground as they walked next to the wagon.

"Stow it, the sooner we're done, the sooner we're back inside out of the damn cold." Their sergeant barked from the passenger side of the wagon. "You'd rather

223

be on shit pot duty, just say so." The sergeant finished, glaring at the two in the back of the wagon.

The two men fell silent and went back to the task at hand. A swift breeze blew around the massive city and cutting through the men like invisible daggers. The sergeant looked to the peasant driving the wagon, "It looks like we're almost done, this should be the last load."

"Look, sir, is that smoke?" The driver asked, squinting in the low light of dusk, pointed out to the horizon, the sergeant turning to investigate in response.

The officer quickly stood on the passenger seat of the wagon and tried to balance himself, peering over the vast farmland. The curvature of the ground obscured his view, as a small plume of smoke rose from a nearby farmstead in the distance. While not unusual, the fact he could see the light of the fire alarmed him.

"Maybe one of the fools dropped a torch or candle?" The sergeant responded, squinting his eyes trying to focus.

Suddenly a bell rang out from a watchtower along the wall, then another and another. The towers chimed over and over, activity along the wall increasing as footmen and archers alike took positions.

"Alright, let's get in the gate. We've been out here long enough." The officer ordered suddenly feeling exposed in the dark.

The footmen, sighing with relief, hopped into the wagon, elated to be heading back. As they made their way onto the main road, heading into the city with the other wagons, the air slowly filled with a foreign and disturbing sound. A low-pitched murmur at first that slowly swelled to an almost deafening moan. "The hell is that!" One footman in the back exclaimed, panic in his voice.

"I'll not stay to find out, faster driver!" The sergeant stood looking back over his shoulder.

The wagoner whimpering in response, "Sir, I can't. The other wagons are in the way; not enough room to go 'round them." He said impatiently searching for a way up onto the mounds but they had fencing along them, or perhaps through the ditch below not sure if the wagon could pull out of the steep incline. The horses whinnied and restlessly shifted in their harnesses. The scent of a predator was near, they could feel it, smell it.

The bells were at a furious pitch now, the walls now brimming with archers. Again the sergeant looked back to the horizon. Something was moving. Their heads bobbing up and down over the ridge as they approached.

"Move your asses!" The sergeant barked at the wagons in front of him; standing at this point, trying to see what the holdup was as his body trembled, he pulled his blade.

In the distance, near the front of the convoy, a wheel of one of the wagons in the front had fallen off. Two serfs were struggling to fit it back into position as footmen lifted the back of the wagon to balance it. The moaning became louder, reverberating through the men with a foreboding tone. The foot soldiers in the back jumped off and began running for the gates, joining others as they passed, everyone running for their lives.

"Sod it all, run men run! Leave the wagon!" The sergeant ordered quickly hopping off his seat, his bulky frame falling with a thud dropping his sword as a pain shot through his leg.

The driver hopped off with more ease, landing agilely on his feet and bursting into a full sprint towards safety, not noticing the sergeant's cries for help. The bulky soldier stood, but a sharp pain almost forced him to a knee. Again he looked behind him. Figures were now appearing at a rapid pace over the horizon, as they were in a full sprint. Their eyes gently reflecting the light of the moon like feral dogs, mouths wide open as they growled and hissed, ready to pounce on anyone who couldn't outrun them.

"Jesus, help me!" The sergeant screamed in total panic as he slowly limped his way to the entrance. "Wait! Wait for me, damn it!" He could barely run, the pain jolting through his leg as he felt something twist again as he grimaced in pain.

The sergeant's screams were drowned out by the constant ringing of the alarm bells. He crossed himself as he watched the horde grow closer and closer, as he could now make out details of the army. Their clothing tattered and torn, soiled with blood and dirt, thorny spikes protruded through their skin. Their eyes sunken in and little spots of silver glowing in the dark. They were screaming, moaning, and hissing, making all types of unnatural animistic sounds no human should be capable of making. Their bodies were twisted masses that twitched and convulsed in pain and rage as they screamed in both agony and pleasure into the air. They were less than a hundred paces from the terrified officer, his body trembling as the ground quaked from their approach. Suddenly to the surprise of the vulnerable soldier they all halted in unison. Like a wave meeting a wall, they stopped, spreading out a few hundred feet from the moat. The hissing and moaning slowly silencing as they looked to the ground before them. *They could sense it, the damn barrier*, he thought. The sergeant wasted no time and scurried to his feet, limping as quickly as he could to the gates, the draw bridge slowly rising, waiting for no one as other men leaped onto the bridge. He looked over his shoulder once more, panting and whimpering. The possessed army was slowly testing the ground. Looking for a thinner section so they may gain access to the city.

"Wait!" He screamed as he lunged, grabbing the edge of the drawbridge as it lifted, trying desperately to heft his weight over the top but his armor hindering him.

Two footmen ran over to his aid, diving onto their bellies to remain on the structure. They grabbed his arms and with a grunt pulled the large officer over, all of them tumbling back as the bridge never slowed. The sergeant sighed as his two kinsmen from the wagon helped him into the gates; the three men, last of the refugees outside the walls, left alive. Behind them two sets of thick reinforced gates slammed shut, as an iron portcullis dropped over the outer door, the drawbridge finishing its ascent covering the entire entrance. The bells finally coming to a stop. The entire city was now silent. Everyone in awe as to the horde that stood before them. Hundreds of men and women, all reanimated wretches, twisted versions of those they knew, waiting for the right moment to swarm the walls.

V

Ayla, Brom, and Rohn finally reached the top of the city's ramparts, alarmed by the bells. They gasped at the sight as they worked their way around to the entrance of Eirburg. As far as the eye could see, figures slowly swayed, twitching and growling. They moved in a single mass. One by one the creatures tried to pass the salted earth and quickly it fell in immense pain, their bodies rapidly shriveling as their forms bubbled and sizzled, shattering as they fell to the ground their vessels brittle and dried out. They were testing for weakness in the barrier, searching for an area where they could cross the minefield of minerals. They snarled and bellowed in frustration at the soldiers along the wall, but then fell silent once more, patiently waiting for something.

Lord Marshal Hendrik quickly made his way to the trio. "The hell is this! Who are they?! What do they want?!" He demanded answers from them, or anyone.

Ayla said, staring down at the poor fools who now served the malevolent entity. Their bodies covered in spines, the thick black sap oozing from their mouths. "They want us," She turned to the Lord Marshal, "And they won't stop until they've killed every last man, woman, and child."

Chapter 15:

Old Grudges

I

The walls of Eirburg stood defiantly before the growling horde, their army still waiting before the salt-laden earth. The ramparts were a flurry of activity now, as war drums reverberated their rapid beat, carrying throughout the city. Archers stood in formation on top of the stone towers, preparing to rain down hell on the Withered below. The walls were lined with footmen, armed with swords and shields, backed by halberdiers ready to protect the wall from any who dared to climb. Slowly, the powerful war machines atop the towers groaned under the strain of being cocked and loaded by the engineers.

Lord Marshal Hendrik walked the ramparts, checking its defenses and making last-minute changes. "Everything looks as it should be. We're ready for this. Let the bastards come." He said with a grin to House Gerhardt.

"This is no normal army, hell-bent on taking what they can carry," Brom said, "They want to kill us to the last man."

"They need to breach the walls first. Double the height and thickness of most, and I doubt the sickly whoresons can swim." Hendrik chuckled. "Look at them, waylaid from the salted soil."

"It won't last long, they can out wait us," Ayla said, looking down on the army as they paced on the other side of the salt, grunting and growling, black ooze dripping from their mouths and eyes.

"We can fix that," Hendrik said, raising an arm in the air. "Sergeant, If you would give our visitors a volley. Promptly send them back to hell."

"Archers at the ready!" the sergeant commanded to his men on the towers, a page waving a flag to signal the others as he raised his arm.

Their bows lifted into the air, aiming at the swarm that paced below. "Loose!" the sergeant at arms bellowed as arrows thumped from their strings, the rain of iron-tipped death casting a shadow on the horde below.

The Withered just hissed as the arrows poured from the sky in a torrent, snapping through the air as they hit their targets. Within seconds the possessed army had become pincushions, as the barrage found its way back to earth. Arrows protruded from their heads and necks, but the invaders didn't flinch let alone fall.

The sergeant at arms looked to the Lord Marshal as panic took hold. "Light em!" Hendrik responded as the sergeant nodded, preparing the next volley.

This time as the bows raised and slowly drew back, their tips were lit, flickering with amber light as they burnt eager to fulfill their purpose. Again, the sergeant commanded, and the air filled with the flickering shafts of death, lighting the sky as they flew. One by one they began impacting their targets thumping into the hardened carapace of the dead vessels that relentlessly gathered, the horde growing by the minute. Thick black ooze flowed from their wounds and slowly smothered the burning projectiles. The silver eyes rose to the ramparts, glaring with hatred as they snarled.

"What are they waiting for?" One of the footmen asked out loud, both frustrated and frightened.

As if on cue to the soldiers' concerns, trees in the distance shuttered and shook. The forest bent and leaned to the side as a gigantic form shoved its way through, bellowing loud enough to shake the stone the soldiers stood on. The men began shifting in their places, hiding behind their shields as birds flooded the sky, running from what was quickly approaching.

"Siege engines. No invading army would forget siege engines." Brom spit to the side, a disgusted look on his face.

Two gigantic humanoid figures burst through the tree line, growling and roaring. They stood almost forty feet and left craters in the wake of their footsteps. Bellowing as they trotted, their bodies of flesh and blood long gone, replaced with vines and roots, their fists intertwined wraps of jagged stone. On the larger Fomorian's shoulder stood Hrothgar, with his spiked two-handed war hammer in hand. The two juggernauts surged towards the walls, the soldiers shifting and slowly leaning back ready to flee.

"Golems! Who would have the power to summon a golem, let alone a pair?" Rohn asked, staring at the encroaching behemoths.

"Fomorian's being exact. The one's Garrett and his men had slain in the fields of Dumont during The Purge." Ayla added, her eyes fixed on the grotesque creations.

The giants were filled with rage, eying the walls of the port city, a monument of the English invasion. They lowered their heads like battering rams as they picked up the pace, now jogging towards the ramparts, the ground jolting with each step.

"Fire on the giants! Fire at will!" The Lord Marshal commanded, fluster in his voice.

The catapults and ballista released their payloads, stone smashing into stone as the ballista bolts bounced from the hardened carapace of the golems. Flaming arrows streamed from the towers, but doused themselves once they embedded into their targets. As another catapult boulder smashed into the chest of one of the animated giants, Rohn spotted something. An amber glow peaking from its chest.

"There's something in them. Inside the chests, they must all be like the Fomorians. It's in their chest!" He yelled to the Lord Marshal. "Strike the chest, the ember in the chest!" Again he emphasized, tapping his heart over the roar of the creatures and the constant barrage of siege engines.

The Lord Marshal nodded and passed down the orders to all his sergeants who quickly began passing the word down the lines. Again the Fomorians took hit after hit and shrugged it off, slowly their stone and black root hides chipping away, as thick ooze splashed to the ground. Hrothgar grinned as his powerful army shrugged the projectiles off. From the belly of the Withered Warlord, a screech poured forth, ripping through the air. The men on the walls flinched at the sound, the archers quickly nocked their arrows, preparing for the next volley. They raised their bows to the sky, taking aim, but hesitated as the clouds themselves seemed to move. The dark, low-hanging miasma writhed and shifted as the sound of a thousand birds cawed, diving to the ramparts as one entity.

"Shields! Shield—" The sergeant was cut short as a bird impaled his throat, the officer dropping, now as dead as the cold granite he laid on.

The men bellowed while they fled to shelter as the birds dove, impaling themselves into anyone they came across, even if it meant their deaths. Soldiers dropped from the ramparts lifeless as the flock screeched through the men, diving into soldiers' mouths and eyes. The footmen quickly formed a shield wall, as the birds slammed into the barriers, falling to the ground their beaks and necks shattered from the impact.

Engineers fled down the stairs of the tower to retreat from the swarm of blackbirds in a panic. Many of them were not so lucky as they fell dead before they reached the safety of the tower slain by a creature less than a hundredth their weight. Several birds impaled their beaks into the men's backs, only to rip free and shake their heads before returning to their brethren, retreating to the dark skies, their unnatural caws fading back into the clouds as they retreated to the safety of the air.

Howling with rage, the first giant lunged into the left side of the wall, opposite the Gerhardt's and the Lord Marshal. The outer curtain shuttered as its head smashed into the stone, its feet burning and slowly decaying. It trotted over the salt, but there was not enough of the mineral to take its massive form down.

"Hold men! Brace!" The Lord Marshal exclaimed, Rohn, grabbed Ayla, shielding her behind a pillar as he and Brom fled for cover.

The gargantuan reanimated Fomorian slammed into the wall just below them, the ramparts shaking violently, as a crack slowly slithered its way down the barrier. The Withered wasted no time seizing the opportunity. One by one they began climbing on the monstrosities, scurrying to the top where they could hop onto the wall.

"Archers, focus on the ones climbing!" Marshal Hendrik said pointing, the archers hurrying to prepare a volley.

Ayla, Brom, and Rohn gathered themselves, now face to face with the massive golem. Its eyes glowing with a hollow hatred as it stared at them. Its enormous mouth opened and roared, the sound deafening as vines protruded from its maw like a tongue. The roots wrapped themselves onto the ramparts, as the giant stone fists slammed into the wall, over and over as it released horrific moans that reverberated the very ground it stood on.

"I'll help the men on the other side, you deal with this one!" Brom said with a grin as he ran off before the two could stop him.

"What? How?!" Ayla yelled as the ranger ran to the edge of the wall.

"I have a plan!" Brom tapped the side of his temple as he leaped over the side of the wall to the city below.

"What in God's name is he doing?!" Rohn said. Ayla just shrugged in frustration, both seeming helpless in the face of the giant.

As the tendrils wrapped themselves onto the ramparts, the Withered poured over their living siege tower. The men on the walls bellowing orders and bracing for the impact as the two armies collided, the wall still shaking as the Fomorians pummeled it with their fists. Chunk by chunk, the wall fell to the moat below with a splash, as the giants acted as a siege tower for their brethren and a battering ram all in one.

II

Brom landed on the nearby roof of a hovel as he leaped from the walls, from one roof to another, quickly descending to the ground where the salt carts had stopped just inside the city. With uncanny agility, he dangled from supports and swung to another roof. Unfortunately, the roof gave way as he made contact, as Brom fell through landing on a table with a thud. Air barely eeking out of his chest as he rolled off the table with a groan. The ranger nodded to the terrified family huddled inside as they stared at the man who had just fallen through their roof.

"My apologies." He said, wincing with a smile as he dusted himself off. "You mind?" He asked, grabbing a mug of ale on his way out from their dinner table.

As quickly as he appeared, he vanished through their front door, leaving the family bewildered and confused as a clay mug sailed over his shoulder, crashing to the floor. Again the ranger continued his descent, roof to roof, running along the walkways, and with a final leap, his feet landed on solid ground, the dirt road of the main gates. He quickly began rummaging through the wagons, tossing empty barrels aside one by one as he searched growling in frustration for his prize knowing time was of the essence.

III

Ayla and Rohn stood fast against the horde as it pushed harder and harder into the shields of the footmen, their spears and halberds hacking and prodding into the unrelenting invaders. The Withered screamed and wailed, their voices unnatural and their bodies smelling of rotten soil. Black ooze sprayed from one of their mouths, blinding a man as he screamed and retreated. Not paying attention in his panic he fell backward over the inner curtain of the ramparts down into the city below, bouncing off rooftops as he plummeted to his death.

Hrothgar plowed through his Withered army, eager for revenge. He barely noticed the warriors swatted aside as he charged onto the ramparts. His war hammer whirled through the air as he roared in a fevered frenzy. The fallen king swung the oversized weapon effortlessly as his hammer smashed into the foot soldiers' shields, splintering both the barrier and their arms behind the force. With a growl, he slammed his hammer downwards. This time a soldier's head splattered within its helm, spraying his comrades with viscera. The line of footmen slowly collapsed as spears, arrows, and blades did nothing to the berserker as he bowled his way through the line of helpless soldiers.

"We need to stop him," Rohn said to Ayla as they watched the huge warrior bludgeon his way through their defenses, the problem obvious but a solution lacking from either of them.

"I'll keep the bastard busy you think of something!" Rohn charged in. Tired of watching his kinsmen fall to the unhinged warlord, at the last moment the squire dropped to his knees, sliding under the warrior's hammer.

Rohn's blade sliced against his hardened, leathery leg, slashing his ankle, black ooze pouring from his wounds, but did little else to Hrothgar. The young man quickly rolled to his feet, his shield up and blade at the ready to strike.

"Foolish boy, I'll pound you into paste!" Hrothgar said snarling at Rohn, as he raised his hammer and lunged for the young scribe.

Brom's lessons flashed in the young man's mind, the way he had charged him like a bull, hefting his weapon over his shoulder. Hrothgar did the same as he barreled forth, Rohn just calmly waited, timing his deflection. At the last moment, Rohn shifted his weight, his shield upright protecting the left side of his face as he thrust the barrier upward. Hrothgar's hammer bounced off his kite shield, swinging wildly over his head, smashing into another foot soldier sending him over the sides of the wall. Hrothgar was thrown off balance from the weight of his hammer, causing his seven-foot frame to wobble.

Ayla quickly reached into a large leather pouch on her belt and pulled a small oil pot, no bigger than an orange. Scanning for a way to light its dried wick, she shoved her way through the crowd of soldiers that were fighting for their lives against the gruesome and relentless Withered. She slid between both soldiers and monstrosities, spotting a brazier the archers used to light their arrows. Deftly dodging through the mayhem that surrounded her, Ayla fought her way through after shoving one of the Withered over the ramparts into the moat below as it screeched in pain from being dissolved in the saltwater. The hemp rope flared to life as she let the brazier's flickering flame dance on its tip and waited. Patience was the key component of a sharpshooter. Patience and focus. Seeing the back of the mighty Hrothgar she reeled back to lob her grenade, but before she could let loose of the pot, a Withered farmer burst through the crowd, slamming into her as he was cleaving his way through the soldiers, the flaming orb rolling to the side on the ramparts of the walls. She quickly drew her short sword and hatchet from her belt immediately held at the ready. The Withered farmer swung wildly, slashing with his claws, hissing furiously. Ayla tried to dodge as many of his blows as she could, but his attack was endless, as he had no muscles to become tired. She moved backward quickly, trying to regain her balance as he lunged forward, her blades doing the best they could to deflect his razor-like fingers tearing into her armor and skin.

IV

Brom had finally found it, a relatively full barrel of purified salt. With his axe in one hand and a barrel of salt over his broad shoulder in his other, he sighed, looking to he would have to climb to get back to the battle. Quickly Brom began taking the steps two at a time, his thighs and calves burning as he ascended the tower, the chaos raging far above him.

V

Rohn countered again, the war hammer ricocheting off his blade as he allowed the momentum to deflect off his sword. The edge gliding across Hrothgar's chest and then the back of his thigh. But the Warlord did not fall, he did not flinch. His body seeped with the viscous liquid, it splashing as he maneuvered around, trying to regain his footing against the young Gerhardt.

Ayla was growing tired while parrying the constant attacks. She couldn't do this for much longer. The lass repositioned herself with her back to the forward face of the rampart walls the invading army roaring behind her from below. She slouched, her body burning from its cuts and bruises, as her muscles ached. The Withered saw its chance and charged her screaming "Trespasser!"

Ayla gasped, winded from the constant barrage of blows or her adversary. Again the thorned farmer charged, his jaw detaching as he screeched, pressing his attack once more, barreling towards the exhausted young woman. Ayla was tired, she was in pain, but she was also smart and at the last second, she rolled to her back. Her hatchet hooking the neck of the Withered with the curved inner head and shoved up mid-roll with her feet to its stomach as her blade impaled into his chest pushing him upwards matching his momentum. The screaming vessel flew over the rampart walls and sailed into the moat with a splash, its body sizzling as it crumbled away as it writhed in agony. Her attention quickly refocused back to Rohn. He too was getting tired from the never-ending assault from Hrothgar. The Warlord never slowed, never relenting just like his possessed warriors.

Ayla's grass green eyes scanned the stone floor of the ramparts, quickly spotting her oil pot, the wick still lit as it smoldered, clinging to life. With the grace of a seasoned fighter, she bobbed and weaved through the crowd of soldiers and

Withered alike, sliding to her rear end as she scooped up the projectile with the speed of a cat.

Rohn was dodging as fast as he could, but more and more of Hrothgar's blows were landing as they smashed against his shield, it was chipping and cracking to the point of shattering as the young man grew tired, as a result, his footwork becoming sloppy. Hrothgar again hefted his hammer up, his unlimited pool of stamina thrusting him forward, ready to crush Rohn under the weight of its gigantic head. Hrothgar swung his hammer once more, a rabid zeal over his twisted face, but was interrupted as his back suddenly detonated in a burst of flames. His enormous form engulfing as the blaze wrapped around him in an amber embrace, even the oozing sap not strong enough to fight the thick, sticky oil.

Hrothgar roared in rage, a towering inferno of burning barbarian spun wildly, his hammer flailing into the surrounding air. Chunks of the wall fell into the moat under Rohn, causing him to lose his balance and fall to his back, his shield finally shattering as it collided with the heavy stone surface. Hrothgar swung his hammer at Ayla as his body roared in flames. The young lass barely dodged the barbaric weapon reeling backward.

She quickly retreated, her legs and arms kicking as fast as she could to avoid the hammer as it slammed down over and over, bits of stone stinging her bare skin as they sprayed from his strikes. Hrothgar, still ablaze, raised his hammer again, snarling, "You will pay dearly, little one. Rejoice, tonight you meet your God."

Hrothgar heaved his weapon once more into the air, its iron-toothed head coated with the gore of those that fell before him. The axe head began its descent, a blur of pig iron death, but missed its mark. Garrett's flail smashed into Hrothgar's face; spraying bone and root covered in black gore, into the air. The barbarian king reeled back, stumbling, struggling to regain his balance. Another flail's head careened into the brute's chest. Burning hunks of the once-mighty warlord shattered into the sky as he stumbled back, leaning against the inner curtain wall.

"Behind me, lass," Garrett said calmly but determined, a flail in each hand. "His quarrel is with me." The knight's eyes locked with Hrothgar's as the fallen king would finally get his vengeance, his eyes welling with rage as he charged forward with a bestial roar.

Brom had finally reached the top of the tower, the battle still thundering on the ramparts as it slowly spilled over into the streets. The Withered Ones had gained enough ground to leap from the walls into the homes below, trickling down on the innocent commoner's hovels.

The resurrected Fomorian bellowed as it pummeled the wall, its tongue of tendrils growing ever thicker. The dexterous ranger bobbed and weaved through the conflict, shoulder butting Withered as he went. In a last-ditch effort, Brom dropped his axe. With both hands, he heaved the barrel of salt through the air, over the heads of his kinsmen. With a thump, the container landed into the mouth of the Fomorian who reactively chomped down on the object that was foolish enough to enter his crushing maw.

Before the giant realized what he had done, the barrel erupted, salt splashing down its body through the various cracks and crevasse as the barrel splintered into kindling. The reanimated giant began roaring, his throat sizzled and burnt as chunks of his body rotted, falling into the moat below. The tendrils from his mouth snapped loose as the salt disintegrated them at the source.

Brom reunited with his broad axe, as he saw his opportunity, and jumped from the ramparts into the gaping wound of the golem. The joyous warden slid down into its core, grinning all the while knowing his ancestors were watching. His feet finally brought him to a slow as he heard a thumping pulse through the body of the golem. It was what Rohn had spoken of. A large seed, the size of a wine barrel, pulsed with an ember light. Roots and vines fluttering out, quickly trying to replace what had been destroyed, but the salt was far too much for it, the mineral eating away at its structure. It reverberated and shuttered as its once-powerful form slowly crumbled under its weight, hissing as chunks fell to the moat below.

Brom aided its destruction as he hacked and chopped the pulsing seed, bracing his legs outwards to the sides, leaning his back to on the giant's structure for leverage. Over and over, his axe sunk into the growth. It squirmed and twitched with each hit, pulsing as black ooze spurt from it. Brom hacked with feverish laughter, the blade cleaving in deeper with each strike.

With a final swing of his weapon, the seed burst like a ripe melon, spraying black sap all over the wild man. The Fomorian groaned and roared weakly one last time before succumbing to its wounds. Its body crashed into the moat with a tremendous splash, the geyser of water almost reaching the top of the ramparts. The men on the walls cheered watching the goliath fall and with renewed hope began pushing back all the harder. Bowmen on the towers began passing the word as they rushed down to grab more barrels of salt. The Lord Marshal roared orders, trying to keep the lines from breaking even further and letting the Withered into the city itself.

"We must hold!" Marshal Hendrik stated as he stood behind his men, guiding them into formation.

VII

Ayla had quickly moved to Rohn and helped him to his feet, the boy weary and sore from his confrontation with Hrothgar. The two found themselves surrounded by the Withered and quickly moved back-to-back as the infected closed in.

"Remember the chest; look for the ember," Rohn said, gripping his sword with both hands.

"Aye, easier said than done!" She replied, as a claw just skimmed past her head.

The two of them spinning around one another, working in cohesion. One of them would unbalance their target as the other would strike finishing the job. They cleaved limbs and heads from the vessels. Spouts of black gushed into the air. *What has no head, cannot see, what has no arms, cannot strike*, Rohn said to himself. The duo worked their way through the crowd, leaving a trail of severed appendages in their wake as the Withered writhed and squirmed on the ground, trying to reconnect with their missing limbs.

VIII

Sir Garrett spun, his flails slamming into Hrothgar one after another in a deadly dance of metal and ferocity, chipping away at him piece by piece as his flails bounced off the warlord's intimidating form. Hrothgar roared in pain as the flames were slowly smoldering, but the damage had been done. His once-powerful body gifted by the Mother was failing him. It was rigid now, dry and brittle. The essence of the Mother in him slowly fading, he could sense Her disgust. Her disappointment. Time after time, he swung his hammer, hoping to strike the Templar, but even in his wounded state Garrett was besting him.

The Templar's flail wrapped itself around the warlord's leg. The knight pulled with all his might, his wounds reopening as his muscles flexed. The twisted barbarian fell to the ground as his leg came from under him, Garrett quickly sent the other flail into his chest as the Withered commander fell to the cold stone. Repeatedly Garrett's spiked headed flails came crashing down, shattering the brittle body revealing Hrothgar's weakness, the pulsing seedling.

Garrett now had his target. He focused as he brought his weapon down once more, but Hrothgar was expecting it. The warlord caught the maul in mid-air with a clawed hand and pulled it backward, sending Sir Garrett reeling behind the once human king. Hrothgar quickly rose to his feet, his body cracking and snapping as he did. He leaned down and picked up his hammer, the head still caked with blood and tissue from those unlucky enough to encounter the massive warrior.

Sir Garrett plummeted to the ground, grabbing his wounded stomach as blood seeped through his quilted surcoat. He heard the roar of Hrothgar behind him and instinctively rolled to the side just in time as the warlord's hammer smashed into the stone, shattering it like ice. The battered knight drew his sword, its sleek form glinting in the dark, paired with his remaining flail still in hand. The two recovered for a moment, glaring at one another. Both wounded warriors knew this was it, the finality to their rivalry. It would end tonight, as they stared at one another, neither one flinching.

"I didn't know until after," Garrett admitted.

Hrothgar snarled, "Would it of changed what you did? Would it of changed you, murdering my men, murdering me for something we had no part in?" His hammer swung once more, shattering a pillar behind Garrett as he just managed to dodge the blow with a painful wince.

Sir Garrett limped in pain as he squared off with the native king. "Yes, It would of," Sir Garrett spit to the side, his saliva thick with blood, the stitches of his wounds tearing with each moment, sending a flutter of pain through his body.

"I failed myself, my order, and above all, I failed God. I didn't wait for an explanation. I wanted you to pay for what had been taken from me and I used it as an excuse to fulfill my vengeance, succumbing to wrath."

Hrothgar offered a twisted smile. "I have yet to begin taking from you old man. When I'm dong crushing your skull, I'll cleave those you love in half from balls to brains and leave them hanging from the shell of this city." His voice was unnatural and inhuman as it reverberated from his body, his mouth barely moving.

"So be it." Sir Garrett said calmly, readying himself.

Hrothgar charged forward, his body cracking and creaking as he flung himself at the Templar once more, his hammer prepped for a powerful blow. Garrett expected nothing less, as the dead king was led by his rage. A spinning flail intercepted the weapon mid-swing, wrapping its chain around its handle. The two fought for control of each other's weapons, as they tugged and pulled in a violent duel for supremacy. Finally, the old enemies drew in, face to face as their bodies slammed together. Hrothgar growling and hissing as he grinned. Sir Garrett stoically stood in the face of the monster who was once a man. Garrett gripped his sword, as it had skillfully found its way through Hrothgar's chest. The small seedling now cleaved in two, as its thick sap poured from its vessel's.

"I'm sorry." Sir Garrett said sincerely.

"I'll see you in hell, Templar." Hrothgar hissed as his body crumbled and the silver light from his eyes faded.

IX

A thunderous roar bellowed behind Ayla and Rohn as a small contingent of Royal Guard unleashed their fire lances. The massive halberd cannons spewed bursts of lead balls and flame through the hordes of Withered. Their bodies shredded to bits, almost disintegrating within the close quarters of the weapons. What was left of the creatures stumbled and collapsed as the Royal Guardsmen moved as a formation to clear the wall, their fire lances now cleaving the invaders in half. The Royal Guard impaled those still standing and discarded them over the sides as if they were nothing more than refuse.

Ayla and Rohn had now returned to the remaining formation of soldiers, the men followed their example and began cleaving the Withered limb from limb the rear guard finishing the job with spear and sword behind the powerful Royal Guardsmen line.

"Well done! Let's finish this! Forward men!" Lord Marshal Hendrik stated as he whirled his blade in the air.

Rohn fell in line behind the wall of black powder bursts that lead to the deaths of the Withered that guards were dishing out generously. Rohn smiled back to Hendrik. The two nodded in celebration to one another, just as a gigantic hand crushed the Lord Marshal like an insect. Rohn cried out in terror as the fist lifted with the smeared Marshal underneath. Stuck to both the stone and the golem's hand Hendrik stretched like putty the look on his face was pure shock and confusion. In the last moments of his life, before the hand again smashed down into the wall finishing what it had started; smearing the Lord Marshal and grinding his armor to scraps. Ayla ran to Rohn's side as he stared in horror, watching the man's life end so brutally. She turned to see the bodies of the Withered regrouping. The torsos, heads, and arms were slowly slithering back to their masters, trying to reassemble themselves.

"The seeds in them, we need to destroy those, or they will resurrect," Ayla said to Rohn, snapping him from his daze.

The pair quickly went to work hacking and slashing as a cloud of white mineral scattered above them and onto the Withered. They looked up confused as the salt got into their mouths, its taste tart and sharp. The bowmen above were tossing hand full's of the leftovers from the barrier onto the ramparts. The Withered screamed and bellowed their bodies reacted violently to the concentrated mineral.

Engineers began loading the salt barrels into the catapults and maneuvered it to face the remaining Fomorian golem. They rushed to pull the arm down, barely one-third of the way, and let the barrel fly. The wooden container slamming into the behemoth, scattering salt throughout the monster's body. Slowly its form cracked and dried out, decaying before their very eyes. Rocks, stones, and chunks of rotted vines began falling into the moat below, joining its brethren as the soldiers pushed back the horde off the wall and into the saltwater moat with a splash. Their bodies hissing and gurgling as the briny water ate away at the vines that crept through them like acid. As the seedlings popping like kettle corn one by one, the bull sharks that patrolled the moat were drawn to the fleshy feast as they swarmed, each taking turns ripping the Withered apart.

Rohn and Ayla saw Sir Gerhardt fall to a knee, leaning only on his blade as he was coughing in pain. They didn't hesitate and ran to his aid. His once white tunic was soaked with blood, his face was pale as cream, and his eyes could barely focus. Ayla grabbed him, placing her own battered body under his arm as Garrett slowly faded in and out, as the fight was far too much strain on his wounds. That last thing Sir Garrett heard as all went black was Ayla and Rohn begging him to hold on, the two most precious people the knight had in this world.

X

Brom's fist burst through the surface of the water, still gripping his battleaxe. The ranger struggled as he pulled himself to the surface and onto the bank of the moat. Rolling out and onto his back as he spat water into the air, trying to catch his breath. He let out a dry laugh as a groan to his side caught his attention. His head flopped to the right and less than two feet from his face was one of the Withered trying to claw its way out of the moat. Brom recognized it as one of the Skadi they had fought at Fort Dumont. It was missing both its legs and one of its arms, flailing its remaining limb fruitlessly as the saltwater dissolved the roots holding it together. Eagerly the nose of a bull shark rose from the water as it gnawed on the remains of the corpse, shaking and pulling it under.

"I wonder what's eating them," Brom said, and began laughing far too hard, more so at surviving yet again than the cringe-inducing joke.

The huntsman just laid there for a few moments, enjoying the view and scent of his dying adversaries. Soldiers on the wall threw the remaining attackers over the side of the front curtain wall, each one landing with a splash sending the sharks into a new frenzied surge. The smell was horrid, like month-old stew in swamp water, Brom thought as he rose to his feet his body completely sore. He looked to the ramparts and yelled for one of the men to lower the gate in a less than polite manner, as he worked a cramp from his leg. The moat sizzling and churning as the last of the attackers slowly sunk to the depths below.

243

Chapter 16:

Give No Rest to the Wicked

I

"Garrett… Garrett, wake up." Abigail whispered.

Slowly Garrett came to as the bright blue sky flooded his vision. He was lying in a field, as small puffy white clouds floated over him playfully in various shapes and sizes. With a comfortable groan, Garrett sat up and saw his stronghold tucked neatly into the canyon of the mountains, the roar of the waterfall behind him, and the air filled with the scent of daisies and wildflowers. Above him, birds sang unrestrained in their chorus, as wild rabbits scurried through the thick green grass. The world was at peace, and he felt safe and carefree.

"Glad to see you up." Abigail, Ayla's deceased mother said as she stroked his hair. "You had us worried."

Garrett looked at her stunned. A tear came to his eye. "How? You're…"

"Yes. I am. But you're not. Not yet, anyway." She smiled mischievously. "Not from your lack of trying."

"I've missed you." He said, a longing in his voice.

"You need to listen to me, my time with you is limited. You're in danger. So is everyone else you love." Abigail said solemnly, dispensing with the pleasantries.

Black clouds slowly billowed overhead as they rumbled with thunder. The once beautiful sky became dark as the weather fouled, the animals fled into the safety of the mountains.

"What do you mean?"

"This is just the start, Garrett. It began when we landed here. We were warned but ignored it. Now She returns." Abigail's voice had become cold.

The sky rolled with thunder and arced with lighting. Torrents of rain began falling from the sky, but Garrett and Abigail remained untouched by the downpour.

"Who returns? We can leave. We can go back—"

"No." She stopped him. "It's too late for that. Events are in motion that will alter more than Voskavia. No land will be safe from Her threat, no city out of reach." She said, as she began to decay before his eyes. Abigail's thick mane slowly falling out of her head as her rosy cheeks sank in, her once vibrant skin turning mottled and gray.

"Dear God! Please don't leave me!" He begged as he caressed her face, tears streaming from his cheeks.

"The source. You need to cut off the source." She said as her body slowly crumbled into dust in his hands, leaving nothing but gray ash.

"Don't leave me! I'm sorry." He wailed his soul in agony at losing her once more, as she crumbled through his fingers.

"We know," Elizabeth said, standing next to him.

"My God..."

Elizabeth, his first love and the mother of Rohn put her hand on his shoulder. The Gerhardt homestead was burning as a fierce storm raged around it. Fiends of all types ravaged the manor as commoners fled. To his horror, those he loved were far too slow to outrun their assailants. Commoner and footman alike were ripped to shreds by enormous red leather-skinned demons that cackled and laughed as they fed on the helpless people.

Garrett knew these monsters were not natural. They were not of this world. His body trembled as the fortress cracked and fell piece by piece. He watched frozen in dread as Brom tried to fight the beasts off, but was overwhelmed as they ripped him to shreds, the lycan warrior no match for their aggression and power. Ayla and Rohn fought valiantly side by side as they had before only to be bathed in the flames of a gargantuan black dragon as it flew over dousing the entire valley in its breath. The heat was suffocating even at a great distance and melted even the stone of the mountain, turning it into bubbling magma.

"How can I stop this?" He said, watching all those he cherished die.

"It is already in motion, some of what you see cannot be stopped," Elizabeth told him flatly. "Unity will save you. Faith will guide you."

"Don't leave me. Not again." He said tears falling freely down his cheek. "I'm sorry I failed you, I abandoned you both when you needed me most!"

"We'll meet again my dear, just not yet," Elizabeth said, gently caressing his face.

He closed his eyes and leaned into her hand. Her warm caress a welcome change in the nightmare that surrounded him. To his surprise, however her soft fingers grew cold, her nails grew long, sharp, and pointed. Garrett grabbed her hand, as it had become scaly and cracked, thick with muscle. Her skin charred and blackened as ebony horns protruded from her joints. Finally, he mustered the courage to look up to his long-gone first love. As ash rained down on the valley, everything around him burning, he wept in desperation.

A massive demon had replaced Elizabeth. The ungodly creature grinned, bearing multiple rows of jagged teeth in its mandible accompanied by a twisting serpent's tongue, as thick black horns protruded from its skull. A pair of massive wings splayed open behind it as it roared into the sky. As Garrett looked up at the heavens once serene and calm and watched the moon creep in front of the sun. The ring of light behind the celestial body seemed to bleed upon the world like an open wound, slowly oozing onto the land like a deep crimson waterfall.

Shadows of more horrors silhouetted in the air as they moaned and growled far above him. Creatures Garrett had never seen or heard of circled above, obscured in the clouds, only revealed as lighting rippled through the red sky.

The gargantuan dragon landed on the rubble that was once his home, crushing it like pebbles under a man's foot. Its wings shook the mountains as Garrett flinched, cowering before it. The beast took a deep breath as its maw opened wide, a red light billowing in its throat as its red eyes glared at the puny templar. With a roar, a searing wind of white-fiery flame bathed over what remained in the valley. The knight screamed in agony as it incinerated his body to ash, his bones flaking into the wind, the flame searing everything it touched.

II

Sir Garrett jerked awake in bed, lying on a puffy, comfortable feathered mattress that billowed around his form. His weary eyes filled with sleep slowly focused as he became more aware of his surroundings. The room was nicely furnished and well decorated, warmed by the glow of burning logs in the hearth. The bed he lay in was large, almost twice the size of his at home, and was smothered with various pillows of different shapes and sizes. He slowly tried to sit upright and although sore and in pain, it was nowhere near as bad as he remembered. At last, he recognized where he was. This was the castle in Eirburg. Lord Harmon's home.

A familiar figure made its way from across the room. "You're up." Ayla said excitedly, in a low tone as she sat on the edge of the bed beside him.

"How long was I out?" Garrett asked happy to see her.

"Almost a week. We thought we lost you there a few times. The city already mourns the loss of so many, including Lord Marshal Hendrik. We feared you would be next to build a burial pyre for." She smiled, holding back tears.

He nodded and laid back as the plush mattress conformed to his body. The knight looked down, his torso wrapped in white gauze, and while he was sore, his bandages were relatively clean. It seems his stitches were healing well, as they felt dry and itchy. His mouth parched as sandpaper.

"Rohn? Brom?" He asked weakly, his eyes slowly shutting again.

"They're well. Brom is, of course, taking advantage of Baron Edric's hospitality, I don't think I've seen him eat or drink this much and that's saying a lot," She laughed gently giving him a sip of water from the table next to him, "Rohn is resting, he was with you for days when you fell unconscious. I've also received word from home. They are well, though Miss Shea was furious they had to use her supply of salt."

"Thank God. And the city?"

"All is calm for right now. We haven't seen any more intruders since the siege. The soldiers even reinforced the barrier of salt around the walls, but the colony's supply is running low. We need Stonestead back up and running."

"Wonderful, perhaps—" Garrett slowly slumped back still pale.

"Aye," Ayla interjected, covering him. "Rest, I'll see to everything else, we need you back to on your feet."

She kissed Garrett on the forehead and then made her way out into the hallway, letting him catch up on his rest. A steward was fast approaching as she quietly closed the door behind her, it uttering a gentle click in response securing itself.

"Lady Ayla." He smiled and gave a small bow. "Lord Harmon wishes to see you and your compatriots in the main hall as soon as possible."

"Of course, is everything alright?" Concern on Ayla's face, "What has Brom done?"

The steward chuckled. "Nothing, my Lady, Lord Harmon just wishes to speak with House Gerhardt."

"Alright, I'll be there shortly." She nodded, making her way to the room she was staying in.

The steward scurried off, his legs rapidly carrying him down the hallway to fetch the others as he dodged a pair of servants not slowing his stride. Ayla couldn't help but wonder what was so pressing as the hairs on her neck stood up. She went into her room and cleaned up before meeting them in the audience chamber as a feeling of dread crept over her. She knew the battle had been won, but she feared the war was just beginning.

The three companions reunited once more in the main entryway of the castle, Brom pulling himself away from the city's many taverns filled with dice games, pleasurable lady folk, and loud music. Rohn spoke with Ayla of Garrett, both happy to see him awake once more and as the three entered the audience chamber to their surprise, were met with applause and jubilation. The royal guards stood to attention their armor clanging as they did. Lord Harmon, Dusan, and Bishop Varik stood behind the table also applauding. Rohn noticed a familiar face in the crowd near the Lord's table. Lady Agatha stood gently clapping, giving the boy a wink.

"Please come forward." Lord Harmon beckoned them to his table.

The trio smiled. Rohn and Ayla were humbled, and a little embarrassed. Brom, of course, was joyous at the attention. The ranger gave the audience a flourished bow, shaking each of their hands like a celebrity.

"Eirburg owes you a debt of gratitude, especially young Ayla, who discovered the weakness of the invading army." Baron Edric said, the crowd slowly falling silent.

"My idea," Brom muttered, Ayla, elbowing him in the side. "Just saying." He added with a wince.

"I am a man of honor and one who recognizes his debts. What would House Gerhardt's request of their Lord for their loyalty and bravery?" Lord Harmon offered a sincere smile of gratitude, waiting for their reply.

"Well, my Lord. My father still needs medical aid—" Rohn began.

"Worry not for Garrett," Lord Harmon lifted a gentle hand to stop the young man, "He is safe here and under my protection. He will be well taken care of until he gets back on his feet at no expense to him or his family. What is it, the three of *you* wish." He smiled generously at the trio.

Brom was overwhelmed. He never had the opportunity to ask for anything he wanted, especially from a Baron. For once he was speechless as he searched for what he desired.

"Well, if I could use the workshop of your castle, there is a new prototype I would like to work on. Also, Ironclad needs repairs and refitting. It was damaged from the siege of Dumont." Ayla said, humbly.

"Of course, my resources are at your disposal, Lady. What about the two of you?" Harmon asked, looking to Rohn and Brom.

"Gold," Brom said bluntly.

"Brom," Rohn said, giving his ally a harsh look.

"Lord Harmon wanted to know, that's what I want."

"So be it. You will be paid well for your part in the battle, I hear you dove headfirst into one of the Fomorian's mouths. Such bravery and selflessness *should* be rewarded." Lord Harmon smiled, preventing the two from bickering.

"Our young warrior deserves a sword of his stature." Bishop Varik said. "Perhaps a weapon more fitting the squire. A master craft blade made by the Lord's craftsmen?"

"And a suit of armor to match." Lord Edric agreed.

Rohn's chest filled with pride as he nodded. "That will be more than generous my Lord."

"Before the two of you go, I have a request. I know you have done so much for us already, but it seems our worries are just beginning. Lady Agatha Du'Vale's fief has been abandoned. Stonestead has been overrun by creatures from its mines disturbed by the digging. This resource is vital to our future in Voskavia, as it not only fuels us with a steady supply of iron and stone, but also the now imperative salt used to destroy the abominations. I told her you would be interested in helping her, as I'm sure she will be happy to fill you in with the details and reward you for your efforts." Baron Edric motioned to Agatha as she nodded gently in reply.

"I would be most grateful," Agatha added, with a spry smile.

"It's settled then. The three of you will rest, recoup, and in two days leave for Stonestead. We are depending on you once more; the mine must reopen. Thank you, House Gerhardt, and God be with you." The Baron smiled.

IV

The two days had passed rather quickly. Sir Garrett was up, but not yet ready to leave his room in the palace. His wounds were still tender and not yet fully mended. This forced him to remain at the castle to recoup and rest against his wishes. He hated letting those he loved to go off and fight without him, however, he had more than enough faith in his family, that they could handle anything they faced so long as they remained together.

Rohn stood in front of the repaired and refitted Ironclad, the squire dressed in his new armor as its fit was custom sculpted for his form. A steel breastplate with a light ringtail tunic worn underneath. Pauldrons, gauntlets, and shin guards to match glinted with a blinding polish in the sun's rays. The armor was lightweight, allowing him freedom of movement, but hardened and resistant enough to withstand earth-shaking blows. His new blade was folded steel, a long sword with an extended handle allowing him to grip with two hands, but balanced well enough it could be used with a shield. The hand-guard was pointed, allowing him to use it to pierce armor, and the pommel was a steel cross that could easily crack a skull with enough force. He loaded provisions into the wagon as Ayla approached, the two smiling at one another in the warm early morning sun.

"You look well-rested." She said, her new crossbow slung over her shoulder as she carried a large pack of provisions.

She was in a new brigantine hauberk. A leather layer beneath gave her protection, including a hood. The armor was specifically designed for an archer, or in her case alchemist. The treated leather would withstand fire and shrapnel, as well as talons and teeth.

"Aye, and better equipped. Though I can see I'm not the only one." Rohn motioned to her new weapon.

"Yes, it took me a few hours to get it right, but it works. Two limbs cocked back with one mechanism, allowing me to fire two bolts rapidly. It reloads almost as fast to boot. I figure this will be a perfect time to test it in the field. That and the scholars gave me several new tombs from to pour over." She smiled, holding her chosen weapon like a favored child.

The two were interrupted as a heavy leather bag of gold the size of their heads clanged into the wagon. "That's mine, don't touch it," Brom said, as he pulled himself up and into the cabin of Ironclad.

"Nice to see he's in a good mood." Ayla chirped, both having a chuckle.

The night before, they shared dinner with Lady Agatha, who explained the situation. The Stonestead mine had always been a perilous place, but commoners were going missing in its depth more than usual over the past few weeks. This all came to a head when they abandoned the town altogether.

Several days ago a scouting party had gone to the village and noticed it completely abandoned. The manor's rooms were splattered with blood and gore, not a soul in sight. While the trio gave their condolences for the loss of Sir Edgar, she seemed only momentarily distraught by his death. Lady Agatha was more focused on getting the settlement back up and running than mourning her late husband. Whether this was her way of grieving, or simply, the three did not press the matter. They received as much information on the situation as they could and then got a good night's rest.

The party loaded into Ironclad once more in a routine they had acquired over the past days. Its frame was reinforced and repaired, the wagon was supplied for days and their four fresh horses reared eager to pull the war wagon. Rohn slid into the driver's cabin and grabbed the reins, Ayla joining him in the opposite seat. "You seem natural there, if I might say so. It suits you." She quipped smiling at him her dimples exaggerated by her happiness.

"Aye, Brom refused to handle Ironclad, but it took to me," Rohn said, preparing the reins getting comfortable in his chair.

"That it has." She nodded. "Shall we?"

"Just don't kill us. I've money to spend when I return!" Brom's voice bled from the back, muffled by the thick armor of the wagon.

The two looked forward as Rohn snapped the reins. The horses grunting as they lurched ahead, mud flanks bursting into the air. Soon Ironclad will once again be on the road. This time to Stonestead, to aid the Empire once more. They didn't know what they would face, but it mattered not. As long as they were together, it would work itself out.

Chapter 17:

Ironclad

I

Rohn brought the horses to a trot as they passed through the brutalized trade post of Dumont on their way to Stonestead. The bodies that littered the ground were now gone, as they had joined the assault of the capital. The air reeked with death as fumes of the dead lingered. Only birds and stray dogs inhabited the old fort, looking for scraps as rats scurried through the vacant burnt husks of both man and hovel.

"Damn shame," Ayla said, peering at the sight through the slits in the driver's cabin.

"Aye, needless destruction. And for what?" Brom muttered. "Let's go, Rohn. I'd like to arrive at Stonestead before nightfall."

"Aye." Rohn snapped the reins of the wagon lurching it forward once more.

They were glad to leave the place of death behind. It reminded them of nothing but hardship and pain. First Ayla's mother, then Garrett being wounded. The fort felt cursed, as if they built it on sacred ground, as it knew nothing but death and misery.

Ironclad roared down the road as the sun lifted towards its apex. Its massive hull a sight to behold, intimidating and formidable. Rohn and the others felt safe in it. It had withstood an assault by Lycans and survived the trek back to Eirburg in one piece. An asset to the family that kept improving with each repair and refit.

"Were almost there," Brom said from the passenger seat he now occupied, as he mouthed a piece of an orange, handing a slice to Rohn.

Thanks to their prudent planning upon departure from Eirburg, the trio had more than enough time to investigate and decide how they would deal with the infestation.

"Last few days, I have been thinking. Those seeds," Ayla said as her head popped into the driving cabin, "The infected acted like a hive, a single organism. Perhaps the seeds were aiding in the control, like a parasite. And the roots, its black liquid, same consistency as sap. Perhaps we need to search deep in the forest? We might find clues to what is causing the growth and infection." She said, taking a measure of the reactions of the others.

"Wouldn't hurt, but we should clear the mine first. We could use the support of Lord Harmon and Lady Agatha." Rohn answered his eyes never leaving the road.

"And how are we to get this monstrosity through? The horses would kill themselves." Brom's mouth dripping with orange juice.

"You could find something stronger. Like an ox, or a bull." Rohn chimed in.

"Durruk," Brom said. "Oh yes. A durruk would do nicely. Big bastards clear forests as they wonder and a full-grown bull would pull the wagon himself with the strength to spare."

"And how do you expect to tame a durruk, females are more violent than males especially when they have offspring," Ayla noted.

"I'll figure something out. I always do." Brom said, shoving another wedge of orange in his mouth.

"We're here," Rohn said, pulling onto the reins as the handbrake squealed, sparks flying from the wheels.

Brom's eyes followed Rohn's, as he gazed on what was left of Stonestead. They rapidly approached the empty fief, Ironclad's wheels grinding into the mud and gravel as it struggled to slow. What was once an industrial powerhouse of the region was now nothing more than a ghost town. The mining village was usually bustling to the brim with workers that slaved away from dawn to dusk, but even animals now avoided the settlement. The ripe smell of death and decay even fresher and thicker here than the fort.

Brom pointed to the Lord's keep. "Let's start there. Perhaps we can take shelter in the manor."

The settlement was in a state of disaster, not even rodents dared to venture within its vicinity as the mud on the ground was stained with what little remains the beasts had left. Ironclad came to rest in front of the abandoned fortress with a groan that seemed to carry for miles. The keep was eerily silent and void of life its doors creaking gently with the breeze, the steps inward smeared in dried blood, as the sound of flies emanated from within. The stench was foul; rotten food and meat were accompanied by the thick smell of feces. Rohn covered his face even before disembarking, the smell making him want to gag. Brom and Ayla quickly hopped from the wagon and scanned their surroundings, checking for signs of what happened and what to expect.

"My God," Ayla said, crossing herself. "This place, it's a graveyard."

"Aye, but all the corpses have been eaten." Brom said, "Small feet, dozens of them if not more." He said as he scanned the dirt.

There were signs he could see most men missed, even seasoned trackers. His senses were far keener from the blood he shared with Skadi and with the damp air provided by the overcast sky, the moisture aided his sense of smell, far beyond that of a man. The area was thick with burning wood and rotting flesh, the mercurial taste of blood on his tongue as it flowed through the gentle breeze that danced through the manor. The stairs were smeared with dried bits of viscera and tattered clothing. Axe in hand, Brom made his way through the double doors of the estate. The tattered banners and tapestries within slowly fluttered in the breeze of the oncoming storm. The ranger's boot squished in something, a foul stench emanating from the pile. Piles of scat everywhere, as it even ran down the walls. The embers in the massive center fireplace were long dead, but the scent remained. Brom moved slowly and with purpose through the keep, his eyes quickly adjusting to the darkness that gleaned of platinum.

Brom pointed to the top of the stairs to the others with a silent warning. The doors to each room were shredded through leaving large holes through the barriers, splinters still resting at their base. Something had clawed its way through the quarter-inch-thick wood as bits of skin remained on the debris. He tried to open the door with a tug, but it wouldn't budge. *Bolted from the inside*, he thought. He crouched down, peering into the darkness. The room reeked, a thick odor of musk, bodily waste, and a hint of rose water stung his nose. Brom looked to the others as he stood, then without warning, he reeled back, sending his broad axe into the door. The force of his blow split the barrier down the middle, his boot finishing the job as the door tumbled to the stone floor with a hollow clunk. Rohn and Ayla scowled, shaking their heads as Brom smiled and took a step into the room.

It was a horrific sight. Gore and bits of bone painted the granite walls, the once elaborate bed was ripped to shreds. Brom noticed a few corpses left. Small green fur-covered bodies. "Goblins," Brom said.

"Small creatures," Ayla said. She moved one of the heads of the corpses with her boot, placing it facing up, its eyes rolled into the back of its head, its oversized mouth agape.

"True, but numerous. They hunt in swarms and breed like rabbits. They cannibalize when resources run dry." Brom added.

"So how do we stop them?" Rohn asked, covering his mouth from the stench.

"They burrow, deep in the ground. Little bastards are afraid of fire, or light. Maybe we can trap the horde, burn them perhaps." Brom shrugged, investigating the remains of the bed.

Ayla knelt next to one of the small bodies, its stomach blowing itself in half when it burst outward. A gold ring was lodged in its ribs, partially digested by the creatures' stomach acids. With a gloved hand, she slowly pried the jewelry from its cadaver to bring it closer to her face for inspection. "They eat metal?"

"Aye, they can digest just about anything. Iron, silver, as they usually just pass it. If you're brave and so inclined, you can find their den. Sift through the scat and you'll find a few treasures left behind."

"What about gold?" Ayla asked, noticing the rare metal was only slightly damaged.

"Maybe, why?" Brom asked, seeing the wheels in her head turn. "What are you on about?"

"A theory. If your kind, Lycans, have a severe, deadly reaction to silver, as humans to arsenic and the invaders to salt. Then our little devourers must also have a similar weakness. These bodies are blown apart. The rib cages are shattered outward, not inward. Their tongues bare pustules. Much to the same reaction you get if you hold a silver spoon." She spoke as she investigated a few more corpses, all bearing the same fate with gold left in or near the remains.

"So how do we find out?" Rohn asked, "How do we get them to eat the metal?"

"Bait." Brom bluntly said. "This place is a death trap. They must've found a way in. Through the chimney, perhaps, as the windows are still intact."

"I have an idea as well," Rohn said, a smile etching across his face. "We're going to release a beast hungrier than them."

Ayla and Brom raised their brows with intrigue, dashed with a bit of apprehension, as Rohn detailed his plan.

III

After finally agreeing to try Rohn's idea, the group had spent the rest of the afternoon preparing rations they had brought with gold dust. To Brom's objection, they had voted to use part of his reward, but Ayla insisted they load the rations with large amounts of gold powder to make sure the beasts ate enough. They had formed a manufacturing line; the trio working in unison as Brom ground down his gold reward complaining all the while. Before the sun got too low, the brawny ranger had gone about preparing a few more things well suited to a large man with an axe such as felling a few trees and running lines to them from the wagon. The three were content they had done all they could to prepare for the beast's return.

As the sun slowly set once more over the mining settlement, the clan could hear squeals and screeches coming from the darkness of the depths in the quarry. The horde of ravenous little creatures was waking up and preparing for an evening outing in search of food for their ever-hungry bellies.

"I hope this works," Brom said, throwing the empty bait bag to Rohn.

"It will, we have no choice. What survives the bait will move to us if they don't run off altogether." He replied, praying they stood a chance.

They had parked the wagon in the old barn, their horses stored safely in the stone keep as Brom barricaded the upper rooms and stuffed the chimneys, while Ayla sedated the steeds so they would sleep through the ordeal and not draw attention. Brom had placed the trail of bait right to them, as they waited in the pitch-soaked walls of the stables. Nothing protected them except Ironclad, its body smeared in a mineral-based jelly mixed with common farming supplies Ayla had found in the barn. While it wouldn't make the wagon fireproof, it would give them time to use the buckets of water to douse any flames that caught, and God willing to use Rohn's escape plan.

"So where did you get this idea again?" Brom asked Rohn, loading another small barrel of water into the wagon, Ayla wiggling the container into place.

"In a book, I read as a boy. Two men wished to fell a massive dire bear that ravaged their farm. So they built a cage from wood and placed it in front of the beast's den, scattering bait all around them as they took shelter within. They had armed themselves with long spears and bows as they waited for the bear to approach, planning to slay the creature from the safety of the cage." Rohn threw a few more handfuls of bait around the wagon, the last of the tainted rations scattered throughout the barn, before he joined his friends, shutting the iron door behind him, sealing them into Ironclad.

Brom raised a brow at the young scribe. "Did it work? Did they kill the bear?"

"Oh yes," Rohn said nodding, "Though the bear got through the wooden cage and mauled them, in the end, they all died alongside one another. I always thought it a tale of how the line between predator and prey is so thin and easy to cross."

Ayla and Brom stared at Rohn with contempt.

"What?" Rohn said with a nervous smile, "It was a wooden cage, nothing like this design. I have faith in your workmanship Ayla, Ironclad will hold firm." He said with sincerity, his voice unusually calm and steady.

"I certainly hope so. I'm not fearful of them getting in as much as burning to death in a giant oven." Ayla pulled the lever on the top of her crossbow, the dual limbs bending back as their strings locked into place with a click.

The sun was setting now, in the final moments of its time gracing the forest with its dimming light. Gentle rays of gold and amber peeking through the canopy, fading as the ball of fire made its way down, giving the night to the shadows and what creatures lurked within them. Brom put a whetstone to the blade of his axe, caressing the edge slowly, almost as if in a trance as he repeated the motion with complete focus. He stared at the crescent axes blade as if watching for a particular sign that he was done and the edge was perfect.

Rohn's leg bounced on the balls of his foot nervously as he sat on a bench inside the wagon. They had done all they could to prepare for the encounter with what little information they had. The bait was placed; the horses sedated and locked away as Rohn racked his brain trying to think of anything he had forgotten. Their war wagon had been smothered in as much gel as Ayla could make. Their cloaks were soaking in a barrel of water ready to be donned at the right moment. As the thoughts raced through his mind, he noticed the surrounding forest had suddenly gone silent. Ayla and Rohn looked to Brom, his face staring out in the distance as he focused his senses.

"They're here," The ranger said. His acute hearing could pick up the chittering and slurping as they fed on the pile of bait in the center of the settlement.

"Let us know when they are done eating," Ayla whispered, Brom nodding in reply.

Rohn crossed himself, kissing his wooden cross, then slowly drew his blade, the steel singing as it slid from its leather-wrapped wooden sheath on his belt. With his free arm he unslung a kite shield from his back, the metal buffer was light and much easier to maneuver in the confines of the wagon. Ayla carefully placed two bolts into her crossbow, her delicate fingers feeling the ammunition notches cup the strings of the bows. Rohn took a defensive position before Ayla on a knee with his friends behind his back and his shield held to his chest, blade held horizontally in preparation ready to stab. The three warriors faced the door of the barn, peaking from the slits of the wagon.

They could hear them now. A low rumble of footsteps vibrated the ground, as the green tide flowed through the ghost town. A blur of teeth and claws as each one crawled over one another, chittering, screeching and yowling. Their tiny bellies bubbled as they digested the bait. Some of the goblins slowed as their meal was beginning to disagreeing with them.

A fraction of them fell to the ground wailing as their stomachs bloated beyond their capacity and like small cherries being squeezed they popped. Their insides bursting from their bellies like macabre confetti over their brethren as they scurried ever forward, the scent of food, flesh, and blood intoxicating. They could smell the new intruders as they followed the trail of tainted treats. Many of the little beasts grinned; remembering the place where they had fed on horse flesh many nights ago eager for another meal of meat and bone. They climbed over one another like swarming ants, all wanting to be the first to bite into their prey, ignoring their detonating kin as they drove forwards too hungry to care. A wave of teeth and claws rolled like a river through the barn door, crashing into Ironclad's stoic form. Blackness doused over the inside of the war wagon as the horde smothered the armored cabin. Small teeth and claws ferociously swiping and biting what bits of the structure they could get in their mouths. The pack growled and screeched at the sweet smell of the trio's fear-filled sweat.

"Now!" Rohn commanded. Seeing the last of the horde pour in, Ayla quickly moved to a rope tied inside the wagon leading up to a beam.

The slipknot slid from its place as four large barrels fell to the ground, their ends tied to another rope that wound itself through pulleys that yanked the barn doors shut with a loud slam. The horde and Gerhardt's trapped within the wooden structure together. For better or worse, only one species would leave this barn alive.

The wagon rocked as the goblins furiously scratched at the wagon, gnawing on its wheels, and eagerly stuck their small arms through the slotted portals. Brom was having far too much fun grabbing the limbs as they reached through the slits and with a yank they popped from their sockets. The ranger was making a disturbing game of it, as the wounded creatures screeched and howled, flailing backward grasping for where their appendage used to be.

Ayla looked to Rohn as the young man gazed at her, his face calm and steady. At that moment she saw it, what Garrett saw. He saw himself in Rohn. Solid as a rock in the center of a storm, his faith unshakable in both his God and kin. He feared nothing, as he was ironclad in his faith and family. Rohn gently smiled at her as she pulled the second slip knot.

This time the rope led to pins placed in the wall as they popped out one by one, releasing the lanterns tied to them that gradually fell to the horde below. The candles within floated to the ground, to the pitch-soaked hay around the side of the wagon, each glowing stick gently tumbling and somersaulting through the gluttonous mob of gnarled teeth.

The goblins hissed and snarled as the wax burnt their coarse coats of fur and singed their green leathery hide. Each one bounding out of the way of the falling embers, heads cocked as the candles slowly rolled to their final destination as the first one graced the black volatile liquid, tip first. Its flame gently kissing the ground as the surrounding area erupted into a violent flurry of flame. The fire roared through the barn, as it scurried to consume and slithered up the walls like a living being, sucking the oxygen from the large space gasping like a resurrected monster starving from its long slumber. The heat blasted through the ports of the wagon; the party flinched as the bright light of the blaze pierced through the carriage, its roar like a dragon's breath.

The goblins knew now what they had walked into. While not sentient, they were intelligent. They knew a trap when they saw one. Their small bodies began to burn, their fur smoldering as they scurried about trying to find a way out of the inferno.

"Cloaks!" Ayla yelled, as it was already getting harder and harder to breathe in the wagon. "Remain low, the smoke will rise."

Brom tugged the shawls from the water barrel and quickly handed them out, each one rapidly throwing in on and fastening it around them as they hid in the hoods of the cloaks. The soaked garments gave a moment's relief from the raging fire that swirled, engulfing the barn. The creatures began screaming and clawing at one another, trying to find a way out from the monster that was now devouring them. They bounded from wall to wall, their feet and hands singing as the fire engulfed all it touched, sucking the air from the barn as it grew rapidly in power.

The goblins had met their match, finally something more ravenous and relentless than them. The blaze feed on anything and everything in its path, roaring as each piece of timber and bale of hay fueled its rage. As the roof moaned and cracked, it began collapsing as the weakened structure slowly gave way. Wood glowing eerily as the primal element consumed it. The three were gasping for air, Rohn fell to his knees and Brom could hardly see. Ayla crawled low to the floor of the wagon. The floorboards began smoking as she pulled over barrel after barrel of water. The smoldering wood hissing as if the fire itself was infuriated at being denied the fuel it craved to feed itself.

Rohn coughed and gagged, crawling along the floor, the water now almost evaporated by the immense heat. Brom grabbed a large chain that lay on the floor of the wagon's cabin. Rohn reached into the driver's compartment his eyes watering from the haze engulfing Ironclad. Blindly he reached for the lever in the driver's cabin and as his hand found its way, he squeezed and jerk the brake, the burning hot metal singeing his hand through the glove. The wagon rocked as it was once again free to move, its axle connected via chains to a large spruce Brom had felled with his axe earlier. The weight of the tree laying on the hill direly wanted to pull the massive wagon down with it, but it needed a little nudge for gravity to take hold. All three souls pulled the chain Brom had been holding and tugged with all their might, the other end of the links wrapped snuggly around an ancient hemlock tree, its thick trunk barely noticing the metal around its form.

"Pull!" Brom yelled, "Damn it pull!" He choked.

Bracing themselves against the smoking hull, the wagon gradually rocked as they tugged the chain in unison. Their cloaks were now smoldering as little white wisps of smoke curled like locks of hair from their mantles. The floor of the wagon began to burn once more throughout the cabin. Flames licked through the tiny cracks of the wood desperately trying to find more fuel to survive.

The walls of Ironclad were now bare, the gel melted away long ago, its structure blackening as the fire desperately tried to engulf it and those within, its hunger never-ending. They tugged and pulled the chain slowly, the tree and chain acting as an anchor as the wagon slowly rolled. The trio growling and screaming, out of fear, out of pain, on the brink of panic as the barn collapsed around them. Brom snarled as the burning hot chain seared through his gloves, but he knew they were moving, just a few more feet he kept saying to himself. Their muscles were pulsating with pain as they flexed and rippled even Ayla bellowed, veins slowly rising from her neck. With a burst of air, Ironclad smashed through the back wall of the barn, embers, and sparks fluttering through the air as the structure collapsed fully on itself behind the now free wagon. The remaining goblins ran from the smoldering heap, their bodies nothing more than small sources of fat for the fire to feed upon. They howled into the night's air, as agony is all they felt falling to the cool soil, their bodies twitching as the life ebbed from them.

Ironclad rolled down the hill, bouncing as it careened uncontrollably, Brom's boisterous laugh filling the cabin as it did. Ayla and Rohn latched onto one another. Safe in each other's embrace as the wagon roared past the hemlock that had aided their escape and splashed into a small creek bed at the bottom of the hill. The war wagon hissed as it rolled into the knee-deep water, its form dousing in the cool rush that flowed past as it came to a stop.

"I'm not sure if I am blessed or cursed," Brom slowly said, catching his breath, "to be in the presence of minds such as yours." The man laughed aloud.

Ayla and Rohn looked each other over, their faces blackened with smoke and soot. Seeing they had survived mostly unscathed, they joined in with their ally, the wagon now reverberating with laughter. The trio collapsed on the now cool floor of the wagon, enjoying the sweet smell of spruce and maple trees that flowed through the fresh air that now enveloped them.

IV

Ayla hopped from the back of the wagon, splashing into the cold creek. The frigid water was refreshing compared to the hell they had just escaped, as she thanked God for every breath of crisp air she inhaled. Her emerald eyes scanned up the hill and stopped at the billowing smoke at its peak. The barn was still burning as it cracked and caved in on itself. The sounds of the creatures had faded, the roar of the dying inferno was the only sound she could make out.

Rohn splashed next to her the two still grinning from their close brush with death and narrow escape. Brom spat a slew of obscenities as he peeled the skin from his palms, although the burns were already healing they still hurt like hell, his hand shaking from pain as he cleaned them in the cool water.

"I knew it would work. Ironclad survived the Skadi. How could a fire take her?" Rohn spoke as she washed his face in the clear water of the river.

"I'll wish to never do that again, thank you. Being in an oven once is more than enough." Ayla grinned glad to be out of the inferno.

"This isn't over," Brom said, his hands freshly wrapped in linen bandages.

Ayla and Rohn looked at him their faces skewed. "They're dead, burnt alive, and if any escaped—" Rohn began before Brom began shaking his head in disagreement.

"They'll breed." Brom interrupted Rohn's train of thought. "Faster than rabbits, even rats. In a few weeks, their numbers will replenish. In a few months, they'll return, a new brood starving and chomping at the bit for fresh meat. They'll mature just in time as Stonestead gets up and running to full capacity, and we'll be here again. We need to stop this, make sure they have no ground to go to. Burn the nest and kill all left."

Ayla sighed, looking to Rohn. "We've no choice. We can't let the settlers be ambushed again."

Rohn nodded his sense of duty overcoming his fear. It was best to finish this. Most of them, at least, had been culled by the fire. The three gathered their gear and waded through the gentle water, leaving Ironclad to rest in the river bed. They made their way to the top of the hill, the smell of the burning barn thick in the air, with a whiff of smoldering flesh and hair assaulting their senses when the wind shifted.

Brom was the first to the top, his axe at the ready. He could do nothing but smirk as he rested his weapon on a shoulder, the two soon joining him at the peak of the hill. The barn still burned with embers fluttering randomly, but now only a bonfire instead of a roaring inferno. The outer walls of the husk blackened to cinders, barely able to stand against the gentle breeze that rolled in from the oncoming storm. Thunder rolled in the air, as small droplets of rain pelted Brom's head. The wild man opened his mouth to the sky sticking out his tongue with a chuckle letting the droplets pepper his face.

Ayla moved to the burning shell that was once a stable for more than a dozen horses. The inside was littered with small, charred corpses. Some of them still moving. The survivors dragged themselves across the ground with what little strength they still had. She almost felt sorry if they hadn't been trying to rip her limb from limb before. A gentle squeeze of her crossbow's trigger put the survivors to rest one at a time. Rohn joined in, putting his new blade to use. This isn't how he wanted to first use his long sword, but life was life and one must respect it even when taking it.

The creatures were just slaves to instinct, to their primal nature. Eat, breed, sleep, and repeat. He shook off an existential debate in his mind; if his life was worth as much or more than the creatures. He looked to Brom. He had to smile at the huntsman's zest for life as he tried to catch raindrops on his tongue when a moment before he was almost burnt alive in a mobile tomb.

They worked their way past the barn, Ayla glazed over her handiwork, the various bodies of goblins splattered across the now muddy ground. They had erupted from the inside, their gizzard spraying into the air as their stomach popped from the methane overload.

"Damn, lass, you were right. Pity them." Brom nudged one of the corpses, the body almost ripped in half, its white spine clear to see. "If I so much as sniff silver near a goblet I'll have your legs." He said half-jokingly as Ayla rolled her eyes.

She looked back down at her doing. A shadow of guilt flowed over Ayla. Though these beasts wouldn't hesitate to rip her apart alive, she couldn't help but feel remorse at how they met their end. Small figures no larger than a human child lay in the mud, their bodies barely recognizable.

"They were monsters Ayla, don't waste your sympathy on them. Save it for those who deserve it." Brom said, giving her a gentle nudge with his elbow.

"I know, it's just…" Ayla tried to put it into words. "Never had to take so many lives before all this. Now it seems like it's becoming a day-to-day chore. I don't know how I feel about it."

"You are still human and not a monster. As long as you can feel, even if your actions are justified, you will feel a bit of guilt. These creatures, the Skadi and even the abominations at Eirburg, felt no remorse, nor guilt for their actions. Reveled in it as if it was second nature and a joyous hobby. That's not you, girl. Remorse is what separates man from beast." Brom said, giving her a rare smile of compassion, knowing what it feels like to lose yourself to the monster within.

"We should move on before the storm worsens," Rohn said with a low tone, placing his hand on Ayla's shoulder.

She nodded and smiled at him. The two made their way to the mine opening, as Brom caught up. He had wanted to check on the horses, the animals still in their herbal induced slumber. The three approached the entrance of the quarry, its portal like an open maw daring them to enter.

"Ladies first?" Brom joked, smiling at the two.

"Really? You'd let me go in first?" Ayla said as her eyes narrowed.

"No girl, I was talking about the pretty lass to your right."

"Very funny, you're just a one-man minstrel aren't you?" Rohn replied, his blade at the ready.

Bromislav grinned and hefted his axe with both hands before him as he disappeared into the dark. No need for the torch Ayla prepared. After the third strike of her flint, the rope had ignited. Rohn lit his torch on her flickering flame. The two joining their friend into the mine's darkness. Their lights gently fading away.

V

They had been walking through the bleakness of the tunnels for close to ten minutes when they came across a large, open cavern. Its walls were covered in wooden scaffolding, the ground littered with tools and rubble, but most of all tiny footprints.

Brom inhaled deep, the place reeked of death. The musk of the goblins wafted in through a shaft below, its scent bitter and pungent. He motioned his young companions to follow as they made their way down to the cavern floor, their boots crushing loose rocks and dirt as they made their way.

The huntsman stood before the open portal; the scent was strong here. He gazed back to Ayla and Rohn, a look of warning. Both of them nodded in response, shifting on their feet, preparing for what the next few feet held for them. Brom's boots crunched in the loose stone, as he made his way through the tunnel, the scent was overpowering, thick in the air lingered blood. This was it, their den. His eyes scanned the darkness below, the recess gliding down a steep slope to the cavern floor below, covered in bones. Brom made his way down to the nest's floor. Bone clattered as he stopped at the bottom. His two companions soon following with slightly less grace.

"My God," Rohn said, crossing himself. The place was littered with skeletons of various animals and commoners both young and old.

They had been feeding for weeks, bringing remains back to their lair. *But for what, for who* — Rohn thought. His answer coming all too soon as low growls hummed through the cavern. The female goblins backed into the narrow alcove that they had dug, placing their backs to the rear of the burrow. Teeth and claws bared as they snarled at the intruders. Rohn and Ayla looked to Brom. He sighed and returned with a resolute but solemn expression.

The goblin's bellies were fat and bulbous, making them sluggish. Filled with the next generation of swarming creatures. There must have been a dozen or so of them. Each one capable of bearing a litter of recruits and a few months later, they, in turn, could bear their litters.

"How do we do this?" Rohn asked, hesitantly, his voice shaking and low.

Brom looked to the ground, a large shovel caught his eye. "As quickly as possible." He said as he set his axe to the side, propped up by a large rock.

He grabbed the shovel and like a spear thrusted it into one of the alcoves; the creatures screaming and yelping. Again and again, he smashed into the darkness, Ayla flinching with each strike.

Rohn made his way to another. This one stood about waist high as he plunged the tip of his blade into the darkness, seeing movement. He could feel his long sword slow as it met bone and flesh. He continued to strike until there was no more resistance in the stone cubby.

Ayla placed her hands over her mouth, tears welling in her eyes as the two finished the job moving from one alcove to another. Brom tossed the shovel to the ground as he spat. The ranger took no pleasure in this, but it had to be done. The ranger held his hand out, and Ayla knew what he wanted. She pulled from her satchel a bundle of pitch pots. Each of the monster slayers lit one with heavy hearts. Almost ceremoniously, the rope's wicks danced with flame. Rohn was the first to toss his pitch pot. The small alcove bursting into light as the grease erupted. Then Brom and Ayla. The room slowly filling with an amber glow as each alcove burnt like a small incinerator, the bodies inside turning to ash.

"Let's go, I could use a damn strong drink," Brom said, offering his hand to the others as he ascended the slope, his friends nodding in agreement.

The three left the mine that night and prayed they would never have to return. They gathered the horses and woke them with smelling salts, the animal's none the wiser to what they had slept through. Brom lead them down to the creek, and with his expertise, he harnessed their mounts in and pulled the wagon to the bank. Ayla had sent word to Lady Agatha with a messenger pigeon, the bird shaken but unharmed during the ordeal well protected in its cage, letting her know of their brutal success. They couldn't but help feel a bit of guilt about what they had done. After all, they were human, not monsters.

Chapter 18:

A Night of Knights

I

Lord Harmon smiled at Garrett who was sitting in front of his fireplace reading a novel as he opened the door partially to check in on his old friend.

"Do you mind?" Lord Harmon asked.

"No, my Lord." Garrett motioned him to enter, his body mending well with the skills of the clerics and personal physicians of the castle.

"Edric will do, Garrett. I am not holding court." The Baron smiled as he entered, making note that the guest quarters had changed little since he had been here last.

Edric made his way to the armchairs that were stationed in front of the flickering flames of the hearth. The aging Baron gave a small grunt as he sat. Both friends couldn't hide their age, their bodies could not hide their obvious secret. The lives they had led had worn them, both mind, body, and spirit. Edric sighed as he eyed the dancing flames in the hearth.

"When did we get so old?" Edric chuckled. "It seems like only yesterday we landed on these shores, wide-eyed and seeking adventure."

"Aye," Garrett nodded with a smile, "But time refuses to be held at bay. It marches forward without hesitation."

"How do you fare old friend?" The Baron asked, turning his attention to his dear friend.

"I am well, though I grow tired of chicken broth and milk." He chuckled as Edric forced a smile, something weighing on his conscience.

"As soon as you are back to your old self, I will hold a banquet in your honor. Your family will be returning home soon. As I've just received word, the mine is clear. The three of them were successful, though Lady Agatha will need to raise a new barn." Edric chuckled.

"Sounds about right. Are they ok, did they—" Sir Gerhardt stopped, almost afraid to ask.

"Oh yes, they were more than capable." Baron Edric answered, putting the knight at ease.

Sir Garrett nodded, relieved and at the same time not surprised. He had faith in his family and friends. The old knight knew what they were capable of, especially together. "Something weighs on you. I see it in your eyes." The Templar said bluntly, the Baron nodding slowly in response.

"I am sending a new contingency of soldiers back to Dumont in a few days. They are to fortify the fort. It will become a forward outpost into the wilds once more. Alistair, as you know is not military-minded. It was a mistake of mine to put it into his hands. I have to do something I thought I never would have to, dear friend." Edric said, sitting up straight in his chair. "I am once again calling you into service. I need you to replace Lord Marshal Hendrik and secure the frontier once more. I know what I promised you, but things have changed. The landscape is rapidly altering, closing in on us. I need your help, so I am expanding your lands. Your fief will now include Fort Dumont. You may tax it as you see fit just make sure it is up and running ready to take on whatever may come as it was once before."

Sir Garrett nodded, "Why not go to the Church? Bishop Varik has a slew of Templars at his disposal, and what of Sir Alistair? What will become of him?"

"I will find a new place for Alistair, perhaps taking over Hweabrea. He is a fool, but he does have a mind for coin, not war. As for the church, we cannot trust them, Garrett, I know of your loyalty to God but sometimes I question theirs.

The Bishop seeks any opportunity to pluck the colony from my control. As we speak, more ships sail from the mainland, filled to the brim with nobility and their servants. The other houses keen on biting into the land I have carved out. I need your loyalty. Enemies surrounded us, outside of our walls and within. Hendrik was loyal but…" Edric said, as he stood from his chair and walked to a nearby window, peering out. "He is no longer at my side. I find myself alone and surrounded. Overwhelmed." He peered over his shoulder to his concerned friend.

"Is power that important to you, Edric? The King knows you, your strength of character, he will not just brush you aside at the first sign of—"

"Weakness? Failure?" Edric interrupted sharply. "This is the defining point of my life. When the history books speak of me, they will know me as a success; the man who tamed the wilds of foreign lands and brought civilization to the uncivil. You know our purpose here is far greater than what meets the eye, Garrett. This colony cannot fail. Will not fail. You know damn well why that is."

Garrett sighed, leaning back into the deep chair, "How much does my family know of our mission?"

"Enough, for now. Ayla knows of the entity. Little more than that."

"So be it. When my family returns, I will inform them. Under one condition. I am to keep training my son, as I want my family by my side." The knight spoke firmly, but with respect.

"Of course, yes. It will be easier for the four of you to travel than an entire regiment of soldiers. I've not even the men to give you, we've lost so many. I need the remaining forces here, to protect the port. However, you and your family should be more than enough to handle what may come until we receive reinforcements." Edric spoke, his tone thankful and finally calm.

"I would not let these people come to harm. You know this, Edric. It is my duty to my kinsmen and, above all else, God. I will do all I can."

"I know you will my old friend, I know you will." Edric gently smiled, as the two shook hands.

"But in return, I ask of one thing," Garrett said, not yet releasing the Baron's grip.

"Name it and it will be done," Edric said.

Garrett smiled at Edric as the sun faded into the sky, the two soldiers once again fighting side by side.

II

Later that night the castle's banquet hall was bustling with nobles, servants, and entertainers. Three new passenger ships arrived, filled to the brim with eager souls seeking new opportunities in the harsh frontier. There was no shortage of people wanting to flee England, as the war was now in full bloom. The ships unloaded vital supplies, a fresh cadre of serfs and mercenaries looking to make their fortune.

Lady Agatha Du'Vale was reunited with her son Jasper and his posh wife Annette, who Agatha found as nothing but an annoyance. However, the Lady needed reinforcements here, especially after the death of Edgar. They wanted to obtain a firm grip on trade in the new colony and had to do so quickly now that their first settlement had been ravaged by goblins and competition was about to become fierce. Especially since the other houses were drawn to Voskavia like flies to a corpse, ready to make their fortune and spread their influence in the new territory.

Bishop Varik, Lord Edric, and Dusan sat at the center, with Sir Alistair Dumont at the end, four empty seats of honor separating him from the others. The chairs were reserved for the monster slayers, the warriors of House Gerhardt, and their patriarch. Arriving back as the sun crept over the horizon in the early morning, the three champions had slept through the day. Only briskly did they greet Garrett, as he was still tired and in pain, Brom groggily growling as he walked past the family reunion, tired and sore from his trip. Each one had quickly made their way into their private rooms, hot baths, and warm beds waiting for them. At dusk, they awoke, washed their faces, and dressed in exquisite clothing that had been laid out for them, custom-tailored to their exact measurements.

Brom, of course refused the garments, and wore his usual sleeveless wool tunic and studded leathers over it. Rohn wore a fine white dress robe, with a matching linen tunic and neatly hemmed trousers, tucked into well-polished boots. Ayla was a sight to see, the gem of the evening, her hair pinned up, small curls falling over her face like red ribbons. Being a tomboy, she couldn't help but blow them from her nose, her eyes crossing as she did. Her dress was lined with white lace, the fabrics dyed in soft rose, and crumpled velvets complimented her hair. The corset she wore gave her curvy figure and ample bosom a smooth and sensual shape.

Rohn grinned, seeing her so happy and in a jovial mood. "You look wonderful, truly stunning," He said as she took his arm.

"Oi, shut it, you're going to make me blush," She said with a shy grin.

Rohn couldn't stop looking at her as he escorted her into the main hall that was decorated with flowers, incense, and flowing banners. The nobles, all dressed in their finest, turned and applauded as the group entered together, Baron Edric and those attending gave them a standing ovation. The huntsman, of course reveling in such attention, bowed and kissed the hands of noblewomen playing into their adulation as the husbands raised a brow glaring at their blushing wives. They made their way to their front through the chamber, Brom to one side and Sir Garrett to the other in his formal snow-white padded coat, smiling ear to ear as he watched Ayla and Rohn walk before him.

The others were far more humble, giving polite waves and nods as they made their way through the crowd. Lord Harmon took his place standing in front of the lord's table, joined by Bishop Varik.

"Rohn, if you would please." Baron Edric motioned to a pillow in front of him, casually laying on the floor. It was made of soft auburn fabric lined with golden tassels and embroidered with House Harmon's emblem in matching stitch.

"Sir Gerhardt." Lord Edric motioned for him to take a place at his side.

With a smile, Sir Garrett moved from his family and stood next to his lord and dear friend. With great pride, Garrett pulled his blade from its sheath as it hummed, the crowd hushing in response. Garrett gently handed it to Lord Harmon with a proud smile and a slight bow.

"Take a knee, my son." Garrett smiled, fighting back tears, as Rohn stood in shock.

With a silent nod, Rohn gently knelt on the plush pillow, it cushioning his knees from the hard gray stone of the feasting hall. He bowed his head humbly before Lord Edric as his hands trembled. Brom and Ayla watched, stepping aside, smiling for their friend, their brother in arms. As he took his rightful place in their home, Ayla wrapped her arms around Brom's burly bicep with joy.

"You are to be commended for your bravery in battle, for your loyalty and service to King, country, and Almighty God. I confer on you the title of Knight of the Realm. With such title comes duty and a substantial burden, but one with purpose. A sworn oath to speak the truth. To obey your lord. To be a devoted servant of God. To be brave in the face of adversity and defend the helpless and above all, you will carry yourself with honor and distinction as you now represent God, your country, and the noble ancestors of ancient Avalon. Do you, Rohn Gerhardt accept such duty, totally and unquestioned?" Lord Harmon asked as those gathered went silent.

"Yes, my Lord, with all my heart," Rohn said quickly, wiping his eyes, trying to hide his emotion.

"Let it be known from this day forth I Edric Harmon, Baron of Voskavia dub thee Sir Rohn Gerhardt," Edric said, as he gently tapped the flat side of the blade on Rohn's shoulders, tears faintly dropping from the young man's cheeks as the hall erupted into cheers.

Lord Harmon handed the blade back to Sir Gerhardt who took it with a slight bow. "You have a legacy to live up to now. Though if it were not for you and your house, we would have lost Stonestead. Again, the city owes you a debt. Let us celebrate your success, and the blessings that have been bestowed upon us."

Brom smiled as he raised a cup to the new knight, the ranger slinking to Rohn's side and whispering in an ear, "If you think I'll take orders from you boy, you had better sit on my axe handle and save me the trouble of shoving it up your arse." Then handed him a cup filled with spiced wine. "Otherwise, congratulations," Brom stated as he wrapped his arm around the young man's shoulder, and the two shared a laugh as they drank together.

The meal was grand and overly lavish. Lord Harmon served pheasant, chicken, and wild pig, roasted in the enormous fireplace of the palace. The cooks scurried through the enormous kitchen, preparing rice puddings, apple cakes, and sweet bread. Stew was boiling in a pot, mixed with carrots, potatoes, and onion. Kegs of wine and cider were rolled in, propped on stands, as the empty ones rolled out by the dozen.

Lord Harmon sat at his table, at the head of the room. He smiled, hiding the fears he held for the future of his colony deep within, clapping along with the minstrels' tunes that chirped through the air. Jugglers danced, tossing colorful balls to one another, and fire-breathers shocked and amazed onlookers blowing flame into the air from a small torch, as finely dressed nobles laughed and carried on, indulging in their strong drinks and rich food.

A few hours later, Lady Agatha politely dismissed herself from the table. She glided with grace along the stone floor, which was adorned with furs and woven rugs. She moved with the grace of a spirit through the outer edges of the dining hall, smiling and nodding to others as she went. When she left the great hall, her pace quickened, as she had to return before her absence was noticed.

"Is all in place?" The familiar voice caught her off guard, causing her to jump.

"Dear God, man! Must you lurk?" She growled.

"I thought it best to catch you here before anyone sees us." Bishop Varik said, folding his fingers over his large belly.

"Yes, all is in place. And I take no joy in doing this, your eminence. I do this for the colony. For the good of the people."

"Of course you do. We all do. But if we stand idly by, Lord Harmon will have us swimming to sea in a few days. You see how easily you lost the mine. As we speak his hamlet is overrun and Eirburg recovers from a horde of abominations that ravaged its walls, what next? It must be done. When he is out of the way, I will recommend House Du'Vale as the replacement." The Bishop said.

Varik knew House Du'Vale was tired of playing second fiddle to House Harmon. For years they were brushed aside and ignored by the Emperor. House Du'Vale had supplied the King with all he had ever asked. Soldiers, stone, lumber, even food from their stores so he could have his festivals. No longer would they stand by while their contributions went ignored. Especially after the loss of her husband.

Lady Agatha made her way back to the table. She eased back into her chair with grace and joined in on the applause of the harpist as the musician finished her melody. Bishop Varik skulked back in through the kitchen and waited for the opportune time to rejoin the nobility sliding in as he introduced himself to one of the new nobles. An influential house that owned taverns and brothels and though they were considered an unsavory source of income, the Bishop knew best to keep all avenues of revenue open.

"Perhaps a toast, my Lord?" Lady Agatha suggested to Baron Edric. She motioned in several servant girls carrying trays of silver wine goblets.

"Yes, a toast!" a voice from the crowd chimed.

Lord Harmon stood, smiling, and with a gentle hand calmed the hall to a mere whisper. The servant girls moving swiftly along the tables of the nobles, each one handed a goblet of wine, brought in from the newly arrived ships. Bishop Varik joined the head table once more, standing behind the Baron, a smile carved into his fleshy face. Brom motioned the lass to just pour the glass into his tankard, as his companions laughed at the inside joke as they took their goblets.

"I would like to make a toast, to those we have lost. To all we have sacrificed and all the promise our future holds. With more houses from the mainland joining us, our resources pooled, I am sure, by this time next year we shall be dining on the opposite side of the continent." Lord Harmon raised his goblet, as everyone followed, cheering and nodding in approval.

The baron took a sip from his silver goblet, the room silent as everyone soon followed suit and indulged in the sweet wine as well. It tingling on the tips of their tongues as its warmth flowed down to their bellies.

However, to one person in particular the wine was laced with a bitter aftertaste. Their tongue tingled and went numb. A sharp pain shot up his left arm as his heart seized. He couldn't breathe as he gasped for air, his face sweating profusely. Bishop Varik clutched his chest, wheezing and coughing, his face beet red. The portly priest fell forward, bumping into Baron Edric as he clambered onto the table, the crowd gasping and shouting. The holy man soon thudded to the ground as beads of sweat splashed from his brow.

Ayla put her glass down and ran to the bishop's aid. She quickly undid the top buttons of his satin vestments, his face as crimson as his robes, white bubbles of froth coming from his mouth. Ayla cradled his head in her lap, trying to see if he was choking. Other clerics quickly joined her, falling to their knees as they tried to help their eminence. They desperately looked up to one another and then back down, putting their head to his chest. Carefully they listened, but nothing. They quickly crossed themselves, and as the crowd did so as well, mimicking the motions. A hushed and deafening silence fell over the hall and those attending as they waited with bated breath. One of the clerics closed Bishop Varik's eyes and whispered something to one of their brethren, the second cleric scurrying off through the crowd.

"My God, what happened?" Lord Harmon's face stricken with shock.

The young cleric stood with his eyes teary. "His heart just ceased my Lord. The bishop is dead." He said crossing himself.

"Clear the hall!" Edric commanded, as dozens of bodies quickly made their way out, looking behind them in shock and disbelief. Clerics ushered in, carrying a gurney to place the swarthy bishop on. Only the Gerhardt's, Dusan, and a few heads of the newly landed nobles' houses remained. The clergy covered his body respectfully with a cloth as four of them heaved his body onto the platform.

"Hell of a way to go." Baron Edric said. Sir Garrett nodding.

"What did he expect, he swilled more wine than I did and indulged in spiced meat all night." Brom blurted, his mouth filled with sweet bread and mead.

"Brom!" Ayla scowled at him. "Show some damned respect."

Brom shrugged, "The man has nothing to worry over now. He has joined his ancestors after an indulgent life. I mean no disrespect. You know, when I was a lad, the party had not yet really begun until a man died."

The group stood in silence, crossing themselves. Men removed their caps as the bishop was carted away. Passing through the crowd outside, women were sobbing into handkerchiefs held to their faces. The feast dispersed afterward; the evening not able to keep its momentum after the sad turn of events. The Gerhardt's returned to their private rooms as well, the evening weighing on their heads.

"Damned horrible what happened to the bishop. You never know when your time is up do you?" Rohn stated. The question was more rhetorical than inquisitive.

"Aye, may he rest in peace." Ayla smiled at Rohn as they made their way down the halls to their private quarters. "But things are looking up for you, Sir Rohn. Should be damned proud. You earned it, to be honest, I wasn't sure the plan would work, but you believed in it so adamantly. "

"Yes, because I knew I had Brom and yourself there with me. I knew the care and effort you and father put into Ironclad. I had faith in those around me. Faith that God would see us through, our cause righteous and just." He added.

She just grinned, patting his arm, hers wrapped around it. "You're a good man, Rohn. I'll see you in the morn." She gave him a gentle kiss on the cheek and carefully closed the door to her room behind her, giving him one last glance with a dimpled smile.

Brom walked down the hallway, swaggering all the while, a tankard in one hand, and a servant in the other. "Please don't tell me you're off to bed already, boy? The night is young, and the city is still awake. Plenty of taverns and women to go around." He grinned as the drunken woman giggled, biting into his beard.

"Thank you, Brom, but I feel I could use a good night's rest. Be safe."

"Suit yourself, Sir Rohn! Just don't grow old with only regrets to keep you company!" Brom bellowed down the palace hallway as Rohn made his way into his room.

The wild man picked up the woman tossing her over his shoulder as she laughed and screamed playfully kicking. "Which tavern shall we be kicked out of first lass?!" He said as he bit her bottom on the way out of the guest quarters.

III

On the other side of the keep, Lord Harmon had made his way to his bed-chamber. The night had taken its toll on his mind. He closed the doors behind him to the illustrious room, complete with a canopy bed, private landing, and a fireplace almost large enough to walk in. The servants had done their job for the evening and he had dismissed them early, as they already had his bed turned down, chamber pots emptied and the fire stoked. Edric made his way over to the alcohol cupboard and pulled two glasses, pouring a sip of strong brandy, the caramel-colored liqueur's vapor wafting into his nostrils as it splashed into the goblet. He took a sip and then finished filling the two glasses.

"Did anyone see you enter?" He asked, lifting the goblets from the table.

He made his way out to the veranda and there sat Lady Agatha, her silver mane flowing freely in the night's breeze. "No one, and what if they did?"

"The palace would be flooded with gossip, you've just become a widow and already in another man's quarters." He smiled, handing her a goblet, as he took a seat next to her, his arm draping around her shoulders.

"Edgar was a fool. You and I both know it. Why do you think I let him go? I knew his greed would overcome his sense of self-preservation. Not to mention he had not touched me since our wedding night. Even then, he was more interested in the stewards than his wife." She took a sip of the liquid the soft taste rolling over her tongue.

"Did he know?"

"Edgar? Perhaps, but he cared little of my wondering eyes."

"No, Bishop Varik."

She smiled at him and kissed him gently on the lips. "No. If the tablet had not stopped his heart, I'm sure the shock of my betrayal would have." She chuckled.

"We must not take it so lightly what we have done, you know. He was a man of God, a powerful figure In the church." Edric added, serious in his tone as he drank deep, looking over the city, its light flickering like fireflies.

"He was a treasonous blubbering lard. He plotted to kill a baron, and if Dusan had not changed the cups at the last moment, we would mourn you instead." Lady Agatha placed her head on his shoulder and nuzzled in. The coastal air filled with a chill. "Soon this will all be ours, together. However, we must keep the new nobles in line. So many fledging houses here now, the competition will be brutal."

"Yes, I need to begin searching for a replacement for the bishop in the morning."

"No need, my dear. I know of a priest eager to fill his place and well suited. He also wishes to see the colony thrive and is more inclined to let the nobility take the lead." Agatha added another sip of the strong beverage slowly loosening her nerves.

"Already taking the lead? So soon. And I've yet to be devoured in my bed." Lord Harmon prodded.

"Poor taste." Agatha poked his ribs, feigning a scowl. "I did care for Edgar, I just did not love him, nor him me. His fate was most regrettable, but, very fortunate for us."

"Yes, the two most powerful houses on the continent combined into one. Voskavia is just the beginning." Lord Harmon added, inhaling deep. "First the continent, then the throne itself."

"All in good time, my love, all in good time." Agatha cooed, as the two embraced into a deep kiss, their legacy just starting.

Chapter 19:

What Dwells in the Deep

I

Dale sat in his hovel staring into his hearth, the flames barely reaching out from under the log that lay on them. Everyone else had fled the hamlet, terrified the hag would take them or their kin in the night. The lake was now too dangerous to fish or farm kelp, as the eels had become monstrous, attacking anyone who ventured into the water. The creatures easily reaching eight feet and over ninety pounds could overtake a man as they ripped and tore into him with their thick, needle-like teeth. Dale cared little though, as he had nothing left. He lost his wife and now his son, their only child. His spiked club was his only companion now, always reliable and always there when he needed it. The witch was a coward when confronted. He witnessed firsthand her reaction when the club bounced off her thick skull. He would kill the devil's daughter or join his family trying. Dale had reinforced his fishing nets. This time they were fit to hold a grown man, made with thick hemp rope. With a deep swig, he finished the bottle of ale he had purchased for a special occasion, as he saw this moment as good as any. This night he would dance with the daughter of evil and meet his loved ones in paradise.

"I don't understand why we keep getting sent to these shit holes," Brom said, as he swung in his hammock dangling from Ironclad's roof as he bit into his apple.

"This particular hamlet you speak of supplies a large portion of herbal supplies to not only the capital, but to England as well, and is the Baron's fief." Sir Garrett corrected him not looking up from his book, as he lounged comfortably on one of the padded benches, his legs crossed and stretched out.

Since the Goblin infestation, House Gerhardt had quickly gained the reputation of dependable monster hunters. Lord Harmon was quick to dispatch them to Hweabrea to combat the witch in the lake. The refugees spoke of a crone which had moved into the swamp and claimed the territory as her own. It started with the disappearances of a peasant here and there, a wondering girl picking flowers gone missing to never return home. Then bold attacks on men in the kelp fields by eels that lurked in the depths of the lake. Soon entire families were ripped from their homes in the middle of the night screaming for help, with few coming to their aid, as their neighbors were afraid they would be next.

Lord Harmon swore to the settlers that the problem would be solved and they would be back to work within a few days. He then did what he does best and dispatched the slayers of House Gerhardt. The family now barreled down the road in a newly repaired and refitted Ironclad, the third design of its type, this time reinforced more heavily and adorned with an ancient Roman Scorpio light ballista turret modified for their needs; capable of firing a harpoon and various other ammunition. The wagon roared down the dirt road pulled with a fresh set of heavy warhorses, young Rohn at the reins and Ayla sitting coach, her crossbow in her lap.

Rohn tugged back on the reins as they arrived at the hamlet. The town was quiet and still. Most of the houses were farther inland, only a few nestled themselves on the lake itself. The young knight set the brake and made his way from the driver's compartment.

"Finally!" Brom said, rolling out of his hammock. "Almost died of boredom before the bitch had a chance to drown me."

"Pity that would have been." Garrett quickly chimed in his tone thick with sarcasm.

"Where do we start?" Rohn asked, looking around. He stood in the center of yet another ghost town.

The place was eerily silent, only nature itself dared to make a sound. Hovels ransacked and looted by either the inhabitants or scavengers. The sounds of the swamp sang through the air. Toads, crickets, and other insects made their presence known. Rohn aided Brom in securing the horses as the two took in the village.

"Ayla, assist me please, I wish to set the turret. Brom and Rohn, search the area for clues but be sure to stick together. I'm sure we're being watched." Sir Garrett instructed.

"Let's go, boy, we've work to do." Brom huffed axe at the ready.

"Boy? Still? I am a knight, had you not heard peasant?" Rohn joked, prodding the dangerous huntsman.

"Oh, funny one are you? I'll bow to you sir knight when you kiss the brown winking eye I sit upon."

Rohn laughed a little too loud at the crass joke, as the two of them wandered off into the night. Nothing but crows and vermin skulked in the shadows of the houses they passed, searching for any sign of life.

III

The odd pair had gone from home to home finding nothing but empty hovels, musty with moisture from the damp swamp. Small specs of dust danced through the shacks as blades of moonlight crept through the cracks in the thatched ceiling.

"No one here. Suppose we should head to the lake, see if I can find tracks." Brom said, as he tossed an abandoned wicker basket to the dirt floor of the hut.

"Aye, we can—" Rohn stopped as Brom lifted his hand, motioning him to listen.

A faint sob reverberated through the walls of the shack, making its way through the empty hamlet. Brom gripped his axe in both hands prepared to meet whatever it was head-on and armed. The two men crept silently, weaving their way through the huts scattered along the edge of the lake. As Rohn rounded a corner, Brom held a hand up for him to stop. Then motioned to the door he was leaning beside.

The cries led them to a small cabin, a few meters from the water's edge. Its door had been shattered and sloppily hammered back together with haste and little skill. Brom could easily peak through the open gaps in the planks of the door. His ice-blue eyes focused on a petite figure kneeling in front of a dim fire in the hearth. A young woman, in her late teens, wearing a drab peasant dress worn from her endless days working the fields, her slender arms wrapped around her body as she sobbed. Rohn moved into place, but his heavy armor made him far less stealthy. A plank of the porch gave away his presence with a loud groan, as the girl jumped to her feet, staring at the door suddenly alarmed.

Brom growled disappointedly at Rohn, giving him a look, as all the young knight could do is just shrug and grin sheepishly. The ranger shoved the knight forward, forcing Rohn through the door as the ranger once again crept off into the shadows.

The youthful swordsman carefully opened the door, eyeing the room, "We're not here to harm you." Rohn said, raising his arms as he carefully entered through the disheveled hut, "Lord Harmon sent us, to aid you. My name is Rohn. Sir Rohn. I mean, I am, I mean I just have been knighted… I'm a knight." Rohn stammered. Not sure how to handle this.

"A knight?" The girl asked, terrified, backing into the hut's rear wall.

"Yes, we came to assist you, are you alright? Are you injured?" Rohn asked as he drew closer to the frightened peasant.

She shook her head no as her blond hair tussled under its cap gently falling across her face, her arms still curled up to her chest as she stood timidly near the fireplace.

"They took my sister," She finally sputtered out her breath quivering as her eyes darted back and forth to the door. "Can you find her?"

"We can try." Rohn offered his hand with a faint smile.

She returned the gesture with a smile of her own. The porch creaked once more. Another disheveled woman stopped at the door frame, breathing heavily.

"Are you alright miss?" Rohn asked. Abruptly he turned to the new woman.

"Sarah!" the new figure said. "I thought they had taken you! The baron has sent us help!"

"They took mother!" Sarah exclaimed, her brown hair a mess as she tried to catch her breath.

The younger lass crept behind Rohn gingerly grabbing his waist, "Please Sir, help us! They will either drown her or force her to make a pact with the devil!

"Where is she?" Rohn asked the sister who was clutching his cloak.

The girl's voice slowly altered, becoming raspy and coarse. "The lake brave little knight. Singing a chorus of bubbles in the pale moonlight." Her face twisted as she hissed.

Rohn spun on his heels. Her blond hair had become black as night, her eyes flickering silver in the dim light of the fireplace. With blinding speed she lunged up at Rohn's neck as he tried to hold her at bay, her skin turning into a sickly pale bluish-green as her gnarled teeth snapped for his flesh.

"Does the young knight wish to no longer aid his damsels in distress?" She cackled as he fell onto his back, trying desperately to keep her at bay, calling for aid looking for Brom.

That's when he saw Sarah, or what used to be the shapely brunette, her form twisted and altered before his eyes. Her nose curled out and her once shapely limbs became gaunt and lanky, stretching to their real form as the spell dismissed. Her fingers and toes were webbed, ending in sharp black claws two inches in length capable of disemboweling a full-grown man.

"What's the matter, Son of Adam? Are we no longer your taste?" The older sister cackled as she blocked the doorway.

"Oh, but you're our taste precious knight! Gut you like a fish and hang you by your toes!" The hag pinning Rohn grinned a long, grotesque tongue ran across her thin pale lips.

The other sister ducked her head, entering the room to aid her sibling with the knight. She shuttered a few feet in and froze in place. Without warning, she let out a screech of pain, rattling the walls of the hut. Frantically she was reaching around behind herself. She spun, wailing in pain, Brom spinning with her as he clutched the handle of his weapon that protruded from her back, the sickle on his axe buried into her spine.

"Damn it, I hate witches! I knew they smelled off, even for trawler's wives!" Brom growled through gritted teeth as he twisted the axes handle, the hag falling to her knees.

Rohn used this time to wrap his right calf over the younger hag's leg, heaving his weight as he shoved her to the right off of him. She flailed her arms, releasing her grip as she fell to the floor. Rohn quickly gained the upper hand with the distraction and straddled her, pinning her arms above her head. Though only just over five feet tall, the woman was stronger than a full-grown man, cussing in a hoarse and unnatural voice, for someone in her petite stature.

Brom deftly swung his axe, cleaving into the side of the neck of the stunned hag, her bellows becoming gargled and rasp. He wiggled his axe loose as her dangling head spewed foul speech. With a grunt, the ranger swung once more. The toughness of the creature's hide surprised him, this time cleaving through, as her head spun to the floor. Thick, pasty goo spurting into the air as her arms flailed and spasmed, looking for her missing head.

The other sister's face was now etched with terror. She gurgled an incantation through her teeth, her body bulging as it ripped through the peasant's dress. Her face too, went gaunt as her black eyes glared at the young knight pinning her, surprise on his face as she contorted underneath him. Her body twisted and bubbled back into her natural form, her skin pale white as veins protruded through her slimy, thin limbs.

"Curse you, we'll split you like a fish. We'll dance to your screams!" She screeched as he thrusted her torso into the air, Rohn tumbled over her head, landing face-first into the dirt floor.

Brom hefted his axe, blocking the door. "Only way out, witch, is death!", he snarled, his eyes flickering silver from the light of the hearth.

Cornered, the hag slashed at Brom, growling and yelping all at once. Her long sharp nails singing off the end of his axe as he parried each blow, her long stringy ebon hair hanging like a curtain over her hideous face.

"Cleave you limb from limb!" She said in a guttural tone, fear slowly dripping into her voice, knowing they would soon outnumber her.

Rohn bounded to his feet as the blade of his sword sung being drawn from its sheath. The hag backed up, quickly stepping over the table in the center of the room. She whimpered and growled. She lashed out at Rohn with a swipe of her left hand. This time the young knight was ready for the witch's attack. With a glint of steel, three of the hag's fingers fell to the floor of the hovel like thin, pale sausages.

She reeled back hissing as thick white goo poured from her wiggling stumps. Brom used the distraction to position himself for the next blow, kicking a stool out of the way, he lunged in swinging the crescent bladed head horizontally, cleaving the hags right arm in half at the elbow, a stream of white blood trailing behind his axe as it thumped into the wall behind her.

The hag wailed in pain, throwing her weight into Brom with a shoulder butt as he tried to free his axe, her lanky legs carrying her out of the hovel in but a few steps. Brom slammed into a pair of shelves from the hag's retreat, as the room spun, stars fluttering in his vision. Rohn swung his blade, slicing a deep cut into her thigh, but barely slowing the retreating witch.

"Pox on you and yours, sons of whores, damn you to hell!" She wailed as she clamored through the door frame leading to the lake.

"Get her before she gets to the water, the hag will heal if she reaches her sanctified grounds," Brom yelled as he clamored to his feet, still stunned by the blow.

Rohn stumbled after the witch, her stride almost two of his. "I am forsaken! Abandoned!" she wailed almost to the waters of the lake.

Rohn couldn't keep pace with the hag in his armor, the weight of it dragging him down as he tried to run in the sand. As the remaining hag charged to the safety of her lake, a glinting harpoon sailed through the air, thumping through her torso, the barbed head poking through the front of her pot belly. The sky filled with the agonizing screech of the hag as she gripped the harpoon with her two remaining fingers, bellowing to the stars above. A snap of leather twirled past Rohn's head, as one of Brom's bolas spun around her bony legs, the Norseman bounding past the young knight with ease as he cursed through gritted teeth. The hag fell to the sandy bank, clawing and wiggling like a worm towards the water, only a few feet from her disfigured hand. She sobbed desperately, trying to reach her sanctuary, but the harpoon was attached to a light chain that held her at bay like a fish on a hook.

"I really, really, hate witches!" Brom growled as he slammed the butt of his axe downward, across the hag's jaw. The creature slumped to the sand whimpering, dazed by the powerful blow.

Brom lined up his next attack as Ironclad roared into view. The chain reeled the wounded hag in slowly with a rattle. Garrett yanked the reins, pulling the brake, as sparks sprayed from the iron bands on the thickly fortified wheels. Ayla grinned, sitting behind the Scorpio cranking the hag in like a giant fish more than pleased with herself.

"Don't kill her! We may need her alive Brom." Garrett instructed as he made his way from the driver's cabin, moving much better now, but still had a slight limp in his step.

Garrett knew while hags were creatures of darkness, they were once human. Power-hungry women who bargained their earthly forms for a taste of power. They traded the souls of the innocent to their patron, slowly losing all humanity as their gifts grew.

"Last time we double date, boy." Brom grinned to Rohn, heading back into the hut for the other hag's head.

Garrett approached with a pair of shackles dangling from his hand. Rohn leaned on his knees, trying to catch his breath from the encounter, as Garrett gently clapped the lad on his back, checking to make sure he was ok.

"Those won't do any good, creatures missing a limb." Brom spat as he made his way back, the witch's head he removed dangling over his shoulder.

Garrett clipped the iron around her ankles and yanked the bolt loose, connecting its chain to her shackles. "Talk witch, sister of sadism." He commanded her. "In the name of God, you will obey my commands."

She lay on the sandy bank, a few feet from the wagon curled in the fetal position. "God? God!? There is no God here, old man. Just pain, death, and misery. You will soon see it. Her roots now grow beneath us. Strong from the death we bring her, the pain we sow, the misery we plant." She cackled, peeking from beneath her thin black twisted hair. Her eyes were almost pretty if they weren't met with a crooked nose and jutted jaw, filled with jagged teeth.

"You sell yourself into the devil's grace and for what? Look at you, you're nothing but a creature now. No better than the beasts that slither in this swamp." Sir Garrett said with condemnation. "Repent women and we will put you to rest so God Almighty may judge you for your sins." He added.

The hag laughed her voice haggard and croaking. "Repent, the son of Adam demands. Repent and be saved? There is no place to be safe. No longer is your Eden protected. She reaches farther now than ever, even beyond our shores. Over the salt sea, her seedlings find new lands. The darkness will soon be all you know, chosen child. Vengeance will be ours."

Ayla glared at the witch as she spoke, the words striking fear into her gut.

"She'll give us nothing. Ramblings of a decayed mind and warped soul." Brom said, hefting his axe to a shoulder tossing the hag's head to the ground in front of her kin. "Give me the order and I'll reunite these two."

The hag retreated into her black mane curling into a ball staring at her sister's head; the mouth moving as if to speak as the eyes rolled backward. While most humans and even animals would die from a wound inflicted from the harpoon, she was already slowly healing. Her limb had clotted and sealed, should she reach the waters tainted with her magic she would be fully restored in but a day or so. Those she had drowned left their life-force in the lake for her to draw upon when needed. She silently began to mutter an incantation under her breath, falling into a trance, hoping to go unnoticed. Brom's swift boot reeled her out of it as it connected with her crooked nose, splattering with white soupy plasma. She wailed again, her voice reverberating across the swamplands.

"I am forsaken. Forgotten. Abandoned." She sobbed, her voice cracking and garbled.

"You sold your soul, witch, of your own free will," Garrett said, staring at the pathetic wretch before him, his palm resting calmly on the butt of his blade.

The monster hunters surrounded the hag now. Ayla dropped a cage from the side of the wagon. It clanked onto the ground with a heavy thud, its barbed bars made of iron. "It's usually used to capture hell-hounds and the like, but we can squeeze her scrawny arse in there with a push." The redhead quipped.

"In." Brom motioned with his axe, malice in his voice.

She scurried on her hands and knees into the cage, shivering with fear. Her scent was foul, a mixture of rotted fish and low tide. "She will come. Hell, you will pay." She cried in a hiss.

"Another hag? How many are there of you?" Brom chided, as he kicked the door to the cage shut and placed the lock with a click.

The hag was curled inside, growling and snarling at her captures. "No tainted one, son of Skadi. The Mother. You met her spawn. The Withered Ones, no longer inhabited by the souls of humanity, she has claimed their shells. She will claim yours as well, Her wrath will be swift and death will be slow."

"Well, I'm sure she knows where to find us, pretty one. Until then, you keep your teeth together, or I'll take them one by one." He promised, crouching down to her level as she reeled back from his cold gaze.

"Alright, we need to make sure we've got them all. Search for survivors. Hags will take prisoners to their lairs to either convert them or eat those who refuse. We must search for their den and make sure none are left." Garrett said to his warriors.

"Won't be able to lure them out, they'll know we're here. Bide their time and wait to strike when it's in their favor." Brom added, leaning against Ironclad, the wagon standing strong and proud.

"We go in after them?" Rohn asked his gaze on Garrett.

"We might have to. They most likely have a lair hidden around the lake, perhaps partially submerged." Ayla said as she prepared her crossbow after double-checking on the cage. The hag curled in a ball whimpering inside.

"We go down there and they hold all the cards. There damned fast in the water and they have beasts to aid them no doubt." Brom growled, shaking his head, "The last thing I feel like doing is swimming with a bunch of bewitched animals and God only knows what else that might serve the witches."

"Aw, don't be so timid, I'll go with you. Think of it as a gentleman's fishing trip." Rohn dared the hunter.

Brom scowled and hefted his axe. "So be it, but we'll need harpoons and short blades, our weapons will only get tangled and hinder us. We'll tow a line, when you feel a tug you real us in." He said to Ayla who nodded and returned to the wagon to gather what they needed.

Garrett made his way to the shore. "Here, help me launch this boat, you can use it to row to the middle of the lake. She'll be in the deepest part, sheltered from intruders." The old knight still moved swiftly, but his torso was still sore and battered.

Brom and Rohn disrobed to their basic attire, their pants rolled up and a leather jerkin is all they wore. They needed to be able to swim fast and quickly surface when they ran out of air. The two placed the majority of their gear in the wagon, leaving their favored weapons behind in place of one's more suited to the watery environment.

"You and your stupid ideas," Brom spat on the sand. "Just had to volunteer us. First, you almost bake me alive, now you wish to drown me?"

"You would send my father? He's barely able to walk, or Ayla? She's strong yes, but nowhere near your stature." Rohn shamed him.

"Aye, but it's not the hag I fear, it's what she might have conjured. These witches can cast spells, unholy magic." Brom warned.

"We'll be fine," Rohn promised him.

"I hate witches. Mother would tell me stories of Baba Yaga, the crone. I wouldn't sleep for days."

"A werewolf, scared of something?" Rohn chuckled as they walked to the boat.

"You've no idea what the dark arts are capable of. Make your toes curl and your teeth grow fur. It summons forth shit, not of this world, boy."

"I'll watch your back and you watch mine. Together we will persevere." Rohn chuckled, oddly calm.

Rohn just shook his head as the two pushed the boat into the water, making gentle waves as it glided out. A tow line trailed their boat tied to the back end, as they vanished into the haze that floated above the water like a soupy cloud. All Ayla and Garrett could do was watch the spooled roped gradually slither out into the water.

IV

They had been rowing for a few minutes, stopping every so often to listen. Nothing, not even ducks rested on the mirror-like surface of the water. It was smooth and flat, as you could easily get eight to ten skips across its surface. All was quiet only to be randomly interrupted by a rare splash out in the distance. The two looked at one another. There was a distraught look on Brom's face, then something nudged the bottom of the boat. Rohn pulled the paddles in, both men readying their short blades. Again something knocked on the bottom of the dingy. A flicker of black flesh peaked from the surface just a few feet away.

With a surge of power an eel lunged from the waters, its narrow fanged maw wide open, Rohn flailed as it went for his face, but Brom's blade had found its mark with a quick thrust. The eel squirmed and wiggled like a worm on a hook as his sword impaled it through its gills. The ranger quickly pinned it to the floor of the vessel with his foot and finished the job. A small spurt of blood shot into the air, its droplets rained on the water creating small ripples as the eel faded into death.

"Be on guard. I'm sure there are more of them," Brom warned, not taking his eyes from the water.

Rohn was alarmed now, the eagerness of youth fading. *Perhaps this was a bad idea* — Rohn thought, as his vision couldn't pierce the muddy water of the lake. Brom stood, carefully balancing himself in the boat, as he grabbed a harpoon.

"I'll grab them, you finish it quickly." Brom readied his weapon prepped to strike at the first sign of movement.

A tail flicked out of the surface of the water, the barbed spear plunged into the black depth as Brom grunted. No resistance as the ranger pulled the weapon from the abyssal lake. It had missed the animal, as they were far faster than Brom had remembered hunting them as a boy. Another eel lurched from the steel-like surface, this time at Brom, aiming for his groin with jagged teeth, its barbed fins flaring. Deftly, Brom grabbed the eel by its lower jaw, but at the expense of his balance, and fell backward, splashing into the black water.

Rohn yelled for his companion rapidly scanning the surface with his eyes, but another slithery beast burst from its depths, latching its fangs into the young knight's forearm. Rohn gritted his teeth as the fish writhed and squirmed its slick muscular body. Blood ran from the young man's arm freely as the creature shook, trying to pull him into the depths, water splashing as it slapped its tail on the surface. The scent of the dangerous animal was almost as bad as the hags, their breath smelt of rotted fish, and their skin was slick with slime that emanated a sharp tang. The water ruptured once again with white froth as another eel sprung from the black glass surface behind the knight.

The small agile creature's bladed fins slashed through Rohn's leather jerkin as it dove over the boat, leaving a bright red streak of red along his back as it vanished into the water. Rohn struggled with the animal latched onto his arm pulling it into the boat, its skin slick with mucus as it twisted and writhed trying to rip a chunk from the lad's limb.

Growling in pain, Rohn pinned the fish, leaning on the beast with a knee, as he drew his short sword from his belt. The mutated fish's jaws flexed as he eyed his prey, quickly realizing he was now the captive, as the polished steel slid into its muscular dark flesh. Rohn snarled and twisted the blade, the creature going limp with a sickening slurping sound as the blade cleaved into the arteries within its gills. Rohn spun on his heels, now on the defensive, ready for the next beast. A ripple swirled in the water as Rohn reflectively braced himself and waited, spotting the eel slither through the shadows of the water. Grinding the ball of his back foot into the bottom of the boat, he waited and watch for subtle signs of movement, noticeable disturbances in the water. The knight spotted the fish making its approach just beneath the surface. The creature's eyes locked on Rohn. With a burst of speed, the young man leaned to his right, as the eel burst from the water once more, flaring its fins, aiming for Rohn's neck. This time his blade found its mark, slicing into the creature's mouth horizontally, getting lodged in its jaw as it almost split the fish in two. The creature's limp body, well over twenty pounds, twitched and writhed for a moment before going limp staring eye to eye with its slayer.

V

Brom wrestled with the fish as he was pushed to the bottom of the lake by its powerful tail. Instinctively he held his breath, struggling with the massive creature snapping at his face, his weapon dropping below to the lake bed out of sight. The animal was strong, even more so, egged on by a fevered loyalty to its Mistress.

It snapped its mouth one last time gripped in the ranger's powerful hands, then with a quick flick of its tail, it slithered over Brom's shoulder out of his grasp. The beast flared its fins as it slammed into his body, leaving a red gash as it fled, his spines slashing into the huntsman like a razor. Brom gathered himself and waited. Still in the depths, he was surrounded by a forest of lake kelp and seaweed. To surface now would be foolish, it would attack him from below where he had no defense. He waited, calming his heart rate so his lung full of air would last longer. He could feel the pressure of the eels as it swam around him, as it displaced water when it flicked its wide tail.

His right hand bolted into the dense jungle of kelp, his nails digging deep into the meat of the eel. It was a powerful creature, almost pulling him as he tightened his grip. The eel's head snapped out of the cover of the kelp and bit Brom's bicep, sinking its needle-like teeth into his skin. Not one to be outdone so easily, Brom clamped his teeth into the neck of the fish, his head shaking like a dog. The water around the two clouded now with one another's blood as the eel struggled for the upper hand. Brom's teeth popped through as it broke the fish's thick hide. The native ripped his head back, feeling a mouthful of the fish gripped in his ivory canines. He could feel the jaws of the beast relax and loosen, as its strength faded from its body. Just to make sure, the wild man grabbed the jaws of the animal one in each hand, and with a brutal tug split them in two like a wishbone. He grinned happily, knowing the eel would never bite him or anything again.

VI

A large hand breached the surface and gripped the side of the dingy, startling Rohn. He quickly recognized the tattoos on the arm and grabbed it, pulling his friend in. Brom surfaced with a gasp, growling and cursing as he did. Both of them falling into the boat with exhaustion and relief. Brom laid on the floor of the vessel, his head propped up by a bench, as he let out a laugh. Rohn collapsed, his arms resting on his knees, grinning at the ranger.

"You alright?" Rohn eyed his shoulder. The wounds were deep but slowly closing.

"Aye, you think that's bad you should see the chunk I bit out of him." He chuckled. "I've always hated the taste of eel."

The two laughed as they regained their stamina, lazily lying in the boat. Something caught Brom's eye. A small piece of land jutted from the center of the lake. "There." He said, pointing. "She has to be near there. The only piece of land I've yet to see on this damn lake."

Rohn grabbed the paddles once more and heaved them through the water, as Brom gripped a harpoon ready for whatever lay ahead. Within a few strokes of the young knight's muscular arms, their boat slid onto the small island. Rohn hopped off, blade in his hand, Brom right behind him wielding both a hatchet left in the boat and the last remaining harpoon. Cautiously they made their way around the island, as the fog was dense. The two could easily vanish from one another's view, even if only taking a few steps away from each other.

Brom gave a slight whistle for his friend, waving him over to the side of a large rock. His keen eyes had spotted a small cave entrance dug under the stone. Only big enough for one man at a time, Rohn volunteered and slid in first. Through mud and roots protruding from the soil raking along his body, he slithered through. Brom took a knee and waited for the lad to wiggle in, then closed in right behind him, his eyes glinting in the dark.

297

The tunnel was pitch black and filled with the putrid musk of corpses magnified by the damp air. A pungent aroma that grew stronger and stronger as they slid down deeper into the belly of the island. The small tunnel finally opened to a large cavern as Rohn rolled out, his body caked in thick mud. A body of water to his left splashed gently against the cavern's bank. The large cave was submerged under the surface, the void in the island acted like a bubble or pocket of air. He stood carefully. The echo of the cave gave away its size, although he could see little in the inky darkness. The ceiling of the cave was a good five feet from his head as the rest of it veered out into various nooks doused in shadow. He could hear Brom slide behind him, the man grunting as he rolled in the mud.

"I can't see a damned thing," Rohn whispered.

Brom stood, his eyes quickly adjusting to the low light. His eyes scanned his new environment, then halted on a figure to the back of the cave. "Follow me." He said in a low tone, as he crouched low, ready for another fight.

As they drew deeper into the cavern, they could hear a gentle sobbing. Whimpering coming from the dark. Brom grabbed a bone from the dirt and wrapped some sackcloth around it, the fabric smeared with old blood. He quickly pulled his flint from his belt pouch and snapped it across his sword. Sparks bounced and danced off the fabric, the rapid flashes shortly illuminating the immediate area for only a second before fading. The damp fabric resisting the warm embers of flint. Then, with a small pop, a dried portion caught and sprang to life. Brom handed the makeshift torch to his companion with a grin. "We need to be quick, that won't last long." He warned him.

Rohn nodded and followed the veteran huntsman, the two making their way to the small slender figure in the corner, curled into a ball. It was a young woman. Her clothing ripped and soaking wet. Rohn wanted to rush to her side, but with caution moved around her, trying to glimpse her face.

"Are you alright, were here to help." He said softly.

"She's in the water, you must be careful. She's resting." The woman replied, a quiver in her voice as she shivered from fear and the cold, wet air.

Brom's eyes moved to the water, small ripples ebbing onto its bank. The room stunk like filth, scat, and decay. His senses were overloaded, as he tried to focus, wafting the air in, his nose raised to the ceiling. Something wasn't right again. Just like the hut. He smelt a human, the sharp mercurial taste of blood thick in the cavern. Rohn tried to cover the frightened woman with a nearby shawl that was damp and muddy.

"Come, we'll get you to safety." He said, rubbing her shoulders trying to warm her up.

"She wanted me to join her, take the vow and swear my loyalty to their mistress." She whimpered, her body heaving as she sobbed.

Brom's eyes gazed through the chamber resting on the corpse of a man dangling from the ceiling, seaweed wrapped around his ankles. His chest was ripped open, ivory bone protruding from the gap. The man's heart had been removed. A nailed club dangled from his wrists by a leather strap. He looked at the frightened woman as Rohn took her hand. Her nails were red, dried with blood.

"Rohn. Step back." He ordered his gaze not leaving the woman.

"What? Why—" Rohn asked, but knew the answer as soon as he heard his companion's tone.

"Step away from the hag boy." He snarled, the stranger's eyes narrowing at Brom.

The woman let out a blood-curling screeched and with blinding speed she lashed out, her fine and soft features warping back into that of a swamp hag. She hissed violently, slashing at Rohn. The young man tripped and fell to his back, trying to retreat by kicking his feet in the slick mud. Brom's harpoon thumped into her chest at the last moment. The rope connected tightly in place as Brom tugged. She slowed only momentarily, spinning with unnatural speed, her arms flaring open, claws outstretched, as she sprinted for the huntsman. Rohn's torch rolled from his grip and doused itself in a puddle. The cavern once again going dark as the walls echoed with screams and bellows.

VII

Ayla paced on the roof of the wagon. It had been some time now since the rope stopped moving. "You think they are alright? I mean it hasn't moved an inch." She asked for the fifth time in ten minutes.

"Aye," Sir Garrett answered, again. "Brom and Rohn can handle themselves. You forget our native friend is not completely human." He said over his shoulder to the nervous girl.

"I suppose," she sighed and crouched down. She looked out into the fog. Helplessly searching for any sign of life.

A small shadow darted through the mist. "There!" She pointed, dropping to a knee behind the Scorpio turret, glaring between two small vertical plates that acted as a shield.

The figure bound from shadows of the fog, quickly over the sand and stopped, staring at the two. The deer's eyes slowly blinking scanning them as they stared back. Garrett let out a chuckle, releasing the grip of his sword. "Be still. God is with them. They will find their way." He said as the doe bounded off into the mist, vanishing into the dark.

Ayla saw the rope slowly slide, barely an inch. Then again, it twitched in the water, leaving visible ripples. "Look!" She pointed, both nervous and relieved.

The knight stood slowly with a wince, his muscles not what they once were weak from the days of bed rest. The rope suddenly unraveled and held taught. Then relaxed and jerked again and again. "Crank lass, quickly!" Garrett ordered, pulling on the rope as hard as he could.

Ayla cranked the spool on the back of the wagon. The teeth of the mechanism clanking as it bounced rapidly as she spun the handle. Both were holding their breath, praying to see their friends appear. Garrett set his hand once more on his blade's handle. He saw a shadow moving through the mist, a vague shape glided on the water.

Slowly the boat came into view, sliding through the curtain of fog. Even the hag watched with anticipation, her long fingers curled around the bars of the cage. The elder sister's head floated into view, resting on the bow of the vessel, her jaw slack and dangling unnaturally. Brom and Rohn sat in the dingy, weary as they were pulled into shore. The men were muddy. Covered in soil and blood. They looked like they had just gone to hell and back. Though they appeared in rough shape, they had smiles on their mud-caked faces. Their eyes and teeth standing out in stark contrast to the blackish mud, as the boat floated into the bank. Brom hopped out and pulled it ashore, Rohn threw the head of the hag onto the sand.

The remaining witch whimpered and groaned at the sight of her sister's twisted face, her eyes still staring ahead, mouth agape and lifeless.

"We're done. I don't want to see a fish, or another lake for months." Brom spat, the five large gashes across his chest almost healed.

"Are you two alright?" Ayla shouted as she hurried to them.

Brom was in pain but gradually healed as his body regenerated the tissue lost in the scuffle, the man starving for something to eat. "I just want to see beer and breasts. Roasted chicken or a blonde tavern wench will do just fine." He quipped.

Ayla rolled her eyes and moved to Rohn. His arm looked bad, it was getting infected as it was swelling with a purple hue. "I'll need to tend to that," she said. "Let's get the two of you cleaned up and in the wagon."

The men washed in the lake's water with noticeable caution. They explained what had happened with the eels and finally coming across the final sister. The hags were well adept at casting alteration incantations; it was an old spell that shamans of Brom's tribe could cast through great effort, but these hags did so with little difficulty, indicating their patron was a powerful one. With focus, the witch would use the heart of the person she wished to imitate and could take the person's form. Garrett glared at the hag's head and crossed himself.

"Magic is of the devil. False powers given to seduce fools to do the wicked bidding of their master." Garrett snarled, disdain clear in his voice.

He glared at the hag in the cage. The last of the monstrosities curled within. Although he wanted to end the creature's life, it was rare for them to be captured. What the scholars and clerics would learn from her could be invaluable.

"We bring the last one back alive. You two clean up, get dressed. Ayla tend to them, please. I'll drive the wagon back to Eirburg. You men deserve some rest, as do you my dear." He smiled proud of his companions.

Again they had performed as expected, like a well-oiled machine. Each one knew their place, their strengths, and tried to overcome their weaknesses. It was all he could ask from anyone. He knew a day would come when he no longer led them or when they were not on the winning side. Hard times find everyone, no matter how far one runs. He took solace though, as he knew hard times made hard men. A sword is forged in fire, not a gentle breeze. Their struggles would mold them into better versions of themselves.

The old templar hoisted himself up into the driver's compartment, giving the caged witch one last glare as he did, the iron crate fastened to the side of Ironclad once more. With a snap of the reins, the horses reared, flanks ripped from the earth flying into the air. Ironclad made its way back through the village and down the road to Port Eirburg. The slayers carried a prize for Lord Harmon that no man had ever brought him.

Chapter 20:

A Time to Reap and a Time to Sow

I

The ship had been out to see for a few days now. Its sails filling with the wind as its crew hustled about, Gravy among them, as the veteran sailor was a boon to any vessel he manned. The old seaman went below deck, skulking through the shadows, to light his pipe with a candle in one of the lanterns. He puffed it to life, white smoke billowing from his mouth as he skimmed over the ship's cargo bay.

Below deck, they had secured a shipment on the way to the mainland. It was filled with fine lumber, gently wrapped in canvas cloth to keep it dry from the harsh water of the sea. Gravy noticed something furry laying on its side between the crates. *One of the cats*, he thought. Taking another big puff as he made his way to the deck of the ship, leaving the animal to its solitude.

If Gravy had been a little more curious, he would have noticed the cat was not alone, nor was it still alive. Flies buzzed around its cadaver; several rats scurried from their victim. Usually, nothing more than a nuisance to civilization this small furry creature would become death incarnate. It slowly squeezed its way through the side of one of the many crates, where it reunited with its brethren. The family of rats that rode this ship were special, chosen vessels to carry a message to the homeland of the settlers. Their small bodies carried a gift, an ember of The Mother faintly glowed in their chests. Within each one a small bulb pulsed with a warm amber flicker, waiting for their chance to sprout.

In the ancient sanctum below Fort Dumont, two figures walked its darkly lit halls. Since the attack on the capital, The Mother's roots swelled and ripped through the soil, now throbbing through the hidden temple as She expanded even further. She had once again claimed the archaic citadel of Her secret servant's thanks to her favored son. The robed silhouette of the Prince of Thorns was most dominant in his ornate crimson garb, as he gently caressed the pulsing vines with his blackened clawed fingers, making his way through its recently restored halls.

The Prince had grown substantially in power, the braziers and torches mystically bursting to life effortlessly at his whim as he casually made his way through his sanctuary. He was shadowed by another figure, a lesser servant of Sytal. The man was nothing more than a pawn. A plaything at his disposal. As a servant of Sytal, the brother wore the customary black robe and a mask of his chosen patron, the raven. The acolyte hurried to keep pace with his Prince and would be king, eager to please the powerful warlock.

"Did the ship make it out of port?" the sorcerer asked, already knowing the answer.

"Yes my Prince," The figure slightly bowed trying to keep pace with his master. "Lord Harmon expects nothing. The only people aware of the shipment's contents were those that are loyal servants. They hurried the shipment off on a small merchant vessel, with your message to the mainland."

"Your ship, is it not?" The Prince added as more of a statement than a question.

The robed figure's stomach knotted as the Prince slowly turned to face his brother. "Did you think your anonymity extended to me? Your lackeys may not know of your deeds, but I know everything about you, Sir Alistair Dumont, merchant knight and coward of the frontier."

Alistair's pudgy hand rose to his mask as he slowly removed it, his hands trembling. "I have served my purpose have I not, loyally and faithfully. I pray the Mother will recognize my efforts and spare me Her wrath? Perhaps a small token for my troubles, to live out my days in peace and good health."

"My dear brother." The Prince's clawed hand laid on the trembling knight's shoulder as Alistair swallowed hard. "She knows of your loyalty. The Mother also knows the only reason you serve Her is that you fear death and the various ways it can be served to you. She must make sure you are loyal to Her for eternity. We must not cling to one form, as Her plan alters, so must we. But fret not, my brother. We still have much work to do. You are more useful as you are."

The merchant knight nodded, relieved for now. "I swear I will earn Her mercy. My devotion is unshakeable."

"Of course you will. I have no doubt… you're dismissed." The Prince said, gently motioning him to the entrance.

Alistair moved hurriedly through the hall, placing his mask back on his sweaty face and balding head, as his legs moved as quickly as they could. The terrified man removing himself from the Prince's presence as quickly as possible. Another figure moved in the shadows behind the sorcerer. This figure moved with the feline grace; her mere walk was enticing to the eye. She slithered behind her one true love, her Prince, and would be king.

"I missed you," He whispered. "I ached to see your face once more, as the summer begs for rain."

Maisie stepped from the shadows, her blackened feet tip-toeing playfully like a dancer over the newly repaired floor, a grin of elation on her face, her black eyes fluttering. The Prince's face distorted and twisted, his mask dissolving back into his veined flesh as a grin grew across his mouth.

Maisie slid into his embrace, her dainty blackened fingers wrapping around his biceps as she stared up at him with adoration. Aiden grabbed his love around her slender waist as he kissed her deeply. Her smell intoxicating, an aroma of lilacs and lilies, her long curly mane black as pitch flowing over her shoulders like a shawl. She remained in the same white linen sleep gown that she had passed in, its thin fabric showing her shapely figure. Her fair skin was now webbed with black veins, blessed with the Mother's life force. Aiden didn't care how she looked however, he would take Maisie anyway he could and the Mother knew this. Aiden slowly danced with his soul mate to the sound of silence. The two lost in the moment, as the Mother's roots gradually squirmed around them, twisting and writhing with joy.

Aiden was chosen for a reason. He knew the forests well. He had played in them as a small child, hiding from the others who bullied him. All he ever wanted was acceptance. He would offer his friendship to those of the fort, and all he ever got in return was disdain and punishment. This festered in him becoming resentment and hatred especially when he lost the two people he ever cared for. The children tortured him, claiming his parents hated him so much they died to get away from him. So he did all he could do and found refuge in the forests. Away from the town where those that persecuted him were afraid to tread. He never feared the beasts that lurked in its woods, and why would he? What was the worse that would happen? The truth was, some days he went into the forest to die, hoping the beasts would devour him quickly and end his suffering. The darkness grew inside the boy and he found it ironic that the commoners who feared monsters so deeply, with no hesitation created one themselves. No, Aiden never feared the forest, as that is where he met the two most important people in his life.

The first was a young woman, who pitied the boy. She showed him kindness to protect his fragile feelings unwittingly leading him on, letting the young man think more of her than she did him. He fell for Maisie, deeply in love with her, but the feelings were not mutual. Yet he followed her like a lost puppy, vying for her attention as the town mocked him. She was his only friend and confidant that remained in this harsh world.

That was until he came across another. This one was but a sapling when he came across Her alone in the woods, dwarfed by the mighty trees that surrounded Her, hidden in their shadows. She whispered to him, making sweet promises of power and revenge, filling his mind with dark purpose. He thought he was going mad until she proved herself, and the entity rewarded the vulnerable young man for his service. She empowered the boy with dark magic pulled from another world, giving him gifts an orphaned serf could only dream of.

When he asked what he was to call., she simply replied "Mother". Her tone soft and sweet in the abandoned boy's ears, soothing his broken heart. She needed his help, as she was starving and weak from the brutal retaliation of a more powerful entity. The sapling needed more than just rain and sunlight. She needed more than material sustenance. She craved negative energy to be exact, that of war, death, and strife as she thrived on it. Pain was Her soil, misery Her sunshine. The boy was all too happy to help the small entity. He had plenty of enemies to offer Her. The frail being, encased in an oak sapling, was carefully dug up and placed before Her in a burlap sack to protect the entity's frail roots. The Mother had told him of a geyser of dark power. A well to the abyss, deep in the woods. Her home that she had been uprooted from so cruelly and without mercy. Aiden obeyed, wanting to please his new Mother, his caretaker and with little to fear with the ancient spirit in his arms, the monsters of the realm left him to his duty.

It took the boy days to reach the fountain of dark miasma; the forest blackened and withered around the unholy breach. Spiritual warriors, The Templar of the One Church called these fissures of raw energy "Hellmaws". Rare portals that tore into the world, giving access to the material plane. Aiden had read of such places in books he bought with his meager wages.

Castle Houska, a palace built over a bottomless pit to the underworld, was one such place. The massive fortress was raised to protect the nearby village from the demons that crawled from it at night. Instead of a castle in this well of darkness, Aiden would plant a little sapling. His much-adored new matriarch. She promised Aiden that as she grew stronger and more powerful, so would he, as they had a bond, just like mother and child. He had become Her little prince; the most favored. So Aiden fed Her, small animals at first, then stolen livestock as she grew, Her roots reaching down into the well of unholy energy eagerly vying for its power. Soon She was large enough to tap into its well and began bearing fruit that Aiden carried as his own, protecting them. Small little acorn-shaped masses that pulsed and squirmed with vile power.

The Mother had taught him how to plant them and nurture them. She explained that they needed vessels, bodies to survive. Aiden used animals at first, then societies unwanted, luring them with the promise of easy coin as no one would miss them. With the Withered, the Mother had servants to attend to Her. Her eyes and ears; an army of abominations. With the Withered's numbers quickly growing, Aiden was free to work on his Mother's dark agenda and formulate plans for Her return. He was tasked with the disposal of the scions of Adam. A powerful bloodline passed down through the generations burdened with both power and purpose. The Mother knew of the Gerhardt's. The scent of the Creator was all over them, a wretched sensation to have them walk on Her soil, causing the Mother's roots to curl with anger. Such a horrid hatred She carried for them, especially Sir Garrett. The monster slayer, the holy man, the stench at Her meal, the thorn in Her shoe. He rallied his kinsmen once before and led a holy crusade as he cleansed Her servants from the territory. Though it worried Her a little, these were but minor setbacks. She was ancient. A being that was here before man and its prehistoric predecessors and would be here long after.

After weeks of Aiden's careful tending and nurturing, She had become a mighty oak, bark as black as night and thorns the size of a man's arm. Her roots pulsed with a limitless source of dark power. The rift feeding Her omnipotent form as she guzzled its essence greedily. She decided it was finally time for Her chosen child's due rewards.

Aiden had followed Maisie's father to the lumber camp and waited for dusk with the Mother's blessing. Maisie's father had never liked him, always said his daughter could do better than a laborer, and she believed him. Aiden enjoyed what he had done that night, cutting the men down like weeds. Splitting them like lumber. After he had dispatched them, he planted the seedlings. The Mother's roots soon took hold of the fresh vessels, just like those before them. Aiden had been critical in Her growth. He was the wind that carried Her, the little embers of sentience she needed to spread, to thrive, to multiply. To awaken Her champions, The Old Ones. As She grew in power, so did Aiden, just as she had promised. The young man used his gifts the Mother granted him to recruit others, preparing them for ascension and the return of the ancient ones. Power attracted ambitious people like a moth to a flame. There were plenty of such ambitious people here on the frontier.

Aiden reminisced over all the events preceding this day. How he had used the looter as bait, luring the troll into the homestead. He filled the fool with rumors of hidden wealth as he told him there was coin to be had under the floorboards. Mother had promised him he would be unharmed, but the Gerhardt's must die. However, She didn't expect them to be in the company of a lycan, a minor setback. While yes, the troll attack had failed, the warlock now knew how formidable Sir Garrett was. The bloodline was strong in him as it was King Arthur, the way he mustered his companions, indeed very impressive. Aiden knew he would need a far stronger and more focused beast. Scavin should have served his purpose well, but also failed to slay the templar. Though Scavin revealed Sir Garrett's weakness and the fact the templar had a son.

The birds' attack had taken a deal of power and focus on Aiden's part, but the results were worth it. It had terrified the outpost, like the other attacks across the countryside, it made his Mother's roots swell and grow, bursting from the soil as they sprouted. All connected to their queen, their goddess. In return for his service, the Mother gave him immortality, true immortality. He had all the gifts the Withered were blessed with, and more. He could hide his true nature and call on Her from great distances. Most of all, she rewarded him with his bride. They would serve Her for eternity as he helped his matriarch spread across the world. Her rightful place as the dominant entity in the realms of man.

III

The priest entered Lord Harmon's private study with a faint smile, answering the lord's summons, as the Baron looking up from a desk covered in documents to the robe-clad wisp of a man.

"You summoned me, my Lord?" The robed figure spoke in a soft tone, just above a whisper, as he greeted Lord Harmon with a slight bow.

"Lady Agatha says you hold much promise. She says that you have been a great help to her during this difficult period of Lord Edgar's passing. She speaks highly of you and that does not come easy."

"I am most honored to serve my Lord, I am glad Lady Agatha speaks of me in such high regard. Be certain my service is to God and my country. I will lead the colony in faith and leave political matters to the nobility." The priest said, his head gently bowing in its brown cowl.

"While it is up to the Archbishop and Pope to deem you worthy to lead this parish, I am putting my full support behind you, as is Lady Agatha. With the two most powerful houses backing your nomination, I'm sure the Pope will be more than content with you filling in Bishop Varik's position." Edric said.

"That is most gracious of you my Lord." Again, the priest bowed low.

"So from this day forward I hear by name you Varik's successor and recognize you as the new acting Bishop of Voskavia. Bishop… You'll have to excuse me my memory isn't what it once was. What was your name again?"

The priest smiled widely, removing his cowl. His pale skin in stark contrast to the various vibrant colors of Baron Edric's study. "Ekart, my Lord. I suppose Bishop Ekart now." He grinned as he shook Lord Harmon's hand.

Chapter 21:

A Storm on the Horizon

I

The Gerhardt's had reached Port Eirburg with no trouble under the guide of their seasoned leader. Ayla had spent the trip tending mostly to Rohn and listening to Brom describe how he slew the Hag in complete darkness boasting of his exploits. He had been ravenous since he got in the wagon; the ranger devoured everything and anything as his metabolic rate kicked in rapidly healing his wounds. Rohn just smiled happily they were all once again together. The group had become very close, and although she was threatened by his presence at first, she was glad he chose to stay. The fiery-haired lass had grown quite fond of the young knight. Ayla shook out of her daze and looked to his arm, finishing her stitching, making sure it was straight and taught. She numbed the area with a salve of aloe and other herbs to promote healing. Ayla couldn't help but smile at Rohn as she bandaged his arm, resting her hand on his. "I'm glad you made it." She whispered. "We've grown attached to you."

Rohn chuckled as Brom snored loudly, bread crumbs in his beard as the night of fighting caught up to the warrior.

"I'm glad to hear that. We've endured so much these past few months." The young man said, his hazel eyes locked to hers.

"Well, It may not be posh or fun, but it's our life." She joked.

"Thank you, Ayla," He said his voice sincere.

"Aye, that's my job."

"No, for everything. For understanding, for sharing your life with me. Your friends, your family. I had nothing when I came here. If it wasn't for father's note…"

"Don't get all soft on me." She said turning her gaze trying to hide her blushing, their hands slowly lingering on one another's.

Their gaze met for longer than they realized. Her deep emerald eyes staring into his. Rohn had grown quite fond of her as well. She was strong, determined, smart, and beautiful. He never met a woman like her. The two blushing as they smiled at one another.

"Were almost there, I can see the city gates." Garrett bellowed from the driver's cabin.

The two snapped from their daze and stood adjusting themselves as Brom snorted and coughed slowly opening his eyes as he awoke. "What I miss?"

II

Ironclad rolled through the capital city with impunity. The common folk scurried from the wagon with haste. The hag dangled from the side of the wagon in her iron cage as commoners gawked at her while whispering in hushed tones. Children rode on the shoulders of their fathers to get a better look at the creature, the fallen witch, the first of her kind to enter the gates of Eirburg. The onlookers were stopped however, at the palace gates as Ironclad rolled through, a full troop of soldiers escorting the war wagon. The footmen moved cautiously alongside the creature; their halberds aimed at the captive should she lunge out. A small contingent of soldiers stood at the ready as the wagon halted in front of the fortress with a groan as the doors opened the audience stepping back as it did. The now-famous foursome was given nods and claps on the back as those around the wagon were most impressed by what they had accomplished.

"Don't worry boys; she's missing a limb and most of her fingers. Just don't kiss her and I'm sure you'll be fine." Brom teased the halberdiers, as he came from around the back of the wagon, soon joined by Ayla and Rohn.

Sir Gerhardt hopped out of the carriages, armored driver's compartment, slowly getting his step back. "Take the prisoner to a cell. Do not release her from the cage and do not speak to her. Is this understood?" He commanded with a raised finger, his eyes deadly serious.

"Yes, my Lord!" The guards quickly slid their halberd poles through the top rings of the cage, giving the hag a wide birth.

As the four men carried her off to the back of the castle, down into its dungeon below the lord's palace, the group huddled together, stretching their legs once more happy to be in the open air. Ayla reached into her satchel and offered a book to Garrett with a bit of hesitation at first, but could no longer hold her tongue.

"I was thinking about what she said to us. It's starting to make more and more sense as to what's happening. You should read this." Ayla said quietly, as she handed Garrett the journal.

"Where did you get this?" His age etched face paling at the sight of it.

"You should read what's in it. Lord Harmon knew of this." She told him, almost pleading in her voice.

Sir Garrett quickly placed the journal in his satchel, ushering the others into the castle. "We'll speak of this later, Ayla in a more private setting."

Lord Harmon appeared at the top of the stairs to greet the returning group, surrounded by an entourage of his servants and nobility. His face was glowing with joy, his arms open as he embraced his old friend. "Thank God, I prayed for your safe return, and not only were you successful, but I hear you captured one of the creatures. Remarkable Garrett, simply remarkable."

"Yes, my Lord." Sir Garrett said with a bow not forgetting his station. "We did as requested and hoped to return home for a while. We need to rest, recoup, and prepare for what is to come." The templar spoke just above a whisper to the baron as the others were distracted by the praise of nobility. "She has returned Edric."

"I was wondering my Lord, if I could once again use your workshop, as Ironclad needs some alterations," Ayla spoke as she bounded up the stairs, giving a slight bow to the baron.

"Yes, yes, of course. But first, might I have a moment of House Gerhardt's time? Please follow me, I wish to speak with you all in a more discrete setting." He motioned the quartet to follow as his legs moved with purpose, leading them to his private study through the grand doors.

"You know Lady Agatha and I plan to wed this summer?" Lord Harmon told Garrett as they walked down the hall side by side, headed to the baron's private study.

"Did she just not become a widow?" Garrett chuckled slightly surprised by the change of subject.

"Yes but, at our age, you can't hinder love." Baron Edric grinned as he opened the double doors to his private library.

The Gerhardt's entered with a grin, only to stop in their tracks at the stranger before them. An old man, dressed in leathers and furs sat in a chair in front of Lord Harmon's oak desk. Edric walked past the visitor without skipping a beat, as he was well aware of the druid's presence. He motioned Brom, Ayla, and Rohn to enter as he closed the doors behind the group and secured them so they wouldn't be interrupted.

Garrett stared at the man, a ghost from their past made flesh. "Lord Harmon…" he said without taking his eyes from the native.

"It is too late, Garrett. We are knee-deep in what we have sown, there is no use hiding from it from your family."

"Edric, I think—"

"Garrett." Lord Harmon interrupted him, raising his hand softly.

The others gazed at the shaman with confusion. Brom sighed and took a seat on a cushioned bench near the gathering.

"What's going on?" Ayla asked, Rohn, stepping behind her, also interested in an explanation.

The old man stood, his face decorated in old Slavic runes and symbols. He spoke in an old tongue not uttered for centuries as he pointed a crooked finger at the aged knight and his liege in a grim tone.

Sir Garrett looked back and forth from the druid to Lord Harmon, "I'm sorry I don't understand…"

The man spoke again his tone growled and foreboding, his finger stricken with arthritis as he pointed it to Garrett.

The room grew cold and the sky's light faded as the wind snapped outside the study's windows. The commoners on the street near the castle shuttered at the sudden change in the weather. They grabbed the hats on their heads and wrapped their clothing tightly around themselves as the winds ripped through the tight confines of the city. The atmosphere changing with the temperament of the powerful druid within the city's walls.

"He asks, what have you done? The earth is again in upheaval, the forests are sick, and the animals are hiding." Brom said, as everyone turned to the ranger.

"I did not know you spoke his language." Lord Harmon said with a brow raised.

"My mother was a Slavic farmer's daughter, my father a Norseman. I was raised in both cultures and educated in their ways. He speaks an old form of Slavic, the same language the slaves spoke that were brought here on the longships of my father's people." He said to Edric as he stood, the shaman slowly gazing over the ranger.

Again the druid grimly muttered, as he motioned to Brom then to Garrett and Edric. Brom nodded and waited for the druid to speak once more. The ranger listening carefully as the sage spoke, the druid's tone harsh and cold.

"He says, you have woken the entity. A creature who feeds on suffering and pain, war and death." Brom said, crossing his arms over his broad chest.

The old man sat down once more. Again he spoke, the words flowing from his mouth were sharp and agitated.

"He says, we have put things into motion that cannot be undone. The Withered Ones once more walk the earth. The land will wipe us clean like an illness. She will bring back the primordial gods who ruled these lands long ago and bring suffering to our homeland and the world beyond. Nothing good can come of us being here, but it is too late to flee. We are damned." Brom looked to Sir Garrett.

Sir Garrett's blood went cold, goosebumps bubbled across his skin. His dream rushed back into his mind like a flood. The horrid images playing over and over. Abigail's warning. It was true; they had brought something back with their intrusion.

"Tell him we thank him for his concern and will take it under advisement." Baron Edric said, smiling at the druid.

The druid spoke once more, as if provoked by Edric's dismissal. He shook his head, and with a mournful sigh, walked out of the study, leaving the group dismayed and confused. Brom stared at the shaman as he left, shaking his head. Lord Harmon waiting for his translation. The ranger looked to Baron Edric and with hesitation, he spoke, "He said to make peace with your God. You will soon meet him."

"What the hell was that all about?!" Ayla asked, still in shock.

"Why don't the two of you have a seat? There is something Garrett and I would like to speak to you about." Lord Edric politely but forcefully motioned to the chairs before his desk.

With hesitation, Rohn and Ayla took a seat on a nearby sofa. Brom once again resting on the padded bench at the side of the study.

"We came here for a deliberate purpose." Lord Harmon began, "Sir Garrett and I had a mission far more important than colonization in the name of England. Finding Voskavia was no mistake, nor is the colony's primary purpose to harvest its resources. Though I am happy to send them back to our King, there is far more at stake here than the conflicts that wage at home. Emperor Arthur's ancient campaign for the chalice was but a cover for his true task, one we carry on to this day." Edric sighed as he sat down in the armed chair behind his desk.

"Sir Ruthger was on a mission, just as Arthur and his knights. He was seeking a source of power, that much was true. However, it was no chalice, no material relic, they sought. The Knights of Avalon were burdened with great a task. A task that would take everything from them, body, mind, and soul." Sir Garrett added staring at the floor, his mind heavy but happy to relieve his conscience of the secrets he had to keep.

"Emperor Arthur was tasked with finding gateways to other worlds, these portals connected our realm to ones of myth and legend. Some of these entities that came forth from these planes were benevolent, kind, and compassionate to humanity. Wishing to aid us in our growth and development, some however are not. They see us as little more than rodents occupying fertile territory. We believe Lilith is such a spirit." Edric said, assessing the reactions of the two.

"Lilith, as in Adam's first wife?" Rohn asked, still somewhat confused and in shock to the revelations.

Edric shook his head and leaned on his desk with his elbows. "Yes, and no. Lilith is far older, much older than man, a pre-biblical, antediluvian being. All corruption, plague, famine, disease, even the fall of Lucifer was of its design."

"We use the term 'her' very loosely, we might add," Garrett interjected. "The entity is beyond mortals comprehension and little is documented of her. Lilith lives only for herself, striving to dominate and corrupt, to make what is, hers. With this into consideration, its first known appearance in human form was that of a female, Lilith. Although she can take the shape of almost anything she desires, we believe she has returned in her first form, the oldest of her avatars. Ancient civilizations and religions, including the bible, even back to the Sumerians, speak of a tree in their historical documents. While there are many variants of this myth, one speaks of a great and powerful tree that feeds the souls of men with unholy desire and lust for power."

"Arthur and his knights knew of this being, they were warned of Lilith's resurrection and rebirth. So they set out on their crusades, searching for these fountains of unholy energy that attracted her. For generations the Templar continued the work of Emperor Artorius, seeking these portals and sealing them. One such fissure is here, in Voskavia. Lilith has claimed it as her own and would bring down her wrath once more on humanity. This time on a biblical scale and we must make sure this does not happen. That is why I will not retreat." Lord Harmon said, his tone calm but firm and resolute.

Brom shrugged, "So we find this bitch and cut her down to size."

"I wish it were to be so easy my friend. She has an army at her disposal, legions of unearthly and bestial abominations if the druids are correct. The Withered, as the shaman called them, that attacked the castle were her pawns. Expendable. I'm afraid we have yet to see the full extent of her wrath."

"You knew this could happen?" Ayla asked tears welling in her eyes as she glared at Garrett.

"Yes. It is why I came here. I knew what my task was when I was knighted before I set foot on Voskavia." Garrett responded apologetically.

"So what do we do?" Rohn asked his tone desperate and shaken.

"We regroup. You may return home, for now, rest and recoup, but your father is right. You must prepare for what is to come. She knows where we are and that is an advantage she has alone. We must locate her if we are to end this, but such a trip will be arduous and dangerous. We will need far more resources and manpower to accomplish this. Our first objective is to aid the settlers and nobles in establishing our foothold on the continent, as there will be safety in numbers. I will think about what to do next and summon you when I am ready to make our next move. May God be with us." Lord Harmon said with a heaviness to his tone.

III

House Gerhardt, at long last made their way back to the family homestead, within safe confines of Ironclad. They left their prisoner, the witch, behind with Lord Harmon to do with her as he wished. The road back seemed darker, the sky bleak and overcast now with black foreboding rolling clouds. The forest was denser. Even Fort Dumont was slowly succumbing to the overgrowth of the forest. Weeds, vines, and even saplings began sprouting in the middle of the outpost. Lord Harmon expected a new regiment of soldiers to retake the fort when his reinforcements arrived from England, which was due any day now. For now, the fort remained empty. A shell of what it once was, a reminder of the wrath that could befall any of them.

A gentle rain fell from the sky, slowly pelting the strong hull of Ironclad. The forest was indeed growing at a rapid rate, as the path to Gerhardt Manor was almost overcome by the rapid growth of the forest. The faces of the monster hunters were haunted by their newfound knowledge and destiny as they peered over the slow but inevitable creeping of Lilith's domain.

Their fears melted away and turned to temporary elation as they rounded the bend and saw the manor still standing. Strong, proud, and defiant against the world around it, much like them. The household rushed out to greet them, as they poured from the front doors of the manor and workers chased the wagon down from the fields. All their familiar faces grinning with exuberance to see them return home, safe and sound.

Miss Shea cried as she hugged them all, pulling Brom's face into her bosom as the family laughed. The fellowship was happy to be home once more, surrounded by those they loved.

Each one celebrated their return in their personal and unique way. Brom made his way back to his remote cabin and was greeted by his mountain dogs Fen and Elka. He noticed the girl had more girth and her teats were dropping. A clear indication she was with a litter. "My Boy!" He congratulated Fen, wrapping his arms around the two-hundred-pound dog as the mountain hound wagged his tail happy to have the attention.

Garrett picked up Rowdy, a small terrier mutt he had rescued from a war-torn encampment a few years back as he shook hands with Mr. Bosc his master engineer.

"Damn good thing you sent that missive," Bosc said, taking a puff of his pipe, "We had no idea what you were on about, but we did as we were told. Kept us safe and sound. Since then, we've been salting a ring around the mansion, using what we can get from the mine and traders. Luckily, Shea keeps around a large supply." Bosc smiled, a rarity for the man.

"I'm glad to see all is well. We were concerned but had faith knowing you and Miss. Shea would keep a tight ship." Garrett smiled, "We have much to catch up on." Sir Garrett squeezed the craftsman's shoulder gently, missing the sight of his home and family.

Though happy and at ease to see those he loved, Sir Gerhardt's contentment was plagued by the dream and the warning of the wildman. It slowly crept back into his mind, the horrors that awaited them. He couldn't help but wonder if they could avoid the fate he saw or was it too late? The words of the druid repeating in the back of their minds, haunting them like a dark shadow that hung in the sky.

Make peace with your God. You will soon meet him.

Epilogue: A Thousand Years of Darkness

I

Songbirds fluttered about their business as the sun rose over Port Eirburg. The town bustled more now than ever. The siege was but a distant memory in most minds as life had to go on. A few months had passed, and the weather relented into a warm summer. The new influx of immigrants had breathed life into the capital, especially with the new noble houses arriving, injecting their wealth into the local economy.

Lord Harmon made his way to the docks with his entourage of servants as he took in the ocean air and crisp breeze. Today Lady Agatha joined him, dressed in a fine gown made of crumpled velvet that her son had brought her from England. Their relationship now an open secret amongst the nobility and even commoners. The two had been spotted many times together over the past weeks.

The new bishop was also fitting in rather well. Ekart had taken the witch into his custody to be examined in a safe and holy sanctum, far from the population. Today he insisted on joining the baron to welcome the new colonists, as he wished to give them a blessing as they disembarked into the new land. The three casually made their way to the top of the stone docks. This vantage point allowed them to see not only the entire port, but far beyond the horizon. The bishop smiled, waiting for the small dots in the distance to approach as he readied his bible to bless those who landed. Lady Agatha stood next to Lord Harmon; her arm wrapped in his.

The two made a powerful couple. There were rumors abound they had something to do with the death of Varik and even Sir Edgar, but the two ignored them as nothing but ignorant gossip. The couple was happy, wealthy, and healthy, all they could ask for. This late in life it was best to grab what joy you had, while you still could. Especially with the continent getting more and more dangerous. Dumont, again, has become a force to be reckoned with under Lord Marshal Garrett's command. The outpost was well-stocked, fortified, and boasting a sizable force to defend Eirburg's borders. The growing frontier was now scattered with homesteads, as nobles and yeoman created settlements of their own. Quick to make their fortune, the new wave of settlers dove into the dark and treacherous forest despite the harsh warnings.

Lady Agatha talked Lord Harmon into giving her more soldiers to secure the mine. The flow of stone, minerals, and precious metals flowing freely into the capital, and to make up for the losses Baron Edric had placed Alistair in charge of Hweabrea. Alistair, although a coward of a man, was a powerful negotiator and merchant. He would make good use of the resources in the lakeside village.

The new colony ships came into view through the mist of the ocean's swells as a watchman called from his tower. Two large galleons, the biggest to arrive on the continent to date, their massive sails snapping taut in the wind as they slowly drifted to port. Those ashore waited patiently to welcome the new settlers to their home and inform them of its peculiar nature.

II

The sailor on the lead vessel stood in the crow's nest, wincing as he stared in the distance. The shape of land appeared on the horizon, teasing those who were sea weary as the ship bobbed on the waves.

"Land ho!" The gravel-voiced seamen bellowed with enthusiasm as a seagull flapped past the scout's nest.

Aboard the passenger ship, settlers excitedly scurry on the deck, thrilled to see their new home. Many had heard the rumors of Voskavia and were more than happy to try their luck on a new continent. A fresh start and a new life. Just like many before them, they dream of what is to come, as their hearts were filled with hope and aspirations.

The watchmen smiled down to the deck below, the crew and passengers tiny from this view. His amusement soon vanished from his face as he saw a large shadow, almost the size of the vessel itself glide under the ship passing in between the two boats. With a shutter the entire craft jilted violently to the left, the smile on the sailor's face turning to terror as he began ringing the bell in his tower as fast as he could.

"Brace! Brace!" He screamed as a massive reptilian head breached the surface and bit into the hull of the ship, crushing it inward.

The animal pushed the vessel sideways in the water as it shook its head, trying to slay the boat with one bite. The passengers aboard screamed in terror as they searched for anything to grab a hold of, many of them falling overboard as the ship rocked violently in the powerful maw of the leviathan. Its two gargantuan claws flailed in the water, sending geysers of white froth into the air. Finally ripping a hole in the vessel large enough to fit a wagon through as the wood shattered in the beast's powerful jaws. A horrific moan bellowed through the water as the sea serpent swam off and circled the now wounded vessel, kicking its legs and snapping its tail, ready to hit the crippled ship once more. The massive blue and black serpent breached the surface, assaulting the ships over and over. Its powerful barbed tail smashing into their sides as it passed. Serfs and nobles alike jumped from the vessel screaming, some of them only to be devoured by the monster assailing them.

Lord Edric watched on the shore in dismay as the creature's wails reverberated through the stone of the docks. The Baron of Eirburg, Lord Edric Harmon, first of his name, watched powerlessly in terror as the ship split in two. Nothing but kindling remained of its hull.

About the Author

Author R A Revis was born and raised in Las Vegas, Nevada. Revis has been a fan of fantasy novels for almost as long as he's been able to read. His first novel, *The Dark Times Saga: The Black Forest*, is fueled by his fascination of the paranormal and the supernatural, including his love of ancient history and religions. Look for more books from *The Dark Times Saga* (series) coming soon.

FORGIVEN & FREE

A HALTED HEART

GENEVRA BONATI

9 781735 383460